Dear Reader,

They say that people are the same all over. Whether it's a small village on the sea, a mining town nestled in the mountains, or a whistle-stop along the Western plains, we all share the same hopes and dreams. We work, we play, we laugh, we cry—and, of course, we fall in love . . .

It is this universal experience that we at Jove Books have tried to capture in a heartwarming series of novels. We've asked our most gifted authors to write their own story of American romance, set in a town as distinct and vivid as the people who live there. Each writer chose a special time and place close to their hearts. They filled the towns with charming, unforgettable characters—then added that spark of romance. We think you'll find the combination absolutely delightful.

You might even recognize *your* town. Because true love lives in *every* town . . .

Welcome to *Our Town.*

Sincerely,

Leslie Gelbman
Editor-in-Chief

Titles by Deborah Wood
(who also writes as Deborah Lawrence)

GENTLE HEARTS
SUMMER'S GIFT
HEART'S SONG
MAGGIE'S PRIDE

OUR · TOWN
HUMBLE PIE

DEBORAH LAWRENCE

JOVE BOOKS, NEW YORK

HUMBLE PIE

A Jove Book / published by arrangement with
the author

PRINTING HISTORY
Jove edition / July 1996

The Putnam Berkley World Wide Web site address is
http://www.berkley.com

ISBN: 0-515-11900-8

A JOVE BOOK®
Jove Books are published by The Berkley Publishing Group,
200 Madison Avenue, New York, New York 10016.
JOVE and the "J" design are trademarks
belonging to Jove Publications, Inc.

PRINTED IN THE UNITED STATES OF AMERICA

10 9 8 7 6 5 4 3 2 1

To Roasane Falcone, Faye Hughes, Jan Ference, Laurie Barnhill and Paula Eddy—artists and writers, remarkable and talented ladies, and compassionate friends.

HUMBLE PIE

❖ 1 ❖

Rocky Mountains, 1873

HANK TURNER'S BEEN livin' on borrowed time. The war had been over for eight years, but he had deserted the Southern cause before then and had begun robbing banks. And killing. Parker Smith vowed to see Turner pay for his crimes.

Five months earlier, Parker had heard a rumor about Turner that led him to Park City in the Utah Territory. It hadn't panned out. He was thinking about heading farther west when he witnessed a woman giving a youth a piece of her mind for attempting liberties. Once the commotion died down, he realized there was something familiar about her and asked her name. He was told: Katherine Turner. She and her mother did laundry and mending.

He didn't believe it was a coincidence that the woman had the same surname as the outlaw he had been tracking. When she and her mother left town unexpectedly, early the next day, it seemed to confirm his growing suspicions. It had taken him two days to discover they had taken the road north.

Their trail eventually led him to the Montana Territory, through Virginia City to Three Forks. He had lost them there and had decided to try some of the mining camps. When he'd stopped in Deer Lodge for a good night's rest and a little sport, Miss Rose had complained most of the evening over the loss of a wonderful seamstress. By the time he rode out of town, his hope had been renewed.

The last days of September weren't a time to linger in the northern Rockies, and he didn't plan to stay longer than necessary. The sky was clear blue, and he hoped the little town of Moose Gulch, in the high country, would mean the end of his four-year vigil.

Moose Gulch was set in a gully between two mountains, and there wasn't much to it. However, the buildings were made of logs or wood, not canvas. There were a couple deserted storefronts along with a livery, general store, saloon, barbershop, and the Grubstake Hotel, a small building with benches on each side of the door and a sign boasting a dining room. He pulled his horse up to the hotel, which must have seen more prosperous times, and went inside and through to the dining room.

The gold wallpaper had lost its luster and the red drapes were faded. He'd seen other hotels like this one, left behind when the miners moved on to better prospects. But the tablecloths were white, the lights bright enough to see the food, and it smelled damn good. Maybe his luck was changing.

After shoving a loose wisp of hair behind her ear, Kate Miller picked up the heavy tray of dishes and carried it to the table. "Here you are, gentlemen. Three steaks, pan-fried potatoes, and creamed peas. I'll bring you more coffee."

She set the plates down in front of each of the men and placed the biscuits in the middle of the table. "Enjoy your dinner. There's fresh apple pie for dessert."

She stopped at the next table, stacked the dirty dishes on the tray, added the cups and flatware. Next to the rumpled napkins, she found two little gold nuggets and slipped them into her pocket.

"Miss?"

A large hand dropped onto her shoulder. She whirled around, her elbow instinctively shot out and upward.

"Whoa!" Parker grabbed her wrist in the nick of time

and arched one brow. ''Do you greet all customers with such warmth?'' The woman's eyes flashed with anger, and he felt a grin tugging at the corners of his mouth.

As she stared at him, she quickly took his measure. His cavalry boots and slim denim trousers were dusty—trail dusty rather than from working a dig. Then she noticed the Colt strapped to his right thigh. She eyed him. ''When one of 'em's dumb enough to manhandle me.'' Smirk all you want, she thought, jerking her arm free.

''I'm sure you'll jog my memory if I forget.'' He glanced around the dining room, pulled out one of the chairs at the table the woman had just cleared off, and sat down. He set his hat on the next chair.

''What'll you have, mister?'' She brushed some crumbs off the table onto her hand.

''A smile wouldn't be bad for a start.'' It was *her*. Katherine Turner, from Park City. And she had to be Turner's daughter. The resemblance was as strong as he'd remembered. A shape any man could warm to, although her brownish hair could have been brushed with a rake rather than a hairbrush, and golden-brown eyes—eyes that seemed to defy or mock him. ''And a name.'' A comment he'd heard about Turner's daughter—''colder than a mountain lion's whiskers in a blizzard''—had stayed with him, and now it made sense. His lucky day had been a long time coming, but when it came, it was pure gold.

Kate peered through her lashes. ''Matilda, Nell, or maybe you'd like Sarah?''

His gaze slowly slid down from her mousey hair to her puckered but well-formed lips, her stubborn chin, the obvious mounds straining against the top of her dress, the flair of her skirt down to her square-toed boots. He smiled lazily, deceptively, while studying her every move. ''How about Katherine?'' She didn't flinch, and he was beginning to think his suspicion of her had been foolhardy, then she glared at him. It lasted for less than a bat of an eyelash, but it was enough. After four longs years of searching, would it end in Moose Gulch?

"Call me anything you like." Why had he suggested *Katherine*? She stared at him, her mind in a scramble to see if he was baiting her or just jabbering to keep himself company. She regarded him with forced calmness. Had she seen him anywhere before? Denver or Deep Creek or maybe Benton City? No. She would've remembered him.

He did have the nicest dark long eyelashes and well-shaped brows, and a measure of fascination about him, but that was no reason to treat him any different than any other man. It was reason enough, though, to pray he was only riding through town. She didn't recognize him, but his type meant trouble—to men and women alike. He rested against the ladder-back chair with a confidence few decent men possessed and brushed an ebony wave back from his brows, eyeing her with a scheming look she'd seen far too often. She sighed. At least once a week some man had to get cocky. This was her lucky day. He was the second. "We've got stew and pan-fried steak. You want some coffee while you decide?"

He leaned forward and rested his forearms on the edge of the table. "How old's the meat?"

"Slaughtered the beast myself, just this morning." She met his gaze with her usual detachment. His eyes were as blue as a summer sky, and unsettling—and that further annoyed her. If he could draw his gun with the same accuracy he could fix a person with his wily stare, the man was certainly deadly.

He chuckled. "Okay. I'll have steak. Is that coffee fresh?" She appeared disgusted with him, but her knuckles were white, her fingers stiff, and she looked ready to take flight. He'd struck a nerve; he'd bet on it.

She nodded.

"I'll take a cup now." He usually didn't have trouble cajoling a smile from a woman. This one was different, but he enjoyed a challenge.

Kate went to the kitchen and returned with a steaming cup of coffee for the stranger. She set it down and quickly turned away, but his deep, soft voice followed her.

"Thank you, darlin'. You sure know how to warm a man's heart."

She gritted her teeth and continued clearing off another table. She felt him watching her every move. Her pulse throbbed in her temples, but she forced herself to keep moving, ignore his disturbing regard and provoking remarks. If he'd had bad breath, missing teeth, or a weak chin, dismissing him would be much easier—but that wouldn't make him any less threatening.

She glanced at him out of the corner of her eye. Could he be a bounty hunter? A chill twisted down her spine. She stacked and carried the dirty dishes to the kitchen. Surely she was making more out of his teasing her than it warranted. When she returned to the dining room, one of the three men at the other table waved her over.

"Ma'am, that was real tasty." The man grinned and belched.

"No denyin' that." His companion quickly added.

The third man gulped the last bite of potatoes and rubbed the napkin across his mouth. "Any of that apple pie left, ma'am?"

"How do you like it? With cream or a slice of cheese?"

"Cheese," all three responded in unison.

She laughed and gathered up their dishes. A few minutes later, she served them generous slices of pie, each topped with a slab of cheddar cheese. The thinner of the three grabbed the fork before Kate set the plate in front of him. She refilled their cups and stepped over to do the same for the stranger.

He noticed the weariness in her eyes. "Will you join me?"

"I don't sit with customers." She straightened her back and stifled a groan. Her day wasn't over yet, and wouldn't you know this fellow expected company thrown in for the price of the meal.

"My name's Smith. Parker Smith. You look like you've been on your feet all day." He shoved the adjacent chair out for her.

"Mr. Smith, I've still got work to do." She pushed the seat back under the table. "Enjoy your stay in Moose Gulch."

He watched as she disappeared into what he assumed was the kitchen. Well, she still had to serve his dinner, and of course, the pie.

By the time Mr. Smith finished his dinner, Kate had cleaned off all the tables but his. "Do you want a piece of pie?"

"Sounds good. The meal was too. You make it?"

"Just serve, mostly." She piled the dishes up and started away, and then paused. "You want cream or cheese on top?"

He noticed the way her hands clutched the dishes. "What do you recommend?"

His voice was deep, smooth, and he used it like a woman would a lace fan, but she was too tired for banter. "You can have it plain, if that makes your decision any easier."

"That'll be fine."

When she returned and set the slice of apple pie down in front of him, he kicked out the chair again and nudged her back onto it. "There's no one else here. Surely you can keep me company for a minute."

"I have dishes to wash." She slid her foot back, starting to rise.

"Wait." He covered her hand with his. "I'm looking for a woman. I thought you'd probably know most everyone around here."

"I keep to myself. Asking questions isn't too healthy."

"Ya, I know." He grinned at her. "I'm looking for Katherine Turner. Saw her father years ago and was hoping she'd put me in touch with him." He'd kept his voice light, but the waitress became tight lipped.

"Turner's not an uncommon name. Why don't you ask over at the store? Most people don't introduce themselves here."

"Don't suppose they do."

Kate saw the cook, Charlie Daws, peer around the

kitchen door and responded before he could call out her name. "I'll be right there."

She shot off the chair and hurried to the kitchen. "I'll get these washed up. You want me to help with the baking, Charlie?" She'd only known him for three months, but it seemed more like they'd been friends for years. He wasn't any taller than she and was probably old enough to be her grandfather with his thinning white hair, but he was as hard a worker as any man half his age and had a heart of gold.

"Nah." He grabbed the broom leaning near the back door and started sweeping the floor. "What's that gent palaverin' 'bout? Was he fussin' ya?"

She almost grinned at his fatherly protectiveness but just shook her head. There were only two men she allowed into her life, Charlie and Thaddeus, an old prospector, whom she had taken to as if he were a long-lost uncle.

She lowered the dishes into the pan of hot, soapy water. "He says he's looking for some woman." She attacked the plates viciously with the dishrag.

"Anyone we know?" He swept the dirt into a pile and opened the back door.

"I told him to ask at the store."

Charlie brushed the dirt outside, closed the door, and watched Kate. "What else did he say that's got yer dander up?"

She took a second pan over to the water barrel and filled it. "You know I don't encourage the men. But he's new in town. I shouldn't have let him rile me."

"That ain't like ya, gal. Ya want me to refill his coffee?"

She spun around, spraying soapy water, and grabbed a towel as she spoke. "I'm not turnin' tail on him."

"I jist wanted to give ya a hand."

"Now what would I do with three?" She grinned and picked up the coffeepot. As if prepared to do battle, she marched out to the dining room, refilled Smith's cup, and returned to the kitchen.

Parker nodded his appreciation, deciding it wouldn't pay to rouse her anger again so soon. By the time he'd finished eating, she hadn't returned. He left four-bits on the table, enough for two meals and a generous tip, he figured, picked up his hat, and went to see about a room.

Kate crossed the distance from the hotel kitchen to the cabin she shared with her mother, Mary Louise. The shack had been claimed by different prospectors through the years and each had added his own touch. The stone fireplace had a good draw, there were two bottle windows for sunlight, and the wobbly sawbuck table worked just fine after Kate had steadied one of the legs with wood chip wedges and scraped the surface down to fresh pine. She also filled in many holes in the chink between the logs and replaced the ropes in the bed frame before putting their fresh corn husk mattress on it.

When she rounded the corner, she saw that the heavy, rough-hewn timber door stood open into the one and only room. Her mother, who managed to maintain her ladylike appearance even in rough surroundings, was crouched on the dirt floor. with her full skirt spread out behind her. "Mamma . . . what in tarnation are you doing with that critter?"

The squirrel ran outside. Mary Louise shook her head and came to her feet. "I don't know why ya get so outa sorts b'my little diversions." She brushed off her skirt and gracefully sat down on her old rocking chair.

Her *Southern drawl*, as the Yankees called it, always got stronger, the words more drawn out when she defended herself or tried to wheedle something from someone, but Kate wasn't amused. "All your furry little creatures have fleas." Seeing her mother's absentminded nod, Kate flexed her fingers in frustration. "I'm not willing to spend the winter with them. If you must feed them, do it outside." After two months of disinfecting, scouring, and using chloride of lime and water for the foul odors, the cabin was pest free and now smelled of food, wood smoke, or the freshly scraped dirt floor.

"You're right, deah. They'ah just so cute."

Her mother had been trying to replace her favorite cat, Lissie, for years. The poor little creature disappeared one night on their second move after leaving their home in Hunt County, Texas. The cat had been more of a childhood friend than a pet. However, her mother had taken the loss the hardest, but one of them had to have more sense than tears, and she had turned out to be stronger willed than her mother. ''One day we'll have a real house. Then we can have another cat, Mamma.''

''I know, deah. Maybe if we lived in the city, you'd meet a nice gentleman. A good man provides for his woman.'' Mary Louise smiled at her daughter.

Kate's immediate response—*A man's responsible for our being in this dirt-floor cabin*—went unsaid. She'd learned crying over their loss did no good and neither did reminding her mother of Hank. ''We don't need a man. I've managed to put away some money. When we have enough, we'll move to a town and live like ladies.'' Although I doubt I'll dress like one, she thought, or do my hair in a waterfall like Mamma's.

After almost three months in Moose Gulch, she had grown fond of the small town. There were times, when she walked through the trees or stopped by a creek, she felt so at peace she couldn't imagine living in a city. Besides, in places like Moose Gulch, she could wear trousers without a skirt on top when she wasn't at the hotel. Her mother was the lady of the family, a true Southern lady.

''Darlin'.'' Mary Louise rose and closed the door. ''I know you're doin' your best. If ya'd only do somethin' with your hair—'' She shrugged.

''I'd better get more firewood.''

Kate went back outside and stared at the woodpile. Since Mary Louise had finagled a couple miners out of an old woodstove two weeks earlier, the cabin had been toasty warm. She made four trips before she had brought in enough wood to last the night.

''I finished mending Mr. Pitt's jacket. Would ya mind

takin' it up to him? I worry about him. He has so few clothes, poor man."

"The walk'll do me good." Kate pushed back the yellow calico curtain that hid their bed and small chest of drawers. The chest was polished weekly and gleamed in the light, a remembrance of her childhood home. Her sewing box sat on the top at one side, her mother's on the other with a small, wood-framed mirror in between. It was only large enough to see her head and shoulders, but she had no need to see more. "I'll finish Morrey's dungarees and go by both camps."

Mary Louise went over to the old dome top trunk in the corner. She withdrew her knitting bag and returned to her rocker. "Do ya still fancy workin' at the hotel?"

"Mm-hm." Kate glanced over at her mother and saw the blue yarn. "I thought you used the last of your wool on Mr. Pitt's socks."

Mary Louise carefully place the old carved knitting sheaths on her lap. Kate was glad they had been able to save a few pieces of their heritage.

Mary Louise peered through her lashes and murmured, "I found more in the trunk." She put the ball of yarn in the bag and pulled the loose end up to her lap. "If we're goin' to remain in this freezin' place, we'll need more shawls and stockings."

"I guess we will." Her mother had never been much farther north than Dallas before they began moving from town to town, and she had complained about the cold winters there. Kate's father also liked warmer weather, which was why she kept moving north.

"With it frostin' this early, I hate to think what January will be like." Mary Louise shook her head.

"Keep knitting, Mamma. If it snows like they say, you'll need a lot more wool." Her mother smiled in her dreamy fashion as she worked the knitting sheaths, and Kate couldn't help wondering why. Now and then through the last few years, she'd had the feeling her mother knew some grand secret. Again, she silently questioned Mary Louise's private beaming, but for the life of her, Kate had no idea what it could mean.

That look. There had been traces of that same look in Smith's eyes. Ye gods, no. She must be mistaken, Kate thought, prayed.

Katherine.

She shuddered. *Why* had he suggested calling her Katherine of all names?

2

After leaving his bedroll, rifle, and saddlebags in his room, Parker led his horse over to the livery. A wiry little man with unruly dark hair came out of the open double doors.

"What can I do for you, mister?"

"Have an empty stall available for a few days?"

"Got a couple." The man motioned behind him. "Pick one." He glanced at Parker. "Don't get too many strangers this time a year."

Seeing three horses in the end stalls, Parker led his mount, Buckshot, into the first one. "Don't imagine you do." He began unsaddling his horse. "I haven't seen another horse pass through here this afternoon. I'm surprised you have enough business to stay open."

The man chuckled. "The missus runs the store. I manage to keep busy and deliver goods to the miners off and on."

"You must be an old-timer here."

"I have a claim down by the creek. Made sense to stay on." The man's attention kept straying to Parker's holstered gun.

Parker spread the saddle blanket along Buckshot's back and patted his neck before he fastened the rope across the stall entrance. "I'll pay for a week."

The man's eyes grew large, and he stepped back a pace.

"That'll be one dollar." He held out his hand, palm up.

Parker placed the coins in the man's hand. "Make sure he has fresh water and plenty of feed."

"That I will." The man slid the coins into his deep trouser pocket before he held out his hand to Parker. "I'm Mac Goody. Folks just call me Mac. I'll take good care of him."

"Parker Smith." They shook hands. "See you tomorrow, Mac."

Parker left the livery and sauntered down the street. The general store and the barbershop shared a boardwalk. There were two boarded-up storefronts; one had a faded sign—SOPHIE'S FINE DRESSES—the other ELMER'S FOOTWEAR. Some high-grade ore must have been found nearby before the claims played out.

He'd seen it happen enough times to know the miners still around were only finding enough dust to keep their dreams alive. Was Turner one of those? Or was he holed up higher in the hills, close enough to see his daughter when it was safe? And now that he thought about her, where had she disappeared to? It occurred to him she might live at the hotel, and that idea appealed to him.

He crossed the road and went 'round back behind the saloon, a good-sized building. Tree stumps littered the ground almost down to the stream, and there was a cabin directly behind the hotel.

With the layout of the town in mind, he went back to the road. A mule and two horses were tied up in front of the Placer Saloon; a wagon stood across the street at the store. Cards and whiskey usually yielded more information than questions, so he headed for the saloon and went inside. Several kerosene lanterns lighted the room with a hazy yellow glow; windows were expensive, especially when there weren't many customers. However, the scarred plank floor was evidence of a more prosperous time, and he wondered how long ago that was.

A man sitting in the far corner strummed a banjo and sang softly, ". . . Away down South in Dixie. Away, away, away . . ." Three men were playing poker at one table.

There was a woodstove, a battered dartboard in back, and several faded prints of well-endowed women, dressed to remind men what didn't seem to be available here, were tacked on the walls.

Parker didn't want to be reminded of home or women, at least not now. He stopped at the plank bar, about as far from polished mahogany with brass rails as you could get. The brawny bartender eyed him guardedly, but most people in small mining towns were alert to strangers. He tipped his hat back. ''Whiskey.''

The bartender set a glass out, poured beyond the halfway point, and set the bottle back on the ledge behind him. ''Six bits.''

It was a generous measure and the price typical, Parker knew from experience, for a mining town. He withdrew the exact change from his pocket and laid the coins on the bar. ''Looks like a storm building up.''

''That time of year.'' The bartender rubbed a towel over the counter. ''You got a claim up here?''

Parker shook his head. ''You probably see more gold than the men digging for it these days.'' He sipped the rotgut. He'd seen men squander months of hard labor on a day's pleasure, but this watering hole had little in the way of entertainment.

''Not much here anymore.''

The bartender moved away, and Parker strolled over to see how the game was going while the banjo player strummed ''Farewell, Old California.'' Other than the occasional ''Christamighty,'' ''Dadburnit,'' or ''Thunderation,'' the men were silent. Neither the game nor the men held his interest.

Parker swirled the whiskey, glanced at the dregs in the bottom, and set it down on the bar. This was no place to pass the winter, he thought, walking back out into the chilly wind blowing through town.

Kate paused a couple hundred yards from Morrey's dig and called out. It didn't pay to surprise anyone out there, especially a miner. Occasional robberies were still talked about. He waved to her, and she went down the trail to his campsite. He lived in a tent he had lined with animal skins.

She smiled and waved a gloved hand in the direction of the recently added log walls outside his tent. "Looks like you've decided to stay the winter after all." He was just a bit taller than she, average build, dusty brown hair, and, as with the other miners she visited with, he was old enough to be her father.

"Yep." Morrey rubbed his jaw. "Aw'most got me a palace and 'nough dust to keep me goin'."

She pulled the dungarees out from under her heavy jacket and handed them to him. "That seam should hold, unless you strike it big and eat your way out of them." She grinned.

"Thanky. Jist might do that." He tossed the trousers inside his tent and handed her two animal pelts. "Like to keep the slate clean."

She rubbed the brownish rabbit fur against her cheek. "No one tans a hide the way you do. Thank you." She looked at the black-and-white fur underneath the rabbit and unfolded it. "This wolf was huge. It's too much. I can't accept it."

He shrugged. "Sure you can. Lay it out across your bed or in front of the fire to keep your ma's feet warm."

"I owe you, Morrey."

He chuckled. "Now, that's what I like to hear."

She continued on up the mountain to Mr. Pitt's camp. If she needed more than the cold temperatures to confirm that summer had indeed passed, the blackened Indian pipes, the once tall, regal plants with snowy white flowers, signaled the change of season.

Every time she saw Mr. Pitt, she wondered why he was there. He didn't dress like the other miners. She'd never seen him wearing anything other than a white shirt, black necktie, and tweed coat. His only concessions to the rough conditions were a pair of sturdy boots and a long heavy overcoat. She called to him and went on into his camp.

Mr. Pitt tipped his bowler hat to her. ''What are you doing up here this late in the day, Miss Miller?''

''My mother wanted to make sure you had your extra jacket back today.'' She handed it to him and smiled. ''How have you been?''

''Splendid, my dear.'' He waved his free hand in an arc. ''Who would not thrive in this beauty? I do believe every young man should be required to spend a year up here in the north country.'' He stared at the nearby cedar trees. ''Would do them wonders, don't you think?''

She stared at the blue-gray-green mountains in the distance, picturing fuzzy-cheek boys, cocky know-it-alls, and nodded. ''They'd be men when they left.''

Mr. Pitt inspected where the tear had been on the sleeve of his jacket. ''Mrs. Miller did a fine job reweaving this. Please relay my gratitude.''

When she glanced back around at him, he pressed a small gold nugget into her hand. ''I can't accept this.''

''It isn't for you. It is for your mother. I regret to say I have rendered another pair of my favorite trousers unwearable unless your mother's magic touch can rescue them.''

He almost makes me feel like a lady, she thought as he stepped into his tent. She shook her head. No, he was just a gentleman.

He returned and handed the pants to her. ''I will be in town in a few days, so you won't have to make another trip up here.''

She tucked the neatly folded pants under her arm. ''They'll be ready, Mr. Pitt.''

The sun seemed to drop from sight come evening in the mountains, and the clouds had blocked the sun even earlier than ususal. She left while she could still see her shadow. She dropped off the gold, trousers, and animal pelts at the cabin and put on her calico skirt before going to the hotel to serve supper. When she arrived, the kitchen was good and warm, and Charlie was stirring a large kettle of soup.

Charlie frowned. ''Yer cheeks're red as cherries. Ya been up at the camps again?''

"I had to get Morrey's dungarees back to him and return Mr. Pitt's jacket." She shrugged out of her coat and hung it on the peg.

He shook his head. "Ya can't be runnin' up to the camps much longer. Gettin' too cold." He stabbed a fork in the skillet and turned over two steaks.

She finished tying the apron strings and peered out into the dining room. She picked up two bowls. "Did you serve the soup?"

"Jist took 'em coffee."

After he'd ladled the beef soup into the bowls, Kate carried them out to the two men seated by the far wall. While she kept busy, she wondered how much longer Charlie would be able to keep her working. The temperature continued to drop, day by day it seemed, and so did the number of customers.

Mr. Bishop, the owner of the Grubstake Hotel, motioned to her, and she stepped into the lobby. "Can I get something for you?" He stood a little taller than her own five feet six inches, kept his muttonchop sideburns as neat as his thinning brownish hair, and had trouble keeping his spectacles in place. He'd been kind enough to give her the use of the cabin as part of her pay and hadn't made any advances toward her. But she didn't trust any man under the age of fifty-five and figured he must be shy of that age by at least fifteen years.

"No, Kate." He led toward the stairs, away from the dining room, and stopped. "Since Mrs. Nunney moved away, I need someone to do the laundry and clean the rooms after the men leave, or twice a week for anyone who stays that long." He stared at her over his spectacles. "Would you take on that job? This time of year it shouldn't be too much extra work. I'll give you five dollars for the laundry and one for each room you clean. How about it?"

She nodded. "I can do the rooms before dinner and the laundry at the end of the week." Every extra dollar would help come spring. "Thank you, Mr. Bishop."

"And you, Kate. I've tried my hand at keeping the

rooms, but I'm no good at it. Besides, I always forget to empty the chamber pots.''

That was something she hadn't considered. As he went back to work, she thought about charging him two dollars a room. While she served thick slices of rhubarb pie to the only two customers that evening, that stranger came in and sat down. Against her will, she remembered his name. Smith. Who couldn't recall such a common handle? But he wasn't a common man, no matter how little she thought of him.

Parker sat at the same table he'd taken for dinner. He took the chair that put his back to the kitchen and didn't let her see him watching her. A few minutes later she returned with a glass of water and set it down in front of him. He met and matched her remote expression. ''What's on the menu for supper?''

''Beef soup, pan-fried steak, potatoes, and pie. Or I could scare up some stew.'' Determined to remain calm, she had kept her voice level and didn't quite meet his gaze, but she smelled that swill they served at the saloon.

He downed half the glass of water to rid the foul taste the whiskey had left in his mouth before he leaned back. ''Fine. And I'd like some coffee, now, if you have the time.''

She nodded and went to the kitchen, her fear he would again tease her subsiding. Maybe she'd been mistaken about him. She returned with his coffee and soup. Suddenly she realized she would have to clean his room. As she placed the bowl down in front of him, he reached for the cup, and his hand brushed hers. She flinched and the soup sloshed. As soon as she set the bowl down, she snatched her hand back.

''Sorry.'' Parker covered her hand to steady it and quickly dropped his hand to his side. ''You okay?'' The timing was perfect, and her reaction told him what he wanted to know. By tomorrow evening she'd be talking to him.

''Of course.'' His large hand had covered hers like a

warm glove. As she went to check on the two men just finishing up, she told herself *he* would be leaving in the morning. He had to, because if he didn't . . .

"Kate, that was mighty good." The shorter of the men belched and grinned.

The other man elbowed his friend. "Mind yer manners in front of Miss Miller." He grinned at Kate. "Did you give any more thought to my proposal, Katie?"

"I told you, Hick, I'd never wait on any man outside this dining room." She grinned at him and reached for his empty plate. "You better find yourself some nice woman who likes cooking, having babies, and cleaning up after her man."

Parker raised his cup in a quiet salute. "Here's to you, *Kate Miller.*"

She stacked the dishes and carried them to the kitchen. Charlie jabbed the fork into the steak and dropped it on the plate. "Any one else come in?"

She shook her head and put the dishes in the warm soapy water. "I don't see how you expect to stay open all winter. This town's almost dead. Hick's been coming in once a week, but he won't be doing that once the snow starts—will he?"

"The miners come in once in a while to jaw and warm up." He put a generous helping of potatoes on the plate. "I told ya there'd be work all winter, 'n I meant it. Now quit frettin'."

She eyed him. "You must be richer than I figured, Charlie."

"Jist call me Charlie Crocker."

She laughed. "And you can call me, Lotta Crabtree." She winked and struck a coy pose, then picked up the dinner plate, biscuits and butter. She served Parker's meal, still grinning.

He moved the bowl aside, wondering at the obvious change in her. Her tawny eyes now reminded him of honey, her cheeks had a peachy glow, and was she actually smiling? "Smells good."

"Charlie works wonders with shoe leather." She picked up the bowl and returned to the kitchen.

Parker watched her sashay away, or so it looked to him. He'd seen her express anger and uncertainty, but he hadn't expected she would actually flirt with him. His interest doubled. He told himself it was because of Turner, but his reaction had been that of a man intrigued by a woman's curious smile. He ate without tasting the food, looking forward to her next appearance.

She enjoyed joking with Charlie. At those times she could momentarily forget who she was and why she was there. She washed up the few dirty dishes, dried them, and sat down on a stool at the worktable across from him. "What do you do here all winter?"

"Same as any other time." He peered down his nose at her. "I still don't know why ya came up here. There's nothin' here fer a young, single lady like yerself, since ya don't seem to be inter'sted in any of the men who'd take ya fer a wife."

"Don't you try to marry me off." She sighed and ran her fingers along the smooth, worn surface of the table. "I was thinking more of work. I don't see how Mr. Bishop can keep the hotel open all winter." This small, out-of-the-way mining town had appeared to be the perfect place to spend the winter and save some of her hard earned money. Suddenly Parker Smith's face was as clear in her mind's eye as if he were sitting across from her instead of Charlie, and she felt her spine stiffen up.

Charlie reached out with his rough hand and patted hers. "He ain't gonna close it. Don't worry."

She jerked her hand back. Embarrassed by her reaction, she immediately bent over to check her boot. Why was she allowing that Smith character to invade her thoughts?

"I never should'a tol' you 'bout that cabin." Charlie glanced at her out of the corner of his eye. "Won't ya think on movin' down to Helena? Heard it was a right proper city now. This ain't no place fer ya. Deer Lodge's better'n this."

Kate was well aware that she fit in perfectly. ''I don't want to move. It's nice and quiet here.''

''Is that stranger devilin' you?''

She shrugged. ''He didn't say anything.''

''Well, he don't look like no self-riser, so he'll prob'ly be movin' on . . . 'less he's up to no good.''

No, Parker Smith didn't have the look of a miner, but he didn't seem like a hardened gunfighter, either. ''He must be done eating. I'd better go see.''

Parker listened to her approach. Her step wasn't as light as before, and when she stopped at his side, she reached for his empty plate without so much as a glance at him. ''Give Charlie my compliments.''

Her attention slid from the dish to his face. His manner was sober, no trace of mockery, but his eyes, those sky-blue eyes . . . Feeling as if he'd actually caressed her, a tremor passed down her back.

He continued holding her with his calculating gaze. ''Cold?''

''No.'' She had to get a grip on herself. ''I'll tell him. Ready for your pie?''

''Not tonight. But I'll take more coffee.''

Was he intentionally speaking softly? She wasn't about to lean forward, though his voice had a velvet quality, a deep, resonating sound she could listen to without caring what he said. She hurried away with the dishes and returned with the coffeepot. She stood far from his side and reached across the table to refill his cup. No more accidental brushing of hands this time, she thought.

''Not many customers tonight,'' he said. She was being overly cautious, which amused him, but he didn't allow it to show.

''There probably won't be many till spring.'' He did it again, she thought as she returned to the kitchen, watched her with an intensity she could almost feel. She quickly washed and dried the last few dishes. There was nothing else to do.

Charlie set two plates on the worktable with generous

servings. "Might as well eat now."

She sank down on the stool and picked up the fork. "I can't possible eat all this. Please, take half. I don't want to waste food."

"Ya better start eatin' b'fore winter hits or ya'll end up with the croup or worse." He shoveled a hearty piece of meat into his mouth and motioned for her to do the same.

She bit back a smirk and cut a piece of steak. She was as fit as could be, but she was also hungry. Several bites later, the door to the dining room opened.

Parker entered the kitchen. "I thought I'd save you a trip." He set the cup down on the table. "You must be Charlie." He looked like a crusty fellow, but the glint in the man's eyes betrayed his spirit. Parker had learned to listen to his instincts, and he liked the old man.

"That's right."

"Parker Smith. Glad to meet you." They shook hands. "Did Kate tell you how much I enjoyed my meal? Haven't had food that good in weeks."

"Thanks."

Parker gave Kate a cursory acknowledgment. "See you in the morning."

After Parker left, Charlie gave a low whistle. "So that's him."

"Mm-hm." Kate set her fork down. "What do you think?"

" 'Bout what?"

Flying pigs, she thought. "Him. Parker Smith."

Charlie shrugged. "He'd be hard to miss."

Kate gritted her teeth. "You're a good judge of character. What do you think about him? Could he be a hired gun?"

"Not him." Charlie took his time chewing the last bite of potato. "That one's his own man." He stood up and added, "But I wouldn't want to cross him. Bet he'd be a real bear if he was riled."

"Well, I don't intend to bother him." She came to her feet, also. "If it's okay, I'll take this to my mother."

"Take it fer later. I've got another plate fixed fer her." He draped a clean napkin over the third plate of food warming on the side of the stove.

She left for the cabin a few minutes later, two plates in hand, still wondering what Charlie *really* thought of Parker Smith. She paused halfway home. How did *she* feel about him? He'd done nothing outwardly threatening, but she had felt . . . exposed, but that could have been her own fear of discovery, couldn't it? Oh, botheration! She'd find herself in an asylum for the insane if she weren't careful.

3

PARKER TURNED HIS back to the window, lit the lamp, and closed the door. Surely she'd left by now. He'd hoped to watch her leave, but his room faced the street, and she hadn't come upstairs or stepped foot outside the front of the hotel. He hung his gun belt on the bedpost and stretched out on the mattress with his hands behind his head.

Kate *Miller* or Katherine Turner? He was betting they were one in the same. She was an interesting mix—defiant and smart mouthed, certainly, but she also had shown a softer side. She was fun to rile, and he wanted . . . Damn. He wouldn't let a female distract him from his reason for making the long trek to this speck in the Rocky Mountains.

He closed his eyes and flexed his fingers. Her white hand had been cool, strong, and accustomed to work. If she'd supported herself all these years, she'd have to be, he knew. He'd heard she was a loner, never married. That puzzled him. Wouldn't it be easier for a woman to vanish if she married? But women weren't always logical, he reminded himself.

It was the same each morning. Kate rekindled the fire in the dining room woodstove and set the tables. When she came to the seat Parker Smith had occupied the last two meals, she hesitated. He not only irritated and worried her, he had made her think and feel. However, she reminded herself, if she weren't careful, all of her planning would have been for nothing.

Later, she served Mr. Bishop and, again, wondered why Charlie kept baking and cooking. It wasn't nine o'clock but she doubted there would be a rush of people in the next ten minutes. She was tempted to check the hotel register to see if there were any guests, when Parker Smith came in and took what was becoming his regular seat.

To her amazement, he simply ordered his meal and ate in silence. When he was finished, he said, "Thank you," and "Good-bye, Kate," then left. She went to the outside kitchen door and watched the livery. A few minutes later she saw him ride out of town. She sent up a heartfelt "thank you" and almost danced back into the kitchen.

All her fears had been for nothing. She felt weightless. For all she cared, he could spend the rest of his life searching for Katherine Turner. Kate grinned. He'd never find her. She gathered the cleaning supplies from the storeroom and went up to clean the two rooms that had been emptied that morning.

She didn't think about Parker Smith again until she served dinner. She hadn't realized she was looking for him until she found her gaze wandering to his empty seat time after time. When she felt disappointed he hadn't returned, she scolded herself. He was handsome, she found herself thinking, now that it was safe.

The evening dragged on. After the few customers left and she had cleaned up, she returned to the cabin feeling restless. She built up both fires, mended, and fetched fresh water.

Mary Louise stopped knitting and sighed. "Kate, why can't ya sit still?"

"I—" Kate shrugged. "I feel as if I forgot to do something . . . but I don't know what."

"I heard there was a stranger in town." Mary Louise watched her daughter. "Did ya see him?"

"I did." Kate paused in her pacing. "I also saw him ride

out of town. How did you hear about him?''

''At the general store.'' Mary Louise began plying her knitting sheaths. ''Mrs. Goody said she saw him pokin' 'round town. Did he say anythin' to you?''

Kate eyed her mother. ''He wanted food and company—like most men.'' She wouldn't tell her mother all of it. That would only upset her and cause more questions she didn't want to answer, or think about.

''Miss Lucy thought he was handsome.''

Kate rolled her eyes. ''Miss Lucy's in her dotage, Mama.'' But she was right, Kate thought. The man would have no trouble finding a willing woman for as long as he'd want her. So why had he been so sassy with her?

Mary Louise smiled dreamily. ''Only a dead woman's heart wouldn't beat a little faster when she sees a good-lookin' gentleman, deah.''

Kate stared at her mother, completely surprised by her admission. ''When was the last time your heart 'beat a little faster,' Mamma?''

Mary Louise laughed softly.

Parker spent the day following trails through the mountains within a few hours' ride of town. He had come across several camps and watched each until he was satisfied Turner wasn't there. Near sunrise the next day, he broke camp without even bothering with a fire and headed back to Moose Gulch.

After stabling Buckshot, he went by his room for his soap and a clean shirt, then to the barbershop. A man a few years older than himself was sitting out front working a piece of wood with his knife. ''That bear looks like the real thing.''

The man nodded. ''I've seen enough of 'em.'' He lowered the knife and looked up at Parker. ''Can I help you?''

''If you're the barber, I need a shave and a hot bath.''

''I am.'' The barber stood up and went inside. ''Where you headed?''

''Staying here, for a time.'' There were two barber chairs

with a mirror in front of each with a shelf of shaving mugs, each decorated with tools or scenes and names, some Parker knew, some he didn't. He didn't believe it would be worth the trouble to put his name on one, but he kind'a liked the idea.

The barber held out his hand. "Earl Wilson. Have a seat. I'll heat up some water."

"Parker Smith." He shook hands with Earl, put his things on the wooden bench along one wall, and sat in the barber chair. Earl's clean-shaven face and neatly trimmed sandy hair seemed like a good recommendation for his work.

Earl returned and put a towel around the front of Parker's neck. "The water'll be hot before long." He picked up a fresh mug and shaving brush, added a little water, and stirred the soap into a lather.

As Earl began lathering his face, Parker settled back with his chin up. Most of the time he shaved himself, but it wasn't the same as having a barber ply the soapy brush. "Were you here when those boarded-up shops were open?"

Earl began stropping the straight-edge razor. "Sure was and before. This town looked like another Alder Gulch or Emigrant Gulch, for a time, though you'd never know it now."

With practiced ease, the barber gently stretched one side of his face, and Parker instinctively pursed his mouth to the other side. The man had a good touch.

Earl wiped the lather from the blade and continued. "Never fails to amaze me when folks take a building apart and take it with 'em. There was a bank next door, but Fordham moved away, bank and all."

"I've seen that happen," Parker mumbled out the side of his mouth.

Earl drew the razor down under Parker's chin. "You got a nice start on a mustache. Want to keep it?"

"Not now." When he was a little sprout, Parker thought, he used to dream about having a full mustache like his granddaddy's. Now he also remembered staring at a crumb of bread or drip of sauce caught in the hair over his granddaddy's mouth. "Take it off."

Earl finished shaving Parker and wiped his face with a wet towel. "I'll check on the water."

Parker ran his hand down one cheek and across his chin. He felt better already. He stood and looked out the front window. A man drove an old wagon up the street and Mr. Bishop left the hotel. There weren't enough people around not to be recognized by someone. Could Turner be so well known in town that he came and went—like any other miner—without notice?

Earl came from the back room. "Bath's ready. Towel's on the chair."

"Thanks." Parker carried his hat and clean shirt to the back room. The tin tub was behind a curtain separating it from another. Wasting no time, he stripped out of his dusty clothes and stepped into the hot bath. This is definitely better than an icy stream, he thought, sitting down in the water with the soap.

Fifteen minutes later he walked through the barbershop and found Earl sitting out front painting Parker's name on the shaving mug. Parker handed him four bits. "Thanks. You have a good hand."

Earl held up the mug. "You sure Smith's your name?" He grinned and glanced up at him. "Just foolin'. Had two other Smiths through here last year."

Parker nodded. "That's why my mother named me Parker."

He crossed the road and returned to his hotel room. A few minutes later he went down to the dining room. Except for an old codger seated near the woodstove, there was no one else in the room. He chose a table in the corner near the kitchen door. The aroma of fresh coffee was so strong he could almost taste it. He drummed his fingers on the white tablecloth, then decided to get the drink himself.

He pushed the kitchen door open. "Charlie, I'd sure like a cup of that coffee." Kate's back was to him, but only a blind man wouldn't have seen her stiffen at the sound of his voice. "Good morning, Miss Kate."

Charlie picked up a cup, filled it, and handed it to Smith. "Here ya are. Ya want some breakfast?"

"Thanks." Parker wrapped his cold hands around the hot cup. "I'll take whatever you have. My stomach hasn't had a good meal since I left here." He glanced at Kate and returned to the table.

Kate didn't move until she heard the door close. She couldn't have even if she had wanted to duck out. She pulled her hands out of the dishwater. Ye gods and little fishes! Why had he come back? She grabbed a hand towel.

"Want me to take his plate out to him?"

"No, Charlie." Kate dropped the towel over the back of the chair and took the plate from him. "I've little enough work to do as it is."

Charlie handed her a second plate, and she marched into the dining room. Parker sat watching the door, his head tilted at a lighthearted angle, his damp hair slicked back. He was as cocksure of himself as a rooster in a henhouse. She set the plates down in front of him and stepped back.

"Biscuits and gravy, with pan fries?" He grinned. "I don't suppose you're interested in sharing this with me?"

"You said you were hungry. Charlie took you at your word." An error on his part, she thought, and returned to get the pot of coffee. She refilled old Bert's cup.

"Thanky, gal." Bert saluted her with the cup. "How come no man's caught ya yet?"

Kate shrugged and grinned. "Guess they're too slow." His shoulder length white hair looked yellowed with age, his back was bent, but his mind was as sharp as a knife point. She'd heard the poor man had wandered the hills with no particular aim in life, until a year ago. Now the town seemed to take care of him. She sent up a prayer she wouldn't have resort to the same. On the way back to the kitchen, she stopped at Parker's table and refilled his cup, too.

He motioned to the old codger. "That your beau?"

When she leveled her gaze on Parker, she had a hard time keeping the offended look on her face, and hissed, "I'm glad my father's hard of hearing."

She pivoted on her heel, and Parker feared coffee would be sprayed around the room. He knew she remembered what he'd said before about Turner. Passing the old man off as her father was laughable, but it gave him an idea.

He pushed his chair back and went over to the man's table. "Would you like to join me for breakfast? It doesn't make sense for us to make Miss Kate run from one table to the other."

Bert stared up at Parker. "Who's payin'?"

"I'll spring for it." It was worth a few cents to call Kate's bluff.

"Why d'ya wanta pay fer my meal?"

"Got lucky in a game last night," Parker invented convincingly. He wanted to see Kate's expression when she saw them together.

"Sure. I'll help ya piddle away yer winnin's." Bert followed Parker over to his table and hunkered down across from him.

Parker picked up his fork and pointed it at his plate. "You want the same?"

Bert dragged his sleeve across is his mouth. "Sure do, mister."

Parker banged his fist on the kitchen wall to his left. Kate came flying out, scowling, as he'd figured she would. When she saw Bert at his table, the color drained from her face; her eyes grew large but quickly narrowed on him, and her lips pressed to an angry slant. "Your father would like breakfast."

The damn fool! She held her fists in the folds of her skirt to keep from slugging him. Bert grinned at her, and she doubted he knew what was going on. She got the plate of gravy and biscuits and set it down in front of him.

Bert grabbed his fork. "Thanky, gal. This'll warm m'innards."

"I'm glad." As she turned to go the kitchen, Parker's

eyes sparkled with laughter in an otherwise bland expression. She wanted to knock his teeth out.

When Kate stomped into the kitchen, Charlie held out a chipped cup to her. "What's this for?"

"Thought ya might wanna chuck it."

Kate frowned at the cup. "Why would I want to do that?"

"My ma used to chuck a dish at the door when she wanted to lambast the old man."

"Did it make her feel better?"

"Guess so. Made her smile."

Kate glanced at the cup and pictured Parker's face. She grinned and hurled it at the far door. The sound of shattering china startled her. Immediately she braced her hands on the worktable and sighed.

"Feel better?"

She shook her head. "I *feel* foolish, but thanks, Charlie." She chuckled and picked up the broom. Too bad she couldn't sweep Parker Smith out of her life as easily as the broken cup.

Parker tended Buckshot after leaving the hotel, giving the animal a good grooming. Around one he returned to the hotel for dinner. He wasn't hungry, but he had to make an appearance. He picked at the food, paid for the meal, and left without saying one word more than necessary.

After dinner he spent the afternoon trekking through the area around town. It was damn inconvenient having to play this game, but the stakes were too high to leave. Supper was a repeat of his earlier meal. By breakfast the next morning he was loosing patience. He took a seat by the woodstove and waited for Kate.

She balanced an armload of wood and walked straight to the stove. Halfway across the room, she spotted Parker. He'd come back. Wary, though not about to show it, she didn't break stride. After she had added wood to the fire, she dusted her hands off on her way back to get the coffeepot.

She'd given up trying to figure out the man. If she didn't see him in the dining room, she looked for him when she left the hotel, fearing he would follow her home. He had even invaded her most private hours, showing up in her dreams, smiling, teasing, and worst of all, last night he had taken her in his arms and kissed her senseless.

As she filled his cup with coffee, Parker noticed her face color. ''Maybe you added too much wood to that fire. Your face's red.''

She glanced at him but saw no sign he was needling her. ''You can change tables if it's too warm here.''

''I'm fine.''

She nodded. ''You want breakfast?''

''Yes, ma'am, but tell Charlie not to empty the pan on my plate.''

She pressed her lips together to keep from grinning. ''I'll tell him.''

This side of Parker, she found herself thinking, she could get along with. She served him and went about dusting off crumbs and straightening the tables. A few times her gaze wandered to Parker. Each time she saw something she liked, a soft wave of hair, the easy way he sat back, as if he were dining with friends, and he didn't even shovel his food into his mouth the way so many of the miners did. She came back with the coffeepot to refill his cup.

He finished eating and reached for his hat. His hand brushed over a smooth seam on the tablecloth where there should have been none. He glanced at Kate. Were those little stitches hers? After leaving the coins on the table, he caught her attention and tipped his hat.

Kate nodded, and she smiled as he left the room, when it was safe. If she could be a normal woman, she might have enjoyed his teasing. She picked up his dishes and started for the kitchen—when he came back and walked over to her.

He hoped appealing for help would succeed where his other attempts had failed. ''I tore one of my favorite shirts. Is there a local woman who would be interested in such a small job?'' It almost worked, he thought, she's considering his offer. Then her eyes narrowed.

The image of her mother, so trusting, chattering away with him, sent chills down her back. ''Sorry.''

He shrugged. ''It was worth asking.'' Since he had told the lie, he decided he'd better follow through with it. He had really hoped she would soften, give him an opportunity to know her, verify his suspicions.

When he returned to his room after dinner, he ripped one of his older shirts. With it tucked under his arm, he walked over to the general store and up to the woman dusting off a shelf. She reminded him of dear old Aunt Effie—at least that's what all the children back home had called her, when anyone over thirty was *old*. The woman turned to him, and her prudent gaze traveled down from his face to his gun holstered at his hip. He took the shirt out from under his arm. ''I'm not too handy with a needle and thread. Would you know if there's a seamstress here in town? Or a woman who does mending?''

The woman inspected the tear. ''Mrs. Miller does beautiful work. The miners swear by her.''

On hearing the name Miller, he felt his heart pumping. ''Would you tell me where I can find her?'' He refolded the shirt, wondering what the chances would be that miss and missus Miller were not related.

''Why, surely.'' She quickly stepped to the front window in the store. ''Go alongside the hotel.'' She pointed to the far side. ''There's a path leading from the back, pass some pines, and go around to a cabin. That's where you'll find her.''

''Thank you, ma'am.''

To thank the woman for her help and sweeten the offer with Mrs. Miller, he purchased a packet of needles and thread to match his shirt. He grinned passing the hotel and felt like whistling when he found the path. He soon rounded the trees and saw the cabin. A part of him couldn't help speculating on the possibility of discovering Turner inside, but Parker knew better than to hope for such luck.

The door opened to his knock, and a woman, who reminded him of his mother, gazed at him as if she'd been expecting someone else. ''Hello, ma'am. Are you Mrs. Miller?'' Her dark blond hair was done up fashionably, nothing like her daughter's, which looked hastily pushed back out of her way.

Mary Louise gave him a tentative smile. ''I am. And who are you, suh?'' She folded her hands at her waist.

He smiled, his heart pounding at the familiar, sweet cadence of her voice. ''Parker Smith, ma'am,'' he said, as if he'd suddenly stepped back into a Southern lady's parlor. He quickly recovered. ''I have a shirt that needs mending.'' He held the rolled-up shirt out. ''The lady at the general store recommended you with high praise.''

Shivering, Mary Louise opened the door all the way. ''Well, suh, come on in out'a the cold.'' After she closed the door, she motioned for him to take a seat by the fire. ''Let me see what ya have there.''

Parker handed the shirt to her and chose the straight-back chair, feeling as if he'd stepped back in time. Mrs. Miller's graying brown hair was parted in the center, looped back over her ears, and fell in a mass of curls down over her shoulders.

''Would you care for a cup o'tea, Mr. Smith?''

''Please, don't go to any bother on my account.''

She smiled sweetly, almost like a young girl, but most Southern women did, he remembered.

''Why, it's no trouble I assure you.'' She filled a cup from the teapot, set it on the tray along with the sugar bowl, and served.

He mustered the stale parlor manners he'd learned at his mother's side, but hadn't had the need for in many years, and accepted the mismatched teacup and saucer. He took a sip and nodded. ''Very good, ma'am.''

''It's nice to have a gentleman to tea. We don't have many callers here.'' Mary Louise sat down on the rocking chair and held up the shirt. The thread and packet of needles fell on her lap. ''This is a nasty rip, but I believe I can repair it.'' She held up the thread and needles. ''Were ya plannin' to try your hand at stitchin' this?''

''In a pinch, if you didn't take pity on me.'' He glanced around the shack. ''You've made this old cabin real nice and homey.'' He muttered her name, Miller, loud enough for her to hear. ''By any chance, is Miss Kate Miller, over at the restaurant, related to you?''

''Why, she's ma daughter.''

He gave her a broad smile. ''I thought she had the same lovely smile you have.'' Deceiving this gentle lady didn't sit well with him, but he had to gain her confidence. ''Surely, you and Miss Kate aren't out here alone, ma'am?''

''For a while. Just a while longer.'' She folded the shirt and absently ran her hand over the cloth. ''How about you? Where are you traveling to, Mr. Smith?''

He chuckled. Was she really as fanciful as she appeared? Or was she a gifted charlatan? Whichever, any resemblance to Kate was slight. Kate didn't seem to care about her appearance and was hard as nails, whereas her mother was carefully groomed and made you think of cotton and lace and warm sunny afternoons. ''Why do you think I'm not one of the miners?''

She cocked her head to one side. ''Your attire isn't as rough, and you, suh, have the look of a man who's used to defendin' himself.'' She smiled, her hand grazing the fabric of his shirt.

She wasn't all that soft in the head, he realized. ''At times, a man has to out here, ma'am.'' He took another sip of tea, deciding the best way to bring up his real reason for calling on her. ''Is Mr. Miller a miner?''

She rocked the chair gently. ''Mr. . . . Miller is gone.''

''I'm sorry. You have my deepest sympathy, ma'am.'' He sat back, staring at the fire while watching her from the corner of his eye. If her husband was dead, he had made a grave mistake and needn't waste any more time in Moose Gulch—which meant he wouldn't see any more of Kate. He wasn't sure if he liked that idea or not.

"Oh, he's not—" She glanced at the door. "He keeps in touch. One of these days he'll send for us."

"That's good news. The winters must get lonely here. I'm about ready to give up trying to find my friend and head back to warmer parts." He drew his brows together, as if he were considering something of importance. "Maybe you can help me."

"Why, ifa can. I, too, would surely like to see the last of the frigid climate, but ma daughter doesn't seem t'mind the cold."

She wouldn't, he thought, it matched her personality. "I've been searching for a man named Turner." He watched her closely. "Hank Turner." Her eyes grew round, lighted from within as if the name conjured warm memories. "I met him a while back. We've been through a few of the same towns." He chuckled. "Seems like I just keep missing him."

Mary Louise stopped rocking and glanced around the room. "I hear from him, time to time, but don't ya tell Kate," she whispered.

"Your secret's safe with me, ma'am," he confided. "Would you send him a message for me?"

She started the chair in motion again. "Can't. Don't know where he is."

"Then how—"

"Oh, I find his little notes hidden here an' there." She raised her gaze to Parker. "I haven't seen him in . . . s'many years."

He shifted on the hard seat. "Then how—"

Suddenly the door burst open, and Kate stood there glaring at him. He came to his feet, still holding the teacup. "Miss Kate. What a surprise. I was—"

"Get out of here!" She shoved the door wide open. Damn, this was her worst nightmare.

"Now, deah, that's no way to treat my guest." Mary Louise put his shirt aside and stood up. "I believe the tea's still warm."

"Mamma, please, I'd like to speak with Mr. Smith—

outside.'' If Kate'd had a gun, she would have used it. She stepped back against the open door and waited for him to leave, then followed him out. ''What in tarnation are you doing here?''

''My shirt needs mending, but you already knew that.'' He ambled several yards away from the cabin, stopped, and eyed her. ''Shame on you, Miss Kate, for not telling me your mamma's said to be a fine seamstress.''

She paced back and forth in front of him, flexing her fingers. ''Leave her alone! I don't know what you're doing here, but keep away from her.'' Now they were in a pickle. Her sweet, often befuddled mother would probably invite the devil in for tea, too, she thought, but he's not going to hoodwink me. That canny smile plastered on his face made her sick inside.

''Then meet me tomorrow after dinner,'' he said. Her cheeks were growing red, and the stubborn tilt of her jaw was magnificent. He wouldn't have been surprised if steam had poured from her ears. She really was something when her temper was up.

''You're out of your mind!''

He sipped from the cup still in his hand. ''This sure is good tea,'' he said, as if reading her mind. But he didn't need to, dismay showed in her eyes.

She ground her teeth. ''That's blackmail.'' And she couldn't afford to have him asking around town about her, spreading suspicion or gossip.

He smiled. ''Two o'clock tomorrow?''

❖ 4 ❖

ONCE SHE WAS sure Parker had left, Kate stormed away from the cabin. She trudged up the steep mountain on the other side of the creek, hastily bundled up against the cold. Plowing through the thick shrubs gave her an outlet for her anger and her fear. In all the towns she and her mother had lived in, she'd been careful not to let anyone get too close to them. Her mother spent many evenings regaling Kate with stories about her many friends, and Kate had wondered at having someone to really confide in, share dreams and memories with—

Parker and her mother had been talking, visiting. How long had he been there? *What* had they talked about before she'd arrived? Surely her mother hadn't said anything she shouldn't have. No one knew—not even Charlie. Oh, botheration, she thought, guessing wouldn't change anything. Neither would getting lost in the woods after sundown.

She hurried back to the cabin. Her mother was sitting in her rocker by the fire mending a shirt. Kate pulled off her gloves, unwound the woolen scarf, and hung her jacket on the peg.

Mary Louise completed the stitch and glanced at her daughter. "I'm nearly finished with Mr. Smith's shirt. Would you take it to him, deah?"

Kate dashed to the bed, grabbed her skirt, and pulled it

over her head, grinning to herself. ''Of course.'' He'll have no excuse to come back, she thought. ''Mamma, what all did you two talk about?'' She fastened the waistband and brushed her hair back.

''Nothin' much. He was just tellin' me 'bout lookin' for his friend.'' Mary Louise tied off the last stitch and snipped the thread. ''If his friend's in these vast mountains, it could take him months, even years to find him.''

''Mmm, it could.'' The sooner he left, Kate thought, the better she'd like it. If she'd been thinking faster that first day, she might've sent him off in a different direction. Evidently, she'd become overly confident. She grabbed her jacket and scarf. ''I've got to hurry, Mamma.''

''Here, deah,'' Mary Louise said, handing Parker's shirt to Kate. ''Careful with that, now. The needle and thread are tucked in there.''

Kate took the neatly folded shirt. The fabric was soft, of good quality, and held the faint aroma of laurel. She'd always liked that scent. She crammed the shirt into her jacket pocket and dashed to the hotel kitchen. Charlie was at the stove. ''Sorry I'm late. I took a walk up the mountain.'' After she hung up her jacket, she peered into the dining room. There was a cup on one table but no one in sight. ''Was Mr. Bishop here?''

''Yep. His steak's 'bout ready.'' Charlie plopped a generous mound of mashed potatoes on the plate, added string beans and the pan-fried steak.

Kate put several hot biscuits on a small plate and set it on the tray with the dinner plate. Then she spooned butter into a bowl and carried the tray into the dining room. After serving the meal, she saw Mr. Bishop at the desk in the hotel lobby writing in the ledger and went over to him.

''Your supper's ready. Do you want Charlie to keep it warm for a while?''

Mr. Bishop glanced at her. ''No. I'll be right in. Thank you, Kate.''

As she entered the dining room, someone came down the stairs and she kept walking straight to the kitchen. Mr.

Bishop ate and left. Old Bert came by for his plate of left-overs. She had dusted the furniture and the molding in the dining room and figured she could have painted the walls and not bothered anyone, when Earl Wilson came into the room. She returned his smile. "Hi."

Earl took his hat off. "Evening, Miss Kate. Am I too late for supper?"

"Just in time. You have your choice of seats." She met him at the table he chose. "Tonight we have steak and chokecherry pie." She guessed Earl was in his late thirties. His appearance and clothes were always neat, and he wasn't bad looking. He'd been nice to her, but when he'd shown her more interest than she wanted, she had made it clear she wasn't looking for a husband.

"Sounds good." He set back, staring at her. "You're looking well. This climate must agree with you."

"I think you've been up here too long," she said lightly, hoping he'd take the hint that she hadn't changed her mind about him. "I'll get your supper." She returned with his food and poured a cup of coffee for him.

"Can you keep me company? I eat alone at home."

He watched her with those puppy-dog eyes, and she came close to pulling a chair out. "Sorry. I still have work to do." She felt sorry for him but not enough to encourage unwanted attention.

When she went back to the kitchen and grabbed the bucket of clean water, Charlie snatched it from her hand. " 'Nough o' this. Sit. Yer supper's gettin' cold."

She stared at the plate of food on the worktable, then eyed him. "Where's yours?"

"Right there," he said, and set a second plate on the table in front of her.

She sat down and picked up the fork and knife. "This's a lot of food when I've only had one paying customer." She needed this job. It was too late in the year to wander the Rockies looking for a position in another out-of-the-way town. "I hope Mr. Bishop can keep me on."

"No use yankin' on a coyote's tail when he's happy to let ya be."

She grinned, hoping to ease the alarm stirring inside her. There was no way she could pack up their belongings and leave without Parker Smith tracking them down within a couple hours. Halfway through her steak, she checked the dining room. Earl was still eating. "Did you serve Smith tonight?"

"Nah. Ain't seen him." He peered over his fork full of mashed potatoes at her. "Worried?"

"It's not my problem if he can't remember when to come for supper." Unfortunately, she *knew* he hadn't left town. She finished eating and served a generous slice of pie to Earl.

He eyed the plate. "Mind if I take that home to eat later? I'll bring the plate back tomorrow."

"That'll be fine." She picked up a clean napkin from the other side of the table and covered the plate.

He stood up and paid for his meal. "Thanks, Kate."

"Have a good evening." She cleared the table and took the plates back to the kitchen.

After their dishes were washed and put away, Charlie handed her jacket to her. "Yer mama's plate's on the table. Take the rest of that pie, too."

She gave him a quick hug, bundled up for the short walk, and left, with both plates. The wind had picked up, and there weren't many stars in the sky as she made her way along the path to their cabin. If not for the smoke pouring from the chimney, it was well hidden among the bushes and tall pines. Inside, it was as warm as a spring Texas afternoon. She set the plates on the table and closed the door. She hesitated only a moment before setting the bar in place.

Mary Louise frowned slightly. "Somethin' wrong, deah?" She set her knitting aside.

"No. I've become overconfident in the last month." Kate hung her scarf on one of the pegs by the door. "We've got to be careful." The bar was a sturdy length of plank and should keep any man or beast out, including Parker Smith, she thought, knowing her mother would never bar his entry. "It's there for a reason. We might as well use it." When she hung her jacket up, she realized his shirt was still in her jacket pocket. Tomorrow's soon enough. He shouldn't need it tonight—there was nothing to dress up for in town.

"The creatures won't bother us less they're hungry." Mary Louise set her place at the table.

"I'd just as soon not be supper for one of them." Kate uncovered the second plate. "Charlie sent nearly half a pie."

"Oh, he's such a deah man." Mary Louise peered under the napkin covering the pie. "I do enjoy a good choke-cherry pie." She sat down and cut a bite of meat. "Katherine Anne, have—"

"*Kate*, Mamma. You *must* remember to call me Kate." Her mother's lips quivered and her eyes filled with tears. Kate softened her expression to ease the chiding. "It's important, Mamma. This's a nice quiet town, and I'd like to stay the winter."

Mary Louise looked away. "I know ya do, deah."

"I'll be cleaning the hotel rooms this winter. We'll be able to move this spring. We'll need to decide where we want to go." Kate wished there were some way she could find out if it would be safe to use their real names—anywhere. But after some man had asked about her by name in Park City, she couldn't take the chance.

"Some place warm." Mary Louise ate a bite of string beans and dabbed her mouth with the napkin. "Do ya suppose we could move back home?"

"I'm not even sure where 'home' was. We'll find a nice town, and you'll make new friends." Kate poured herself a cup of tea.

"Oh, darlin,' don't ya remember ridin' over to Dallas and browsin' in the shops?"

While her mother recollected a life Kate barely recognized, she worked on an old dress she was remaking. They had never been so far north, and from the recent early frost, she believed it would indeed be a very cold winter. She had saved nearly half of every penny she'd earned for the last four years. She'd hoped to put away enough to purchase a modest little house. Now, older and more experienced, she knew they wouldn't move into a new life but would have to create one.

Later when she noticed her mother yawning, she banked the fires. They changed into nightdresses and climbed into bed. "Night, Mamma."

"Night, darlin'. Sweet dreams."

Kate curled up on her side and her mind drifted as a patchwork of fickle thoughts blended. There was a small house with a garden; Betsy, the mare she had when they left Texas and had to sell, trotted by. She felt as if she were eight again, safe in her mother's arms, until a man stepped out of the shadows.

Parker sat in the corner of the dining room, not far from the door to the kitchen. Mr. Bishop was seated closer to the woodstove, and Bert was sitting next to it. Parker sipped his coffee wondering how the hotel *and* dining room managed to remain open with so little business. It was a safe bet no one besides himself was registered, and he was probably the only paying customer in the dining room. Kate served his breakfast. "Have time for a cup of coffee with me?"

"I have work to do." She avoided meeting his gaze. After awakening that morning with piercing blue eyes, as clear in her mind as his rugged masculinity and the scent of his hair tonic fresh in her mind, she felt as if they'd spent the night together. She didn't need any more complications in her life—especially him.

He continued staring at her. She fidgeted with the tablecloth, the salt shaker, and her skirt, but she wouldn't look at him. He nodded. "I'm sure you do."

She returned to the kitchen for the coffeepot. He hadn't pressed her, and she should be glad or at least more at ease.

She wasn't either. Two o'clock loomed ahead of her as if it were a noose, and she could almost hear a clock ticking the minutes away. She grabbed the pot and returned to the dining room.

Mr. Bishop didn't speak until she had refilled his cup. "Smith's the only one here now. Cleaning twice a week's enough."

"That'll be fine with me." She hadn't cleaned his room the day before, but she knew she'd have to do it in a day or so—hopefully after he left town for good.

Parker finished eating all but the last piece of bread and lingered, waiting for her to return. He checked his pocket watch several times. Thirty-seven minutes later she looked around the room from the kitchen doorway. "I was beginning to think you'd left."

And I'd hoped you had, she thought. "More coffee?" Was he a bottomless pit? Or had he set out to make her miserable? They were alone. Maybe they wouldn't need to meet later.

He shook his head. She ducked back into the kitchen. He was pushing back from the table when she returned.

She handed his shirt to him. "Mamma thought you might need this."

When he held it up, the spool of thread fell to the floor, but he ignored it for the moment. He inspected the tear and nodded. "Your mother has a way with a needle and thread. Please thank her for me. How much do I owe her?" No wonder Miss Rose was mourning the loss of Mrs. Miller.

"Four dollars." That was an outrageous charge, but she didn't care. Let him pay for my discomfort, too, she thought.

He pulled a handful of coins from his pant pocket, picked out four silver dollars, and held them out to her. "Your mother is a lovely woman. Please give her my best."

Men usually found her mother charming, probably because she was so fawning and tractable. Kate tucked the money in her pocket and placed her hand on the chair opposite him. "Mind if I sit down?" He raised one dark, expressive brow, and she waited for his reply.

"What about your work?"

Her fingers tightened on the back of the chair. "I can spare a few minutes."

"In that case, why don't you pour yourself some coffee?" She'd aroused his curiosity. He had the feeling she rarely made a rash decision.

"It shouldn't take that long." She pulled the chair out and perched on the edge. "Since we can speak now, there's no need to meet later. What did you want to talk to me about?" Her arms were at her sides, and her fingers gripped the seat.

She faced him head on, but ready to run, as if they were about to duel. He cleared his throat. "I just wanted to talk. And I rarely hold a woman at gun point." Although she might be the exception. She cocked her head at a charming angle, and he had to remind himself she was most likely the daughter of a killer.

She narrowed her gaze. "What about?"

He shrugged with deceptive nonchalance. "The town, weather, maybe about the miners in the hills." He eyed her. "Surely, you're acquainted with the art of conversation." She seemed to prefer meeting a challenge rather responding to a social request. So be it. He'd give her one.

"As well as you." She was in no mood for chitchat. "If you walk from the livery to the saloon, you've seen the town. The people are nice. Winter starts early here. It'll snow any day." Or so she'd been told, but he didn't need to know how long she'd lived there. "Most of the miners have moved on. The ones that've stayed don't take to nosy strangers. There're no entertainments and traveling medicine men rarely stop here." She leaned forward and stood up, her fingers almost painfully cramped. "Enjoy your visit, Mr. Smith."

He hid his smirk and came to his feet within an arm's length of her. "Oh, I intend to, Kate." He dropped the price of his meal on the table along with a tip for her. "I'll come for you at two.'' He flashed an easygoing smile. ''If it snows, maybe Mac will let us picnic in his livery.''

After Kate finished at the hotel, she went over to the general store. With so little money and that only for necessities, she didn't spend much time in shops, but she liked the hodgepodge of the Goodys' store. The aroma of fresh ground coffee filled the air. Mrs. Goody was at the post office counter. She was middle-aged, and her brown hair pulled back into a knot that usually looked a little careworn. She was an easy woman to like with her friendly manner, but Kate had learned long ago not to get too close to anyone, because she and her mother never stayed in any town very long. She greeted Mrs. Goody and went to the shelf where the bolts of yard goods were stacked.

Their flannel petticoats were getting thin, and as thrifty as she'd been, scrimping on warm clothes for winter would be foolhardy. She ran her hand between two bolts of flannel, one ivory, one lavender. One wouldn't stay clean long and the other hardly seemed to go with her plain skirts. But it would be fun to have a bit of color, even though no one would see it.

She pulled the lavender bolt out and paused. Her mother firmly believed every lady must have a red petticoat in her wardrobe, and hers was threadbare. Kate slid the red bolt out, and Mrs. Goody came over.

Mrs. Goody smiled at her. ''I haven't seen you for days, Kate. Did Mr. Smith find your mother?''

''Yes, he did. She asked me to thank you for recommending her.'' Kate only stretched the truth a tad, and her mother would've approved. She had hoped moving to such a small town in the Rocky Mountains would be safe. Moose Gulch probably wasn't even on any map, but she'd been wrong to think they'd be any safer here. So very wrong. There was no place to hide, no crowd to get lost in or even a way to slip out of town.

''I'm glad. He seemed nice enough, not like some of the shooters I've seen.''

Kate glanced around and changed the subject. "How's Miss Lucy doing? I thought she was helping you out here?" Mrs. Goody's mother was of a certain age, but she was good company for Mary Louise.

"She felt like baking today. This afternoon this place will smell like a bakery."

"Please give her my best. Mamma does enjoy their visits."

"I surely will, Kate." Mrs. Goody ran her hand over the fabric. "How much do you want, Kate?"

"Six lengths of the red and twelve lavender. We'll need warm petticoats."

Mrs. Goody flipped the bolt, unwrapping the red fabric. "That you will. By January I'll be wearing six, two pair of woolen stockings, and a wool dress." She measured out the six lengths. "No way to avoid drafts up here."

"It's reassuring to know our cabin isn't the only airy building in town. Morrey lined his tent with pelts."

Mrs. Goody nodded. "He'll be toasty, but I wish he and Mr. Pitt would move in town for the winter." She set the red bolt aside and reached for the lavender one.

"And leave their claims?" Kate chuckled. "We both know they won't, but I'll check on them."

"You're such a dear, but the snow gets deep. It won't be easy to get to their claims." She cut the material. "They say freezing to death isn't so bad. You feel warm and just go to sleep."

Kate shivered. "I'll keep that in mind." She added thread to the folded yard goods. "How are your girls doing?"

Mrs. Goody beamed. "Lizbeth and Sarah are doing fine at Mrs. Goodwin's school for girls." She tied the string around the bundle of cloth wrapped in a piece of calico. "I surely hope we can get down to Helena for the Christmas."

Last winter Kate and her mother had been in Frisco in the Utah Territory, but there was never more than a foot of snow on the ground. "Does it snow that much?" She paid Mrs. Goody and pocketed the change.

"We have a sleigh, so unless there's a blizzard, we'll get down to see them."

"I'll keep my fingers crossed." Kate left the store and returned to the cabin. Her mother was outside feeding scraps to some of her critters. "You're spoiling them. They should be getting ready for winter, not moving in with us."

Mary Louise passed out the last crumbs. "They aren't eatin' all of it. See," she said, pointing to one fluffy squirrel. "His cheeks are full to poppin'. He's takin' most of it back to stash it away."

"I hope he does." Kate went inside and put the yard goods on the bed. There was enough time to start cutting the fabric before she had to return to work. She measured four lengths of the lavender. Skimping on the fullness would yield three petticoats instead of two.

When Mary Louise came in and closed the door, she noticed the fabric spread out on their bed. "Oh, that red's bright as cherries. What's all this for?"

"Petticoats. Mrs. Goody said she'll be wearing six by January. You can have one of these and the red. Your old red petticoat's faded and worn thin."

"Thank ya, deah. You're so good to me, but ya don't have one. We'll share it."

"For a special occasion, I just might." Kate made the first cut. "You know, Mamma, we can't continue using so much wood in the fires. It's getting harder and harder to find pieces I can chop."

Mary Louise tsk-tsk-tsked. "That's no work for a lady. I'll ask Mr. Smith if he'd do us a kindness."

"No—we'll manage with a little less heat." Kate glanced at her mother. "And a few more clothes."

Mary Louise held the red flannel at her waist. "Yes, deah, we'll be fine." As she watched her daughter's quick movements, she frowned. "Kate, slow down. Ya ain't makin' feed sacks."

"Don't be too sure," Kate muttered, well aware she didn't have the patience to make the small perfect stitches her mother did with ease. She snipped the edge of the flannel, and her hands trembled as she ripped the flannel, separating the last two panels. It was nearly time to get back to work, but that wasn't what caused the anxious feeling in the pit of her stomach. She quickly folded the pieces of fabric and set them on top of the dresser.

"Your cheeks are a bit flushed, and ya seem agitated." Mary Louise carefully folded the red flannel. "I do hope you're not comin' down with the fever."

"Mamma, I'm fine. There's so much to do."

"There'll be plenty of cold nights to knit and sew by the fire." Mary Louise looked through her lashes at her daughter. "If we had the yarn and yard goods, we could have new wardrobes by spring. Mrs. Goody does have some nice fabric."

Kate grabbed her jacket and opened the door. "I'll see what I can manage, Mamma." Her mother's concern lay with their clothes, while she was worried about their home and safety.

She'd given up trying to force her mother to admit that their lives hadn't been grand all those years ago. Her father had been a gunsmith. But her mother was a dreamer and remembered the past she'd probably dreamed of from childhood.

Kate paused a few paces from the hotel kitchen. Banjo music drifted from the saloon, and she leaned against the trunk of a cedar tree. She acknowledged the one gift her father had given her. Marksmanship. Before he had joined The Rebellion, he had made sure she was skilled with a pistol and a rifle. Oh, there had been other times she'd felt cherished by her father, but those memories began to dim after he'd left her mother and her to fend for themselves, left a twelve-year-old girl to be their protector and provider.

5

PARKER WATCHED KATE cross the road and go around the hotel before he went to the kitchen. Charlie was putting a napkin over the top of a basket. "That mine?"

Charlie pushed the basket toward Parker at the end of the table. "No one else 'round here crazy 'nough to want a picnic dinner this time of year."

Parker paid him. "Guess I'm feeling adventurous."

"Must be," Charlie mumbled, pocketing the coins. "Nearest doctor's in Deer Lodge."

Parker picked up the basket and started around the table. "I'll keep that in mind."

He left by the side door Kate had used and followed the path back to her cabin. He rapped on the door twice. And he waited. When he began wondering if she had left, Mrs. Miller opened the door.

Mary Louise smiled. "Please, come in, Mr. Smith. Kate's almost ready."

He removed his hat and stepped inside. "Thank you, Mrs. Miller." The curtain blocked the bed area, but it was a good bet Kate wasn't dressing in her Sunday best for him.

Mary Louise glanced at the basket and noticed the blanket roll under his arm. "Please be seated." She took her rocking chair by the fire, and her attention briefly returned to the basket. "The weather's been unseasonably pleasant.

I can't imagine what it'll be like by Thanksgiving."

While he listened to Mrs. Miller, the curtain shielding the bed area flapped, and he hoped his amusement didn't show. "I understand the snow gets quite deep up here." He noticed Kate's boots below the curtain and wondered if she ever slipped into her mother's soft way of speaking. "Getting supply wagons through won't be easy." And if Kate or her mother couldn't—or wouldn't—help him, he might tag along with one of those wagons.

"Oh, deah. I hadn't thought of that." Mary Louise drew her brows together and darted a glance at the curtain. "Now that ya mention it, the squirrels' coats are gettin' thick. Kate, do ya think we should move on b'fore we get snowed in here?"

Oh, Mamma, why do you have to say whatever pops into your head? Kate wondered, shoving the derringer into her pocket. She turned to the curtain, sent up a silent prayer her mother wouldn't ask what she'd been doing since she hadn't changed clothes, and stepped around the curtain. Parker looked as comfortable sitting with her mother as if he were in a saloon, which she was sure was more his element. "I'm ready, Mr. Smith."

Mary Louise stared at her daughter. She opened her mouth as if about to speak, when Kate sent her a wordless signal. "Will ya be warm enough?"

Kate smiled. "I'll be just fine, Mamma." She went over to the door and lifted her coat from the peg.

Parker stepped up behind her and took the jacket from her hand. "I don't mind helping a lady on with her coat." She stiffened, but he held the heavy jacket out and eased it up her arms. When he settled the collar around her neck, his knuckles looked so dark compared to her pale tender skin. Then he picked up the basket, his hat, and gave Mrs. Miller a smile. "I'll see she doesn't get chilled."

He closed the door, and Kate glared at him. "Smith, what do you think you're doing? You act like we're keeping company." She started along the path at a brisk pace.

He caught up with her and grabbed her hand. "You're

going the wrong way.'' He didn't release her but turned to follow the creek. ''Looks to me like we're keeping company.''

She raised his hand slightly, then snapped hers down and back, freeing herself from his grasp. ''I'm no wayward child. Just tell me where we're going.''

He glanced sideways at her. ''Why, Miz Miller. Didn't yer mamma tell ya you'd catch more flies with honey?'' Her cheeks turned crimson, and her stubborn chin jutted out.

She came to an abrupt halt and scowled at him. ''Poking fun at the way my mother talks will not endear me to you.'' As if *anything* he could do, she thought, would change her mind about him.

''Point well taken,'' he said sincerely. ''I meant no harm, and I'd never mock your m . . . other.'' He'd nearly said *mamma* the more familiar term, but he didn't think she needed to know that their background wasn't all that different.

She turned her back to him and faced the creek. Something about him niggled at her, as if she had seen him before. But that was impossible. She would never have forgotten his beautiful eyes or his deep voice. ''Does this spot suit your needs?'' She glanced over her shoulder at him and saw the smoke from their cabin rising above the trees. She didn't want to get too far from town, not with him.

He motioned up the creek. ''I found a nice sunny place just ahead.'' He stepped past her and continued on where the creek narrowed. With a quick sideways glimpse at her, he crossed to the clearing on the other side.

She followed him, stepping from the rock in the middle of the creek to the opposite bank. He spread out a blanket on the dried grass, and she stared in disbelief. ''What is that for?''

He set the basket on the blanket and looked at her. ''To sit on. I thought it might be more comfortable than perching on a log or rock.''

He's out of his mind, she thought. He must be. She sidestepped the blanket and sat on the ground. He had hunkered down by the basket unpacking it, and he looked for all the world as if they were on a friendly outing. But blackmail, to her way of thinking, wasn't grounds for companionship. "I'd like to get this over with."

He tipped his hat back. "Charlie packed a nice dinner for us." He took out a plate heaped with fried chicken. "Smells good."

The aroma drifted over to her. She grudgingly and silently agreed. The sun was to his back and in her eyes, reason enough not to look at him. She rubbed her moist palms on her skirt. "Why are we out here?" The sun was bright and felt good. She opened her jacket and wished he would have his say.

"It's a good day for a picnic."

It is, she realized with a touch of sadness. "Have a nice time." She started to get to her feet.

He set out two plates, the flatware, and two cups. "Don't you like picnics?"

She had taken one step, when he raised a plate with a browned chicken breast, biscuit with butter oozing from it, and a spiced peach.

"Keep me company?" He pressed the dish to her hand. She slid the palm of her hand under the plate and balanced it with her thumb. She looked unsure and edgy. He'd known she would be, but he could be as patient as Job, if need be. His hunter's instinct told him it would be worth the effort. Add to that his growing curiosity about her, and there was no doubt about his staying in town until he had answers to his questions.

"Since Charlie went to the trouble . . ." She heard a wren and thought it sounded lonesome. She felt that way sometimes. The food smelled good, and she was hungry. And more than anything, she had to find out what he wanted or she'd be awake all night fearing what he might do about his suspicions. "I might as well." She sat back down on the ground.

He filled the cups with hot coffee from a jug. "I asked

for cider.'' He leaned over, held out one of the cups to her, and removed his jacket before he stretched out on the blanket. ''I guess Charlie didn't approve.''

''He wouldn't've.'' She took a sip and set the cup down.

He picked up the chicken with his fingers. ''Is he related? Or a good friend?''

''Friend.'' She ate a bite of biscuit. He seemed at ease. She was certain she hadn't understood his invitation. ''Why?'' Her judgment couldn't be that far off the mark.

He shrugged one shoulder and stretched the truth a little when he said, ''He reminds me of someone.'' He ate another bite of chicken. ''It's nice up here in the mountains. What was Moose Gulch like before the claims played out?''

Good question. She didn't know but, she realized, neither did he. ''The saloon was busy day and night. Everyone was. The miners left nuggets for tips.'' She sipped the coffee, recalling other towns. ''There were more women here then and fights, too. It was a boomtown for a while.'' She glanced at him. ''It wasn't so different from others around here.''

''I'm surprised you stuck around.'' He picked up the biscuit. ''Mac mentioned he had a claim. Did you try your hand at panning for gold?'' Her fingers were long, slender, and work roughened. He looked away, determined to remember why they were sitting by the creek.

''I tried it once—ended up sitting in the icy water with nothing to show for my effort but mud. I—'' *Am saying too much*, she thought. ''I didn't try again,'' she said with forced ease. He had a pleasant manner that had loosened her tongue.

''Good idea. Not many miners left the hills with full pockets.'' He stabbed his fork into a peach half. ''I'm surprised Bishop's hung around so long.''

''So am I,'' she said softly and reached for the last piece of chicken. ''Why are you here, Smith?'' She didn't like cat-and-mouse games, especially when she felt like the mouse, and wanted this meeting over with.

He met her steely gaze. ''I told you the other day. I'm

looking for Hank Turner. He has a daughter—Katherine. She's around your age.'' He paused, giving her time to think it over. Her attention shifted for a moment and returned. ''I'm hoping she'll help me locate him.''

She slipped her hand under the edge of her skirt and made a fist. ''Which are you—outlaw or marshal?''

''Are those my only choices?'' Remaining straight faced was hard to do. She'd slipped. He'd given her no cause to believe Turner lived outside the law.

She glared at him. Sometimes there wasn't much difference between the two.

''Neither. Why?''

Her gaze involuntarily veered to the gun resting against his thigh. ''You don't look like a digger or farmer or ranch hand.''

''Do you always make such harsh judgments?''

''That's a new Peacemaker with a cutaway.'' Only shooters wanted the trigger guard cut away to save a second when drawing and firing their gun. He wore the weapon as comfortably as he did his shirt or pants, and in her experience, only a skilled shooter thought of his pistol as part of himself.

''You have a good eye.'' Her knowledge of guns surprised him. Could she work with her father? He hadn't thought of that before and didn't like the idea.

She hated asking, but she needed to know. ''Do you know this Turner's daughter?''

''I've seen her. I'd know her anywhere.'' He eyed her, adding, ''Has her father's hair and nose,'' to provoke her.

She gritted her teeth. She didn't look anything like her father. Nothing. Her mother said she resembled her grandmamma. And she certainly didn't get her father's underhanded ways. ''She might not be flattered to hear she looks like a man.''

''Thanks for the advice.'' He saluted her with his cup and sipped his coffee. He already had her animosity. It was time to switch tactics. ''I remember the first time I was told I looked like my father.'' He looked up at a pine tree. ''I felt ten feet tall.'' Had his voice wavered? Given away feelings he strived to keep to himself? ''But I guess it would be different for a girl.'' His father was shot and killed ten years ago, and Parker had dealt with his loss. This was the last step. After his obligation was taken care of, he would move on and not look back.

She rolled her eyes. ''Not many girls'd like to hear they look like men.''

''Oh, I see what you mean.'' He refilled their cups. ''What do you remember about your father when you were growing up? I don't have any sisters.''

''I didn't, either.'' Her arm brushed against her pocket. ''Mine taught me how to shoot,'' she said with an edge to her voice.

I'd better not forget that, Parker thought. ''What else? Did you chase after your brothers when they went fishing with your father?''

''I haven't any brothers.'' And if I did, she thought, I wouldn't be here. She ate the last of her peach, wiped her mouth, and pushed her plate closer to the basket.

He stacked the dishes and began repacking the basket. ''Come to think of it, neither did Katherine.'' A movement in the brush caught his attention. He picked a couple ripe currants from the nearby bush and tossed them to the ground.

Kate had rolled to her knees when she noticed Parker watching the squirrel. She paused, regarding him out of the corner of her eye. This meeting was different from what she'd expected. If he weren't searching for her father, she might have enjoyed talking with him. Once again, her father intruded into her life, and she vowed to find a way to end his interference. Parker posed a greater threat than she'd first thought. She quickly stood up. ''I have to get back.''

''I'll walk you home, if you wait a minute.''

''No need to trouble yourself. I know my way around the mountains.'' At least this area, she thought, crossing the creek. She took three long strides and called out, ''Hope you get Turner.'' With her back to him, she smiled. He just might be the answer to her problems after all.

Kate's parting words haunted Parker all afternoon. He'd first believed she was pestering him. But the more he thought about it, heard her repeat ''Hope you get Turner'' again and again, he changed his mind. There'd been an edge in her voice. He was sure she had meant it—unless she was better at dissembling than he'd given her credit for.

That evening, when he walked into the dining room, there were two men he hadn't seen before seated at separate tables. The older of the two was dressed in buckskins, mountain style with an otter collar and cuffs on his heavy coat, and the other wore a gray jacket, purple vest, and blue shirt. He took the table in the corner, where he could keep them in sight and waited for Kate. She carried a large tray over to the older man.

She balanced the tray with one hand while she served the hearty meal. ''Think that'll warm your belly, Coop?''

''Ah, Katie, you know me too well.'' Coop picked up the knife and spoon.

When she flashed him a grin and turned, she noticed Parker sitting in the corner. He gave her a nod, and she returned it. He hadn't changed clothes, but there was something different about him. She pushed a wisp of hair behind her ear and carried the tray to the stranger's table. ''Hope you're hungry.'' She set a generous serving of stew in front of him and a plate of biscuits. ''If you need anything, just call out.''

''Thank ya, ma'am. Looks real good.''

She moved over to where Mr. Bishop had eaten and stacked the dirty dishes on the tray before she stopped at Parker's table. ''Evenin'. Tonight it's stew and sourdough biscuits, berry flummery for dessert.'' She made the mistake of glancing at him. Did he have his daddy's firm chin and straight nose? And which of his parents had his sky-blue eyes? she wondered. Oh, thunder, she shouldn't even think about him.

"That's fine with me." He watched her mouth as she had looked at him. Her lips had softened, as if to smile, then suddenly thinned out. "Business is picking up."

She picked up the tray. "Looks like it." She went back to the kitchen and scraped off the dishes. "Smith wants some stew."

Charlie ladled stew onto a plate and set it on the worktable. "Coop 'bout ready for his puddin'?"

"Most likely." She dished out the flummery and put it on the tray along with a plate of biscuits and stew. When she looked up, Charlie was watching her. He hadn't mentioned Parker or the picnic basket and neither had she. "You outdid yourself with that dinner you fixed." She set the coffeepot on the tray and smiled at him. "Thanks."

"It warn't free. Smith paid good for that dinner." He shrugged. "Did he treat you right?"

"Yes, sir," she said with a wink. "You know I don't put up with bold-faced foolery." She opened the dining room door and carried the tray to Parker's table.

After she served his food, Parker gave her an appreciative nod. "If I keep eating like this, I'll have to punch another hole in my belt."

She picked up the tray. "You don't have to eat it all," she said, walking away. She knew no more about his plans than she had that morning. As she set the tray down near Coop's table, she shot a quick glance over her shoulder. Parker was watching her. With a deliberate unruffled manner, she set the flummery down within Coop's reach and picked up the coffeepot. "How've you been?" she asked, refilling his cup.

"Right tolerable as allus." Coop pushed the last half of a biscuit around the plate, sopping up the gravy, then handed her the plate. "I surely missed Charlie's puddin'."

"I'll tell him."

"Nah. Don't." Coop stuck his spoon into the pudding. "Let's keep it betwixt us."

"Won't say a word." She winked and went over to check the fire in the woodstove. Parker's interest in her was unsettling. She was tempted to ask him if he would be leaving tomorrow, but she decided that'd be foolhardy. Besides, she had to clean his room in the morning in any case. That thought made her smile as she stepped over to the stranger.

Parker broke open a biscuit and dipped it into the gravy. Kate had been distant with him, but with the old man she laughed and smiled. Strange. But come to think of it, she was friendliest with older men. He ate a chunk of venison and observed her speaking to the duded-up newcomer. When she was guarded with the man, he grinned.

Kate cleared dirty dishes, refilled coffee cups, and served dessert. The stranger left, and she went over to Coop. ''Ready for another helping of flummery?''

Coop shook his head. ''You tryin' to fatten me up?''

She laughed. ''No chance of that. We only see you once every few months.''

He paid her for his meal and stood up. ''When I'm an old codger, I jist might move to town.'' He stepped past her. ''See you in the mornin'.''

On her way back to the kitchen, she paused at Parker's table. He'd only eaten part of his meal, but he had pushed the dish away. ''I'll get your dessert.'' She reached for his plate, refusing to wonder what he was up to now. Maybe he'd given up on her. That would be a blessing, wouldn't it?

He stood up, pushing his chair back. ''I'm full.'' She stepped back, and he picked up his hat, wondering what was going through her mind. ''Why don't you take the flummery to your mother?'' He took a couple coins from his pocket, gently grasped her hand, and closed her fingers around them. ''So long, Kate.''

He put his hat on and left the hotel. The town looked deserted, and wind whistled between weathered boards on abandoned storefronts. He raised his collar against the bone-chilling cold and paused at the narrow lot between hotel and saloon. There was no place for him to work while he kept watch over Kate and her mother. He didn't need the cash but a place where he could blend in and move about unnoticed.

Mac seemed to spend a good deal of time at his claim; Earl carved bears, elk, and mountain lions to fill his time between occasional baths or haircuts, and the bartender had no trouble handling the saloon by himself. Parker could handle a gun, not a unique ability, had worked in saloons, for the Union Pacific for a time, delivered goods and mail to miners, and even posed as a huckster once, while tracking Turner.

He opened the heavy oak door and stepped into the smoky saloon. The bartender was talking to the banjo player wearing the same patched and tattered reb shirt. The bartender nodded, and Parker stepped up to the center of the plank bar. "Whiskey."

The bartender poured the drink and pushed it over to Parker.

Steeling himself for the first foul taste, Parker gulped down half the shot. "Quiet tonight."

The banjo player nodded. "If yer wantin' a game or some sport, ya'll have't go down to a hurdy-gurdy house in Deer Lodge." He smacked his thigh. "Sounds right inter'sing, don't it?"

Parker came close to smiling. "That it does."

The banjo player drained his glass and set it down with a thump. "If ya'll go me another beer, Smith, I'll play ya a tune."

"Sounds fair," Parker said, putting the price of two beers on the bar. Finally, he thought, a name for the big, dark-haired bartender. "I'll take one, too." It couldn't be worse than the whiskey. Ralston nodded, refilled the other man's glass, and filled one for Parker.

The banjo player reached for his glass. "Thanks. Any man who buys me a drink has a right to my moniker. Tullie James." After he drained the glass, he picked up the banjo and began strumming "Goober Peas!" "Folks call me Tullie."

"I like the sound of your banjo, Tullie." As Parker

sipped his beer, he decided he'd have to stop by each night for a drink. There was little else to do, and eventually he might overhear some helpful comment. He stared at his glass and listened to the verse "Lying in the Shadow underneath the trees . . ." He wondered if Kate had ever wiled away a hot, lazy afternoon under a sycamore.

6

KATE CLEANED THE room the stranger had used. Parker's was next. She stepped up to his door, set down the bucket of water, and knocked on his door. When she didn't hear a sound, she reached into her pocket for the key.

Suddenly the door opened, and Parker eyed her as if she'd drawn her pistol on him, then he gave her a curious look.

"I'm here to tidy up the room."

"I should've known it wasn't a social visit." He stepped back. "I was beginning to think I'd have to change the linens myself." She marched into his room with the assurance he had come to expect and appreciate. She fascinated him because she possessed an odd combination of traits, he reassured himself. He discounted the fact that she was pretty, forthright, and fun to tease.

She set the bucket and rags down. "I'll get fresh sheets and be right back."

"I'm not going anywhere."

I didn't think you were, she thought, going down the hall to the linen closet. After she picked up the sheets, she grabbed two more blankets. She didn't mind giving him a piece of her mind, but she wasn't a cruel person. At least she didn't believe she was.

He had just moved his Winchester carbine away from

the bed when she returned with an armload of bedding. Having no desire to test her skill with the weapon, he set it in the corner, butt down, and stood in front of it. ''Do the extra blankets mean we're friends?''

''It means winter's coming.'' He was like a dog with his jaw locked on to a bone. She put the bedding on the chair and opened the window to air out the room. ''I don't like finding frozen bodies in beds I have to change.'' After she set the chamber pot out in the hall, she dusted the top of the pine bedstead and the old chest of drawers.

He stayed out of her way. She darted around the room attacking the dust as if it offended her, then she stripped the covers off the bed with a vengeance and grabbed the side of the mattress. ''Is this necessary?'' he asked, quickly moving to give her a hand.

''It is, unless you're partial to a hard-packed mattress.'' It flipped over, and she moved away from him as she plumped it up. She couldn't figure him out. She liked things plain, uncomplicated, and he was more like patchwork gone amiss.

When she shook out the clean sheet, it cracked as if it were a whip. He shifted his weight and leaned his shoulder against the wall. The sheet floated out over the bed and settled in place. Since when had bed making become so interesting?

She smoothed out the under sheet and tucked it in securely. As she brushed her hand over the upper sheet, she caught a glimpse of his pants and black cavalry boots. Until that moment, she hadn't *really* thought about him stretched out between the sheets, sleeping in the bed she was making. When she picked up the blanket she'd taken off the bed, the cold breeze coming in the window cooled her cheeks. ''I can manage this alone. You must have something else to do.'' The blanket slid to a cockeyed angle, and she yanked it off the bed. Oh, please, Parker, just leave me *alone*.

He grabbed the carbine and his hat. ''Sure you won't need my help?''

She leveled her gaze on him and picked up one of the pillows, ready to pitch it at him.

Her proud face was so expressive, she didn't need to say a word. "Guess you don't." He tipped his hat and left her to her work.

His rich laughter drifted back to her, then she got a whiff of laurel from his pillow. Four-thumbed numskull, she thought, heaving the pillow across the room. When she was ready to leave, she closed the window and looked around one last time. He'd left nothing sitting out, no sign that he'd used the room.

She walked to the door and paused. He must have some of his things in a drawer. She could take a peek, she thought; he'd never know. But she guarded her privacy, and snooping through another person's belongings was against her nature.

She stepped into the hall, closed and locked the door. Besides, if he didn't leave town, she'd be back to clean his room in a couple days. As she gathered the dirty linens to take to the cabin, she realized she may not feel so honorable by then.

Kate checked the dining room for the fifth time and turned back to Charlie. "Mr. Bishop's the only steady customer we have, and he left."

"Ya might as well git, too. No call fer ya standin' 'round here." Charlie looked at the mound of biscuits. "Want'a take these to yer ma?"

She knew he always served fresh biscuits with each meal and didn't seem to like making bread pudding with the leftovers. "Mind if I take some to Thaddeus? I haven't seen him in weeks."

Charlie shook his head. "Summer's long gone and we're in fer a blow. Ya don't want'a git lost up there."

She dumped the biscuits into a clean piece of linen and tied the ends. "It's sunny. If I wait, that storm you're worried about may come, and I won't get up there." She put her jacket on and winked at him. "I'll be back before supper."

"I'm too old t'track ya down." He followed her to the door. "If ya git lost, I'll send that Smith fella after ya," he called out.

She paused at the bend in the path to her cabin. "An' I thought you liked me, Charlie Daws. See you later." He meant well, but the sky was clear. It wasn't all *that* cold; the wind just made it feel that way. She dashed into the cabin and surprised her mother.

Mary Louise stared at Kate, then continue checking the shirt and pants drying by the fireplace. "My goodness, deah. What's all the fuss about?"

Kate tossed her jacket on the empty chair by the fireplace. "I'm going up to check on Thaddeus." After bundling up against the stiff breeze, she pulled on her other petticoat and a second pair of stockings, then wrapped an old woolen shawl around her shoulders.

Mary Louise watched her. "If it's so cold out, maybe ya should rent a mount from Mr. Goody? And deah, do wear your cotton gloves under the heavy ones."

"You know I like to stretch my legs." Kate found the gloves tucked in the corner of one drawer and put them on. "I'll return well before sundown," she said, shrugging into her heavy coat. "Oh, I almost forgot. Charlie wanted you to have some of these biscuits."

Mary Louise smiled. "I swear, that man must think I eat like a ranch hand." She watched Kate set four biscuits out on the table. "When we have our li'l house, I'll keep a crock o' honey butter."

With her hat in hand Kate went over and kissed her mother's soft cheek. "That'll be real nice, Mamma." She straightened the crocheted fascinator draped across her mother's shoulders. "Would you like to eat at the hotel tonight?" She gave her mother an encouraging look. "I bet Charlie would like to see you."

"That'd be nice, deah." Mary Louise patted her daughter's hand. "Ya take care, now."

"I will, Mamma." Kate put her hat on, slipped the chin strap in place, and grabbed the bag of biscuits on her way outside.

She cut through the trees and walked along the road for over a mile, then followed the barely noticeable path leading down a small ravine, across Moose Gulch, and wound up near the summit of Pudding Mountain. It had taken longer than she'd remembered to reach the cave Thaddeus claimed for his home. She stopped near a large rock several yards from the opening and called out to him.

Thaddeus appeared in the narrow opening. "Kate, what a treat."

She met him in the clearing, and he enfolded her in a bear hug. He'd lived in the mountains so long, he came close to resembling a great hairy bear. "I've missed you." He was only a half a head taller than her, but his girth and powerful arms made him a giant in her eyes.

"You've been on my mind, too, but you shouldn't have come up here." He released her and tied back the heavy buffalo skin.

The narrow entry led to a space half the size of her cabin. She took off her gloves and heavy coat and sat down on a seat carved into a chunk of tree trunk, the wood as smooth as glass. She set the bag on top of a rough three-legged table at her side. "Charlie sent some biscuits."

"How's the old codger doing?" Thaddeus filled a tin cup with water from a bucket and handed it to her before he sat in his hide chair.

"Thank you." She still hadn't gotten used to the drier air in the high mountains and gratefully sipped the cool water. "He never complains. How about you? Given any more thought to moving closer to town?" She had met Thaddeus her first day working in the dining room, and for some reason, it was as if they'd been longtime friends. If she were pinned down for an explanation, she'd guess they had much in common.

He shook his head. "Moose Gulch's too citified for me. I've been my own counsel, livin' out up in these hills for close to thirty years. I couldn't take all those people yammering day 'n night."

She burst out laughing. "Then I guess Deer Lodge or Helena's out of the question."

"Got that right. Tell me, what's new in town? The Goodys are still there, aren't they?"

"Yes, enough miners come through for supplies, though I can't say the same for the hotel. Most never take a room." She looked over at his hide trunk and at the wall of the cave. There was a map of the area drawn on a piece of elk hide and a pair of snowshoes. He'd explained how the snowshoes were made and used, but she knew she'd have no need for them. She'd be stuck in town till the snow melted.

He nodded. "And how's your mother takin' to mountain life?"

"Thanks to that woodstove you gave us, she's snug as can be. She does laundry and mending for a few miners and makes a shirt once in a while." She drank more water. "She talks about living in a city where her friends will come to tea and go to luncheons."

"Mm." He eyed her with one raised brow. "Deer Lodge might be more to her liking, if you're determined to stay in the territory."

"I . . . I'm not sure yet." She looked at his weathered face. "Thaddeus, what will do you up here when the snow comes?"

"Hunt 'n trap. The animals' fur gets thicker for winter." He motioned to the cave opening. "The wind's kickin' up. I don't meant to be inhospitable, but you better start back."

She set the tin cup down and stood up. "I got a late start, but I do like coming up here." She put on her heavy coat and gloves.

He grabbed his great coat. "I'll walk you part way."

She grinned at him. "I thought you would."

"You're gettin' too sassy, miss." He chuckled. "Glad you haven't lost your spunk."

She stepped outside. ‘‘I’d think this territory would breed spirit.’’

‘‘Doesn’t always work that way in the high country.’’

The wind nearly ripped the hat from her head. She stopped under the protection of a tall spruce tree and pulled her shawl up over her hat. ‘‘Is this what they call a ‘blow’?’’

‘‘It surely is, an’ you better get back to town as fast as your legs’ll carry you.’’ He took her hand and bent forward into the wind.

She caught a glimpse of clouds moving over the mountaintops. This wind felt different from the tornado that had swept through Mackey’s, Texas, but just as alarming. They were walking into the ice-cold wind, and it seemed to suck the air from her. She tugged one end of the shawl across her mouth and forced Thaddeus to stop. ‘‘I know the way. You get back to the cave.’’

‘‘Kate, you’re not used to this weather.’’

‘‘It’s downhill all the way, won’t take me half as long.’’ She leaned over and pressed a kiss to his cheek. ‘‘Stop by the cabin if you get tired of your own company. Mamma keeps the fireplace and woodstove going all day.’’

‘‘I appreciate the invitation.’’ He patted her back. ‘‘Now get your tail down the hill.’’

She wasn’t about to argue with good sense. At the first bend in the path, she paused, turned back and waved, then hurried on down the mountain. Giant trees bent under the force of the wind, and she had to keep her mouth covered to breath. When she turned down the road, the wind was at her back, and she had to fight to keep her footing.

She figured she was within a quarter mile of town when the first snowflakes began falling. She slowed her pace and watched the white flakes blanket the dark green trees. Knowing she was almost home, she could appreciate the beauty of the weather. She looked back the way she’d come. Her tracks had already been covered over and it was quiet. So quiet and peaceful she felt safe.

* * *

After following a trail down the mountain, south of town all afternoon, Parker returned that evening to find the town covered with snow. He knew winter would come early there, but he'd hoped he wouldn't still be there to see it. After he gave Buckshot a good rubdown and put a blanket over his back, Parker went to his room to wash up.

The bed was neat, but he couldn't help wondering if Kate had booby-trapped it somehow. He was grateful she had closed the window. Everything appeared to be just as he'd left it. He slapped a little laurel balm on his hair, slicked it back, and went down to supper. He heard people talking before he reached to doorway. That's reassuring, he thought. There was something unnatural about eating alone in a large dining room.

Old Bert was in his seat by the woodstove, Bishop was sharing a table with a man Parker hadn't seen before, and Mrs. Miller was at a table near the door to the kitchen. Kate paused to speak to her and darted through the doorway. He stopped at her table on the way to his. "Good evening, Mrs. Miller. You're a pleasant sight this evening."

Mary Louise smiled and momentarily lowered her lashes. "Why, Mr. Smith, how nice of you. I was hopin' Kate could sit with me, but she's too busy. Would you share my table?"

With only a quick glance over her shoulder at the door to the kitchen, he smiled. "It would be my pleasure, ma'am." He took the seat to her right, which gave him a full view of the dining room and lobby.

"Mr. Daws made his wonderful parsnip soup," she said, as if trying to entice a child to eat. "It'll warm you right up."

When she sat demurely with her hands in her lap, Parker gave her a devilish grin. "Please, don't let the soup get cold on my account." While she ate, he waited for Kate.

Mary Louise patted her mouth with the napkin. "What do you think of this fair town, Mr. Smith?"

"It's nice 'n quiet. What do you like most about it, Mrs. Miller?"

She smiled, a peculiar, almost childlike smile that softened her features and lighted her eyes, and he could only wonder what thoughts had filled her mind. "Everyone's so friendly and warmhearted, but we won't be stayin' here much longer." She picked up her spoon and dipped it in the soup.

As he remained outwardly calm, his heart seemed to pound in his ears. "I'm sorry to hear that. Moving this time of year won't be easy. If I can be of help, Mrs. Miller, please don't hesitate to ask my assistance."

"You're such a kind man, Mr. Smith." She gave him a coy look. "I just may do that."

He was taking a chance, but she appeared to be in such a genial mood, it was worth the gamble. "Have you been in touch with Hank lately?"

Mary Louise shrugged. "Not directly, but I know he'll help—"

As Kate shoved the door back and stepped into the dining room, she saw Parker and heard her mother's words in the same instant. "Mamma! Here's your supper." Avoiding Parker's gaze, she quickly exchanged her mother's soup bowl for the dinner plate. He watched her. She *felt* it and hated herself for paying him any mind, for noticing how good that blue chambray shirt looked on him.

Parker grinned, not to taunt her, but because he could almost hear her thoughts. "Good evening, Kate."

While she set a plate of biscuits and a small dish of butter on the table, Kate recited, "Tonight we have parsnip soup, pot roast of beef, and spice cake," in a flat voice. She picked up the small teapot from the tray. As she refilled her mother's cup, a tremor jostled her hand.

"Sure smells good." Parker exchanged glances with Mrs. Miller. "Your mother gave the soup high praise."

Mary Louise nodded. "Yes, Kate, you must tell Mr. Daws it was as good as I've ever made myself."

Kate balanced the tray on her hip. "I'm sure Charlie'd rather hear that from you, Mamma." She hurried over to Mr. Bishop's table and served a generous slice of cake to him and one to the other man, then she set a piece in front of Bert. "I know you must be full, but would you taste that for me?"

Bert stared at the cake and smacked his lips. "Miss Kate, you sure are kind to a old no-'ccount."

"Don't you talk about yourself that way. You're my best customer." She winked and started back to the kitchen with the tray of dirty dishes. Her mother was carryin' on with Parker as if she were walking out with him. Kate came close to slamming the tray down on the kitchen worktable. "I need another supper." She grabbed a bowl and stepped over to the kettle of soup.

Charlie watched her a moment. "What's gotten into ya?" He dished out a portion of beef and vegetables.

"Mamma can't keep her mouth shut around Parker. It's revolting."

Charlie set the plate on the table. "Smith's sittin' with yer mamma? No wonder ya got a bur under yer tail." He set another tray out for her and started scraping the dirty dishes. "Ya know ya shouldn't ort'a let him see he's gettin' to ya."

She put Parker's food on the tray, straightened her back, and took a deep breath. "By the time he finishes eating, I'm sure he'll be bored with hearing Mamma's stories." She raised the tray in a mock salute.

"If no one else's come in, we can join them."

She grinned at him. "I like the way you think. Just soup for me." She carried the tray into the dining room. As she reached around Parker's shoulder and served his soup, she caught a whiff of laurel and gritted her teeth. Why did he have to wear that scent? And why the devil did she find it so appealing? She set his supper plate off to his right. "I'll get your coffee."

"Thanks, Kate." He had heard the flutter in her breath and wished she'd settle down around him. After learning her mother was still in touch with Hank, he felt a surge of goodwill.

She stopped by her mother's chair. "Need anything?"

Mary Louise looked up, dabbing her mouth with the napkin. "I'm fine, deah, but can't y'all sit for a while? I'm sure Mr. Smith'd enjoy your company, too."

He nodded. "Indeed I would."

"Just like the spider watching the fly," she muttered. That was the last thing he wanted from her. "I'll sit down in a minute." She got the coffeepot and a cup. After she had served Parker and refilled the other men's cups, she sat between Charlie and her mother. And across the table from Parker.

Mary Louise passed the plate of biscuits to her daughter. "I was just telling Mr. Daws what a wonderful cook he is. We certainly are fortunate he likes workin' here."

Charlie shrugged off the compliment and glanced at Kate. "That soup's not sa good cold."

She dipped her spoon in the creamy parsnip soup. "You know I never waste food, especially not yours."

"Oh, my goodness no, Mr. Daws," Mary Louise quickly added.

Each time he took a bite, Parker looked at Kate. Her mother had trapped her into joining them, and he didn't mind at all. Somehow, he had to break through that uncompromising veneer. He usually had no trouble finagling his way into a woman's good graces. Not so with her. He caught her gaze and held it a moment, as if he were trying to calm a wild animal, then looked away.

Kate broke open a biscuit and slathered butter on it. He was putting on quite a show for her mother and Charlie, but she knew what Parker was after. She'd wished him well in his search for her father, so why hadn't he left? She ate a bite of biscuit and decided to ask. "Mr. Smith, I understood you were leaving to find your friend. Or have you already found him?"

As if to say, point taken, he gave her a slight nod. "Not yet, but I have the feeling he's not too far from here." She pushed her hair back behind her ear and glared at him. The spark was back in her pretty eyes. For a few minutes there, he had thought she was going to play the wallflower.

Oh, you great oaf, she wanted to scream, if I knew where he was, I'd draw you a map. "There's a lot of territory to cover in these mountains. I don't envy you."

He finished eating and sat back in the chair. "Kate, would you like to ride out with me your next day off? You must know your way around better than I do."

Her fingers bit into the remaining piece of biscuit. She'd left herself wide open for that, she realized all too late. "I do laundry on my days off." She felt the toe of her mother's shoe against her leg and added, "But thank you for the invitation."

Mary Louise looked at Parker. "She'll be takin' clean clothes to the miners tomorrow. You might walk along with her, Mr. Smith, and meet the men. One of them could be your friend or know of him."

Parker gazed at Kate. "I would be happy to keep you company." Her eyes resembled black onyx nuggets, and she looked ready to spit bullets. "I'm a fair shot . . . should you need protection."

Lord preserve me from fools and silver-tongued devils, she thought, and her mother. "You can tag along if you like."

"Oh, how nice," Mary Louise cooed. "Maybe Mr. Daws can pack a few biscuits and bits of meat for you to take along."

"That won't be necessary, Mamma." Kate narrowed her eyes at Parker. "If we get hungry, I'm sure Mr. Smith can shoot a bear . . . or something."

Parker shoved his chair back and stood up. "What time should I meet you, Kate?"

"After breakfast." She was used to coming and going as she pleased, and she didn't like being pinned down by him.

He left the price of the meal by his plate. "See you in the morning." He looked at Mrs. Miller. "Good evening, ma'am." He nodded at Charlie and left the hotel.

As soon as he stepped outside, the wind stung his face and cut right through his trousers. The snow was deeper and three mules were tied up in front of the saloon. He tramped over and entered the warm smoky room. Tullie was picking on his banjo and three men had a poker game going at one table. Parker waved to Tullie and stepped over to the bar. "Evening, Ralston. I'll have a beer."

"Smith." Ralston drew a glass of beer and set it in front of Parker. "The Grubstake busy tonight?"

Parker nodded. "You seem to be keeping busy, too." He took a drink of beer and listened to Tullie play "The Old Oaken Bucket." Not a gambling man, Parker was content to watch the game.

Ralston served fresh drinks to the poker players, refilled Tullie's beer, and went back behind the bar. He wiped the bar off and stood across from Parker. "Have you heard about that bridge they're building across the Missouri?" He drew a glass of beer and set it on the bar for Parker.

"That's some project." Parker paid for his beer. "Where's it going up?"

"Atchison, Kansas." Ralston shook the rag out. "I sure would like to see that."

"If I get down that way, I'll write and tell you about it." Parker chuckled, picked up his glass, and sat down at a table near the game. He nursed the beer until it turned warm, and Ralston had just brought him a second one when Charlie came in the saloon.

Charlie got a beer and joined Parker.

"I'm surprised you're not sitting in on the game," Parker said, motioning toward the game table. "You strike me as a wily gambler."

Charlie shook his head. "Done my share 'n lost more'n I care to recall."

Parker nodded, his thoughts returning to Mrs. Miller. She was his best contact to Turner, but he would welcome any information. Earl came in, got a beer, and Parker motioned him over. "Have a seat—or were you going to join the game?"

Earl pulled a chair out and sat down. "Not tonight. I used to sit in every night." He drank some of his beer. "I had money to throw around, then.''

With a glance at Charlie, Parker chuckled. ''First hand I sat in on I lost a month's pay in less time than it took me to finish my whiskey.'' He drew a circle in the sweat on the side of his glass. They were close enough to the poker game to overhear the players' conversation. One of the men in the game mentioned a miner up the mountain who'd been robbed of his stash.

''Poor old Pan Handle, he'd jist put away 'nough t'make a trip t'Deer Lodge.'' The man gulped his whiskey and banged his shot glass on the table.

''Heard 'bout some trouble o'r in Cedar Creek. Some feller hit Barrette and Lanthier,'' another man said. ''Wonder if'n it were worth his trouble.'' He coughed and spit a stream of tobacco juice on the floor. ''You boys hid yer stash, didn't ya?''

The third man spoke softly. ''Ain't nobody gonna git their hands on my hard-won find.''

Parker looked at Earl. ''You hear about that?''

Earl nodded. ''There's always some no-account sneaking around the claims.''

Charlie raised his beer. ''It's not as bad as in forty-nine. Varmints who couldn't find spit on their boots were as thick as fleas.''

Parker watched another man come into the saloon and walk up to the bar. The man's rough clothes were covered with a dusting of snow, and when he tucked the side of his coat back, his Colt was within easy reach. Parker never went anywhere without his Peacemaker, but he only made a show of it if he thought he might have to defend himself or was ready to issue a challenge. ''You know that fellow at the bar?''

Earl looked at the man. ''He's never been in my shop—or anyone else's by the look of his hair.''

''Ain't seen him in the hotel, either.'' Charlie drained his glass. ''Well, gents, I'll leave ya to yor fun.''

''Night, Charlie.'' Parker sipped his beer, watching the stranger, hoping the man wasn't out to prove himself.

❖ 7 ❖

PARKER LINGERED OVER his second beer until the poker game broke up. Earl left when he'd finished his drink, and the new fellow walked out a while later. Sure Earl had gotten home before the stranger could've followed, Parker still felt uneasy and stayed on to see why. After the poker game broke up and the players had wandered out, he set his glass on the bar. "Night, Ralston. You better lock up tonight."

"Always do."

Parker stepped out onto the boardwalk. A door rattled across the street, and he halted in his tracks. The mules were gone and there wasn't a horse in sight. He started back to the hotel. Another noise came from the abandoned buildings across the road, and he paused. It had sounded like a groan or maybe someone falling down. The wind blew the snow so hard his tracks didn't last a minute. He darted over to the last storefront and eased his way around to the back.

It was black as pitch and quiet, until he heard scuffling noises and a voice asking, "Where—" from inside. Drawing his pistol, he lightly stepped forward until he came to an open doorway. There was a deep groan and a thud. He darted inside, and his eyes slowly adjusted to the darker room. Someone was gasping, and it sounded as if the person was on the floor. He could barely make out a shadowy figure standing six or eight paces ahead of him and pointed his pistol at him. "Party's over."

The dark figure didn't move.

Parker stepped farther away from the doorway and cocked his Peacemaker. "Throw your gun outside!" He had learned that it was safer to assume a troublemaker was armed, and he wasn't going to second-guess his experience.

"This'uns mine. Go find yor own."

"Drop your gun or take your chances. Makes no difference." Parker spoke in a deep voice. A voice that meant he was deadly serious, or so he'd been told. A gun landed on the floor. "Kick it outside."

The person on the floor groaned. "That you, Smith?"

"Who's there?"

"One Finger." He scooted to the other side of the door. "I was in the game o'r at t'saloon." He got to his knees.

"You okay?" Parker didn't recognize the name but took the man at his word.

"I'm alive. I thank ya mightily, Smith." One Finger coughed. "Did Dusty git away?"

"Who's he?"

"T'other one in t'game."

"Called himself Jay."

"Haven't seen him." Parker nodded. "Who's your friend?"

Something hit the back of the building and Jay moved. "I wouldn't do that. You'd be hard to miss at this range."

"Ya the 'Smith' from Cheyenne? They say ya shot a guy in a poker game."

"Walk over to the doorway . . . turn around. Put a hand on each side. Now!" Parker kept the pistol trained on him. "One Finger, can you find some rope?"

"Yes, siree!" One Finger scrambled around in the darkness. "Ain't no rope, but I found somethin' silky like. Will this do?" He handed it to him.

Staring at the other man, Parker rubbed his fingers on the material and smiled. "A ribbon?"

One Finger chuckled. "Used t'be a ladies' shop in here."

"It'll do just fine." Parker took one step toward Jay. "Is Jay your name?"

The man answered with a harsh laugh.

"Makes no difference to me, but it's as good as any. Turn to your right and put your forehead on the wall, Jay, with your hands behind you." The man slowly did as ordered. Parker motioned One Finger forward. Without saying a word, Parker handed his gun to him and quickly bound the man. He took his pistol back. "I don't suppose there's a jail in town."

"Nope." One Finger inched forward. "But Ralston has a cold cellar with a lock on the door."

"Go tell him what happened. We'll follow." One Finger limped away. Parker checked the man for hidden weapons. He found a derringer in one boot and a knife in the other. "Kick the boots off."

"Yor crazy."

Parker really didn't want to fire his pistol and alarm the whole town, but the derringer wouldn't disturb anyone. When the man didn't move, he shot at the toe of his boot. The man quickly got his boots off. "Let's go back to the saloon. You know the way."

"Those boots cost me four dollars."

"Pick them up. I don't want them." Parker watched him shuffle around. "Hurry up."

"What's all this to you?"

Jay finally grabbed a hold of his boots, and Parker shoved him out the door. "I don't like scum like you."

"Ya ain't no marshal."

Parker prodded him across the road. "You're smarter than I thought."

Ralston stood in the saloon doorway watching. "Hey, he was playing poker with One Finger."

"Can you lock him in your cellar? You must have a town committee to deal with rabble like this."

Ralston smiled. "Sure can." He led them to the back room and opened the trapdoor.

Parker grabbed Jay's arm. "Better make sure there's

nothing down there he can use as a weapon. I'd just as soon not have to do this again tonight.''

Ralston went down and brought up a hatchet and two shovels. ''He should keep till morning.''

Parker gave the man a nudge. ''Get down there.''

''Yor crazy. I'll freeze to death!''

''Ralston, you got a good length of rope? We'll tie him to that tree out back.''

Jay dropped his boots into the cellar. ''I'll break my neck goin' down that ladder tied like this.''

''If you don't move, I'll give you a hand.'' Parker shoved the barrel of the pistol in Jay's back. ''Move.''

The man made it down to the third rung, teetered, and fell the rest of the way. ''You son of a bitch!''

Ralston slammed the trapdoor shut, bolted and put the padlock on the door. ''He's not going anywhere.''

One Finger let out a long sigh. ''I owe ya, Smith.'' He gave out a nervous laugh. ''Ya know, I thought you'd a jumped me. Surely glad I was wrong.''

Parker slid the Peacemaker back in the holster and looked at One Finger. He was a short man, thin with jet-black hair and past his prime. ''Tell me something. How'd you get that handle?''

One Finger gave out a harsh laugh. ''Shot m'finger off, I did. See?'' He held up his left hand.

The first finger was missing. ''You sound like a dangerous man with a pistol.''

''This calls for a drink on the house.'' Ralston went back to the bar and poured each of them a generous shot of whiskey. After he handed the glasses out, he held his up. ''Thanks, Smith. The town owes you.''

Kate stepped from the warm cabin and into wind-driven snow. Leaning into it, she fought her way to the side kitchen door. In this weather there would only be one or two meals to serve. And, she slowly realized, she'd have to put off her trip to the mines. She opened the side door to the kitchen, hurried inside, and had to lean against it fasten the latch.

Charlie gave her a crooked grin. "What'd'ya think of our blow?"

"As long as I can keep us in firewood and get over here to work, I don't mind." She hung her coat on the peg and brushed the snow off her hair. "Has Mr. Bishop been in yet?"

"He's still in the dining room." Charlie set the pot of coffee on the worktable. "So're the Goodys, Ralston, and Wilson."

She stepped over to the table. "What's everyone doing here? And in this weather?"

He eyed her and set out a towel. "Big doin's last night. One Finger got hisself bushwhacked, and Parker saved his hide."

She clenched the towel with both hands. "Did he shoot someone? Or get shot?" She struggled to fill her lungs. "Is he all right?" She wanted Parker gone, not dead or in jail—just out of her life.

"By gum, no. Not him." He waved his arm at the door. "They'll be wantin' more coffee. Mebe some food."

She quickly wrapped the towel over the hot handle on the coffeepot and hurried into the dining room. Had Charlie heard right? She'd been in Moose Gulch over three months and there hadn't been a lick of trouble, except for a fight or two that broke out in the saloon. Mr. Bishop, Mr. and Mrs. Goody, Mr. Ralston, and Earl Wilson were seated around the woodstove.

Mrs. Goody saw Kate and waved her over. "I was hoping you'd get here. Sit down, dear. No reason why you shouldn't be in on this. You've probably seen more of Mr. Smith than most of us."

Kate refilled Mrs. Goody's cup. "Just as soon as everyone has fresh coffee." The men continued talking as she filled their cups. Mr. Goody's brown eyes were as bright as polished copper. Kate had never seen him so excited—or any of the others, either—and decidedly curious.

Mac held his cup up for her. ‘‘We’ve talked about hiring a sheriff for almost four years.’’

Bishop nodded. ‘‘But we haven’t had much call for one the last two years.’’

‘‘Heard talk last night about some miners being robbed over Missoula way.’’ Earl smiled at Kate. ‘‘Good morning.’’

‘‘Don’t usually see you here so early,’’ Kate said softly as she filled his cup. After she did the same for Mr. Ralston, she went back to the kitchen, asked Charlie to join them, and took a seat near Mrs. Goody.

‘‘I think Smith’s the man for the job.’’ Ralston took a sip of coffee. ‘‘I saw the look on his face. Cool as the wind. I say we ask him.’’

Charlie joined them. ‘‘Where’s old One Finger? He’s the one that knows what happened.’’

‘‘Reckon he’s still sleeping it off.’’ Mac glanced around the circle.

‘‘Well, are we in agreement?’’ Bishop looked each man in the eye. ‘‘We’ll ask Smith?’’

Kate looked at each of them. She wasn’t surprised Parker had the men’s respect, but she dreaded what they were suggesting. ‘‘Is that really necessary?’’ Six pairs of eyes stared at her.

Bishop nodded. ‘‘This is an easy place to reach, and everyone knows we don’t have a sheriff. Smith doesn’t strike me as a man who’d shoot first like some.’’

‘‘That’s a fact.’’ Ralston raised his cup. ‘‘He could of shot that coyote and none of us would’ve thought twice about it.’’

Mac shared a look with his wife. ‘‘We can’t pay him much. I’ll give him a ten-dollar credit each month and free stabling for his horse.’’

‘‘I’ll throw in baths, haircuts, and shaves.’’ Earl glanced at Bishop.

Bishop sat back. ‘‘Room ’n board and ten dollars a month, cash.’’

Parker won’t accept their offer, Kate thought. He wants

Turner, wants him too much to stay holed up here. At least she hoped so. She couldn't imagine facing him every day for the next four or five months—or more.

"He can drink on the house, but he doesn't seem to be a heavy drinker. I'll add another twelve dollars a month." Ralston drained his cup. "Who's going to ask him?"

Kate refill Mr. Ralston's cup and Mac's. "Where's the man now?"

"Who?" Ralston breathed in the steam rising from the cup. "Locked up in my cold cellar. If we leave him there much longer, he might freeze."

Might? Kate wondered. Seemed more than likely to her. "What're you going to do with him?" The dining room was warming up, but she sure didn't want to invite the thug in for breakfast. She'd known from the first that Parker could handle himself and that his Peacemaker wasn't for show. He may keep the town safe, but who was to protect her from him?

Charlie cleared his throat. "Who's gonna ask Smith?"

They exchanged glances, then each one turned to Kate.

"What're you looking at me for? I don't know him any better than the rest of you." She prayed Charlie wouldn't mention the picnic.

"He ate with your mother last night, and you sat at the table." Bishop looked at her. "I don't mind that. Anyone could see he's not indifferent to you. How about it, Kate. Want to ask him for us?"

Kate shook her head. "No. Not me." Ye gods and little fishes! I won't do it. I'm the only one who doesn't want him here. "He'll think I was joking." She sent Charlie a quick glare, but he was grinning like a fox in a henhouse.

"I'll talk to him." Ralston glanced at Kate. "Guess I'd better have breakfast. Might as well eat while I wait for him to come down."

Charlie got up. "Be ready right soon."

The meeting broke up, and Kate couldn't believe her ill fortune. Her last hope was that Parker wouldn't be interested in the job. But even she had to admit twenty-two dollars a month with credit all over town wasn't bad for doing nothing.

She washed up the dirty cups while Charlie fixed Ralston's breakfast. No one in town knew she was a crack shot, but even if they did, they wouldn't ask her to be sheriff. She could do it in her spare time.

Charlie set the hot plate on the worktable. "It's ready. Parker's is, too."

She set a fresh cup of coffee on the tray with the food and carried it to Mr. Ralston's table. Bert had come in, but he sat by himself in his usual place. She served Mr. Ralston and hesitated. "If Smith turns you down, I can do the job. I'm a good shot. Learned to shoot when I was eight."

Ralston stared at her. "You're serious?"

"Yes, sir."

"I'm sorry, Kate. I don't think the others are ready for a lady sheriff."

"Don't see why not. My pistol can shoot a man just as dead as Parker's. If you want a demonstration, I'd understand." She got Bert coffee and his breakfast. Before she added wood to the stove, she glanced at the stairs. Parker usually came down early. Since he hadn't, could that possibly mean that he'd taken her advice? "Mr. Ralston, are you sure Smith hasn't left town? Did Mac check the livery this morning?"

Ralston lowered the bite of ham to his plate. "He didn't say. Why do you think he's not here?"

"He asked me about a friend he was trying to track down." She went to the woodstove and added several small logs to the fire.

Ralston raised the fork again. "If he doesn't come down by the time I finish eating, I'll go check on him."

She refilled his cup and went back to the kitchen.

Charlie looked up at her. "Smith down yet?"

"No. Has anyone seen him?"

"Not since late last night." Charlie refilled his cup and started a fresh pot of coffee. "You still set on gettin' him out of town?"

She shook her head. ''How could I run him out?'' Lord knows I've tried everything short of pulling my pistol on him, she thought, but maybe the town's offer would drive him away. If she had to spend the winter with him questioning her about a man she hoped never to lay eyes on again, she just might shoot him.

Charlie set a breakfast plate on the worktable and put on two more slices of ham to cook. ''Ya should eat. Need to keep yer strength up.''

She laughed, and it felt good. ''I'm not as thin as a fence post, but I am hungry.''

''Good. Ya haven't been eatin' much lately.''

She grabbed a clean fork and sat down. ''Where's yours?''

''Ate just b'fore all the commotion started up.'' When the coffee was ready, Charlie poured her a cup.

She had eaten half her meal when the door to the dining room opened and Parker stuck his head inside.

''Morning. Have any coffee left?'' Parker smiled at Kate, but the look she gave him only added to the curiosity Ralston had initiated a moment before. He stepped into the kitchen and peered over her shoulder. ''Mm. That looks as good as it smells.''

He hadn't left town, and his grin was boyish. It would have been endearing—if she were at all interested in him, which she was not. In spite of her disinterest, when he stood behind her, her heart beat faster. She jabbed her fork into a piece of ham. ''I'll bring your breakfast in to you in a minute.''

Charlie handed Parker a cup of coffee. ''Ralston's been waitin' to talk to ya.''

''Thanks. So he said.'' Parker raised his cup to Kate and joined Ralston at his table. ''Is Jay still locked up?''

''Was when I left.'' Ralston washed his last bite of biscuit down with coffee and sat back. ''One Finger found his horse tied to a tree and put it in the livery.''

''Where's the nearest jail?''

''The territorial prison's in Deer Lodge. A huge stone

building. Opened up last year, but there's no one to get him there.''

''I can take him if it comes to that.'' Parker sipped his coffee. ''Sure wish it wasn't snowing.''

Ralston nodded. ''It was past due. Will you return after you deliver that guy?''

''Most likely.'' Parker glanced at the kitchen door.

''Did you hear about the town meeting this morning?''

''Nope. Must've been a quiet one.'' Parker took another drink. He couldn't leave yet, not until he'd softened up Mrs. Miller enough to learn where Turner was hiding out.

''I volunteered to speak for the others.'' Ralston looked at Parker. ''We've needed a sheriff for some time, and we'd like you to take the job.''

Parker stared at his cup. Who would've thought? No wonder Kate acted strange. ''You're serious? You don't know anything about me.'' And aren't likely to, he left unsaid. ''I might be a wanted man.''

''I know what I saw. That's enough. 'Sides, the pay's bad, unless you happen to run into someone with a price on his head.''

Parker swirled the coffee. ''Don't suppose many wanted men ride through here.'' It would be perfect. There wouldn't be much to do, and he could watch Kate. He heard the kitchen door and waited for her. After all, he didn't want to seem to be too anxious to accept the offer.

She served his meal and refilled both of their cups. She had thought he'd be laughing by now, but he wasn't. Ralston didn't seem disappointed or especially happy. Maybe he hadn't asked him yet. ''Would you like biscuits and preserves?''

Ralston shook his head. ''I'm fine, Kate. Thanks.''

''So am I.'' Parker scooted his chair over. ''It doesn't seem too busy right now. Why don't you join us, Kate?'' He pulled out the chair on his right. ''You might be interested in this conversation.''

''I'll get my cup.'' She went over to Bert and refilled his cup.

Bert motioned her closer. ‘‘He gonna be our sheriff?’’

‘‘I don’t know yet.’’

Bert patted her arm. ‘‘I’d vote fer you, Kate, any day.’’

‘‘Thanks, Bert, but I’m not in the running.’’ She set the coffeepot down on the next table. A front row seat. The day was sure starting out like no other. She returned with her cup, refilled it, and sat down between Mr. Ralston and Parker.

‘‘I suppose you know he’s asked me to be sheriff.’’ Parker took a drink of coffee. ‘‘Think I should?’’ He cut a piece of ham.

She stared at him. ‘‘Are you going to be here that long?’’ Beneath his loose, offhanded attitude, she caught a glimpse of his serious side. She shifted on the seat. Heaven help her. When he looked into her eyes, the way he was right then, she almost forgot his reason for being there.

‘‘I could be.’’

‘‘But—’’ She glanced at Ralston and knew she shouldn’t sound so set on Parker’s leaving. ‘‘I thought you were passing through.’’ I was depending on it, she thought, taking a drink of coffee.

‘‘My plans’ve changed.’’ She was close to scowling at him. ‘‘That isn’t a problem, is it?’’

‘‘No—’’ She swallowed the wrong way and choked. ‘‘What difference would it make to me?’’ That was a stupid thing to ask *him*, of all people. I shouldn’t take this so seriously, she told herself. He wasn’t. Maybe he was just teasing her.

‘‘Bishop hasn’t rented my room, has he?’’

‘‘Not that I’ve heard,’’ she said idly. ‘‘But I seem to be the last to know anything.’’

‘‘The position’s yours.’’ Ralston leaned forward and looked from Kate to Parker. ‘‘The pay’s not much. Twenty-two a month, but everyone’s donating goods. Mac said he’ll stable your horse and give you ten dollars in credit each month. Earl said your baths, haircuts, and shaves’ll be taken care of. Bishop’s offering room and board, and your drinks’ll be on the house at the saloon.’’

Parker whistled. ''Sounds like a sweet deal. Are you sure there isn't something else I should know?'' Kate pushed her hair back from her face as if impatient, and he wondered if she'd tried to talk everyone out of this cockeyed notion.

''This's a quiet place most of the time.'' Ralston grinned and shook his head. ''But with the robberies in the area, we'd feel better if it were known we have a sheriff.''

Parker sat back, as if pondering the decision. ''I may not stay all winter,'' he said with a sideways glance at Kate. ''But I'll stay here long enough for word to spread.''

''Good!'' Ralston gulped down the last of his coffee. ''Glad to hear it.''

Parker eyed Kate. ''If there's trouble, can I count on your help?'' Her eyes did flash in a most becoming way when she was taken unawares, like now.

Bert ambled over to their table. ''Ya sure kin, mister. She's pure gold.'' He tipped his rumpled hat at her and strolled out.

She grinned at Bert and met Parker's fixed gaze. ''I suppose. Would you trust me to guard your backside?'' She stared him in the eye. He didn't need to know she wouldn't feed him to the wolves. She couldn't do that to anyone, save one man.

''I think so.'' And when I face Turner, I won't need your help, he thought. As much as Parker wanted to see him dead, he didn't want her there to witness it. ''So does Bert.''

She grinned and stood up. ''I'll practice my fast draw after breakfast.''

''What about the laundry? I thought we'd be delivering it this morning.'' He had no desire to walk several miles in a blizzard, but he wouldn't let her go alone.

''Not in this weather.'' She picked up the coffeepot and left him to talk with Mr. Ralston.

8

PARKER HAD JUST finished eating when he saw Bishop in the lobby and waved him over to the table. "Seems Ralston, you, and the others got an early start this morning."

"That we did." Bishop sat down with them. "Have you decided?"

Parker nodded. "I'll do it for a month or so. Long enough for word to spread."

"Glad to hear it. What do you want to do about that low-life in Ralston's cellar?"

"I'll go along with what the town wants. He didn't steal a horse and One Finger seemed okay, so hanging's out. He could be whipped or taken to the prison in Deer Lodge, or I could escort him out of the area." The last had the most appeal for Parker. He looked at Bishop, then Ralston.

Before he spoke, Ralston exchanged glances with Bishop.

"As long as he doesn't come back this way, I see no reason for you to make a trip down the hill."

Bishop nodded. "If you need anything, just let one of us know."

"I will." Parker shoved his chair back and stood up. "Ralston, after I talk to Mac, I'll take the prisoner off your hands."

"Any time. I'll be leaving in a minute."

Parker reached in his pocket to pay for his breakfast.

Bishop chuckled. "Meals come with the job. You better hold on to what cash you have."

"Right." Parker left two coins for Kate, put on his hat, and shrugged into his jacket as he went outside. The wind had let up and the snowfall was light. His first stop was the livery to check on his horse. That done, he went to the general store. Bert was sitting by the woodstove and gave him a nod.

Bert tipped his hat. "Howdy, Sheriff."

Mrs. Goody came from the back room and smiled at Parker. "Good morning. Have you seen Mr. Ralston?"

"Just left him. Thought I'd see if you'd had any trouble here I should know about."

"You accepted the offer. Oh, I am glad. Can I get you something?"

"A box of forty-five cartridges will do for now."

She reached to a shelf below the counter and set the box out for him. "If you need snowshoes, we have a few pairs in the back."

"I hope I won't be needing them soon."

She brought out the ledger and turned to a clean page. "I'll need your first name, Mr. Smith . . . for the record."

"Parker." He picked up the box and noticed she added *Sheriff* after his name. He never thought he'd see that.

She neatly wrote cartridges and forty cents in the right column. "Mac said your badge should be here next week. He's ordering it special."

"Badge? I don't need a badge, Mrs. Goody. I think my pistol's enough. But tell Mac thanks." He started for the door.

"We don't want any doubts about your position, Mr. Smith. We're right proud to have a sheriff." She closed the ledger.

"Bye, Sheriff," Bert said with a nod.

Parker waved and hurried outside. Him sport a badge? When he faced Turner, he never thought about doing it with the law behind him. He wasn't sure that's what he wanted, but he'd have time to think it over. Shoving the box into his coat pocket, he tramped across the road to the saloon.

Ralston set a clean glass on the bar. "Want a drink?"

"Too early for me. I'd rather get the trash out of your cellar." Parker started for the back room. "Has he given you any trouble?"

"Not a bit." Ralston unlocked the padlock and slid the bolt back.

Parker drew his pistol and nodded to Ralston.

Ralston raised the trapdoor and held a lantern over the cellar.

Parker looked down at Jay crouched at the foot of the ladder. "You got your boots on. Good. Come up slowly."

Jay climbed two steps and stumbled back down. "Son-of-a-bitch'n jackass!"

"Unless you want to spend the winter down there, you'll haul your butt up here." Parker stepped back.

Jay made two more attempts and finally climbed out on his third try. "Ya gonna untie me?"

Jay had pissed his pants, and he reeked. "Not just yet." There was no way Parker would take him to the hotel for a last meal. He looked at Ralston. "Thanks for the use of the cellar." Parker motioned to the door with his free hand. "Go on."

"Where're ya takin' me?"

"Out of town." Parker took him around to the side door to the kitchen, opened the door, and called to Charlie.

Charlie pulled the door back. "Why don't ya come in?"

Parker motioned to Jay. "I can't bring him in there. Can you put together a few cold biscuits and a couple slices of ham? If he leaves here hungry, he'll just steal some poor miner's supplies."

"Sure." Charlie grabbed a towel, tossed the cold biscuits on it, plus some ham and a tough chunk of raw venison. He handed the bundle to Parker. "This should keep'm fer a spell."

Parker nodded. "It had better." He nudged his prisoner. "Thank him."

"Yer crazy."

Parker waved the food past Jay's face and held it out to Charlie. "Guess he's not hungry."

Jay lurched sideways into the muzzle of Parker's Peacemaker and froze.

"Did you hear him say anything, Charlie?"

"Not a word."

Parker his shoved pistol into the man's gut. "Guess I'll have to teach you some manners." He handed the towel back to Charlie, holstered his pistol, and wrapped his arm around the man's neck in an instant. Bringing him down to his knees, Parker tightened his hold on the man's neck. "What do you say when you're given something?"

Jay made a gurgling noise, then choked out, "T-an-ks."

"Good." Parker stood him up and took the food. "If anyone asks, Charlie, I'm showing him the way out of town."

Charlie nodded. "He better keep a goin' 'less'n the Blackfeet or Flathead Injuns git'm." He winked at Parker.

"Good advice, but he may be too smart to take it." Parker marched his prisoner over to the livery and saddled their horses. Once they were mounted, he led the second horse west. It stopped snowing and the sun came out.

When he thought they were a good distance from any camps, he stopped the horses and hauled Jay down to the ground. "This road continues west. Stay on it. Don't turn back. There's enough food here to get you to the next town." Parker drew his pistol, pulled his knife out, and cut the silk bonds. They'd held good and left angry marks on the man's wrists. He stepped back. "If you're half as smart as you look, you'll take my advice. Next time I'll shoot first. It'd be easier to bury you than feed you."

He watched him take off up the road as if the devil were on his tail. Parker rode to the top of the ridge and surveyed the road to make certain the thug hadn't doubled back. There was a valley beyond. It looked like a pen-and-ink drawing he'd seen once. In the distance a magnificent elk also noted the rider. The animal appeared to have caught that troublemaker's scent. The fellow was lucky it wasn't a mountain lion. He turned back to town.

Kate swung the ax and finally divided the log in half. After chopping wood for an hour, she had enough to last them the night. How was she going to get through the winter? She pulled her scarf off, tossed it over near her coat and stacked the pieces along the cabin wall by the door. It was a poor showing for all her effort. She dragged a large broken tree branch over to the stump and began hacking it into useable lengths. Suddenly a large hand covered hers on the ax handle and another landed on her shoulder.

"Why not let me do that?" Parker tugged the ax from her grasp.

She sighed, relieved it was him, then spun around, furious he'd given her such a fright. "Why in tarnation can't you just say hello or hi?" He stared into her eyes, his expression as dry as day-old bread, but that didn't fool her. Oh, why couldn't he leave her alone?

"And startle you with a weapon in your hand?" He slid his hand down her stiff back and took off his hat. She was wearing a green shirt and course brown trousers minus the skirt, but no one would mistake her for a man. Not with her curves.

She moved away from him. "You must have something else to do besides pester me. If you're hungry, Charlie probably saved some dinner for you." Now that you're the *sheriff,* she thought. He came close to smiling, and she realized that might be as deadly as his pistol.

"Why don't you drag some more logs over here." He dropped his coat by hers, rolled up his sleeves, and made short work of the branch.

She watched him, wishing she had his strength. His arms were powerful and his hands . . . they were large, his fingers long—capable of working the kinks out of her tired back and holding her so close their heartbeats would sound as one. She was losing her mind. When he looked over at her, she frowned. ''There's a fallen log over there. Think you can walk that far?''

He shrugged. ''A smile would do wonders.'' She pursed her lips. That was a start. He began working on the tree trunk. As he split it off into smaller pieces, she added them to the stack. ''Won't any of the miners trade firewood for laundry or mending?''

''I never asked. It's a thought, though.'' She wiped her brow and picked up two more chunks of wood. ''How about you? I'll wash your clothes in exchange for your help.'' She owed him something for chopping so much firewood, and it seemed she'd be seeing him every day.

He tossed two more pieces aside. ''Sounds fair. I could use some clean clothes.'' Was this the chink in her armor he'd been waiting for? He grinned and swung the ax. ''If the weather clears, we can make that trek to the mining camps tomorrow.''

''Let's see what it's like then.'' Ye gods, he was persistent. Well, she could be just as stubborn. She simply had to remember to keep her distance from him. ''What happened with that no-account?''

Parker tossed another section of the tree trunk aside. ''Last time I saw him he was heading west through a nice little valley with enough food to last him the day.'' He glanced at her. ''If he's careful.''

''Is it true he was playing poker with One Finger?'' She added two more pieces of firewood to the stack.

''Yep. I heard One Finger talking as if they were on friendly terms.'' He drove the ax down and severed another chunk. ''I don't think he'll be that careless again.''

''He's one of the trusting souls. Is he all right? I haven't seen him this morning.''

''As far as I know.'' He shoved another piece away. ''I didn't think he'd run off. Is his claim near here?''

''Not too far.'' The stack of firewood grew. She owed Parker more than one washing. She always paid her own way, but she wasn't sure how she'd settle with him.

He split the last section and leaned on the ax handle. Her

hair had come loose and invited someone to tame it. ''Want to take a walk?''

She looked at the sky. It was midafternoon and the sun drifted out from behind a cloud. When he was agreeable, like now, she realized she enjoyed his company. ''We'll have to leave now.''

He set the ax down by the cabin door. ''It won't take me long to rinse off.''

''Me either. You might as well come inside and use warm water.'' She opened the door for him. Her mother was pouring a cup of tea. ''There's more hot water, isn't there? We need to wash up.''

Mary Louise looked up and smiled at Parker. ''How nice to see ya, Mr. Smith. Can you stay for tea?''

Parker closed the door behind him. ''Thank you, Mrs. Miller. I can't today, but I'd sure like to call another day.'' The only time he would be able to talk with her was while Kate was at the hotel.

''Oh my goodness, I nearly forgot. Kate said ya'd been made sheriff.'' Mary Louise gave him a playful once-over. ''I think that's wonderful, Mr. Smith. I feel much safer now. I really do.''

''I'm glad. If you need anything, please tell me.''

As her mother fawned over him, Kate poured hot water in a large bowl, added a little cold to it, and got a clean towel for him to use. ''We're going to one of the camps, Mamma.'' She quickly washed her hands and face.

''I'm glad ya aren't goin' alone, deah. Those camps are no place for a lady.''

Parker stepped over to Kate's side at the table and said softly, ''Don't forget your pistol.''

''I won't.'' Out of pure stubbornness, she walked to the other side of the cabin and pulled the curtain across the bed area. Then she took her pistol out of the drawer, checked the chamber, even though it was always loaded, and put it in her trouser pocket.

As she recrossed the room, Parker noticed the butt of her pistol poking out of the right side of her trousers. He turned to her mother. "It was a pleasure seeing you again, Mrs. Miller."

Mary Louise smiled and looked at Kate. "Ya leavin' already?"

"See you later, Mamma." Kate snatched her hat from one of the pegs by the door, went outside, and picked up her coat. When he reached for his, she jerked hers on. "You really are something with your 'ma'ams,' 'if you need anythings,' and 'pleasure seein' yous.' Playing up to her won't get you the time of day."

"When did good manners go out of style?" He settled his hat on his head and held his arm out to her. "Couldn't we argue while we walk?"

"We've found something to agree on." She led him through the trees and came out on the road. Snow crunched beneath her boots in the silence. The crisp beauty helped soothe her irritation with him. Besides, she regretted bringing up her mother and didn't want to discuss her with him. "What exactly happened to One Finger last night?"

"He must've been jumped when he left the saloon. I found him in the abandoned building across the street. He took a good thrashing, but he seemed okay."

She left the road and pried her way between thick spruce tree branches. "He must've been happy to see you."

"He was, once he realized it wasn't me beating on him."

She looked over at him. "Why would One Finger think it was you?"

They came to a path and followed it down to a small ravine. "He saw me in the saloon. I wasn't as friendly as his poker-playing buddy."

"Does that happen often?" She was guilty of that herself. It'd been his bearing and the pistol. Guns were commonplace, but he possessed a deadly calm that most people would take as a warning—or a possible challenge.

Her voice lacked its usual conviction and sass, and he wondered if she really did care just a bit for him. "Usually after a shooting. I've never been accused of chasing down an old-timer and clobbering him senseless."

"That won't happen here again. You're the sheriff, now." She stopped at a bend in the path and called to One Finger. "His camp's just down there."

Parker stepped behind her. His coat brushed hers and jostled her old hat. She reached up to set it right, but he brushed her hand aside and straightened it. Her hair was tucked under the hat, and he realized he'd like to see it free of its bond and floating in the breeze.

When he settled the hat in place, she took a deep, steadying breath, completely unprepared for his nearness. She had been careless, and she knew couldn't afford to make the same mistake with him again.

He lowered his hands. After a moment he spotted the camp. It was well hidden. Turner could easily be in just such a camp, and it could take a year or more to comb the mountains for such a speck.

One Finger appeared in a clearing. "Come on down."

Parker followed her surefooted descent. If he hadn't known different, he wouldn't have doubted her claim to be from the area. He smiled at One Finger. "I expected to see you at breakfast."

"Nah. Don't cotton t'them fancy vittles Charlie dishes up. Have a seat. Got some chicory brewin'."

"How're you feeling?" Kate brushed a thin layer of snow off of a log and sat down. "From what Parker said, you took a good pounding."

One Finger poured a cup of hot liquid and handed it to her. "Not the first time, but I surely was glad Smith here came t'the party."

Parker accepted a battered cup and smelled the rising steam. He hadn't tasted chicory in years, not since the war. "Glad to be of help." There wasn't much to the camp—a shelter made from a tent perched on top of a short rock wall.

"Too bad you didn't stick around this morning. There was a town meeting, and Parker was made sheriff."

"By gum, that's good news." One Finger grinned at Parker. "That's right smart of 'em."

Parker shrugged. "How's your gut?"

One Finger rubbed his belly. "Still a might tender, but I got me plenty o' mush. Be right as rain in no time." He filled a tin can with chicory for himself.

"Glad to hear that. I was concerned when you left town so early." Parker sipped the chicory.

Kate warmed her hands on the cup. One Finger was a wiry little man, and he often skittered around with an edginess she figured came from living alone for so many years. He wasn't today, and he looked a little peaked.

"Jist like my own bed." One Finger gulped down some coffee.

Parker finished his drink. "He didn't get any of your gold, did he?"

One Finger beamed. "Not a grain. My high grade's safe." He nodded as if to stress the fact. "If'n he'd come here, he'd a found t'fool's gold. It's not hid sa good."

Parker chuckled. "You're a wily old fox." He wandered to the southern edge of the clearing. "You have a sweet spot here. Well protected."

"Cain't argue that."

Kate stood up and set her cup on a flat rock bordering the fire. "Can we bring you anything? A tonic for your belly?"

One Finger shook his head. "Got me some o' Doc Inglebright's Elixir."

She raised her hand and hid her grin, then quickly sobered. "I have to get back." She didn't want to wound his pride, but she didn't like leaving him, although there wasn't anything she could do about it. "Thanks for the coffee. Take care of yourself now."

After glancing at the clouds moving over the ridge, Parker thought they'd better hightail it back to town, too. "Let me know about your next poker game. I'll be there."

"I will, Smith. Surely will."

When she and Parker reached the path, she waved at One Finger and continued on. She felt oddly pleased Parker had come with her. Old One Finger respected him. It was *al-*

most reassuring. "Do you think he'll be all right?" As the sun disappeared behind the clouds, it started snowing.

The path became wider, and Parker moved to her side. "He's getting on. It'll probably take him a little longer to mend than it would've a few years ago. I'll check on him in a couple days."

"Careful." She pushed the thick spruce branch aside. "You might spoil your reputation." He chuckled and the deep sound felt as if it had grazed the back of her neck.

He caught the branch and stepped clear of it. "Think I should shoot targets in front of the general store? Or we could hold a contest."

Not on your life, she thought and laughed. "Do you really think that would better your good standing?"

When she looked up at him, several flakes of snow landed on her lips, and he watched them melt. "If you're issuing a challenge, I think I can hold my own with you." With or without pistols, went unsaid. She had a nice laugh, a suggestive laugh, the kind of laugh that could inspire a man to pursue a woman no matter the cost to his pride. For all her mannish ways, she was very much a lady, and at times he found himself responding to her in a way he was determined to avoid. If her voice were whiny instead laced with sultry tones, or if she smoked cigars, or if she had a beard down to her . . . it would be easier to think of her as only a means to an end.

She stopped at her cutoff. "I'll see you at supper."

He wrapped his hand around her arm, halting her steps. "I'll walk with you."

"There's no need. It's getting cold." His hand still held her, and she gazed at him. His thoughts were unreadable. "Something wrong?" She stared at his lips, the lower a gentle curve, and wondered what they would feel like pressed to hers.

"Not a thing," he said, his voice huskier than he'd expected, "unless we stand out here much longer. Come on." He took her hand and walked her to her door. She glanced up at him with slightly parted lips, lips on any other woman that would've begged to be kissed. "Better get inside." He tipped his hat and headed back to the hotel before he did something that might breach the fragile truce they were forming.

Kate carried the tray of dirty dishes into the kitchen as Charlie set out two more plates of food. "Having a new sheriff certainly is good for business. At least three men heard about him at the saloon and came over to get a look at him." She grinned and began scraping the dishes. She didn't think Parker was expecting so much attention.

"Yep, biggest t'do in months."

"It's amazing how fast the news spread. We aren't on the main road and don't get that many people riding through here." She set the dishes in hot soapy water, dried her hands, and picked up the coffeepot.

Charlie set the two suppers on the tray. "Don't ferget. Bishop said Smith gets all his meals free."

She set the coffeepot on the tray and picked it up. "I won't."

As she served the meals and refilled cups, she repeatedly looked to the doorway. He'd had the strangest expression on his face when they parted earlier. She had been about to invite him in for coffee, but he'd nearly bolted away. Mamma always said I could catch more flies with sorghum than vinegar, she thought. She'd have to remember that—the next time she had any use for a fly.

9

KATE GRABBED HER coat from the peg and hesitated. "You don't like the snow. Why do you insist on going to the store with me?"

"It's sunny out, an' I'd like to see something b'sides these four walls." Mary Louise wrapped her woolen scarf around her neck and fastened her coat. When they stepped outside, she took her daughter's arm. "Isn't it lovely? Everythin' looks so clean. Even that disreputable saloon seems less offensive."

When she caught a glimpse her mother's new red flannel petticoat, Kate smiled. Her mother was in one of her poetic moods and spoke softly, drawing out her words. It was a pleasant sound and reminded her of Sunday afternoons before her papa left to fight in the Rebellion. They entered the general store. As they were assailed with the delicious aroma of cinnamon rolls, the little brass bell over the door rang out. She smiled at Bert sitting in his chair by the woodstove. "Hi. You keeping warm?"

"Sure am, Miss Kate."

Mary Louise's first stop was the postal counter. "Good mornin,' Mrs. Goody. Isn't this a fine day?"

"That it is." Mrs. Goody sifted through the handful of letters and looked up. "I'm real sorry, Mrs. Miller. There isn't anything for you this week. Maybe next."

"Thank ya for checkin'. Are those Miss Lucy's rolls I smell? I haven't seen her in ever so long."

Mrs. Goody smiled. "Indeed they are. You can go on back. She's been asking about you."

"I will, right after I take a peek at the yarn."

"You go right ahead, Mrs. Miller. Look to your heart's content." Mrs. Goody went over to Kate. "How are you doing, Kate? Did you get the petticoats made in time?"

"Yes." Kate patted her shirt. "Thanks for the advice." She meandered by the kitchenware—an egg fryer, a lipped frying spider, and a long-handled griddle—on her way over to the two shelves of boots. One pair with was lined with fur.

"We have snowshoes, too. If you keep going to the mines, you'll need a pair, Kate. But I hope you won't." Mrs. Goody dusted off one of the lamps. "Men have frozen to death in snowstorms."

Kate chuckled. "After I return this batch of laundry, I think the miner's'll have to deliver and pick it up."

"They come in for supplies anyway, or Mac can help if he delivers supplies."

"Thank you for the offer. I'll have to wait and see if any of the miners want their laundry done." The coffee smelled good, but it was the aroma of sweet cinnamon that teased Kate's appetite. She glanced over to where her mother had been perusing the yarn, but she wasn't there.

"Your mother went back to visit mine. She still bakes enough for a railroad crew, but she doesn't get around so good now." Mrs. Goody took a look outside. "Why don't we have some coffee and rolls? Half the time my dinner is whatever she's made that morning."

Kate smiled. "Sounds good. Thank you." She followed Mrs. Goody through the doorway leading back to the parlor and kitchen. Kate's mother was sitting with Miss Lucy. The dear soul's thin white hair was tucked under her lace-trimmed mobcap. The sparkle in her hazel eyes didn't seem quite as bright as it had been in July, and she looked a few pounds lighter, too. Kate stepped over to her. "Hello, Miss

Lucy. You've been busy this morning.''

Miss Lucy nodded. ''A body's got to keep going or lay down and die.'' She grinned up at Kate. ''I ain't ready to go just yet.''

''That's good news. You keep right on baking, Miss Lucy.''

''I'm glad you left some for Kate and me, Mother.'' Mrs. Goody set several cinnamon rolls on a dinner plate, picked out two napkins, and set them on a small side table before she poured their coffee and joined Kate in the parlor.

''There's always plenty. Just leave some for Mac.''

Kate bit into the sticky roll and licked her lower lip. Her cooking could fill and warm a belly, but it wouldn't bring the pleasure Miss Lucy's did. ''These are delicious, Miss Lucy. Would you share your secret with mamma?''

Miss Lucy considered the request a moment and grinned at Mary Louise. ''You come over after breakfast one day, and we'll bake rolls all day.''

''Why, thank ya, deah. I'll do that.'' Mary Louise sipped her tea and leaned closer to Miss Lucy. ''Did ya see the pretty green yarn in the shop? It'll make a lovely shawl.''

Miss Lucy's glance darted to Kate, then she whispered, ''I'll set some aside for you to take home after we're finished baking.''

Mary Louise grinned and murmured, ''Thank you.''

Mrs. Goody raised her cup to her lips and softly said, ''I wonder what they're plotting.''

Miss Lucy eyed her daughter. ''I heard you, missy. We're planning to take over the town, make the menfolk wait on us hand 'n foot. Ain't we, Mary Louise?''

Mary Louise giggled and nodded.

''Don't start without us,'' Kate said, sharing the joke with Mrs. Goody.

''Landsake, wouldn't they be put out?''

''We'd never starve them into agreement. Charlie's too good a cook.'' Kate popped the last bite of sweet roll into her mouth. If she ate like this every day, she'd weigh as much as a horse.

The bell rang in the store, and Mrs. Goody sprang to her feet. ''Don't hurry, Kate. I won't be long.'' She grabbed a roll and dashed into the store.

She's good to old Bert, Kate thought, and looked at her mother. ''I have to get back and serve dinner. I'll walk you home now.''

Mary Louise shared a glance with Miss Lucy. ''Ya needn't do that, deah. I know m'way back.''

''But the snow—''

''Dahlin,' '' Mary Louise said with a touch of sternness in her voice, ''ya just go along. I'll be leavin' when we finish visitin'.'' She looked at Miss Lucy. ''Sometimes I think she's fa'gotten which of us is the child.''

''I know just what you mean,'' Miss Lucy said with a glance toward the store.

Kate carried her cup over to the dry sink. ''It was nice seeing you again, Miss Lucy.'' Then she faced her mother. From the day her father left home, she'd had to be the strong one, make the decisions, and see they earned enough for food and shelter. She didn't choose to be the ''parent''; she slowly took responsibility when her mother did not. ''Enjoy your visit.'' She went into the store. Bert had dozed off, and Mrs. Goody was showing Parker ready-made shirts. As she continued to the door Kate motioned to her, hoping to escape without being noticed.

''Leaving already, Kate?''

I was trying to, Kate thought, pausing at the door. '' 'Fraid so.''

Parker turned around, holding a deep blue wool flannel shirt in front of him. ''What do you think? Or brown. It wouldn't show the dirt as much.'' It was plain to see she was out of sorts. This time he didn't think it had anything to do with him.

The blue was almost the shade of his piercing eyes, perfect for him. ''That looks fine.'' It was better than fine, but she had no intention of feeding his vanity.

Bert opened his eyes and looked over. ''Does fer a fact, Sheriff.''

Parker grinned, walked over to her; and held it out. "Think it'll wash up okay?" She sighed. At least she was listening to him. He handed the shirt to her and turned back to Mrs. Goody. "I'll take a pair of those Levi's jeans, too."

Mrs. Goody eyed his trousers. "The duck or blue denim?"

"Denim. Two pairs and another shirt like that one."

Kate walked over and handed the shirt back to him. "It's a good shirt. You do know that those Levi's'll shrink, don't you?"

He nodded. "I'm sure Mrs. Goody will help me find the right fit." Mrs. Goody watched them with a matronly eye, and he smiled at her.

Mrs. Goody laughed. "It wouldn't do to have your trousers too tight to sit in, now would it?"

Kate pictured him in skin-tight pants and quickly glanced away. Her imagination was too vivid to abide. A short walk outside was what she needed. "Thank you, Mrs. Goody. I'll see you later." She hurried to the door.

"Kate," he called as her reached for the doorknob. "Wait up a minute. I'll walk with you." She started to open the door, then released it and dropped her hand to her side. He smiled.

Mrs. Goody handed him a pair of jeans. "Hold these up. Let's see if they'll do."

He did as she asked. "You must be used to fitting these." He watched Kate as she wandered to where three pairs of boots sat and picked up one. High-pitched laughter drifted from the back of the store. She stiffened and replaced the boot.

Mrs. Goody tossed that pair of jeans onto the counter and tried another pair. "These're better. Kate, what do you think?"

She regarded the pants. "They should shrink to the right length." Now for the waist. She raised her hand and hesitated. Oh what was wrong with her. It was just a pair of pants. She grabbed the waistband and wrapped it around his waist. Her face came closer to his chest and she breathed in the scent of laurel. She snatched them away from him and straightened up. ''They'll do.''

She blushed, and he struggled to hide his grin. ''Thanks, Kate. Would you shrink these for me?''

''Sure.'' At least he won't be in them, she thought, avoiding his eyes.

Mrs. Goody wrapped up the jeans and shirts and set the parcel in front of him. ''Can I get something else, Sheriff?''

He reached into his pocket. Would everyone forget his name and use his new title? ''How much do I owe you, Mrs. Goody?''

She brought out her ledger. ''I'll put these on your account.'' She dipped the pen into the inkwell and listed his purchases. Closing the book she said, ''There. All taken care of.''

''Thank you.'' He stuck the package under his arm and went over to Kate. ''See something you want?'' She was staring at the same boots. ''Why don't you try them on?''

''No . . . not now.''

Bert barely opened his eyes and said, ''So long, Sheriff.''

''Take it easy, Bert.'' Parker stepped outside with her. ''Does he have a place in town?''

''He's fixed a room to sleep in the building next door.''

''I'm glad you told me.'' He glanced back at the store. ''I thought I heard your mother laughing, but I didn't see her.''

Kate nodded. ''She's visiting with Miss Lucy, Mrs. Goody's mother.'' She inhaled deeply and felt better. ''I should get back to work. Want me to take the jeans with me? I can wash them out this afternoon.''

''That would be nice.''

She thought he'd open the parcel right there in front of the general store, but he started across the road. ''Where're you going?'' She caught up with him at the side of the hotel. She had to take two steps for every one of his. He strode along the path to her cabin as if on a mission. ''I asked—''

''I heard you, Kate.'' He didn't stop until he reached her

cabin. He tipped his hat back and looked at her. "Maybe I should have handed my pants over to you in the middle of town. It would've made for interesting gossip."

She glared at him and pushed the door open. "We should be safe in here—unless you think someone will see you entering with me." She marched inside, pulled off her jacket, and muttered, "Give 'im a badge, and he becomes righteous."

He smirked at her. "It would only raise my standing. I'm not so sure about yours."

That was hard to believe. She'd spent too many years defending her innocence against men who thought it was long gone. "Do you want those jeans washed or not?"

"Yes, ma'am."

His voice was sincere, but his eyes were almost smiling. "Then come inside and close the door. You're letting the heat out." She added another log to the fire.

He went in, dropped the package on the worktable, and untied the string. "I appreciate this." He set the pants on the table and carelessly rewrapped the shirts.

She stood with her back to the fireplace. The cabin felt small. She stepped back and bumped into the hearth. What had possessed her to invite him inside? He wasn't any more interested in her than she was in him, so why was she so wary of him? He was tall, handsome, and could be charming. She took a deep breath. He'd leave in a moment, and she'd be fine.

He glanced at her. "You feel okay? You look a little pale."

"I'm fine."

He took a step toward her, and she flinched. "I'd better let you get to work."

When he left and closed the door behind him, she dropped down to the hearth, her heart pounding in her throat. What the devil was wrong with her? She hugged herself and closed her eyes, but he was so clear in her mind's eye it was as if he were standing in the room watching her. She licked her lips. He meant nothing to her, and she would keep it that way.

She'd vowed ten years earlier not to become like her mother, a sweet but weak woman without her man. No man would do that to her. Especially Parker Smith. She giggled. There was no danger of that happening with him. The last thing he wanted was some female panting after him.

When Parker entered the dining room, he heard Kate's husky laughter. She was talking with a man seated by himself, an older man wearing a tweed jacket with a white biled shirt and black necktie. When she turned and saw him, her full-mouthed smile slipped to a distant although pleasant expression. She certainly was one complicated lady, he thought, walking over to the corner table he preferred.

"I'll get your gingerbread." Kate left Mr. Pitt's table and met Parker at his favored seat. He'd put on one of the new shirts, and he looked even more handsome, in a devilish way, than she had supposed he would. "I'll bring your dinner."

"Thanks." He motioned to the man she'd been talking with. "I see you have another admirer."

"Indeed," she said, her humor restored. "We've had an understanding since summer." She didn't dare look at dear Mr. Pitt and could only hope Parker's voice hadn't carried that far.

He raised one brow. "Are congratulations in order?"

As a burst of laughter threatened, she coughed and regained her composure. "No. You see he's rather shy, and I'm happy with the way things are now." Please, Parker, she thought rushing into the kitchen, leave well enough alone and don't speak to him. She quickly returned with his meal, the plate filled from rim to rim.

He stared at the plate, then at her. "Don't you think the jeans'll shrink?"

"What're you—" She shook her head. "Charlie must've taken a liking to you." She left his table before he could say any more and served a sizable slice of gingerbread to Mr. Pitt.

Mr. Pitt smiled. "Miss Miller, you are far too generous. But I do appreciate your kindness. I have heard about the new sheriff. Would that be the gentleman seated in the far corner?"

"Yes, that's Mr. Smith." She wasn't about to encourage any conversation between them. She didn't believe she'd fooled Parker with that inane tale and certainly didn't want him asking Mr. Pitt.

Mr. Pitt picked up the fork and hesitated. "Would it be all right if I called on your mother? I wanted to pay my respects."

How sweet of him. It would do her mother good. "She called on Miss Lucy before dinner, but she should be home by now." Anyway I hope so, Kate thought. "I was going to bring your trousers up to you, but Mamma can give them to you."

"Splendid. I am glad I have saved you a trip in this frosty weather." Mr. Pitt cut a neat bite of gingerbread with the edge of the fork.

"It's no bother going up to the camps. I look forward to my trips." She refilled his cup and moved on to the next table.

While he ate, Parker watched Kate from time to time along with everyone else. He didn't like surprises and was therefore cautious about his surroundings. As far as he had seen, this town was about as safe as any could be. So why couldn't he rein in his suspicious nature? After spending his adult life honing his skills to bring Turner to justice, he wasn't sure if he would ever be able to simply live without feeling as if he had to be prepared to guard his backside.

Kate cleared a table. On her way back to the kitchen, she barely glanced at Parker. Keeping busy helped keep her mind off him. She left the tray of dirty dishes on the work-table and sliced a piece of gingerbread for him.

Charlie chuckled. "Why don't'cha give'm the pan?"

"Were you saving this?" She looked down at the gingerbread pan and inwardly cringed. She'd been about to give Parker half of it. ''Sorry. Guess I wasn't paying attention.'' She set a decent portion on a clean plate.

Charlie handed her another clean plate. ''Why don't ya have a piece with him?''

''Now, why would I want to do that?''

''Ya gotta eat sometime.''

''I will,'' she said, grinning. ''In here, as usual.''

Charlie cleared his throat. ''Ya cain't. Gonna roll a pie crust out on the table.''

She glowered at him. ''Than I'll balance the dish on my lap. For Pete's sake, what's gotten into you?''

He shrugged. ''Don't like crumbs and such fallin' into my pie crust.''

''Then I'll try not to dribble.'' She picked up the plate, a clean fork, and took it into Parker. ''Your dessert.''

''Is Charlie trying to spoil me?'' He gave her his most innocent look. ''Or are you?''

You sure know how to dish out the foolishness, she thought. ''I wouldn't want you complaining about the service. After all, you are the sheriff.''

He gave her a highbrow nod. ''Indeed I am, ma'am. And I thank ya fer remindin' me o' my place.''

She laughed. She couldn't help herself. ''Your mother must've had a dickens of a time raising you.'' Suddenly all silliness disappeared and his expression was as deadly serious as any she'd seen. ''Something wrong?''

He shook his head and quickly became interested in the gingerbread. Her remark hit too close to home, but he wasn't about to explain. Long ago he had learned that he rarely owed anyone an explanation for his behavior. Neither did he talk about his childhood, or rather his youth. ''This is good. Give Charlie my compliments. Haven't had gingerbread in years.''

''I'll tell him.'' He was fond of questioning her, and she wondered how much she could learn about him—if she put her mind to it.

* * *

As Kate returned to the cabin, she decided to take advantage of the clear sky and deliver the miners' laundry. She pushed the door open and found her mother and Mr. Pitt sitting in front of the fireplace.

Mr. Pitt jumped to his feet as if he had been caught in an embarrassing situation, his teacup still in his hand. "Miss Miller, you startled me. You did say it was all right to call on your mother."

She smiled. "Yes, of course. You don't need my permission. I'd forgotten." She smiled at her mother and back at him. "Please, sit down. I don't want to interrupt your visit."

Mary Louise smiled shyly at Mr. Pitt, then looked at Kate. "What's ya hurry, deah?"

"The weather's so nice, I thought I'd go up to some of the camps and check on One Finger."

Mr. Pitt perched on the edge of his seat. "I was told Mr. One Finger was not harmed. Did I misunderstand?"

"No," Kate said, shaking her head. "Par . . . the sheriff said One Finger had been beaten. We checked on him yesterday. I'd just feel better seeing him again."

Mr. Pitt nodded.

"Well, make sure ya relay our concern, deah."

"I will, Mamma. And don't forget to give Mr. Pitt his trousers. He'll need them this winter." Kate didn't bother taking off her coat but gathered the men's laundered clothes. It was just as well she had somewhere to go. The only way to give her mother and Mr. Pitt any privacy was to leave. She overheard him ask her mother to take a walk and grinned. Her mother was one of those women who blossomed in the company of men. And at that moment, she was happy for her.

"What are ya takin' him, Kate? Ya know ya shouldn't go calling without a li'l something."

"Yes. I remember. You two have a nice visit." Kate left the cabin and went back to the kitchen. Charlie was filling three pie plates with filling, and Parker was keeping him company. It must be my day for surprises, she thought.

Charlie looked up at her. ''Miss me sa soon?''

''Charlie, not in front of him,'' she said, darting a glance at Parker. ''We don't want a scandal, do we?''

Charlie broke out laughing. ''Girl, nobody'd b'lieve it.''

Parker eyed Kate and played along. ''You're wrong, Charlie. Why, you'd be the envy of every man in the mountains.''

''Only these mountains? I'm disappointed.'' She set the bag of laundry on the stool. ''I thought I'd take some gingerbread to One Finger while I'm up his way.''

''Good idear.'' Charlie pointed to the dry sink. ''Might as well put it in that old pie tin.''

''Lucky for you I was here.'' Parker grinned at Charlie. ''Saved a trip around town looking for me.'' She sent him an 'I don't think so' look that he chose to ignore. ''You didn't forget your pistol, did you?''

''I didn't think I'd need it. Thought I was going by myself, but I can get it easily enough.''

''Don't bother. I'll lend you mine, if you need it.''

Charlie glanced from one to the other and shook his head. ''I wish the both of yous'd get 'n leave me t'my bakin'.''

''You're right, Charlie. It's getting crowded in here.'' Parker shrugged into his coat and slung the bag of laundry over his shoulder.''A good cook's harder to find than a sheriff.''

She finished wrapping up the pie tin. If he'd carry the bag, she wouldn't complain. ''Thanks, Charlie. See you at suppertime.'' She opened the door and stepped outside.

Parker joined her, closing the door behind him. ''It's a good day for a walk. Everyone seems to think we're overdue for a big storm.''

''Let's hope it holds off until tonight.'' She wouldn't tell him, but she wasn't anxious to be stuck in town with him and his infernal questions.

Her stride was brisk, and he wondered if she was trying to avoid him. ''You must know your way to all the mines within miles.''

"Hardly. Miners don't stay on a played-out claim. They keep to themselves. I've only gotten to know a few. Not many prospectors are overly concerned about clean clothes." She'd seen a few she felt sure only took a bath every spring and probably with their clothes on. Others spread their flea-or lice-infested clothes over ant hills to rid them of the pests.

He chuckled. "Business must've been good during the town's heyday."

"Mm-hm," she said, continuing with her fabrication. "When the bathhouse was busy, we were, too. And of course the saloons." Wasn't he ever going to give up fishing for information? She turned onto the shortcut to the path they had taken before. "Since you're going to be here a while, you could try your hand at mining. You might get lucky and strike a vein." And find something else to do besides following me, she thought.

He glanced sideways at her. Nice try, Kate. "I don't believe in trusting luck. If I have any, I think I'll save it for something else."

He didn't sound bitter, just down to earth, and she felt the same way. The path narrowed, and she took the lead. He'd roused her curiosity, too, and she couldn't pass up this chance to find out more about him. "What did you do before you started looking for this Turner fellow?"

He stared at her back. He should've expected the question. It had been asked before but not usually so directly. In fact he had witnessed two shootings because of such interest. However, because of what he would do when he found her father, he felt he could afford to be more generous with her than he would with anyone else. His mother had lived long enough to see that he completed his schooling, but Kate wasn't interested in that. "For a time I worked for the *Virginia City Chronicle.*" That first year he'd had high hopes of locating Turner more easily through stories in the newspaper. "Rode on a cattle drive to Abilene, worked for the Union Pacific, and I've worked in a saloon.'' He tried to see her expression, but she kept her face hidden. ''What about you?''

He was a real jack-of-all-trades. That pleased her, although she had no idea why it should. ''Mamma's the seamstress. I've worked in dry-goods stores, dining rooms, mucked out stalls in a livery, and cleaned the working girl's rooms over a saloon.'' That was her most interesting job and where, at the tender age of fourteen, she first learned what men and women did together in bed. Of course her mother had no idea where she was working at the time.

He had never struggled so hard not to laugh. Kate in a brothel. It must have shocked her sensibilities. . . . Could that be why she was so very reserved around most men? He sobered. ''Have you thought of opening your own shop?''

She came to a halt at the bend in the path and looked at him. ''What kind of shop? Can you see me selling lady's hats? Or dresses?'' She chuckled. She'd never worn or owned a dress fancier than the plainest calico, and she'd *never* be hungry enough to earn her keep on her back. ''How about you? What'll you do after you find Turner?''

He hadn't thought that far ahead, at least not after the first fruitless year of searching. ''Moose Gulch won't need a sheriff for long. I'll have to think about it.''

She glanced at him, wondering if he were teasing, but his expression held no hint. ''You'd really consider staying on?''

He smiled at her. ''I'll consider most anything, Kate.''

❖ 10 ❖

KATE STEPPED INTO the big wooden tub and sat down with her knees up near her chin. The warm water barely covered her breasts, but it felt wonderful. She dribbled water along one arm and thought how wonderful it would be to have a bathtub long enough to stretch out in with bubbles up to her chin. She overheard talk about hot springs, down in Wyoming Territory, but boiling hot water didn't sound any more inviting than an ice-cold stream. When we have our own house, she thought, we'll have one of those big tin bathtubs like those fancy ladies had in Canyon City.

Mary Louise looked up from her sewing. "Don't ya fall asleep now."

"I'm folded up like a hanky. How could I?" She washed one shoulder, then the other. "Did you want to use the tub when I'm done?"

"No, thank ya, deah. I bathed just the other day." Mary Louise sighed dramatically. "Ya did, too. It doesn't do a body good to soak it like dirty clothes."

Kate laughed. "It does wonders."

"Well, ya better keep warm. I don't want ya comin' down with the croup or worse."

"People get cold all the time without getting sick. Besides, if I didn't wash, I'd stink." Before washing her hair, she closed her eyes. It had been four days since she visited several of the miner's camps with Parker, and she still didn't know how to take his comment about staying in town. Did he really want to settle down?

"Katherine Turner, ya know ladies don't 'stink.' One may need the use of rose water, but you should never mention it."

Kate groaned. "Mamma, you *must* remember *not* to call me that." She stood up and stepped out onto the oilcloth by the tub. "Could I suggest the lady bathe?" She moved the small bucket of fresh water closer to her and knelt by the tub to wash her hair.

"Oh!" Mary Louise stared wide-eyed at her daughter. "Oh, Kate, ya're foolin' me." She set back. "At times you're so like your papa. He used t'tease me somethin' awful."

Kate worked the coarse soap into her hair. "Yes . . . he did. I'd forgotten."

"Mm-hm. I fear your memory of all the good times we had together with him have faded, dahlin'." Mary Louise worked the needle through the fabric.

"What about the other memories—when he was running from the law? We were shunned, called names, and lost our house." Kate rinsed her hair, squeezed out much of the water, and wrapped a towel around her head. "He left us penniless, Mamma, with only his reputation as a bank robber to warm our hearts."

Mary Louise glanced at her daughter. "If you'd only talk—" She didn't complete her thought but lowered her hands to her lap. "Your bitterness's made ya old b'yond your years. Oh, I do wish he would—"

Kate raised her hand, silencing her mother. "Don't say any more about him, please." As far as I'm concerned, she thought, he's dead. It didn't take Kate long to dry off in front of the fire. After putting on her nightgown, she soaked Parker's jeans in the tub. It could take them a day or two to dry out.

She sat on the hearth and combed out her hair. He had suggested she open her own shop. She had scoffed at the idea, but the more she thought about it, the more appeal it gained. After all, she didn't want to serve meals or clean rooms until she was in her dotage.

Parker returned late in the day from his ride to Deer Lodge and walked Buckshot into the livery. Mac wasn't there, but the weather had been fair, most of the snow had melted, and he was likely at his claim. After giving Buckshot a good rubdown, Parker returned him to his stall and stepped outside. There was hardly any difference from one week to the next here, he thought, but there might be in the next few days.

He smiled. Impatient with the normal course of events, he rode to Deer Lodge and talked with James Mills, the editor of *The New North-West* weekly newspaper. Businesses advertised, and Parker thought a small item in the local paper announcing that Moose Gulch now had a sheriff would spread the good news faster than word of mouth. He'd been tempted to add that his deputy was Katherine Turner but decided that wouldn't accomplish anything.

Before leaving Deer Lodge, he had arranged for a rider to bring a few copies to town. He also saw the new territorial penitentiary. It was a large facility made of stone and resembled a castle more than a prison. Moose Gulch didn't have a jail, though he probably could use one of the abandoned storefronts if needed. As he walked past the general store, Mrs. Goody called to him.

She met him at the door and stared at his jacket. "Haven't you seen Mac?"

"No. He wasn't at the livery."

"Oh." She looked up and down the street, then beamed at him. "Your badge arrived! Mac has it. Wanted to pin it on you himself."

"That's good news, Mrs. Goody." He hoped he sounded more impressed than he felt. Somehow, he'd never imagined sporting a badge on his chest. "I'm sure I'll see him before long." And much sooner than he'd like.

Mrs. Goody stared off into space, frowning. "Maybe we

should have a supper. Invite everyone in town.'' Her expression grew bright-eyed. ''We'll have a pining ceremony. We can do it tonight . . . at the hotel, after supper. Well, I have a lot to do. I'll see you later, Sheriff.''

''Yes, ma'am.'' He continued down the boardwalk until he came to Earl sitting out in front of the barbershop. ''Anything exciting happen while I was away?''

Earl lowered his knife and laughed. ''Saw an elk up the hill and a couple squirrels behind the shop.''

''Sounds like a busy day.''

Earl leaned back against the wall. ''I heard what Mrs. Goody said. You going to that dinner she's planning?''

Parker nodded. ''I wouldn't want to disappoint her or Mac. They're good people.'' Besides, he hadn't eaten since breakfast and wasn't about to miss supper. ''I think I should clean up for such an affair.''

''I'll heat the water. It'll be ready when you are.''

''Thanks. I'll be back.'' Parker crossed the road and went into the hotel. Bishop's office door was open, but the lobby was empty. Parker went on up to his room. Kate had cleaned while he was gone. The bed was neater than he'd left it and his laundry was gone. He got his last pair of clean stockings and drawers, grabbed his comb, and returned to the barbershop for his bath.

Later when he entered the dining room, he found everyone in town waiting for him. Three tables had been pushed together. Mr. and Mrs. Goody, Earl, Ralston, Bishop, Bert, who never missed supper, even Mrs. Miller and an older woman he hadn't met were smiling at him. It was more attention than Parker had expected and certainly much more than he wanted.

Bert waved. ''Howdy, Sheriff.''

Parker walked over to the table. ''Evening, Bert, everybody.'' He smiled at Mrs. Goody. ''You've been busy.''

Bishop smiled at Mrs. Goody, seated across from him, and pushed out the chair at the end of the table. ''Have a seat. Kate will be serving supper any minute.''

''Something smells good.'' Parker sat down. Mrs. Miller's earbobs winked in the light as she spoke softly to the older woman. Ralston eyed him as if on the verge of laughing and drained his glass of water. "Do you folks have these get-togethers often?"

Ralston laughed. "You seemed to've drawn us together, Smith. Everyone just wanted to show their appreciation."

"I haven't done anything, yet. Are you expecting trouble?"

"That's just it," Mac said, looking around the table. "You're our insurance. Who'd wanta squabble with you or your gun?"

"No one with a grain o' sense," Bert said, with a broad grin.

Mary Louise wagged her handkerchief at Bert and Mac. "Now, now, gentlemen. That's nothin' to be discussed with ladies present."

Miss Lucy tut-tutted her friend and fixed each of the men with a stern expression. "At least speak up, gentlemen, so a body can hear what you're saying. I for one would like to know what's going on."

Bert nodded. "Me, too."

Parker glanced at the door to the kitchen, hoping to see Kate. As he was looking away, she came into the dining room carrying a large tray ladened with dishes. Just in time, he thought. There were two empty seats he figured were for Kate and Charlie, between Earl and Ralston. Anyway he hoped so.

Kate set the tray down and met Parker's gaze. His hair was slicked back and still damp. He smiled. She did, too, as she set the first plate of boiled ham, potato cakes, and turnips in front of Mrs. Goody. After serving the ladies, Kate walked around the table to Parker, the guest of honor. When she reached around him to set his plate down, she inhaled the aroma of his hair tonic and abruptly stepped back. "Since you missed dinner, Charlie gave you an extra portion."

"I'll be sure to thank him." Parker glanced up at her. "Did you miss me?"

"No," she whispered. "I ate your meal."

He chuckled and noticed her cheeks turned the color of ripe peaches. "Careful. Someone might think you like me."

"You know better, I trust." It took her three trips to bring everyone's supper out, then she poured the coffee and tea. Charlie brought a tray with three bowls of butter and two plates piled high with biscuits.

As Kate passed her mother's chair, Mary Louise tapped her arm. "Where's your plate? Aren't ya goin' to join us, deah?"

"In a minute."

Miss Lucy crooked her finger at Kate. "I think you've caught our new sheriff's eye. Enjoy the chase, honey. He looks like a rascally sort."

Kate quickly looked up to see if anyone had overheard her outlandish comment. She leaned closer and softly said, "I think he's more interested in you, Miss Lucy." This is how gossip starts, she thought, hoping the dear woman would forget about matching her with Parker.

"Oh, Kate. If I were forty years younger, I wouldn't ignore him."

Kate smiled and gave Earl a hasty glance. Miss Lucy wasn't exactly whispering. Kate stepped away before the sweet elderly woman said any more. She wasn't able to ignore Parker, but she didn't want it to become common knowledge. She quickly checked the table to make sure she hadn't forgotten anything, then went back to the kitchen for hers and Charlie's suppers. He was sitting next to Mr. Ralston when she returned.

Parker gave Kate a slight nod when she sat down between Charlie and Earl, then his attention returned to Bishop and Ralston's conversation.

Ralston picked up his cup. "What do you think about those outlaws in last week's paper?"

Parker cut a bite of ham. "You have my attention. What about them?"

"Seems these bandits moved in on the Idria mining

camp—professional gamblers and thieves took over.''

Parked glanced at each of the men. ''Do you expect that'll happen here?''

Ralston shook his head. ''That mine's in California. I can't recall any bands coming through here.''

Kate heard Mr. Ralston say something about ''outlaws,'' then Earl had bumped her arm.

''Sorry, Kate.'' Earl moved his chair to give her more room. ''Do you think Smith'll catch that thief hitting the miners?''

She swallowed her bite. ''Don't know. I thought he was just suppose to watch out for the town.'' She scooped up a bite of potato cake. ''Did he say anything about it to you?''

''No.'' He glanced sideways at her. ''He's pretty tight-lipped with most of us.''

She continued eating. She didn't want to discuss Parker or further Earl's interest in gossip. ''How're your son and his wife doing?''

Earl beamed. ''I'll be a grandpa before summer.''

''Congratulations! That's wonderful.'' She ate her last piece of ham. They were about done eating, so she refilled their cups and began clearing the table. She reached for Miss Lucy's plate.

Miss Lucy crooked her finger at Kate and waited for her to lean down. ''Dear, will my two cakes be enough for all of us?''

Kate grinned. ''There's plenty and they look wonderful. I'm sure Par . . . the sheriff will be pleased.'' She worked her way around the table to the Goodys and paused. ''Should I serve dessert? Or wait?''

Mac looked at his wife. ''Might as well pass it out. Ralston's got Tullie watching the saloon, but I know he doesn't want to be gone too long.''

''I'll have the tables cleared in a couple minutes.'' Kate was doing fine, until she came to Parker. ''Finished?''

He glanced up at her. ''Just about.''

He was being recalcitrant. The only thing left on his plate

was half a biscuit, and she was certain he'd rather be anywhere than at that table. She leaned down until her mouth was near the rim of his ear and reached for his dish. "If you want that biscuit, eat it because I'm taking your plate."

Her voice felt the way he imagined liquid gold would feel sliding down his spine—fiery, tantalizing, inviting—and he wondered if that was her intention. "Save it for me, Kate. I'll eat it later."

She noticed her mother and Miss Lucy watching her and quickly removed his plate. She left the dirty dishes in the kitchen and carried the tray with cakes, clean dessert plates, and forks back to the dining room.

When Mac stood up, his wife quieted everyone. "Well." He looked around the table and grinned. "This sounded like a good idear. But I'm not real good with words."

Bert rested his arms on the table. "Then just give him the danged star."

Mac frowned at him. "I will. I will." He pulled the badge out of his coat pocket. "I—Parker, we want you to know we're right proud you're our sheriff."

When Mac started around the table toward him, Parker stood up. He had never involved himself in community affairs. But here he was with all these good people looking at him as if they thought he was a miracle worker, except for Kate. She seemed amused.

Glancing around one last time, Mac held up the badge and fumbled a moment before he successfully pinned it onto Parker's coat. Holding out his hand and shaking Parker's, he said, "Now it's official. You're the first sheriff of Moose Gulch."

Parked stared at the badge. It was a simple silver star in a circle with SHERIFF in black on the top and DEER LODGE CO., MONT., underneath. It certainly looked real. "Thank you. I hope things stay as peaceful as they are now."

Bert squinted at the badge. "Yep. It's gen-u-ine."

Kate cut the last pieces of cake and began passing them out. She actually felt a little sorry for Parker. Although his expression didn't betray it, she believed he was as uncomfortable with the attention as she would be. She set a slice of cake in front of him. ‘‘Miss Lucy made Jenny Lind cake for dessert. It may be a bribe so you'll walk her across the road once in a while.’’

He smiled at Miss Lucy. ‘‘It would be my pleasure, ma'am.’’

‘‘Oh, Kate. You are a one.’’ Miss Lucy giggled and whispered to Mary Louise, ‘‘I think she's sweet on him, too.’’

Mary Louise seemed to consider her daughter for a moment. ‘‘If she is, she has a strange way of showin' it.’’

Parker sat back down and tasted the cream-covered cake. ‘‘This's a prize winner. You'll have to enter it in the county fair.’’ He came close to asking Kate to confirm that there was such a fair in the county but thought better of it. They both knew she hadn't been there for more than a few months.

Long after everyone had left, Kate was still cleaning up in the kitchen. The supper had gone well and broke up after dessert. When Ralston returned to the saloon, Parker went with him. She grabbed the last kettle and began scrubbing. Everyone was so happy about his being their sheriff. Hadn't anyone thought he might draw more trouble than the town would otherwise? What if Hank showed up? She hoped that wouldn't happen. Ye gods, she really hoped he was far away—Mexico or even Canada. She heard the door to the dining room open. ‘‘You still here, Charlie? I'm about done.’’

Parker smirked and stepped into the kitchen. ‘‘Did you save my half biscuit?’’

At the sound of his voice, she whirled around. ‘‘Why aren't you drinking at the saloon?’’

He arched one brow. ‘‘Would you rather have me swagger in here all liquored up?’’

‘‘No, of course not.’’ And after that meal he put away, he's not starving for that darned biscuit, either. She turned back to finish cleaning the kettle. "Don't let that badge go to your head."

"Isn't much chance of that." He flipped the side of his coat back, hiding the badge, and shoved his hands in his pants pockets. "And there isn't much around here if you aren't a drinking man." He leaned back against the door.

"You must like to read. I saw an old *Harper's New Monthly* in your room." She opened the side door and dumped the water out.

"You can borrow it if you'd like." He walked over to the stove and shook the coffeepot.

She set a clean cup on the worktable for him. "I think it's still warm. And Miss Lucy insisted we keep the last slice of cake for you." After she dried the kettle, she draped the towel over the side of the dry sink.

He emptied the pot into the cup. "Wanna share?" He took a drink. She looked tired. He pulled out the chair she usually sat in and motioned to her.

She tried to stifle a yawn and ended up laughing. "I'll take a sip of coffee." She dropped down to her chair, and he sat in Charlie's place.

He ate a bite of cake, cut one for her, and scooped it up with the fork. "This is good. Have a bite." He held it up to her mouth.

The spicy apples smelled good, and she opened her mouth as if she were an obedient child. If she could bake as well as Miss Lucy, she could open a bakery shop, and if she had the brass, she'd open a fancy bathhouse—clean towels, hot water, and good-smelling soap but no bawdy women. Lordy, she was tired.

She looked sleepy, cuddly, and for one split moment, he imagined her curled against his chest. He handed her the cup. "You have a nice smile. Want to share what was so funny?"

She shook her head. "Just a silly notion—not worth mentioning." She took a sip of his coffee. "Anyone interesting over at the saloon?"

He offered her another bite of cake. "Bert and Earl

stopped by and a fellow passing through from Missoula. And Tullie. He picks a good banjo."

She grinned. "We should've had the supper at Ralston's."

"Tullie wasn't at supper. Was he invited?"

"I don't know him very well, but he doesn't seem to like being around folks much. I've never seen him in here."

He nodded. There were men like that, and he didn't want to become one. That was another reason he needed to settle with Turner. "He's got the saloon and a friend in Ralston. That's more than many have."

"True." She covered another yawn. "I'd better get home. Would you put out the light when you're done?" She stood up and stretched her back.

He offered the last bite, but she shook her head. He finished it and stood. "I'll walk with you."

❖ 11 ❖

SATURDAY MORNING, PARKER was finishing his breakfast when the young man he'd hired hurried into the hotel lobby. "Ned, in here." Parker smiled at him. "You're early. Must've made good time." The boy couldn't be over sixteen—an age when his weight hadn't kept pace with his height and the world seemed exciting.

Ned plopped the stack of newspapers down on the table. "Mr. Mills gave me the first papers off the press."

"That was considerate of him." Parker motioned to the chair across the table. "Sit down. You might as well eat before you go back."

"Yes, sir." Ned took a seat across from him.

Parker went to the kitchen. "Kate, would you bring another breakfast for my young friend? And a glass of water."

She looked over her shoulder at him. "Sure. Be right there." After the door closed, she glanced at Charlie. "Who could that be? I thought he didn't know anyone around here."

Charlie grabbed a clean plate and dished up fried ham, potatoes, and eggs. "Ya'll find out in a minute."

She carried the tray with biscuits, a cup and glass of water, the coffeepot, and the plate Charlie handed her to

Parker's table. She smiled at the boy across from him. "Good morning."

So young men were also safe, Parker thought. "Kate, this is Ned. He works for James Mills, the editor of *The New North-West*. Ned, this is Miss Miller."

Ned grinned at her. "Mornin', ma'am. This sure smells good." He picked up the glass of water and gulped it down.

She took the empty glass. "I'll get you some more."

When she returned, Parked pulled out the side chair. "Why don't you join us. Ned brought the latest edition of the newspaper." He set a copy in front of her with the news item face up and waited for her reaction.

Ned swallowed hard. "There's a story in there 'bout a gent who coughed up a gold dollar. Seems he went t'sleep with it in his mouth." He shook his head. "Can't imagine why he done that."

Kate glanced at Ned as she sat down wondering if he was joking, but he seemed to be serious. She looked at the paper. The first bold-print headline she noticed was "New Sheriff in Moose Gulch." She met Parker's gaze. "How did they know?"

"I went down and introduced myself. Fastest way I know to spread the word." Parker was happy with the announcement. It was listed on the front page under Territorial News.

She quickly read the notice. It was plain to see he was pleased with it, but she wasn't sure why. "It's nice, but your name isn't mentioned." He was a quiet man, kept to himself for the most part, so why would he want the attention?

"That isn't important. The office is." He had been careful not to garner a reputation. In case Turner recognized the name, Parker avoided situations that would be noticed. Smith was a common name, which he came to appreciate.

She nodded, but she couldn't help wondering if there was more to it than that. He was confident, possessed an assurance that she believed rarely came without having been tried and proven. He seemed pleased with the newspaper.

"Why didn't you tell us?" She tapped her finger on the paper. *Modest* wasn't a word she would've used to describe him—*calculating*, *charming*, and a *tease*, yes.

"There wasn't any reason to make it sound more important than it is." Parker drank his coffee. "Think the others will approve?" He realized he had hoped she would, which was unusual for him. On second thought, he realized he should've known better. She guarded her feelings with the same fierce protectiveness that he did.

She nodded. "I think they will."

Ned pointed to the newspapers. "I brought ten copies. Will that be enough, Mr. Parker?"

"Fine. I'll pass them around town."

"Oh, they'll be all around." Ned beamed. "We have subscribers all over the territory."

"Glad to hear that." Parker glanced at the paper. He was counting on the paper's widespread circulation.

"Oh, almost forgot." Ned stabbed his fork into the last piece of ham. "Mr. Mills said he wants you to let him know if there's any trouble up here." He looked from Parker to Kate. "He likes to print all the local news."

Glancing at Kate, Parker said, "Be glad to oblige, but I hope there's nothing worth reporting."

"Not just bad news, sir. Everyone likes to read good news, too. That's what Mr. Mills says. An' he knows what people like to read."

Kate watched Ned clean his plate. "Do you write any of the stories, Ned?"

"Not yet, but Mr. Mills's trainin' me. I'm workin' on an obituary."

Parker raised his cup and sat back. "I hope it's not mine."

"Oh, *no*, sir." Ned gave them a sheepish look. "Actually, the man's not real. Made him up, just for practice. Mr. Mills said I could practice on Governor Potts, but I couldn't write about his death." He shuddered. "What if he did die? I'd feel like it was my fault."

Kate patted the boy's arm. "I'm sure Mr. Mills only

wanted to be prepared, in case Governor Potts met an untimely end."

"Just the same, ma'am, it'd feel like I was walkin' on his grave." He dragged the napkin across his mouth. "Thanks for the good meal, Mr. Smith, but I gotta get back. I was told not to dawdle 'round."

"You haven't, son." Parker gave him another two bits. "Please thank Mr. Mills for me."

Ned jumped to his feet. "Thanks. Nice meetin' you, Miss Kate."

She had barely smiled, let alone say good-bye, when he ran from the dining room. She burst out laughing. "Think he'll make a newspaper man?" The boy had better learn to slow down, she thought, or he'd leave before the news even happened.

"He has the enthusiasm." Parker finished his coffee. "Guess I'd better hand these out."

She eyed the paper. "Mind if I borrow this copy? Charlie'll want to see it, too."

"That's yours." He put his coat on and picked up the other newspapers. "Don't forget that story about the gold dollar." She looked a little nonplused. His campaign to keep her wondering about him appeared to be working. He tapped his hat brim and left.

It was Monday. The day Kate set aside to do their laundry. She strung the line between two fir trees that were in the sun and managed to hang two bed sheets, one of her mother's dresses, and two of her own skirts on the line. It wasn't much above freezing outside, but the sun was bright and the gentle breeze helped dry the laundry. She went back into the cabin. Their underclothes were drying in front of the fire, and the room still held the smell of lye soap.

Looking around the single room, she wondered where her mother could be. The curtain near the bed fluttered, and she heard a soft sigh. "Mamma, what are you doing?"

Mary Louise pushed the clothes back in place and closed the drawer. "Just straightenin' my small clothes, deah."

She stood up, shook out her skirt, and stepped over to the dome-top trunk in the corner.

"What did you misplace?" Her mother seemed to be in a dither about something. Kate went over to her side. "Let me help. What are we looking for?"

"Nothin'," Mary Louise said, quickly closing the top of the trunk.

Kate pulled her hand out of the away in the nick of time. Taking her mother's arm, she started walking her back toward the fireplace. "Why don't you make a pot of tea?" It would keep her busy and hopefully calm her down.

Mary Louise freshened the pot of tea, poured herself a cup, and began rummaging through their small store of supplies. "I know they're in here."

Kate rearranged some of the garments on the clothes horse. "What?"

Reaching all the way in the far corner, Mary Louise said, "Oh, nothin' deah." She pulled out a pouch, poured the contents onto the palm of her hand, and smiled at the walnuts. With her cup of tea in the other hand, she went outside and sat down on a tree stump.

As Kate changed clothes, she put the skirt and shirtwaist she removed in the tub to soak, then ran her fingers through her hair. She tossed a wool shawl around her shoulders, picked up Parker's laundry and the stack of hotel linen, and walked outside. Three squirrels were sitting in front of her. "I'll see you later."

"Of course, deah."

Kate took a step and paused. "Please don't let those critters in the cabin. They aren't housebroken and mess everywhere."

"Don't ya worry, deah. They're stuffin' the nut meat in their cheeks to take back to their nests." Mary Louise glanced over at her daughter. "Go along with ya. We're fine."

"I know, Mamma." Kate walked along the path to the hotel. It almost felt like springtime. The side door to the kitchen was wide open, and Charlie was standing at the stove. "Nice out, isn't it?"

"Surely is."

"Are those meat pies I smell?" She draped her shawl over one peg.

"Yep." He looked into the kettle and turned back to the worktable.

I wish the miners could smell it, she thought. They'd rush right down here. She put the kitchen towels on one shelf and the tablecloths on another. "I'll be right back." Between cleaning the room and doing the laundry, she was putting away a tidy sum each month. After she put the sheets in the linen closet, she left Parker's clean clothes in his room and returned downstairs.

As she crossed the lobby, gunfire broke the silence. She ran to the door and peered up and down the road. Parker ran toward the livery. Two more shots rent the air. She stepped out onto the boardwalk and saw Hick, one of the miners, standing at the western edge of town firing his pistol in the air. The old fool.

When Parker passed the hotel, he noticed Kate staring up the road. He slowed his pace and stopped across from the livery, several paces from the man. "What's all the ruckus about?" He'd seen the man before but not in the last couple weeks.

"Struck a vein!" The man fired his gun again.

"Why don't you put that away before you hurt someone?" Parker could understand the man's need to let off steam. He hadn't even heard anyone bragging about finding color, small bits of gold left in the bottom of the pans used along streams. The man swung his gun overhead, and Parker ducked.

The man started laughing and lowered his gun.

Parker looked back at the gathering crowd, everyone in town, standing in front of the hotel and the general store. But no one looked especially concerned, and Kate was grinning.

Mac advanced on the man and called out, "Hick, what

in tarnation're you doing a fool thing like that? You could a hit somebody.''

''Not less'n they was up in a tree.'' Hick looked at Parker, then he squinted. ''What's a sheriff doin' here?''

Mac grinned at Parker. ''This's Sheriff Smith. He's our new sheriff, so you better b'have yourself.''

''Good, he kin per'teck my vein.'' Hick shoved his gun in the waist of his trousers.

''Where's this claim?''

Hick frowned at Parker. ''What'd wanna know fer?''

Parker chuckled. ''How am I suppose to protect you if I don't know where it is?''

''Hm.'' Hick rubbed his chin. ''Guess ya got some'p'n there. Ya go up t'road t'the big ol' red cedar, go north and west at the scrubby pine.''

Parker nodded. ''I'll find the path.''

''Ain't no path. Come out dif'rnt e'ry time.'' Hick rocked back on his heels. ''That'a way it's harder t'find.'' He looked at the hotel and waved. ''Hi, ya, Kate. Be there directly.'' He grinned at Mac and Parker. ''I gotta git over t'the hotel. Don't wanna keep m'gal waitin.' ''

As he watched Hick saunter over to Kate, Parker spoke to Mac. ''Think he did hit a vein?''

''Could be. Never known him to brag overly. He did hit a small one a couple years back an' swore there had to be a bigger one.''

''Thanks, Mac. See you later.'' By the time Parker reached the hotel, Kate and Hick had gone inside. When Parker walked into the dining room and saw her standing at Hick's table, he remembered where he'd seen him—right there, and she had been serving his food.

Kate grinned. ''Hick, I'm really happy for you. Have any special plans for all that money?''

''Always want'd to git a look at that Pac-ific Ocean. Think I'll git me some new duds next spring an' ride in one of those railroad cars all the way to Caly-forny.''

''Good for you! Would you send me a note, tell me what it's like there?'' She and her mother had lived in many little towns, in the hills, in farm country and in valleys, but they had never gotten farther west than Utah.

"I will, Kate, an tell you all 'bout it."

"Thanks." She started for the kitchen as Parker pulled out the chair at his corner table, and she went over to him. When he glanced at Hick, she said, "He's okay. When he finally struck it big, he wanted to celebrate."

Parker nodded. "I was just wondering if he'll tell everyone he sees."

"He's usually careful, but I'll speak to him." There was something different about Parker. He was taking his new position seriously, more so than she expected him to, and she admired him for that.

"Good. He seemed to think I'd be his personal guard. I'd hate to have anything happen to him because he believed I was guarding his backside."

"The miners have a right to be a bit edgy about the robberies. If I had any gold, I would be, too." She smoothed the tablecloth. "You ready for dinner?"

"Just coffee, now." He sat back, watching her. "That way I can come back later and maybe you'll sit with me."

That's not a good idea, she thought. "I'll get your coffee." She left and returned with his cup and served Hick's dinner. "The sheriff's worried you'll tell the wrong person about your good fortune. You know he can't protect your claim."

Hick nodded and grabbed a biscuit. "Any strangers in town?"

"No. Did you hear about what happened to One Finger?" The miners were so isolated, she doubted he had and thought he should know.

"He's okay, ain't he?"

"Yes. It seems he said too much during a poker game. One of the other men followed him and almost beat the stuffing out of him. Smith broke it up. He's concerned the same'll happen to you."

"Who was the vermin?"

"No one knew him, but he should be long gone. Parker made sure he left town."

Hick grinned at her. "Parker?"

Oops, she thought. "The sheriff, Parker Smith." She picked up the tray. "If you need anything, just call me." Without a sideways glance at Parker, she went back to the kitchen.

Charlie refilled her cup and his. "Who stepped on your tail?"

She burst out laughing, mostly at her own embarrassment. When she finally quieted, she said, "I fear it's going to be a long winter."

Mary Louise gave Parker a sheepish grin. "Ya really shouldn't've brought me a gift, Mr. Smith."

"It's only a token, Mrs. Miller." To keep within the boundaries of propriety, he hadn't taken off his jacket, just loosened the buttons. The cabin was stifling, but she appeared to be very comfortable.

Mary Louise held the small wooden box a moment longer before she eased the clasp free and raised the hinged lid. "Oh, my, what lovely buttons." She beamed at him. "I'll have to make a special dress for these. Thank ya so very much, Mr. Smith."

When he'd seen the delicate yellow roses on the buttons, he hoped she would like them. She was a nice woman. If his mother had met her, they might have become friends. However, he needed to find out if she had heard from Hank recently. "Mrs. Goody thought they might go nicely with the yard goods you'd purchased."

"Yes, yes, indeed they will." She held up one, nodded, set it back in the box and closed the lid. "How do you like being sheriff, Mr. Smith?"

"It still feels a bit strange, to be honest. Everyone's pleasant, and so far there hasn't been any trouble." He watched the fire a minute. "How's Hank doing?"

"Fine—"

She looked as if she'd been about to reprimand him, but

she didn't. He was confident Kate had warned her not to talk about Turner, but Parker wasn't about to give up so easily. "I hope he has a sturdy cabin for the winter. They say it's going to get mighty cold up here."

"He'll be fine. He takes good care of himself." She ran her fingers over the length of the box.

"Glad to hear that. I guess the miners who are staying are used to the harsh climate."

"Mercy, yes. They've been oh, so helpful. I hope they all find the gold they so desperately seek." She sipped her tea. "Are ya sure you wouldn't like a cup?"

"Thank you. I'm sure. In fact, I'd better get dinner before Charlie runs out of food." He stood up stepped over to the door.

She joined him, the box still in her hand. "It was so nice of you to call."

He opened the door. "Take care, now, Mrs. Miller." Turner was still nearby. It was turning out to be a very interesting day.

He smiled and walked up the path with the sides of his jacket pulled back. No wonder Kate needs so much firewood, he thought, that cabin's hot enough to roast a turkey in the middle of the room. He walked around the side of the hotel and entered the dining room from the lobby. Kate was clearing off the table next to the one he preferred. She shoved a hank of hair behind her ear. He grinned. "Is Hick spending the night here?" She wasn't interested in impressing people, and he found that strength very attractive.

She finished brushing the crumbs from the table onto the tray and glanced over at him. She felt his gaze touch her in a way no other man's ever had. His voice reminded her of the way cut velvet felt when she'd once brushed a piece over her cheek. Even though Hick had left and they were alone, she felt self-conscious about her growing interest in Parker. "He didn't say. Why?"

"Thought I'd watch out, make sure he doesn't run into any trouble." He hung his coat on the back of the next chair and sat down. She was timid instead of the bold, the take-charge woman he enjoyed teasing, and he couldn't resist asking, "Did you eat my meat pie?"

With her back to him, she smiled, picked up the tray, and turned around with a straight face. "Only part of it. I'll bring you what's left."

"Then we might as well keep each other company and finish it together." Kate, he thought, what is going on in your mind? Whatever the reason, he was glad her spirits had lightened up.

She went into the kitchen and began emptying the tray. "Parker's ready for his dinner."

"Okay." Charlie took two plates off the warming shelf and set them on the work table. "Ya better eat, too, b'fore this ain't fit fer a dog."

"We don't have a dog." She was hungry. She'd nibbled that morning, but she hadn't even munched on a biscuit since then. "Might as well." She set the cups, plate and coffeepot on the tray. "Why don't you come sit with us for a while?"

"Mebe I will." He stacked several small pie pans and set them with the dirty dishes.

She carried the tray over to Parker's table, set out the napkin, flatware, and his dinner plate. He watched her every move. She poured his coffee, then met his gaze. "Something wrong? Didn't I set the table right?"

"It's neat—as always." He came close to smiling. "That's why I keep coming back." He winked and broke the pie crust open with his fork.

I wish you wouldn't, she thought, but knew she didn't mean it. She set her place across from him. They were alone, so why shouldn't she enjoy his company? "You needn't. I don't think anyone would mind if you cooked over a fire pit near the creek."

He raised one brow and fought smiling. "Interesting thought. While the meat roasted, the fire would keep me warm in the snow." He chewed a bite, glad he was dining with the old Kate. "Has Hick ever pulled a stunt before like he did today?"

She shook her head and swallowed. "Not that I recall." It wasn't a lie, but it wasn't the complete truth, either. She'd told so many near-truths, she wondered if she would continue out of habit when there wasn't any need.

"At least it was midday." He stabbed a chunk of beef. "Have many miners in this area struck it rich?"

Not in the last four months, she thought. "Not lately. Only the most stubborn ones have stayed on. Why? Change your mind about filing a claim?"

He chuckled. "I wouldn't recognize a vein unless it had a high polish."

"Don't tell Hick or the others." She wagged her fork at him. "That news'd spread faster than your being sheriff."

"If you won't say anything, I'll keep quiet." He took a drink of coffee. "I haven't seen Bishop today."

"I haven't, either. Do you need something I can help with?"

He shook his head. "With so few people in town, it's easy to notice who's missing."

She stared at her plate. That was one problem with living in a town with a population of ten. He was curious about Mr. Bishop. She and her mother couldn't suddenly leave without notice. After moving from town to town for the last eleven years, she wanted nothing more than to stay put for a while. She peered through her lashes at Parker. Did he feel the same? She wanted to know. "You haven't mentioned Turner recently. Have you given up looking for him?"

"No." Had he heard her correctly? He looked at her; only years of disappointing leads gave him the wherewithal to remain calm. "Did you change your mind? Want to help me find him?"

She gulped. "What could I do? I don't know him." Lying went against the grain, but on occasion it was her only means of protecting herself and her mother. Besides, she really didn't know the man her father had become and wasn't sure she ever did.

❖ 12 ❖

EVERY EVENING AFTER supper Parker walked from one end of town to the other and checked the abandoned buildings. It rarely took him longer than ten or fifteen minutes no matter how he varied the route. Being sheriff of such a small town was almost highway robbery, but the folks seemed satisfied. There were four horses and a mule in front of the saloon, his last stop. He hurried inside, eager to get out of the cold wind.

He stepped up to the bar and took his gloves off. Tullie was playing "Lorena" on his banjo, and Ralston was serving drinks to the four men playing poker. Another man sat alone. Parker recognized one of the men, Morrey, from his trip with Kate to some of the camps.

Ralston returned to the bar and stepped over by Parker. "Whiskey or beer?"

"Beer, unless you have a hot toddy." Parker rubbed his hands together, then unbuttoned his coat. "That wind's straight out of the north."

"You still look a might cold." Ralston drew a beer and set it in front of Parker. "The toddy's a good idea. I'll think about it."

Parker took a drink and glanced at the men playing poker. "Kate introduced me to Morrey, but I haven't seen the others before."

"The tall, scrawny fellow's from over Missoula way. The heftier one claims to be from Drummond. I don't know the other two, either."

"Hey, you with the banjo," a stranger in the poker game hollered, "stop playin' that cursed ballad."

"That song got me through many a lonesome nights after the fightin' stopped," the lanky man said.

"Not me," the hefty man put in. "Nearly drove me home."

Tullie switched to "The Blue Tail Fly."

Parker set his glass down and pulled back the sides of his coat so his badge wouldn't catch the light. If there was going to be trouble, he'd just as soon let them discount him as another patron. "Is Morrey playing with gold dust or cash money? I didn't notice when I came in."

Ralston chuckled. "He always exchanges his dust for coin."

"Here?" Parker took another sip of beer.

"Been doing it since I opened."

"Glad to hear that." Parker glanced at the game again. "You ever get away for a day or so?"

"Yeah, I leave for a few days each month." Ralston chuckled. "Ever been to the south end of the Last Chance?"

Parker thought a moment, but he didn't know where that was. "No. Where is it?"

"Helena used to be Last Chance Gulch before they were quite so genteel." Ralston winked and added, "Miss Hattie 'keeps house' near Main and Bridge streets, and I surely look forward to my visits there."

"I'll keep that in mind." Parker sipped his beer. A month ago he probably would have given thought to visiting Hattie or another fancy lady, but now he'd rather have Kate sass him and see her smile.

"If you can tear yourself away, I wouldn't mind the company." Ralston drew another beer and took it over to Tullie.

Taking his beer to the table near Tullie, Parker sat with

his back to the wall. The fellow sitting by himself left. None of the poker players appeared to have much at stake. Except for an occasional laugh or curse, their voices didn't carry over to him.

The heftier of the poker players pushed back from the table. " 'Nough for me. My old women'll tie me in a knot if'n I'm not back b'fore she puts the light out."

They laughed, then the lanky man raised his glass of beer. "Here's to your manhood."

Parker shook his head and wondered what women said in private about their men. Kate's opinion of men would be enlightening. The game broke up and he ambled outside to make sure they went their own way. Morrey headed west, the others southeast along the road. Parker buttoned his jacket, raised the collar, and pulled on his gloves as he walked down the road. He kept to a brisk pace, making sure none of the three men doubled back.

A mile down the road, where it joined the main road between Missoula and Deer Lodge, Parker turned back, satisfied the men were halfway home. Besides, it was damned cold out. The sky was black. He couldn't find one single star. When he was within sight of town, the snow flurry began. The road through town was pristine, and the hotel was dark.

For the first time in his adult life, he wondered what it would be like to have a wife to go home to. If she were like Kate, he thought, it might be real interesting. More than likely she would have been with him. He couldn't picture her sewing by the light of the fire content to wait for him to come home.

Kate awoke the next morning with her teeth chattering. She pulled her hand from beneath the covers and touched her nose, half expecting to find an icicle. She slipped out of bed, put on her heavy coat, and stepped into her boots before she stirred the embers in the fireplace and woodstove. She rubbed her arms to warm up a bit. When she opened the door to get more firewood, there was a snowdrift over two feet deep in the doorway. It was still snowing. Everything was white, the coating so thick it resembled cotton batting. It was beautiful. And it was cold.

Mary Louise sat up in bed. ''Katie, what happened? It's freezin' in here.''

''It snowed during the night, and it's still coming down.'' Kate got her mother's cape and put it around her shoulders. ''Where'd you put that wolf hide? Morrey said it'd be good for a covering on the bed.''

''It's . . . No, look in that box in the far corner.'' Mary Louise pointed to the other side of the worktable.

Kate found the hide and spread it out across the bed. ''I hope it keeps us as warm as it did the wolf.''

Mary Louise ran her fingers through the pelt. ''I don't know if I can sleep with this on top of me.'' She shivered. ''Doesn't seem right.''

Kate started a pot of coffee and heated water for tea. ''We need it, and the wolf doesn't.''

With the cape wrapped tight around her, Mary Louise got out of bed and sat on the hearth to put on her shoes. ''I wonda if the critters're warm enough.''

''I believe they're more used to this climate than we are, Mamma. They'll be fine.'' Kate set her clothes in front of the woodstove and dressed quickly. Before she could leave for the hotel, she had to clear the doorway. Using a large bowl, the only thing at hand, she scooped snow and pitched it aside to start a path. That done, she brought in a good supply of firewood for her mother. ''I'll bring you breakfast. A hot meal will help.''

''All right, dahlin'. I'm not leavin' this spot for a while.''

Kate waded through the snow to the hotel. She stepped into the kitchen and shook the layer of white flakes off of her hat before closing the door. ''Hi, Charlie.'' The room was warm as always. ''What're we having this morning?''

''Mush, apple fritters, and hash. Rib-stickin' vittles.'' He grinned at her. ''Think that'll warm ya up?''

''Mm. Smells wonderful. Mind if I take my meal to

Mamma? The cabin was freezing.'' She opened her coat and took off her gloves.

''Course not.'' He reached for a bowl.

''I'll do that after I get the fire going in the dining room.'' It didn't take her long. When she returned to the kitchen, Charlie had set a plate and bowl, each with the same dish upside down to keep the food warm, on a small tray. ''Thank you.''

He handed her a heavy towel. ''Put that overtop. It's still snowin'.''

''You're an old softy.'' She bundled up again, took the tray to her mother, and hurried back. ''It's getting worse. I'll have to buy a shovel just to get out the door.''

Charlie grinned at her. ''Ya'll git used to it. Jist dress warm. Ya don't want'a git frostbit.''

She nodded. Moving here definitely wasn't one of her better ideas. ''I'll remember.'' The tables were set and the chill was off the dining room by the time Mr. Bishop sat at a table near the woodstove. She brought his cup of coffee and meal. ''Good morning.''

''Hello, Kate. Looks like we finally got a good snowfall. Was the cabin warm enough?''

He wasn't charging her any rent and the weather wasn't his fault. Anyway, beggars shouldn't be too particular. Besides, it wasn't that bad. ''We weren't prepared. It'll be warmer tonight.''

''If you need anything, let me know.'' Bishop sipped the coffee. ''I'll be gone for a while, so I'd like to make sure everything's okay here before I leave.''

''Who'll be running the hotel while you're gone?'' When she started working there, Mr. Varny ran the hotel, but business was better then, too.

He gave her an appraising look. ''Do you want the job? There shouldn't be much to do this time of year.''

Surprised by his offer, she stared at him a moment. He wasn't in the habit of teasing her. ''Sure. I won't be going to the camps.''

''Good. You'll be fine. If there's any trouble, I'm sure

the sheriff will help you out.''

She returned to the kitchen and poured herself a cup of coffee. ''Mr. Bishop'll be out of town for a while. He wants me to . . . run the hotel for him.'' She grinned.

''Good for ya.'' Charlie moved the hash around in the skillet. ''Ya ready to eat?''

''Just a couple fritters.'' She handed him a plate and peered around his shoulder at the skillet. ''That's a lot of hash for the five of us.''

''It's not sa bad baked in crust.'' He handed the plate back to her.

She ate a bite of apple fritter. It tasted better than usual. After a second bite, she went in to check on Mr. Bishop. ''Everything okay?'' She refilled his cup.

''Fine. Where's Bert? He's usually in here before me.''

''I haven't seen him.'' She glanced at Bert's empty seat. ''Think he's all right?''

Bishop looked at her. ''He's lived in these mountains longer than any of us. But I'll check on him.''

''Thanks. I'd feel better.'' She set the coffeepot down, went to the front door, and looked outside. There were no tracks marring the snow, and it seemed a little eerie, as if the town had been deserted. Then she saw smoke rising from the Goodys stovepipe and smiled.

As Parker came downstairs, he saw Kate standing in the doorway and stepped up behind her. ''Peaceful, isn't it?''

She tensed for only a moment. Ye gods 'n . . . was she getting that used to him? His voice? ''Mm-hm.'' She shivered. ''And cold.'' When she stepped back to close the door, she bumped into his chest, his warm, solid chest.

He put a hand on each side of her shoulders to steady her and felt her tremble. She smelled as clean and fresh as the snow outside. He reached one arm around her and pushed the door closed. ''I could use a cup of coffee.'' He lowered his hands, but she didn't move.

''Me, too.'' His hands were large and strong but gentle. She drew a ragged breath, wondering why her defenses weren't working with him—why his touch or the sound of his voice should be different from any other. Then suddenly she realized he'd released her, and she walked back to the dining room. He only wanted information from her, she reminded herself. He must've touched hundreds of women, so it didn't mean a thing. She had to believe that because she also knew he couldn't possibly be interested in her.

He followed her in but paused when Bishop approached. "Morning."

"Hello. That was a good item in the paper," Bishop said, tapping the newspaper under his arm. "Glad you came up with the idea."

Bishop glanced through the open kitchen door at Kate. "Do you have a minute?"

"Sure. Something wrong?"

Bishop shrugged. "Bert hasn't been in this morning, and Kate was concerned. I'm going over to check on him."

"Want company?"

"Sure."

"I'll be with you in a minute." Parker went to the kitchen. "Morning, Charlie. Kate, I'm going with Bishop. We shouldn't be long. Save that for me."

She had just poured his coffee. She dumped it back into the pot. "It'll keep. Go on." After he left, she looked at Charlie. "Bert's usually here long before now. Mr. Bishop said he'd check on him."

"He's prob'ly fine. He takes a few nips to keep warm in the winter. Nothin' to worry 'bout." Charlie gave a raspy chuckle. "Bet he'll be sup'rised to see them."

"But he's getting on in years." She dropped down on her chair. "And he's all alone over there. He could freeze to death."

"Yep. We hav't'go sometime, an' goin' in yer sleep sounds best t'me."

"It would be . . . easiest, but don't talk that way. There aren't so many people in town that we wouldn't miss one." This wasn't something she wanted to discuss early in the day.

"Ya got that right." He raised his cup in a mock salute.

"I don't plan on goin' anytime soon."

She grinned. "Thank goodness." She ate the last two bites of the fritter and cleared Mr. Bishop's dishes from the table. Mr. Bishop and Parker hadn't returned by the time she finished drying the dishes. "Charlie, mind if I run over to the store? I'll need a shovel to get back into the cabin. I had to use a bowl this morning to get out."

"Go on. I'm gonna have this fritter."

She hurried to the general store and returned a few minutes later with a secondhand shovel. She came in the side kitchen door and left the shovel outside. Charlie was frying more fritters. "It's snowing so hard, my tracks in the snow are probably filled in by now."

Charlie nodded. "Ya ain't thinkin' 'bout goin' to the camps, are ya?"

"No. If I want to get out for a while, I'll clear a path to the cabin." She hung her coat and hat on a peg by the side door and went over to the stove to warm up.

"They're back," he said, motioning to the dining room. "I poured 'em some coffee. Ya can take their plates in when these're done."

She went to the doorway and saw Bert. He was seated near the stove in his usual spot, and Parker was across from him. "Bert looks okay. Did he just sleep in?"

Charlie grabbed a plate and dished out two fritters. "Nah. A couple boards blowed off the roof and snow blocked the door. He couldn't get out."

"It's a good thing Mr. Bishop and Parker went to check on him." She set the coffeepot on the tray with the dishes, biscuits, and a small dish of prized huckleberry preserves. Charlie'd told her he'd had to wrestle the bears and coyotes for the favored berries. As she served their meals, she realized Bert was fine, and Parker didn't look at all concerned. "If you want a second helping, just tell me."

Bert stared at the plate. "Thanky, Miss Kate, but this here's 'nough to pop my belly."

"Maybe she's trying to fatten you up for winter." Parker grinned at her. "Do you like your men big and brawny?"

That restored her spirit. Her eyes flashed a moment before she leveled a reserved gaze on him.

She leaned down and spoke softly. "I like well-seasoned men, who know how to treat a lady and when to be quiet."

He burst out laughing. "You tell a good tale, Kate. But we both know you'd be bored sick with a man like that." She needed a man who could stand up to her, laugh with her, and love her fiercely.

"Like what?" Bert asked. "Ya lookin' fer a man, Miss Kate?"

The urge to thrash Parker battled with an equally strong impulse to laugh with him. "Not me, Bert. I've got enough to do without the care and feeding of a man, too."

Parker leaned forward. "I think she's holding out for some rich gent."

Bert nodded. "She'll ne'r find one o' them here."

I'm counting on that, Kate thought as she refilled Bert's cup. "You got that right." She was tempted to ask Parker what kind of woman would hold his interest, but she didn't want to give him the idea that she cared.

After three days of snow, at times so heavy it was difficult to see and other times so light she could watch individual flakes drift in front of her face, Kate figured she must've shoveled enough of the stuff to clear a road halfway down the mountain. Once there was a clear area in front of the cabin, she left the shovel by the door and went inside.

The fires in the fireplace and woodstove were down to hot embers, and her mother wasn't there. As she rekindled the flames, she wondered why her mother had left. Mary Louise had never been the adventurous type and didn't like the cold. Kate went to the general store to see if her mother had called on Miss Lucy.

Bert looked up at her. "Howdy, Miss Kate."

"Bert." With one quick glance she knew her mother wasn't there.

Mrs. Goody came from their quarters in back. "Hi, Kate. How're you doing?"

"Fine. Is my mother visiting Miss Lucy?"

"No. Your mother hasn't been in today. Is something wrong?"

Kate forced herself to calm down. "Probably nothing. Thank you, Mrs. Goody. I'll see you later." As she crossed the road, the snow started coming down harder. She went around the hotel and passed the cabin. Since her mother never left town, the only other place she could be was nearby feeding the animals.

After a quick walk around the cabin, she went to the creek and saw her several yards ahead, sitting on a tree stump with a bucket nearby and a big furry black dog by her feet. She ran up to her. There was at least a half an inch of snow on her mother's shoulders and the scarf over her head. "Mamma, how long have you been sitting here?"

Mary Louise looked up and blinked. "Katie?" She glanced around, as if she had been expecting someone else and sighed.

Kate put her arm around her mother's shoulders. "Come on back to the cabin. It should be warm in there by now." She picked up the bucket and helped her mother to her feet. "Where'd the dog come from?"

Mary Louise smiled at the animal. "I don't know, deah. He just showed up. He looks hungry, doesn't he?"

Not really, Kate thought. It hadn't missed many meals. "Why did you come down here?"

"Thought I'd get some fresh water and . . ." Mary Louise shivered. "It was so peaceful and pretty, I sat down, but my little friends didn't come to see me." She held her hand out to the dog and smiled at it. "I fear this mongrel scared them away."

Kate walked her mother back to the cabin, and the dog followed. "They'd freeze, Mamma. You could've, too." Even the dog couldn't stay outside in the freezing snow for long. Her mother usually adopted small creatures, never a dog before—and not now.

Mary Louise went into the cabin and sat in her chair by the fireplace. ‘‘Would you pour me a cup of tea, deah?’’ She pulled her gloves off and rubbed her hands together.

Before Kate could close the door, the dog darted inside and laid down between her mother's rocking chair and the hearth. She opened the door and spoke to the dog. ‘‘Get out. Go on. You don't belong here.’’ The dog looked from her to her mother without raising its head. Just what they needed, a dirty dog that would probably smell, once it thawed out. ‘‘Come on,’’ she said, reaching for the scruff of the dog's neck. The dog made a low rumbling sound, but he didn't bare his teeth.

‘‘Why don't ya leave him be?’’ Mary Louise ran her hand down the dog's back. ‘‘He's got ice on his fur. Ya can't put him out, deah.’’

‘‘Your scarf's icy, too.’’ Kate loosened her mother's scarf and hung it over the back of a chair. She rinsed out her mother's cup and took it over to the kettle sitting by the fire. After she handed the tea to her mother, she got a blanket off the bed and wrapped it around Mary Louise. ‘‘Feeling warmer?’’ The dog rested one of its large front paws on her boot. Great. Another mouth to feed, if she knew her mother. The dog was kind of cute, though, with shaggy black fur, floppy ears, and overly-long tail. He looked at her with big brown eyes, as if he knew he'd won her over, and wagged his tail. She fixed him with one of her no-nonsense expressions and said, ‘‘Once the weather clears, you'll be on your way.’’

‘‘He needs a name. What shall we call him?’’

Kate hung up her coat and sat down. ‘‘Is it a ‘he’ or ‘she’?’’

‘‘Oh, it's a boy.’’ Mary Louise scratched the dog behind its ears. ‘‘The males are the wanderers.’’ She watched him a minute. ‘‘What do ya want us to name you, huh, boy?’’

‘‘How 'bout Blacky?’’ Kate said in a gruff voice, pretending to speak for the animal.

Mary Louise glanced at her daughter. ‘‘He's a fine animal and deserves a better name than that.’’ She thought a moment. "How about Beauregard?"

Kate eyed the animal. "He doesn't look like a Beauregard. He's too—" *Scruffy* came to mind. "Rough looking." She sat back and closed her eyes. Her life seemed to be getting much more complicated than necessary. First Parker and now this hound. "He must have a family—somewhere."

"What do ya think about J.D.?"

Without opening her eyes, Kate asked, "Why J.D.?"

"Jefferson Davis, of course. It's a fine name."

Kate chuckled. "Do you think he'd be flattered to have a dog named after him? The beast followed us in here. How about Shadow?"

Mary Louise leaned down to the dog. "Shadow? Do ya like that name, boy? It isn't such a bad name."

Kate couldn't resist watching them through her lashes. The dog actually raised its head and licked her mother's hand. It was amazing. "I think he approves."

"Well, Shadow, I think ya need t'be toweled off, and we have to find somethin' for ya to sleep on tonight." Mary Louise looked at her daughter. "He'll be filthy if he sleeps on the dirt, and he'll spread it ev'ra-where."

Kate sat up, completely alert. "That wolf pelt'll keep *us* warm; don't even think about letting that dog sleep on it." She sat back and added, "Besides, I don't think he'd like to sleep on his cousin's fur."

"Cousin? Why that's positively indecent, Katherine Anne." Mary Louise scratched Shadow's neck. "We'll make ya a nice warm bed. An old piece of carpet would be nice."

"I wouldn't mind having carpet instead of dirt, either." Kate stood up. If she sat there much longer, she'd doze off. "I'll get some fresh water." She bundled up, grabbed the bucket, opened the door, and looked at the dog. He didn't budge. If he'd been a cat, he'd be purring. After she got the water, she chopped more firewood and cleared the snow away from the door, again, before she went back to work.

When she walked into the kitchen, Charlie was slicing a

large rib roast. "Are you expecting a crowd tonight?"

He chuckled. "Nah, but it'll make a lot o' meals."

She added wood to the stove in the dining room and closed the drapes against the cold. Bert came in, and she served his dinner. Mr. Bishop was next, and she found herself stealing glances at the lobby, expecting to see Parker. It galled her to realize she was actually *waiting* for him. After Bert and Mr. Bishop had finished and left, Parker came in and sat at the corner table.

She brought his cup of coffee and set it down, harder than she intended, and sloshed some on the tablecloth. "You're late tonight." The moment she said it, she knew it was a mistake.

"I didn't realize I had to show up at any particular time." He set his hat on the next chair, delighted with her irritation. He glanced around the room, knowing they were the only ones there. "Did you miss me?"

"Like a thorn," she mumbled. "I'll get your supper."

He grinned at her. "Join me?"

"I already ate." It was a bald-faced lie, and she didn't rightly care at that moment. She had taken one step away from his table, when Charlie came out of the kitchen carrying two supper plates.

He set one down in front of Parker and the other across from him. "Thought ya might as well eat now. Don't think anyone else's comin' in tonight."

She stared at the food. "Thanks." It was tempting to take her food and leave, but if she did, she'd embarrass Charlie. She pulled out the chair and sat down. Parker wasn't trying very hard to cover his amusement. Sometimes she could happily throttle the man. In fact, just thinking about it made her feel better.

Parker smiled at Charlie. "Thanks for the personal service. Why don't you sit with us?"

Charlie glanced sideways at Kate. "Thanks for the invite, but I've gotta pack up the roast 'n store it out in the shed."

She stared at her plate. The least Charlie could've done was sit at the table with them.

Parker cut a piece of roast and glanced at her. ''Lose your appetite?'' He ate the bite. ''Mm. Good.''

I'm not a child was on the tip of her tongue, but she was acting like one. She began eating. ''Catch any robbers today?'' He raised one dark brow but his eyes were sparkling, and she felt her irritation with him soften.

''No. Should I have?''

She shook her head. ''Will Bert be all right tonight in his room?''

He nodded. ''I shored up the loose boards. They'll hold unless the snow gets too heavy.'' He scooped up a helping of mashed potatoes. ''Did he stay there last winter?'' It had slipped out without thinking. He knew she wasn't and hadn't meant to lead her on—this time.

She'd just taken a bite and nodded. ''Mm-hm.'' She hoped it was true.

''When the snow lets up, I'll climb on the roof.''

She almost smiled. Parker's honestly a nice man, she thought. ''I wouldn't want to see him try that.''

''Me, either.'' He finished eating and sat back. He couldn't remember enjoying mealtimes as much as he did with her. One of these days he'd settle with Turner. Then what? He couldn't imagine her ever wanting to see him after that, but he couldn't forget the wrong done to his father and mother. Now, he could lay another wrong at Turner's feet. ''What's for dessert?''

''Spice cake. I'll get it.'' She carried their dishes to the kitchen. Charlie had washed the dishes and was putting on his coat. ''You didn't need to clean up for me. Thank you.''

He nodded. ''Say, did ya see a dog today?''

Uh-oh, she thought. ''Yes. It latched on to my mother and followed us home. He didn't bite you, did he?''

He chuckled. ''No, but he ate the scraps I was goin' to bury when it thaws.''

''I'll give him what I didn't finish. Maybe he'll leave tonight.'' She could always hope. She cut two slices of cake. The mongrel'd probably get most of hers.

He put on his hat and unlatched the side door. ''He's a

friendly sort. Your ma might like the company.''

She hadn't thought about that. He was probably right, especially this winter when she couldn't get outside very often. ''Night.'' He left, and she took the cake and coffeepot in to their table. When Parker looked at her, her stomach tightened up, and she knew they could easily be more than friends. He was a double-edged saber, and he had cut through her resistance like a silk scarf. She set his plate down and refilled his cup.

''Thank you.'' He waved his arm in an arc. ''We really should invite our friends over. The rooms too large for only the two of us.''

She laughed softly. ''If we issued invitations to everyone in the area, it would only be half full.'' She sat down across from him. ''How do you like our little town?''

''Nice. Wish I'd seen it in its heyday.'' And I wish we'd met under different circumstances, he thought. Killing her father, even in a fair fight, wouldn't recommend him to her.

''Maybe Hick's strike will bring some of the miners back. It doesn't take much to start a gold rush.''

''True, but I thought you wanted to keep it a secret?''

He nodded. ''At least until he's taken a good portion out to confirm the mine's worth.''

She laid her fork on the plate of half-eaten cake and yawned. ''I'd better finish up in the kitchen. Stay as long as you want.''

''I'll give you a hand and walk you home. The snow's pretty deep, and it's dark as pitch out.''

She washed and was surprised when he picked up a towel and dried the dishes. It seemed as if they were done in a couple minutes. She dried her hands and put on her coat. ''I can get back all right. It isn't far. Would you put out the lights?'' She plucked her hat off the peg and opened the door. The dog was there looking up at her with those big brown eyes and his floppy years framming his face. ''Shadow. What're you doing here?''

''Who's your friend?'' The big mangy dog's tongue lolled out of the side of his mouth, and he looked at her with complete adoration. From her smile, he guessed she felt the same. The lucky dog.

"He followed my mother home and seems determined to stay." She picked up the pan of table scraps and set it on the threshold in front of him. "Eat up, Shadow." She met Parker's gaze and laughed.

❖ 13 ❖

KATE SMILED DROWSILY, unwilling to wake completely. Adding those extra logs to the fire in the fireplace and covering the bed with the wolf pelt made all the difference. She started to stretch, but she couldn't move. Her mother must've curled up behind her.

A while later she felt an elbow in her back and almost tumbled out of bed. She woke with a start and pushed back, but her mother didn't budge. "Mamma, do you need the whole bed?" It was time she got up, but what a way to be roused.

She swung her feet to the floor and turned around. Her mother was clinging to the far side of the bed. Shadow was stretched out in the middle with his head on the end of her pillow! She raised her hand to give him a sharp whack, then thought better of that idea. He could easily snap at her.

"Shadow—" She stood up and jiggled the mattress. "Come on, boy, get down."

"What's the commotion about, Kate?" Mary Louise said, raising up on her elbow. She blinked and stared at the dog. "What's he doin' on the bed?"

Kate shivered and grabbed her shawl. "Ask him. I didn't bring him to bed." The dog stretched, yawned, and looked at both of them. "Good morning, Shadow. Did you sleep well?" She rekindled the fires and added wood.

Mary Louise petted him and smiled. "You're the one who kept me so snug and warm."

Kate started a small pot of coffee. "And took up most of the bed. He's not sleeping with us, Mamma." She added water to the kettle and put it over the fire to heat. "You used to have a hissy fit when you found Lissie asleep on my bed, and she was a little cat."

"Ah, well," Mary Louise said, waving her hand. "Everyone know cats'll suck the very breath out of babes."

"That makes no sense. Besides, I was eight years old, not a baby." Kate went over to the bed, clapped her hands to get the dog's attention, and pointed at the floor. "Get down." Shadow jumped off the bed. He walked to the door and looked at her. "Good, boy." As soon as she opened the door, he bounded over the piled-up snow. "After a big supper and a night in a warm bed, he'll go back home."

Mary Louise got out of bed, pulled her shawl around her shoulders, and sat in her chair by the fireplace. "I think you're wrong, deah. He may have lost his people. It's clear he isn't wild."

"I agree." Kate completed her morning ablutions and dressed.

There was a scratch at the door, and Mary Louise smiled at her daughter. "Do ya want me to let him in?"

"You'll get to tend to that chore while I'm working." Kate opened the door. Shadow walked inside, shook himself and sat by her mother's chair. "Pretty sure of yourself, aren't you?"

"He knows we like him. He's a shrewd judge of character." Mary Louise spooned tea into the teapot and added hot water. "Do ya think he'd eat plain porridge?"

Kate stared at Shadow. "He'll eat anything you give him." She sipped her coffee while she brushed her hair and put on her boots. "I'll try to set aside the scrapings and bring you some biscuits."

"Thank ya, deah." Mary Louise coughed and pulled the shawl tighter. "I'm not too hungry this mornin.' "

"You may be later." Kate bundled up. "Keep warm. I'll

see you in a little while.'' After she shoveled a clearing in front of the door, which was beginning to seem as futile as dusting, she walked to the hotel.

Charlie looked up when she came inside. ''Saw yer dog this mornin.' Have ya named him yet?''

''Shadow.'' She hung up her coat and hat. ''It suits him better than Beauregard.'' She built up the fire in the dining room, tied back one of the drapes to let a little daylight in, and dusted the chair rails.

Mr. Bishop, Bert, Parker, and even Earl came in for breakfast. She made sure she was too busy to dawdle at Parker's table. Somehow, she had to think of him the way she did the others, but it wasn't easy. Her body reacted to him, even against her will, and he invaded her thoughts as surely as Grant took Richmond.

After taking a plate to her mother and the old tin pie pan with scrapings for Shadow, she dusted the empty rooms and cleaned Mr. Bishops, then Parker's. She had finished with the room and was taking the chamber pot down to empty it, when she met him on the stairs.

With his mind on Earl's living conditions, Parker nearly walked into Kate halfway up the stairs. He stepped aside. ''Sorry.'' He had just checked the building where Bert stayed. Boards on the floor, roof, and walls had come loose. The repairs wouldn't be that difficult, but Parker wondered who owned the building.

Her glance didn't meet his, but it was enough for her to note his bright eyes and parted lips. ''I'd just as soon not spill this.''

He glanced at the familiar earthenware pot. She was all business, as if they were barely on speaking terms. ''By all means,'' he said, motioning down the stairs. ''How's Shadow doing?''

She paused in the lobby and looked back at him. Don't try so darned hard to be friends, she thought, it's fruitless. She wished it wasn't so but wishing was for children. ''Fine.''

She went out back to the area set aside for such waste,

dumped the contents from the chamber pot and hurried back inside. She started to open his door, then remembered to knock before she opened the door.

He watched the door open, instinctively wary until he saw that it was Kate. ''Back so soon?''

''It doesn't take that long,'' she said, drawing her brows together. ''I'll just put this under the bed.'' His gaze felt like a hug, and she wondered how he could look so at ease, when she felt anything but composed.

Her expression reminded him of someone's maiden aunt. He leaned back against the windowframe. ''Did you read that article about the gold piece?''

She pushed the pot just under the side of the bed and stood up. ''Mm-hm. You?'' She stepped back and her leg bumped the bed. She was standing in his room with him—not the thing to do when she was set on keeping her distance from him.

He nodded. She brushed at her skirt and looked everywhere but at him. ''I guess he was glad he found that gold piece he thought he lost *and* cured his cough all at once.''

''Yes . . . he must've.'' She went to the door, opened it, and paused. ''Will you be eating dinner here?''

''Yes, ma'am. You serve the best food in town.''

She stepped into the hall and met his gaze. The gleam is his eyes was nearly irresistible. ''That's easy. Charlie's a good cook. And we're the only restaurant in town.'' He had a way of drawing her into his silliness, even when she was annoyed with him. But she knew she'd never see him again after he found her father, and she had no intention of allowing him to become too important to her.

As he stepped over to the door, he said, ''Save my seat for me.'' She darted down the hall, and he listened to her brisk pace as she hurried down the stairs. She seemed as skittish as a doe. If she had found out about his visit with her mother, she more than likely would have been furious, not wary.

Kate slowed down to a walk in the lobby and continued on to the kitchen. The last time she'd been fool enough to believe she could be like any other woman—fall in love, marry, and have a family—he'd turned out just like other men she'd fended off. Mostly young men who'd heard about Hank's reputation as a bank robber and wanted to bed his daughter to learn where he was. Damn, she hated being Hank Tucker's daughter. That's why she took her mother's maiden name on the last move, and it had worked. For a few months she'd just been Kate Miller with no past—until Parker had shown up.

Kate fixed a tray for her mother and headed for the cabin. As she came around the trees, the dog raced up and ran circles around her. The animal was trying his darnedest to charm her. "I brought you something, too." She heard her mother cough and found her standing in the bushes beyond the end of the cabin. "What're you doing?"

Mary Louise pushed her foot around under the low branches of the bush. "Just wanted a some fresh air, deah. I wasn't expectin' ya so soon." She shivered and clutched her woolen shawl.

"Let's go inside. Looks like you've been out here too long." Kate opened the door, and Shadow ran in ahead of her. She set the tray on the table. When her mother didn't follow her in, she went out and saw her poking around in the bushes. She linked arms with her and started walking. "Did you lose something?"

"I thought I saw one of my squirrels," Mary Louise said, entering the cabin.

"They're fine." Kate closed the door and uncovered the dishes for her mother. "Charlie warmed the roast—said it'd be cold by the time it reached the table."

Mary Louise pulled her cape tight around her and shivered. "I'll eat it later, deah. I'm not very hungry right now."

"Make sure the dog doesn't get into it." Kate left the tray on the table and picked up the battered pie tin. "Come on, Shadow." She opened the door. As if he understood, the dog trotted outside and sat down at the edge of the cleared path. She smiled and set the pan down. ‘‘Eat slowly. You’ll have to make do with scraps.’’ You great lolloping beast, she thought with growing affection.

When she went back inside, she was surprised to see her mother had dozed off while sitting in her chair. She spread the lap robe over Mary Louise’s chest and kissed her cheek. It was dry and hot, a fever. No wonder she’s so tired. Kate returned to the hotel. Charlie was dishing out potato cakes onto two plates. ‘‘Can I buy a chunk of beef from you?’’ she asked, shedding her coat and hat.

‘‘If it’s fer that mutt, I set the ribs aside fer ’im.’’ Charlie added slices of beef to the plates.

‘‘Thank you. He can have them after I’ve boiled them, but I’ll need fresh meat, too, for a rich broth.’’ She set cups on the tray with the two dinners.

He stared at her. ‘‘Are ya feelin’ peak’d?’’

‘‘I’m afraid mother’s coming down with the fever.’’ She picked up the tray. ‘‘She’s not eating. I thought she may drink beef tea instead.’’

‘‘The miasma,’’ he said shaking his head. ‘‘I’ll start it now. Don’t’cha worry. I got a special receipt that’ll fix her up good as new.’’

‘‘I think she spent too much time out in the snow and took cold. She was ill last winter, too.’’ Kate didn’t want her mother going through that again. ‘‘You don’t need to trouble yourself. I’ll do it soon as I serve this food.’’

‘‘Go on with ya.’’ He set a pot on the stove and pointed to the dining room.

She gave him a nod. ‘‘Thank you, Charlie.’’ When she stepped into the dining room, she glanced to her right, expecting to see Parker. He wasn’t there. Mr. Bishop was, and also a man she hadn’t seen before. After she served their meal, she poured coffee and went back to the kitchen to help with the beef tea.

Charlie didn’t look up when she set the pot back on the stove. ‘‘Anyone else out there?’’ He finished cutting the meat, dropped the pieces into the pot and reached for an onion.

"Not yet, but Parker said he'd be down." She set the tray down and added salt to the boiling pot of tea. When she turned around, she noticed a basket of peas. She'd once read somewhere that they were considered a healthful food. "Mind if I use a handful of those peas?"

"Go ahead. Wish we had some fresh rhubarb." He shook his head. "Ya know this won't be a fit till supper time, don't ya?"

"Mm-hm." She scooped up the peas and dropped them into the pot. "I'll see if Mrs. Goody has sassafras. That might be even better." She refilled coffee cups, served dessert, and had washed the dirty dishes before Parker came into the kitchen.

"Have anything left?" Parker gave Kate a playful grin, but she merely nodded.

He sounded so blamed happy it galled her. She'd never known another man who could irritate her so easily. "I'll bring it right in." Two minutes later she set his dinner plate in front of him, a cup of coffee to the right, biscuits nearby, and suet pudding to his left.

He glanced at the dishes, then at her. "In a hurry? Or is it my company?"

She lowered the empty tray to her side. Was he teasing? "I just have a lot to do." He wasn't smiling. Maybe he was serious or maybe she wanted to believe he was. "Sorry. I have to go." She dashed back to the kitchen. "Parker shouldn't need anything. Mind if I see about the sassafras and check on my mother?"

Charlie waved the spoon he was holding. "Git goin'."

"Thanks. I won't be too long." She grabbed her coat and pulled it on as she hurried to the general store. Mrs. Goody had a supply of sassafras. Kate purchased enough to make a dozen pots of tea and went back to the cabin. Her mother had gone to bed and the dog was asleep at her side. At least her mother wasn't alone.

She set to work. While the tea steeped, she roused her mother and bathed her face with cool water. "Feel better?"

Mary Louise pulled the covers up to her chin. "Thank

ya, dahlin'. I just need some rest.'' Shadow licked her hand, and she gave him a weak smile.

''You must drink some tea before you rest.'' Kate helped her mother to sit up in bed and plumped the pillow behind her back. ''It's ready. Don't go to sleep now.''

''I won't. I'm parched.'' Mary Louise shivered and pushed her hair back from her face.

Kate poured a cup of the tea and steadied it for her mother. ''You need to drink as much of this as you can. Charlie's making beef tea for supper. It smells wonderful.'' She smiled, hoping it would help her mother's spirits. ''I may have some myself.''

''He shouldn't a bothered. I'll be right as rain after I rest.''

Her mother finished the tea, and Kate refilled the cup. She pulled one of the chairs over to the side of the bed and set the teapot and cup on it. ''I have to get back to the hotel, but I won't be long.''

Mary Louise patted her daughter's hand. ''I'm fine. Ya go on, now.''

After she encouraged her mother to drink more tea, Kate refilled the cup. ''See if you can drink this and another one before I get back.'' She set the chamber pot out, hoping her mother would need it. If she did, it would be a good sign.

''Don't ya fret about me.'' Mary Louise patted Shadow. ''If I need anythin', I'll send him to get you.''

''All right.'' If that thought comforted her mother, Kate wasn't about to argue. She kissed her mother's hot forehead and prayed the tea would bring down the fever. When she returned to the hotel, Charlie was sitting with Parker in the dining room. She grabbed the coffeepot and joined them.

Parker held up his cup for her to refill. ''Charlie said your mother wasn't feeling well. How's she doing?'' Kate looked a little pale herself.

She poured the coffee. His gaze felt comforting, for a moment, but she had to remind herself he was simply being polite. ''She drank some sassafrass tea.'' She refilled Charlie's cup and added, "She's resting."

"Wait'll she tastes that beef tea. She'll be herself in t'mornin'."

Kate nodded. "How can she not be?" She returned to the kitchen and stirred the kettle of beef tea. The color was a rich brown, and the rising steam held the aromas of beef, onion, and sage.

Her mother used to like beaten biscuits, and she decided to make a batch. While she was at it, she might as well make enough for supper. She got out the big bowl, scooped flour into it, and added pinches of salt. As she dropped a measure of butter and another of lard into the bowl, the timbre of Parker's voice carried into the kitchen, and she smiled. It was almost as if he were keeping her company.

Later that afternoon Parker walked back to Kate's cabin and softly tapped on her door. It opened partway, and she peered out. "I'm glad I caught you before you left for the hotel. I have something for your mother."

He was covered with a dusting of snow, and she smiled, before she recalled she shouldn't be so happy to see him. "You didn't have to do that." When she opened the door for him, the dog came over and stood at her side.

Parker returned her smile and eyed the animal. "Shadow, I see you're earning your keep." The dog wagged his long tail and trotted outside as he entered.

She closed the door and motioned to her chair. "Please, sit down." She hung his coat on one of the pegs and perched on the edge of her mother's rocking chair across from him. The fire crackled, and the little cabin had never felt so homey before.

He opened the small package he had brought. "I remembered my mother believed sage tea was a certain cure for fevers. A little whiskey and honey in tea's preferred by some." He set the items on the small table. "You might try the last one. No use your taking ill, too."

I can't afford to miss work, she thought, but it was kind of him. "I am rarely sick, but it was thoughtful of you."

She glanced at the curtain hiding the bed and back at him. ''I'm glad she likes tea. I intend to see she drinks her fill tonight.'' Kate settled back on the chair and started rocking. ''Have you seen One Finger lately?''

He nodded. ''Rode out there after dinner. He's back to his former self. Guess that elixir worked for him.'' Some of her hair had come lose from the knot at the back of her head. As she rocked, the strands fluttered softly and swayed against her smooth cheek. He wanted to reach out and see if her hair felt as soft as it looked. Instead, he rubbed his palm on his trouser leg.

Mary Louise roused and mopped her face with the edge of the sheet. ''Kate, why's the curtain pulled?''

Kate was on her feet in an instant. ''Parker came to call.'' She stepped over to the bed. Her mother was flushed. ''I'm glad you woke up. I'll get you a fresh cup of tea.''

''Thank ya, deah. Would ya also bring me a damp cloth and hand me my hairbrush?'' Mary Louise fingered her hair. ''I must look a fright.''

Kate removed the pins from her mothers hair, wrung out the cloth from the bowl of water, and handed it to her mother. She poured the cup of tea and stepped around the curtain. ''Parker, would you stay with her a couple minutes? I'd like to get her supper.'' Her mother always brightened in the company of men, and he might distract her mother—he certainly was having that effect on her.

''It would be my pleasure.'' While she tended Mrs. Miller, he stepped outside and brought enough firewood in to get them through the night. The dog galloped up from the creek. When he bent to pick up a log, the animal managed to drag his wet tongue over Parker's cheek. ''Does this mean we're friends?'' He made a snowball and threw it. The dog ran after it but looked disappointed when he bit into the ball. Shadow lost interest in the snow and darted into the cabin. Parker followed him.

Kate finished brushing her mother's hair back. ''There. Much better.''

''Dahlin', would ya get my bed jacket from the trunk?

The embroidered muslin one.'' Mary Louise frowned. ''I think it's near the bottom.''

Kate tried to find the jacket by feel. She soon gave up and set two of her mother's old dresses on the bed. Underneath she found one of her mother's new petticoats, a small wooden box with pretty new buttons, yard goods and yarn she'd never seen before. She glanced over her shoulder at Mary Louise. When she was well, they'd have a long talk about where these things came from. Kate had almost emptied the trunk when she finally found the bed jacket.

She tossed it onto the bed. When she started to repack the trunk, she noticed that the bottom was lined with small canvas bags. She pick up one and almost dropped it. Lord, it was heavy, as if it were filled with lead shot. What on earth, she thought, pulling the tie loose and opening the bag. She poured the contents onto her hand and stared in horror.

Gold. Dust and flakes and nuggets . . . of gold.

❖ 14 ❖

As SHE RETURNED to the cabin with her mother's supper, Kate couldn't stop thinking about all that gold she'd discovered in the bottom of the trunk. Her mother had used the trunk since they moved more than she had. She was angry, and she was so very disappointed with her mother. Shifting the tray to unlatch the door, she caught a whiff of the broth and her stomach churned. The gold must've come from her father. There was no other explanation. She unlatched the door and shoved at it with her shoulder. Suddenly Parker was there and opened it for her.

He closed the door behind her and glanced at her back. When she left, he suspected she was upset. Now, she was clearly piqued. "Smells good."

"I hope she thinks so." She set the tray on the worktable and went to check on her mother. "You drank the tea. Good. Charlie fixed his special beef tea for you, and I made beaten biscuits."

"I'll try some." Mary Louise leaned over to Kate and whispered, "Is Mr. Smith stayin' for supper?"

Kate shook her head. "I just brought your meal."

"Do ya mind if I eat here in bed?" Mary Louise straightened the blanket over her legs.

"Of course not." Kate unwrapped the towel around the jug and poured the beef tea into the cup.

Parker walked over to the table and stood next to her. "Need any help?" He started to raise his hand. Resting it on her shoulder would have been natural, except she seemed to avoid touching anyone, especially him. He dropped his hand to his side.

"No—I'm fine." She buttered three biscuits and set them on a small plate by the cup. She couldn't look at him, not after finding that gold. Ye gods 'n little fishes, if he knew about that, he'd *never* believe she didn't know where her father was hiding. She had to get Parker to leave so she could talk with her mother. "Thanks for staying with her. Would you tell Charlie I'll be there in a few minutes?"

He patted her shoulder before he gave it a second thought. "Yes, be glad to." He put on his coat and called out, "Mrs. Miller, I hope you're feeling better by morning. I brought fixings for a hot toddy that'll help you sleep good and sound."

"Thank ya so much for keepin' me company, Mr. Smith. I hope ya didn't miss your supper."

"No, ma'am." He stepped to Kate's side. "I'll see you later."

She nodded and picked up the tray as he left. Thank goodness. She set the tray on her mother's lap and took one of the biscuits for herself. "You haven't worn that bed jacket for a long time, have you?"

"No, no, I suppose I haven't." Mary Louise took a sip of the broth. "This isn't at all as bland as my beef tea. It has a tangy flavor."

"I'm glad you like it. I'll tell Charlie." She ate a bite of biscuit. "He said he added something special."

"See if he'll tell ya what it was." Mary Louise drank half the cup and reached for a biscuit. "Don't ya have to work tonight, deah?"

"Yes, I do." Kate broke the last part of the biscuit in half and popped one piece in her mouth. She didn't want to put off their talk, but there wasn't time now. Getting straight answers out of her mother took patience. She added more tea to her mother's cup and set the jug on the chair by the bed. "Will you be all right?"

"Of course, deah. Ya run along so Mr. Daws won't worry."

Kate added wood to both fires and grabbed her coat. "I'll make you a toddy later."

Mary Louise finished the tea and refilled the cup. "I'm feelin' much better. I may not need it, deah. This beef tea's better than an elixor."

"I'm glad." Kate held her skirt up as she tromped through the snow to the hotel. If the weather didn't clear, she might think about getting a pair of snowshoes.

She served coffee and meals, and she thought suppertime would never end. Just when she least expected it, she'd remember the small canvas bags of gold and become angry all over again. The only way they could've gotten in that chest was if her mother put them there, which meant her mother had kept in touch with her father—deceived her. That hurt. A knife twisting in her gut couldn't have any more painful.

Charlie frowned at Kate. "Yer gonna wear a hole in that pot if ya keep scrubbin' it." He picked up a plate and put two slices of meat on it.

She blinked. How long had she been standing there stewing?

"Ya haven't eaten." Charlie set a the plate on the work table. "Sit down."

She glanced over her shoulder at him. He'd never ordered her to do anything before, and she realized it was more bluff and bluster or peevishness than anger. She dried the pot and put it away. "What about you?"

"I had four o' yer biscuits with beef, but I'll keep ya comp'ny." He refilled his cup and sat down with her. "Did ya talk with Bishop?"

She stabbed a piece of meat with her fork. "Mm-hm. He said he wouldn't be leaving after all."

"Do ya want'a take more of that beef tea to yer mother?"

"Yes. She really liked it." Kate broke a biscuit in half.

"What's your secret? She drank two cups before I left."

He chuckled. "Whiskey. Put it in right before you came in."

She stared and slowly grinned. Her mother would be horrified to learn she'd imbibed spirits—or would she? "How much?"

He shrugged. "I jist poured some in." He took a drink of coffee. "Ya say she liked it, huh?"

"I didn't smell the whiskey."

"There was a fair measure of sage, too," he said with a wink. "Didn't want her frettin' over the spirits."

Her mother wouldn't need a toddy tonight, she realized. She folded a slice of meat, put it in the biscuit, and absently ate it. If her mother had any more "tea," it might loosen her tongue. Now she was even more anxious to get home.

Her mother was sleeping soundly, but Kate was determined to speak with her before going to bed. Doing needlework at night usually made her drowsy, so she read the newspaper. "A prominent attorney addressed the jury as 'Fellow Citizens.' " She couldn't help wondering if he was humbling himself or hoping to impress the jury. "Work is progressing finely on the Virginia City and National Park Free Wagon Road." "The many friends of Sheriff Marion will be glad to learn that he had recovered from his late illness and is again attending to 'biz.' " She mulled over the last word and chuckled.

Mary Louise aroused. "Katie?"

"Yes?" At last. Kate left the newspaper by the chair and took her mother a cup of beef tea. "I kept this warm for you."

"Thank you, deah." Mary Louise sat up and petted Shadow. "I do believe I'm feeling better. Mr. Daws really should bottle this potion."

"Part of it already is," Kate mumbled, and placed the back of her hand on her mother's forehead. "You do seem a little cooler." The dog scooted over on his belly and licked her fingers. She rubbed behind his ear. "I didn't forget you.'' She got the tin plate from the table and opened the door. The dog came over, looked outside, and sat down by her side. ''You're right.'' It was snowing again, and she closed the door. ''You might as well eat in here.''

Mary Louise watched her daughter. ''I knew you liked him.''

If he's like most males, he won't stay long anyway, Kate thought. She went to the trunk, raised the lid, and saw a large bundle of cloth, enough green muslin to make a dress. She hadn't seen that before and held it up. ''When did you purchase this?''

Mary Louise brushed at the bed covers. ''I don't rah-tly ree-call, dahlin'.''

No, you don't. You can drawl your words all you want, Kate thought, but I won't give in so easily. She set the small wooden box on the end of the bed. ''And the buttons with the yellow roses?''

''Mr. Smith gave me those,'' Mary Louise said softly.

Kate set a skein of yarn on the bed. ''And where did this come from?'' She added the others until there was a pile. ''And these?''

Mary Louise stared in silence.

As Kate continued unpacking the trunk, her anger grew. Piece by piece, she slung the contents onto the bed. ''Did you wish for all this and, as if by magic, it simply appeared?'' She stared at her mother, defying her to lie, but Mary Louise smiled that dreamy, I-know-a-secret smile.

''What do ya want me t'say, dahlin'?''

''The truth, Mamma. Only the truth.'' Kate reached into the trunk again and brought out two canvas bags. She searched each for a mark some of the miners used, but there wasn't any. ''What about these?'' Her mother looked genuinely unnerved. ''Did you forget they were under your bed jacket?''

''I——'' Mary Louise began crying and covered her face with her hands.

''Am I suppose to believe your admirers have been giving you this gold?'' Kate dropped one pouch onto the bed, opened the other one, and poured several nuggets onto the palm of her hand. "There must be twenty or more bags just like this one." She waited, listening to the crackle of the fire and the thumping of her heart, for her mother to admit where the gold came from, admit that *he'd* robbed the nearby miners.

"K-Katherine, you're s-such a hard g-girl," Mary Louise sobbed.

"One of us had to be strong after Pa—Hank left." Kate clamped her teeth together.

Pulling her handkerchief from her sleeve, Mary Louise dried her eyes and cheeks. "He wants to help us—he always has—" She shook her head. "But ya wouldn't listen. I've never seen such pride in a girl as ya have, Katherine Anne. Sometimes, you're so like Papa."

Kate had never known her grandfather. He had died just before she was born. "I'm glad," she said softly. When she was little, she had pretended he'd been a jolly man with sparkling eyes and a big comfortable lap, who had helped her catch frogs, bait her fishing hooks, and told her wonderful stories about brave men and women. Her mother had distracted her once again, damn it all. "How long have you been seeing *him*?" Suddenly her mother's smile, that dreamy secretive one, made sense now.

"I haven't!"

Kate raised her brows. "Do you expect me to believe fairies hid the gold in the trunk?"

"That's enough, Katherine Anne Turner. Mr. Turner's tried to help us all along, but ya refused t'listen t'me." Mary Louise sank back against the pillow.

Kate gasped. "You mean he's been giving you gold or money all these years?! No!" She shook her head. Shadow barked, but she ignored him. "It's not possible. There were times we hardly had enough food to eat. . . . The hovels we've lived in . . ." She held up her hand. "The hours I've worked to keep us going—" Suddenly she thought about the recent mine robberies. The thief had never been caught! "Is *he* the robber everyone's talking about?"

Mary Louise stared at her aghast. "How can you say such a thing about ya'r own papa?"

Kate narrowed her gaze. "Everywhere we've lived, there's been trouble—and now this. What else am I to think?"

"You're wrong, Katie, so very wrong."

Kate stared at her hands and curled them into fists, refusing to give in to tears. "Where was he when we needed him?"

"Never too far away, dahlin'. He's always watched over us, Katie. I've tried t'tell ya he—"

"Was the perfect papa?" Kate retied the pouch and threw both back into the trunk. Shadow scratched the door and looked at her. As she let him out, she realized she'd have to learn which miners had been robbed. Heaven help her. How could she return all those bags to the rightful owners without being caught?

"He tried, Katie." Mary Louise took a drink of the cool beef tea.

Kate narrowed her gaze. "What about Mr. Pitt? You led him on a merry chase. Why? How could you trifle with his affections like that?"

Mary Louise shook her head. "We're just friends. He understood. I b'lieve he enjoyed my company as much as I did his." She looked at her daughter. "I'm not like ya, Kate. I couldn't cut myself off from people the way ya've done all these years."

Suddenly Kate was tired, bone weary. She tossed everything into the trunk willy-nilly and didn't give a fig how it landed. When she had cleared off the bed, she grabbed her coat and went out to join the dog for a few minutes. The sky was clearing, and the night was so still she could hear the crunch of snow as Shadow tromped around.

She wandered down near the creek. Her mother had managed to keep the gold secret, now she had to figure out how to return it without being caught. If Parker found out about the gold, he'd never believe she wasn't working with her father. She wrapped her arms around herself. It was easy to imagine the cold look in his eyes, hear his deep accusing voice. She shivered. That wasn't going to happen, not if she could return the stolen gold.

Parker was beginning to wonder if his new-found patience was working with Kate. She said her mother was much better, but she was even more distant than yesterday. She had cleared the dinner dishes, but he lingered over his coffee watching her rifle through several newspapers as if her life depended on her finding something. She slapped the papers back where they had been and marched back to the kitchen. He drained the cup and followed her.

Charlie kneaded the mound of dough. "Ya might as well leave. There's nothin' fer ya t'do till supper."

"Okay." She had just washed the newsprint off of her hands when Parker came in and set his cup in the dry sink. "Thanks."

"I thought I'd take a walk. Would you like to go along?" From the way she stared out the window, he was sure she wanted to go. Her expression softened, and her lips parted almost temptingly.

It would be so easy to say yes, she thought, but could she put that *little problem* out of her mind? He'd called on her mother at least once, when he'd taken her the buttons. She glanced sideways. Had her mother said anything to him about her father?

Parker glanced at Charlie and back to Kate. "Should I have another cup of coffee while you make up your mind?" He really did want to talk with her away from there, where she couldn't hide behind the coffeepot or tray or in the kitchen.

He must be as tired of tracking Hank, she thought, as she was of running from his reputation. Maybe they could call a truce. "I'll need a couple minutes. Meet me outside?"

He nodded. "I'll be there." He went up to his room. After he put on his coat, hat, and stuffed his gloves in his pocket, he strolled outside. The sun was bright and the tracks in the snow were turning slushy.

He paused at the front corner of the hotel as she walked up to him. She was a sight wading through snow with her hat in hand and her skirt dragging along just below the bottom of her coat. "Which way do you want to go?"

She motioned beyond the general store to a pristine knoll a short distance away. "Want to see what the town looks like from up there?" His jacket was open and her attention was drawn to the snug fit of his jeans. It was a good thing she didn't shrink those pants a second time, she thought, they'd be positively indecent. She loosened a few buttons on her coat. It was warmer than she'd first thought.

As if he hadn't noticed where her gaze had settled for a long moment, he held his hand out. "Let's go." So she wasn't as uninterested in him as she let on, he thought, walking with renewed energy.

She'd taken four steps and was almost running to keep up with him. He strutted along as if he expected her to simply gallop at his side. "Sheriff—" She dug in her heels and yanked her hand free of his grasp.

Her hand slipped from his, and he glanced over his shoulder. "Something wrong?"

Not a thing, she thought, if you like racing through the snow. "Weren't we suppose to be walking together?"

"Yes." He grinned. He didn't know what had provoked her, but her back was up again. He did like her spirit. "Did you change your mind?"

"If I had legs like a bull moose, I might be able to match your stride."

He tapped the brim of his hat and murmured, "With that getup, it's hard to tell what your legs look like." She shot him a glare that might be considered deadly. Evidently her hearing was good, too.

She gathered her skirt, looped it over her arm and tromped forward, muttering, "I suppose you'd like it better if I wore skin-tight jeans like yours?"

He grinned. "I wouldn't object." When she came

abreast, he kept pace with her. "Have you heard anything about Pan Handle?"

She stared straight ahead. "No . . . Have there been more robberies?" Oh, please, no. She had enough to do covering her father's past thievery. Would it never end? she wondered. They started up the slope, and she slowed down.

"Haven't heard of any, but news travels by word of mouth. And I'm a stranger, sheriff or not."

"You probably hear more in the saloon about goings-on than I do in the dining room." She avoided a mound in the snow. The next moment the ground must've slanted down because she sank to her waist in the snow.

He stopped an arm's length behind her. "Are you standing on solid ground?"

"Yes." She twisted around. "Give me your hand. I can climb out." Elbowing her arms loose, she reached up to him. He looked huge from her vantage point—and strong.

"Grab on to my upper arm," he said, clasping hers. When he felt her fingers grasp his arm with surprising strength, he stepped back, pulling her with him. He halted when she stepped clear of the hole.

She didn't realize he'd stopped and walked right into his chest. His arms surrounded her before she could move away. She glanced up at him and their lips nearly touched. His coat held a hint of her favorite scent that he wore. His breath warmed her cheek, and his eyes—oh, they had the strangest effect on her insides, and she couldn't seem to get enough air.

He didn't know how long he gazed at her sweet face and held her close. A man could forget his good intentions staring into her tawny eyes. He ran his hands over her back and shoulders, brushing snow off. Then he traced his thumb along her jaw to wipe away the last trace of flakes. "You all right?"

I've never felt better in my life, she thought, or more confused. "Fine." His large hands loosely held her arms, and she had no idea why she didn't mind. She trembled, from the cold, she believed. However, she was warm, very warm. "You don't have to hold me up. I won't fall."

He lowered his hands, reluctantly. "How much farther are we going?"

"Not far," she said, tearing her gaze from him. "To that rise." She stepped to his side and shook out her skirt.

He took her hand in his and started off. She didn't need his help, but his hand was warm and strong. For the moment, it felt good to trust in his strength. Sometimes she wondered what it would be like to lean on someone else when she was tired or wanted to be comforted. When they reached the level rise, she turned on her heel and looked down at Moose Gulch. "Isn't it pretty?"

". . . Indeed." In twisting around, she had drawn his arm across her shoulders. He held her close. She didn't struggle, and he liked the way she fit against his side. From the way his body responded to hers, he liked it too damn much. "This would be a good place for a house." What the hell was he thinking about? She's Turner's daughter, he firmly reminded himself, an outlaw's daughter. The outlaw he would someday find and kill.

Kate pulled the gray skirt over her shirtwaist and fastened the waistband. Her hands were still trembling. She didn't know what had possessed her on that knoll. She acted as if she'd been moonstruck or besotted with Parker. It wouldn't happen again because she wasn't going on any more picnics or walks with him.

Mary Louise watched her daughter. "Why're ya wearin' that awful old thing? Wasn't that relegated to the dustbin ages ago?"

"It's comfortable." Kate brushed at her sleeve. The fabric was worn soft and felt good, enough reason to wear it.

Mary Louise gave her an calculating look. "It would make a good start on a rag rug for Shadow."

Kate smiled at the dog. "He looks content there on the bed next to you." She poured more sage tea and felt her mother's forehead. "The fever's better. Now, will you tell me what you were searching for under that bush?"

Mary Louise rubbed Shadow's neck. ''I told ya, deah. I thought I saw some nuts for the squirrels.''

''Do you want the last few biscuits? I'll bring your supper back after work.'' Kate pulled on her coat.

''Thank, ya, deah. I do b'lieve your beaten biscuits're better than mine.''

That was high praise, Kate thought, handing the plate to her mother. ''I'll see you in a bit.'' She kissed her mother's cheek. ''Come on, Shadow, you can take a walk. Mamma'll let you back inside.''

Shadow ate the piece of biscuit Mary Louise offered him. She grinned at the animal. ''I think he'd rather stay here with me.''

''You'd better let him out before long.'' Kate left them and returned to the hotel. She built up the woodstove fire, lighted the lamps, and was ready for supper by the time Bert took his usual seat. She poured him a cup of coffee and set the pot back on the woodstove. ''How're you this evening?''

Bert grinned at her and held the cup with both hands. ''Jist dandy. What'd Charlie fix fer supper?''

''Fresh baked bread, potluck stew, and apple pudding.''

Bert tucked the napkin under the neckband of her shirt. ''I'm ready.''

She chuckled. ''I'll tell Charlie.'' Mr. Bishop came in, and she greeted him. She returned to the kitchen and set the tray on the work table. ''Bert and Mr. Bishop need stew.''

Charlie picked up a plate and reached for the ladle. ''We can count on Bert bein' one o' the first to eat.''

She set two plates of sliced bread, bowls of butter on the tray. The bread smelled so good she quickly buttered a slice for herself, folded it in half, and bit into it. ''Mm. This's delicious.''

''Yer hungry.'' He set the plate of stew on the tray and dished up the second one. ''Think yer mama'd like some?''

''I know she would. I'll take her supper when I leave.'' While she served Mr. Bishop and Bert, two men came in and sat at separate tables. The one she'd seen last summer; the other was new in town. She stopped by the nearest table where the stranger was seated. "Evening."

"Evenin,' ma'am. Sure smells good in here."

"Fresh bread and stew. I'll bring you a plate." She went to the other man's table, then to the kitchen. "I hope you made enough bread. Two more just walked in."

"Made plenty. Don't'cha worry."

When she returned to the dining room, there was a man and woman seated on the other side of the woodstove from Bert. She served the men and made her way to the couple's table. "Good evening. Would you folks like supper?" The woman pushed her heavy cape off her shoulders. Her handsome dress had to be made of alpaca. It was beautiful, and so was the tall, shapely blonde wearing it. The gentleman sported full muttonchops with a beard down to his stiff white shirt collar.

The man glanced at the woman. "We would like to see a menu."

"I'm sorry. We don't have one. After the first snowfall, we don't usually get many travelers through here. Tonight we have fresh baked bread, potluck stew, and apple pudding for dessert." That wasn't completely true, but she hoped to avoid trouble. Out of the corner of her eye, she saw Parker sit down at his corner table. She was glad to see him, even though she shouldn't be.

The woman laid her gloved hand on the man's sleeve. "Please, that will be satisfactory."

He nodded. "As you will, my dear."

Kate waited, but when he said nothing more, she asked, "Would you like coffee? We don't have many calls for tea, but I can check if you like."

"Coffee will be fine," the woman said softly.

The woman sounded weary, and Kate smiled. "I'll be right back." She had feared the night would drag on. It never occurred to her she'd be so busy. She paused at Parker's table. He gave her a slight smile, but his eyes fairly sparkled. Had he misunderstood her friendliness that afternoon? "I'll get your supper."

When he looked at her, he wished they were back on that knoll, and he suddenly felt like a randy youth. "Take your time." She hurried away, and he shifted on the hard seat. Glancing around the room, he wondered if any of the newcomers were there because of the recent gold strike. At least it was something to think about—besides Kate.

She returned with a cup of coffee, and her glance barely met Parker's. She did notice his hand, though, and remembered how firm and reassuring it felt clasping her shoulder. "Your supper'll be ready in a minute."

She dashed back to the kitchen. Charlie wasn't there, so she dished up three more suppers. Earlier, she had wondered how she would stay awake until her mother had gone to sleep and it was late enough to make her trip to Pan Handle's camp without being seen. Now it wasn't a problem. As she served meals, refilled cups, and cleared tables, her attention repeatedly drifted to Parker. He'd been unusually quiet, and she'd been too busy to talk. On one trip back to the kitchen, she paused at his table. "I'll get your dessert."

He stood up. "None for me, Kate. See you in the morning." He wasn't sure if she was glad he was leaving or disappointed, but he knew if he was to survive facing down Turner, he'd best not become attracted to her—as if he wasn't already.

Varying his route, he stopped by the saloon first. One of the two men he had seen in the dining room was at the far end of the bar. Tullie was strumming the banjo. Parker looked at Ralston. "Quiet in here tonight."

Ralston nodded. "Dead. Heard the dining room was busy."

"Kate didn't stop all evening." Parker glanced around again.

Ralston set a clean glass on the bar. "Beer or whiskey?"

Parker shook his head "I'll need it after my walk." He stepped back from the bar. "I thought you were going away for a few days."

"I'm leaving in the morning. When you return, I'll give you a key." Ralston looked at Parker and shrugged. "In case you nab another thief or want a drink."

"All right, but I don't think we'll need your cellar again." Parker visited a while and left. He checked the abandoned buildings, the general store and had walked up to the livery, when he noticed someone darting between the trees along the side of the road just outside of town. He watched until the man was almost out of sight, then followed him up the road.

The man turned up a path. Parker had about decided he was trailing a miner, when he saw a campsite ahead. The fellow crept through the trees up to what resembled a tent, darted inside, then back out and scurried away.

Parker stepped behind a bush. When the fellow came abreast, he reached out, wrapped his arm around the man's midsection, and hauled him back. "Forget something?" The fellow squirmed and twisted, grunting and trying to jab with his elbow. He was small, either a wayward youth or a wiry man. Suddenly he thrashed violently.

When Parker tightened his hold, his fingers bit into a soft mound. He instantly lowered his arm, holding her around the waist. A woman? She screamed, and he quickly muffled her. He was breathing hard, but he knew her voice as well as his own, and his body reacted to her squirming body the same way it had that afternoon. "Kate?"

15

KATE'S HEART POUNDED in her throat as she fought to get free. Her hat had fallen off and her breast hurt like the devil, but she couldn't worry about that now. Try to do what's right and this's what I get, she thought. As she struggled against the powerful arms pinning her against him, he squeezed her tight around the waist. She stood still, gasping for breath, and hoped the hammerhead would loosen his grip so she could escape. His breath fanned her ear, and he said something—that voice. It was deep and . . . Parker? It couldn't be him. He was in town.

She had looked like a man from the back. If she hadn't been creeping through the trees, she wouldn't have aroused his suspicion. ''Kate—'' he repeated, turning her around within grasp. He had first thought she was still in touch with her father. However, now he wondered if she could be working with him? My God, could my judgment have been that wrong about her?

It was him. Anger replaced fear. ''Let go of me,'' she said in a deadly calm voice. ''What do you mean manhandling me?'' He held on to her, not as roughly as before, but much too close to him, close enough to feel the heat of his body. Her heart still pounded but now for a different reason, one she didn't want to believe.

"Come on," he said taking her with him, "before we draw attention."

She aimed a kick at his knee, but he sidestepped her, and she fell into his chest. "Don't ever turn your back on me again, Smith." She refused to look at him, but his heart thumped wildly beneath her ear. "I'm not leaving without my hat."

He held her arm in a vise grip while she reached down for it. She'd barely put in on her head, when he grabbed her free arm. He nearly dragged her back to the road, then stopped in a small clearing. "Why were you skulking around? Sneaking into that tent?" She glared at him with an arrogance that wasn't surprising considering her spirit. He watched her with equal strength.

"Returning wash," she said and suddenly twisted, hoping to break free. It was a disastrous move, one that landed her with her back against his chest and their arms locked across her chest. Being winded didn't help the predicament, either. "I . . . didn't . . . know you were that inter-ested in . . . wash."

"You never snuck into my room to return laundry." If she had, it might have proved interesting, he thought. "Try again." She was strong and clever, and when she tried to break fee, she made it painfully difficult for him to remain angry with her. But this was no game, and what his body desired was less important than their problem.

She attempted to jab her elbow into his stomach, but he held her too tight. "I just came up to see Pan Handle, but he was asleep." She swung her right leg around and hooked his ankle with her boot. At last!

She caught him by surprise, and he tumbled into the snow on top of her. If this didn't stop, he'd have to tie her wrists just to keep some distance between their bodies. He raised up, pinning her upper arms to the ground. "Now, let's start over. You weren't taking a stroll or chasing your dog or hiding from me."

"Get off me, you jackass."

He grinned. "Now, now. Would your mamma approve of such language?"

"Is this how you treat women? Or maybe it's the only way you can get close to one." She glared at him, but inwardly she cringed. It had just spilled out. He didn't have to hog-tie women to get attention. Hell's bells, they probably followed him around towns larger than Moose Gulch, flapping their fans and giving him sly glances.

His grinned as he recalled their earlier embrace. "The last time I held a woman, she wrapped my arm around her."

"You insufferable oaf!" He didn't need to remind her. She didn't think she'd ever forget that feeling of warmth.

He gazed down at her, wishing it wasn't so dark. Her hips pressed against the top of his thighs, and her leg rubbed the buttons down the front of his jeans. He stiffened and all but groaned, then he smiled and shifted his weight intimately. "Back to your reason for being here. Have you thought of another one?"

I'm lying under you because you're insane, she thought. And I must be, too, to have come out here in the middle of the night. "It's none of your business. I wasn't breaking the law." His weight touched her in places no other had, and the feeling was unlike any other. She'd had no idea a man's weight would make her want to snuggle even closer to him. She took a deep breath and moistened her dry lips. Didn't he feel it, the excitement flowing like a rain-swollen stream? She glanced at him as his open mouth came down on hers. His tongue darted and flicked and skimmed hers. A tremor passed through her, and the most heavenly tingly feelings flipflopped in her belly.

He hadn't realized how very much he wanted to kiss her until their lips touched. Her innocence was evident, and his mouth caressed hers with barely concealed intensity. After a moment of calm she came alive beneath him. He moved his mouth over hers, deepening the kiss.

It was as if he'd opened up a door somewhere inside her and set free a hunger for him she couldn't have imagined.

She wanted to wrap her arms around him, but they were still pinned down. She moaned and rocked her hips. His heat covered her, and the snow crunched beneath.

He framed her face with his hands and kissed her jaw. She was warm and soft, and he wanted more. He rested his cheek on hers. ''We have to talk, Kate.''

She wrapped her arms around him and rested her hands on his back. Slowly she became aware of the hard ground. ''Can we stand up?''

He kissed her forehead, came to his feet, and brought her up in front of him. Snow clung to her hair and clothes, and he brushed it off.

She picked up her hat and slapped it against her leg to knock off the snow. ''How did you find me?''

''I saw what I thought was a man sneaking up the road and followed him. I didn't know it was you until—'' He took her hat, stuck it on her head and held her arm, so she couldn't lead him on another merry chase. ''As sweet as that was, I have to know what you were up to, Kate.''

He stood with his feet apart, as if he thought she might run away. ''I . . .'' She was tired and cold without his warmth. ''It's not what you think. I didn't take anything.'' He knew who she was and now he believed the worst of her. The truth had to be better than that. Didn't it? ''I was giving it back.''

''This sounds interesting. What was *it*?''

She shrugged. ''A bag of gold.''

He stared at her. ''You snuck into his tent to give him gold? Your excuses are getting more fanciful, I'll give you that.''

''Pan Handle was robbed. I was returning what he lost.''

''That was very generous. You must earn more in tips than I guessed.'' It was such an outrageous story, he decided she might be telling the truth.

She waved her free hand in frustration. ''Can we walk? It's getting cold just standing here.''

With his hand still holding her arm, he led the way back down the path. ''Where did the gold come from?''

How could she answer without mentioning her mother? ''It was hidden away.''

He halted within sight of the roadway and stared at her. ''The *truth*—or you can spend the night right here.''

''You wouldn't.''

''There's Ralston's cellar.'' He was about out of patience. ''I'm sure he's cleaned it since the last prisoner. It smelled pretty bad the next morning.''

''You can't do that! I didn't do anything wro—''

He cut her off and motioned for her to be silent. The sound of crunching snow came from several yards up the hill.

She listened and whispered, ''It could be a mountain lion.''

''Or a coyote.'' He led her to the road. ''I don't think it'll bother us. We don't have any food.'' On the way back he kept going over what she had said and only came up with more questions by the time the town was in sight. ''I *know* you are Katherine Turner, daughter of Hank Turner, bank robber, thief, outlaw. Why should I believe you? You working with your father makes more sense.''

''You can't mean that.'' Did he really think so little of her? She stamped her feet and rubbed her arms to keep warm. ''Can't we go the hotel and talk over a cup of coffee?''

The note of resignation in her voice caused a twinge of regret, but he had been on Turner's trail for too many years to give it up now. Not even for her. He released her arm. ''Lead on.''

She entered the hotel by the front door. There was one lamp lighted in the lobby. She walked through the dining room and lighted a lamp in the kitchen. ''You might as well sit down.'' After rekindling the fire in the stove, she put on the pot of coffee. As she saw it, she had two choices: allow Parker to believe she was a thief working with her father, or confess the truth and trust he would understand.

He closed the door to the dining room and removed his gloves. ''Can't we talk while the coffee boils?''

"Of course." She unwrapped a half loaf of Charlie's bread and set it on the table with a knife. "Preserves or butter?" She finally met his gaze. His eyes weren't sparkling now, and he looked as grim as she felt. He didn't like this any more than she did.

"Plain'll be fine for me."

She grabbed the jar of preserves and bowl of butter. The one thing she had always taken pride in was her honesty, her reputation. Suddenly she realized his respect was terribly important to her. *If she had it,* that is, she didn't want to lose it.

She was deep in her own thoughts, he realized, and hadn't heard him. "Looks good."

"I told you I didn't know where Hank was." She picked up the knife and whacked off one slice of bread. "That's the truth. I have no idea where he is, and I don't think Mama does, either." As she spoke, she sliced the rest of the bread. "But she must be in touch with him, somehow." She set two small plates out for them and sat down.

He nodded. "She told me he gets messages to her."

"That's more than she told me." If screaming at the top of her lungs would've done any good, she would have. She still didn't want to believe that all her hard work was for nothing. The coffee came to a boil, and she moved the pot off to the side of the fire.

"She seems to enjoy secrets." He was beginning to suspect the answer he had demanded of her was more complicated than he realized. Kate looked miserable, but he couldn't help her until he understood more about her problem. He took off his jacket and hung it on the back of the chair.

She'd never had anyone she felt safe enough with to share her fears with or the truth about her father, but she did feel safe with Parker. Maybe now was the time. She poured their coffee and set the cups on the table. "Last night when I was looking for Mamma's bed jacket, I discovered canvas bags lining the bottom of the trunk. Each one was heavy. I opened two and found gold." She shivered. It still horrified her. "She finally admitted he's been giving her gold for . . . I don't know how long it's been going on." She sipped her coffee and spread preserves on a piece of bread.

That must have been a hell-of-a shock. No wonder she had been acting so strange. "Your mother just kept putting it away? She never said a word or spent any of it?"

"Nothing. But I found some things she made, and I didn't pay for them. I've also been remembering odd little things. She always had enough yarn and yard goods." Kate shrugged. "She did mending. I thought she spent her earnings. I should've asked, but—"

"Why? I think most of us believe the best of our mothers." He ate a piece of bread. "How long have you and your mother been on your own?"

"Eleven years, this December." The kitchen was warmer, and she pulled her coat off.

He gazed at her, trying to guess how old she would've been. "You must've been a child. How did your mother manage?" When he faced Hank, Parker realized, he would have another score to settle with him.

"I'm not sure what she did the first months. Then we lost the house to the bank. The gossips had a field day talking about us. We moved not long after that. We lived in a boardinghouse, and I was able to work for the lady who owned it. I think that's when Mamma started sewing dresses for ladies."

"I'm surprised your mother didn't want you to complete your schooling."

"I did—well, most of it." She smiled. "Mrs. Finley, the schoolmarm, was also a resident at the boardinghouse. She tutored me in the evenings."

"At least you had that. Was Hank in touch with you then?"

She shook her head, staring into her cup. "When we lost our home, I swore I'd never speak to him again. Every time I saw a poster with his name on it, we moved." She looked directly at him. "This last time we changed our name. I had the foolish notion we could be free of the past.'' He was no longer angry, but did he feel sorry for her? She didn't want his pity, just his understanding. As she stared into his eyes, she recalled their first meeting and wondered how he had known who she was. ''How did you recognize me?''

He washed the chunk of bread down with coffee. ''I saw you in Park City.'' He chuckled. ''You were dressing down a young man. You caught my eye. After a few inquiries, I learned your name. I knew Hank had a wife and daughter. It took a while to sort out the gossip, but there were too many coincidences not to follow you.'' He swirled the coffee in his cup. ''It was your eyes. They're your father's, you know.''

She groaned. ''I don't want anything to do with him. Nothing!'' She continued in a softer voice. ''I've spent nearly half my life trying to escape his reputation. How far do I have to go to get away from him?''

He covered her hand with his. ''I don't know, but if he came here and robbed the store, no one would have a reason to believe you had anything to do with him.'' The pain in her voice was too real to ignore. He believed her, and he finally breathed easier. He hadn't wanted her to be guilty of his charges.

''No.'' She stared at him. ''But you would've—just because he's my father.'' She waved her hand. ''It's happened before. I don't want it to happen again, but it could. Hank must've stolen that gold from the miners—that's why I was putting that gold in Pan Handles's tent.''

The idea had occurred to him, too, but Turner wasn't the only thief in the territory. ''Why Pan Handle? There have been others.''

''His camp was closest, so I started with him.'' She broke a piece from the slice of bread. ''I've looked through all the newspapers I could find for any mention of robberies. There were a few notices, but I have no idea where the mines are.'' She finished the end the bread and the last of her coffee.

''Did you make a list?'' He drained his cup.

''Not yet, but I'll have to.'' She carried their dishes to the dry sink and rewrapped the uneaten bread.

''You're trying to do the right thing, but I'm not sure this is the way to do it.'' He stepped over to her. She'd been through so much and looked weary. ''We don't know it was your father who robbed those miners.''

''Who else, then? He's close enough to get word to Mamma. He hasn't been caught—he must be pretty cocksure of himself.'' She glanced up at Parker, saying, ''Doesn't that make . . . sense?'' His gaze seemed to shimmer in the lamplight and roam the length of her body. She wanted to feel his mouth on hers, his arms holding her.

He leaned closer to hear her softly spoken words, like a moth to a flame. He was spellbound by the fragile desire in her eyes. This woman didn't think twice about standing toe-to-toe with him, and she now gazed into his eyes as if she were longing to be kissed. He wrapped her in his arms and held her close as he pressed his lips to hers. Less timid this time, she moved with him, gave him greater access to her sweet mouth.

She slid her arms around him and felt his strength beneath her fingers. She snuggled closer, molding her body to his, and trembled with a wave of desire. His lips were firm and oh, so very persuasive. Her pulse surged. She'd never been closer to heaven than she was at that moment. He spread his fingers on her back, slid his hand down to the base of her spine, and pinned her hips against his. Unable to resist a need she was only now beginning to understand, she clung to him.

He groaned at the sudden burst of desire he thought was under control and raised his lips to her brow. He rarely lost command of his emotions, but she came close to crushing his restraint. He filled his lungs and waited for his heart to stop thundering in his chest. ''I'll help you get the gold back to the rightful owners.'' The thought of some thug overpowering her in the middle of the night sent an icy shiver down his spine.

''You'd do that for me?''

That and more, he thought, but not what you will eventually ask of me. ''You can't do it alone.'' He brushed his lips across hers.

She couldn't remember the last time someone's concern was so comforting or meant so much. ''Thank you.'' She heard herself, surprised by her willingness to share her heaviest burden with him. For one fleeting moment, she considered taking back her words. But as she gazed into his eyes, she decided she really could count on him.

When Kate served Parker breakfast the next morning, she had never felt so mixed up. She wanted to believe he hadn't changed his mind about the offer he'd made early that morning, and yet she waited for him to deny it. ''Good morning.'' For someone who'd been accused of saying too much, she was at a loss for words.

''Morning. You're looking especially bright today.'' Her cheeks turned a nice pink, and she had done something different with her hair. She looked as good as he felt. ''I seemed to have worked up quite an appetite overnight. What did Charlie fix for breakfast?''

Last night'd had a different effect on her. She wasn't hungry, and she felt overly edgy. ''Eggs, flapjacks, and smoked ham.''

He gave her an approving nod. ''How about some bread and preserves, too?'' Her pink cheeks turned red, and he grinned, then he noticed Ralston walking over to the table.

She heard someone coming up behind her and quickly said, ''You should've had some last night.''

Ralston glanced from Parker to Kate and back to Parker. ''Morning. Mind if I join you?''

''Have a seat.'' Parker motioned to a chair. ''Kate was just telling me about breakfast.''

Ralston sat down. ''You can bring me one, too.''

''Be glad to.'' She went to the kitchen and set the tray out as she spoke to Charlie. ''Parker and Ralston are here for breakfast.'' She got the cups and poured the coffee.

He picked up a plate and started dishing out the food. "Thought Ralston was leavin'."

"He isn't moving away, is he?"

"Nah. Jist goes t'town fer a few days." He set the plate on the tray and fixed the second one.

"Thank goodness." She put the slices of bread from earlier that morning on a plate and added the preserves to the tray, also.

"Didn't know ya was so fond o' him." He handed the plate to her.

"Miners come to town to drink and play poker, or whatever they do over there in the saloon." She put the dish on the tray and picked it up. "He's a nice man, and the town needs him."

"Yer right 'bout that."

She served Mr. Ralston first, then Parker. She set the bowl of preserves down last. His hand brushed hers, and her pulse raced. It seemed their kisses had a lasting effect, one she hadn't expected.

Parker grinned at her. "Ah, you found the preserves. I'll share if you want to join us." He pulled out the chair between his and Raltson's.

"I'll leave you to your talk." She set the empty tray on the next table and returned to the kitchen. She'd noticed Mr. Ralston watching them and didn't trust herself to remain matter-of-fact around Parker.

Ralston waited until the door to the kitchen closed. "I'm sorry if I interrupted something."

"Don't give it another thought." Parker pushed the bread and preserves to the middle of the table. "I'm sorry about last night. I noticed a fellow stumbling around not far from the livery and didn't remember seeing him in town." He shook his head. "Turned out he was liquored up and thought he'd reached Missoula. By the time I saw him up the road and got back, you had closed."

Ralston pulled a key out of his coat pocket. "I wanted to give this to you. Help yourself. If you have any rowdy affairs, you clean up the mess."

"I'll do that." Parker dropped the key into his pocket and ate a bite of buttered flapjacks. "Hope the weather holds for you."

Ralston winked. "Miss Hattie's worth the trip."

Parker understood. He'd been like a schoolboy himself around Kate, until last night. As he started to recall how she had felt beneath him in the snow, he shifted on the hard chair and took another bite. Now wasn't the time for such reverie.

"Do you want me to bring anything back for you?"

Parker thought a minute. Anything he came up with, he would rather pick out himself. "Newspaper? By the time they arrive at the general store, they're almost a week old." He reached into his pocket and set two bits on the table.

Ralston shook his head. "I like to catch up on what's happening around the Territory, too." He stabbed the last piece of ham. "Sorry I'm in such a rush."

Parker laughed. "Don't apologize. I understand." Did he ever, he thought. Kate returned with the coffeepot. He didn't envy Ralston his trip at all.

❖ 16 ❖

KATE DID EVERY chore she could think of with renewed energy, but it didn't help the time pass any faster. The morning dragged by, as did the noontime meal. Parker rode over to Missoula after breakfast and said he'd see her when he returned later that afternoon. Mr. Bishop had taken his dinner into his office. The dining room was empty.

She looked over her coffee cup at Charlie. "You might as well put dinner away until this evening. We seem to be the only ones eating here."

"I think yer right." Charlie poured himself more coffee. "Why don't ya fix yer mama a plate? Take some fer yer-self, too. Ya hardly ate a bite."

"I might as well." She left a few minutes later and found her mother sitting by the fire sewing a new dress with the yard goods she'd seen in the trunk.

Mary Louise glanced up at her daughter. "Ya're back so soon. Anythin' wrong, deah?" She folded the bodice and set it aside.

"No." Kate uncovered the tray and set their meals out on the table. When Shadow sat up and stared at the tray, she shook her head at him. "I'd already finished cleaning. There weren't any customers to serve and nothing else for me to do." She took her skirt off and dropped it on the bed.

"Y're always runnin' around, deah. We haven't spent an afternoon together for ever so long." Mary Louise poured another cup of tea and sat down at the table. "Ya can put together that petticoat ya cut out last week." She glanced sideways at her daughter. "An' ya could use a new dress or two."

"Whatever for?" Kate sat down across the table from her mother and looked her in the eye. "Besides, we haven't any extra coins to fritter away." She picked up her fork and added, "I've saved every penny so we can purchase a house."

"We have plenty of gold to purchase what we need," Mary Louise murmured and sipped her tea.

Kate gulped. "You can't mean that. It isn't ours."

"Why, of course it is, deah. Mr. Turner gave it to me for our needs."

"Mamma, you cannot use *any* of that gold. It was stolen. It isn't ours." She watched her mother wondering what had happened to her. She had learned right from wrong under her mother's guidance and didn't understand what could've changed her thinking. "I'm going to return that gold to the miners it was stolen from—or try."

"Katie, ya can't! It's ours." Mary Louise shook her head. "Mr. Turner didn't steal it. How can you b'lieve he'd give us ill-gotten gold? Or that I'd accept it?"

"How else did he come by it?" It was ridiculous. Kate jabbed her fork into a piece of venison. "There's enough gold in the trunk to build you a fine house with the nicest furnishings. Why didn't he do that for you, Mamma?" It was too much to swallow. She looked at Shadow and got his tin plate.

Mary Louise avoided looking at her daughter and laid her fork on the plate. "I didn't raise ya to be so cruel, so disrespectful, and I'll not discuss this further until ya've come to your senses, missy."

Kate set the dog's plate on the floor for him. "I agree. But you're blind where he's concerned—always have been." She shoved the chair under the table. "What I don't understand is how you can approve of robbery and murder.''

''He *never* killed anyone! Where'd ya hear that?'' Mary Louise pulled out her handkerchief and dabbed her forehead and cheeks.

''Don't you remember *where*? Don't you remember my coming home from school in tears because the other children called me an outlaw's daughter?'' Kate couldn't believe her mother had forgotten the tears, her own scraped hands and torn dresses after a fight on the way home from school. ''And what about you? I overheard the snickers and nasty comments when we walked down the street and in the stores or saw people turn away from us. I wasn't the only one crying at night.'' He'd never had the courage to come back and face her, explain what had happened. Besides being an outlaw, her father was also a coward. She grabbed her jacket and opened the door. ''Come on, Shadow. Let's take a walk.''

After talking with the sheriff in Missoula, Parker visited the land office, livery, a few stores, and several saloons hoping to overhear some mention of the robberies. He heard different versions of the same theft, and it had taken place early last summer. Before leaving town, he bought two copies of the *Montana Pioneer* newspaper. Even if it didn't help them, it was something to read.

The ride back to Moose Gulch was pleasant. There were snowdrifts in the shady areas, but the road was clear. If he and Kate could locate the robbed miners, they shouldn't have any difficulty getting in and out without leaving tracks. When he dismounted in front of the livery, Mac came out to greet him. ''I didn't see you when I left.''

''I was taking advantage of this mild day.'' Mac walked back into the livery with Parker. ''How 'bout you? There's not much to do around here, especially this time of year.''

Parker loosened the cinch strap, pulled it free, and lifted the saddle off of Buckshot. ''Rode over to Missoula,'' he said, hanging it over the plank with the other saddles.

"Good. Might as well get to know the area."

Parker nodded. He had been surprised by the flat expanse of the valley where Missoula was located. For some reason, he'd thought of the entire area as mountainous. "Find any color?" He started rubbing-down Buckshot.

Mac chuckled. "A bit. Enough to keep me looking for that pocket."

"I hope you hit the mother lode, Mac. Couldn't happen to a nicer man." When Parker finished with Buckshot, he put him in the stall and gave him an extra measure of oats. "I forgot to ask Ralston. What does Tullie do when Ralston's out of town?"

Mac shrugged. "Might go down to Drummond. Don't really know. He keeps to himself." He looked at Parker. "Any reason for asking?"

"Just curious. I never see him outside of the saloon." Parker slung the saddlebags over his shoulder. "See you later."

After leaving the saddlebags in his room, he took the newspapers with him and went to find Kate. She wasn't in the kitchen, or at her cabin, but Mrs. Miller told him Kate had taken the dog with her. On a whim, he headed up along the creek. He noticed paw prints and picked up his pace. A few minutes later he passed where they had shared the picnic dinner. He kept walking.

The sun hovered over the western mountain peaks. He thought he must be at least a mile from town, when Shadow bounded from a clump of bushes with a stick in his mouth. He whistled and the dog came running. He ruffled the animal's shoulder. "Where is she?"

"Right here." Kate watched him from the middle of the path. He sure was a welcome sight. "How did your trip go? Learn anything helpful?" She suddenly felt better than she had all afternoon.

She was wearing trousers without the skirt. He gave her a lingering, appraising gaze. "Nice legs." She stood with her weight on one leg, with the other off to the side, her coat slung over one shoulder and a sassy grin lighting her face. He hadn't seen her figure so clearly before, but after last night, he would've recognized her nicely curved shape from any angle.

Still grinning, she repaid him by giving him a once-over that momentarily paused at the buttons on his snug pants. He didn't seem to mind at all, but it had the strangest effect on her belly. "You aren't bad, either." She threw a stick, and Shadow ran after it. "What're you doing out here?"

"Looking for you. I got a couple newspapers." He pulled them out of his coat pocket and held them up. The dog ran back with the stick, dropped it and jumped for the folded paper. Parker said, "No—" and the dog planted its butt on the ground and stared at him. "He listens. Someone's worked with him."

She walked down the path to Parker and petted the dog's silky head. "I'm surprised he's stayed so long."

"Why shouldn't he? He's happy with you." Smart dog, he thought. "Want to read through the paper?" He handed one of them to her.

"Thank you." As she took the paper, his long, blunt fingers brushed hers, and she remembered their strength, the delicious feelings they'd aroused. She lowered the paper to her side and gazed at him. He seemed to be amused by something, but she didn't want to ask what. "Have there been any more robberies?"

"Not that I heard about." Shadow trotted back along the creek, and they fell into step behind him. Parker motioned to the clearing where they had picnicked. "There's a good spot." He glanced at her, but she didn't seem to be paying much attention. "I stopped by the cabin a while ago. Your mother didn't open the door, but she sounded . . . out-of-sorts. Is she all right?"

Kate nodded. "We had a disagreement." She crossed the creek and looked around. The picnic. She grinned to herself. "You must be partial to this clearing." He had been so annoyingly charming that day, stretched out on the blanket, chatting and asking questions.

He eyed her. "Guess I am." He reached down, plucked

a small dead plant, and held it out between them, saying in a dramatic voice, ''Only a few weeks ago there was a delicate orange bloom on this stalk.''

She burst out laughing and brushed her hand over his arm. Her heart seemed to leap to her throat, and she curved her fingers around his arm to steady herself. ''There'll be more next spring.'' As if either of them really cared, she thought, but she had to say something.

When her hand slid from his arm, he sat down on the log and motioned for her to join him. ''You'll have to write and tell me when they bloom.''

Did he mean to keep in touch with her? She dropped down by his side and flipped the newspaper open on the ground. His leaving wasn't news. She would be, too, but she never dreamed he'd give her another thought after he left. She stared at the print, wondering if he would even remember her next spring.

He skimmed the first page. ''There's a new gold field in British Columbia.'' He glanced at her. ''Maybe we should try there.''

She thought a moment and shook her head. ''From what Mamma's said, I don't think he'd go that far away from my mother.''

He continued looking down the page. ''Did you know the only living thing in the Great Salt Lake is a worm about a quarter of an inch long? Seems storms wash them ashore to be eaten by black gulls.''

''Would you be serious?'' She didn't understand his lighthearted attitude. Didn't he want to find her father? That thought was a slap in the face. He'd asked for her help and seemed to be happy when she'd finally agreed. Shadow ran up to her dripping water and dropped the stick on the paper. ''Get away—'' She threw the stick into the bushes on the other side of the creek.

''Why so edgy? Don't you enjoy reading snippets about people?'' He traced his finger down the page, pointed to the item on her paper and read aloud. '' 'The most romantic of all numbers is the number nine, because—' '' he said, lowering his voice, "it can't be multiplied away or got rid of anyhow." He glanced sideways at her. "Now, did you know that before?"

She quickly read the rest of the short article. "His idea of romance is a bit farfetched." She grinned and concentrated on the Brevities column.

"Oh, well, maybe the writer has nine children."

She chuckled. "Then his wife has my sympathy."

He skimmed the Court Proceedings column, but Turner's name wasn't mentioned. "We could put an item in the Personals. 'Hank Turner, contact long-lost daughter. Urgent. Please reply.' " He was teasing, but on second thought, it might be worth a try, he realized.

"What makes you think he reads the newspaper? He'd probably never see it, or it could be months before he did." And we'll be long gone by then, she thought. She arched her back and sat up. He was so different from other men, she found herself really enjoying his company.

"Ah, the editor has been kind enough to list the new subscribers for us." As he skimmed the names listed with the city of residence, the dog tossed the stick at him. He pitched it upstream. "He's enjoying the outing."

She smirked. "Do you honestly think Hank would take a subscription? *And* use his real name?"

When she beamed like that, he wanted to take her in his arms and—He leaned close to her. "No, but neither will I ignore the list in front of me." He slid his hand around to the back of her neck and pressed his lips to hers. She returned his kiss with a hunger of her own.

His fingers caressed the back of her neck, stroking, teasing, and sending shivers of delight down her back, she thought she'd melt or her heart would burst. Each time they came together like this, he discovered a new place on her body that was sensitive only to his touch. She wrapped her arms around him, holding him close. But close wasn't enough. She wanted more. She had never felt more like a woman than when she was in his embrace and his heart beat against her breast.

No other woman had ever aroused him with the strength she did, almost to the point where he might be careless. He nibbled his way down to the hollow of the neck and pressed one more kiss to her smooth skin. "See what your smile does to me?"

She grinned at him. "I'm not complaining, am I?" He was so handsome, it was hard to believe he could feel such fondness for her.

"You should." He grazed her mouth and sat back, a safer distance from her. "It's getting late. We've only read the first page."

"Then we'll have to look at the rest after supper." She refolded the paper and picked it up. "Unless you had other plans . . ." She was being reckless for the first time in her life, and it wasn't as frightening as she had imagined. It was exciting. She didn't want to die an old woman who had never known the love of a man. She didn't think she was in love with him, yet, but she'd never find out if she held him at rifle length.

Kate took her mother's supper tray to the cabin and set the table. "Charlie cut you a generous piece of spice cake."

Mary Louise sat down at her place at the table. "Please thank him for me."

"I did." Kate set the dog's dish on the floor. The deceit was too raw for her to forgive her mother, but she didn't think she could tolerate this cold, lonely silence between them, either. "I may be late. Will you be all right?"

Mary Louise nodded. "We'll be fine," she said, looking fondly at Shadow.

"Good. Don't forget to let him out." When she passed by her mother, she put her hand on her mother's shoulder and gave a gentle squeeze.

Earl came into the dining room and sat with Mr. Bishop. They were her only customers until Parker showed up. After Charlie had left, and she had finished cleaning up the kitchen, she sat down with Parker. They went through the rest of the newspaper and even read the list of new subscribers in the old papers, but they didn't find her father's name.

She refilled their cups. "Now what do we do? I can't pass those bags out like Christmas candy."

"I agree. We could take a ride each afternoon, follow a different path or trail each day." He sipped his coffee. "What man wouldn't sympathize with a daughter searching for her father."

"I don't want to *see* him. All I want is to return the stolen gold." She drew lines on the tablecloth with her fingernail.

"I've spent four years tracking your father. I *will* see him. I thought it would be easier with your help." He shrugged. "Either way, I will find him."

"Four years? Why?" She stared at him and realized she'd never asked him. "What's so important?"

He lowered the cup and stared at her. "He killed my father eleven years ago. I swore Hank would share the same fate." She sagged back on the chair and the color drained from her face. He reached for her hand, but she pulled away.

She didn't want to believe it, but he was deadly serious. Her hands shook, and she clasped them on her lap. My God, she thought, what do I say? "I—" The look in his eyes was cold and distant. "I'm so sorry. I had no idea. How could I have known?"

He let out a long sigh. "I never thought you did, but I hoped you'd lead me to him."

She hadn't believed she could feel any worse. She was wrong. "You were using me to find my father—to kill him?" She held her breath. It felt as if she were caught in a horrible nightmare.

"In the beginning—but I would use the devil himself if I had to. My mother never recovered from his murder. I watched her die with a broken heart. Hank Turner will pay for our loss."

"I thought—I trusted you!" She jumped to her feet. "I should've known you didn't really—" She ran through the kitchen and down to the creek. She'd been such a fool to think for even one moment that he had cared for her. That's what cut so deeply. He didn't give a rat's tail for her. If he'd told her the truth, she probably would've helped him. She crumpled down to a heap on the ground crying.

During the next few days Kate's emotions swung like a pendulum, going from wanting to shoot Parker to using the pistol on her father. Half of the time she still wondered if she'd dreamed the whole thing up, but seeing Parker several times each day made the situation all too real. She understood his need for justice. In his place, she'd probably do the same.

She tried to remember her father's face, but her memory had grown blurry over the years. If he came into the dining room, would she recognize him? By the end of the week, she had decided she needed to confront him with the pain he'd caused her.

She wasn't fool enough to wander these mountains alone—but with Parker, they just might accomplish what they both wanted. And they would be working together. She liked that idea. He had kissed and held with tenderness, not brutally, as if he were punishing her for her father's deeds. Maybe Parker really cared for her.

She mulled over her idea for another day. She wasn't like her father, only his daughter, and she'd prove it, if only to herself. She would help Parker.

Her mind made up, she planned to speak to Parker after supper. As much as she'd wanted to hate him, she couldn't. He wasn't a liar or thief or a murderer. He was a man who wanted justice, and after eleven years she didn't really blame him for using her. No. If it had been her, she would've done the same.

Mr. Bishop and Bert were the first to arrive for supper, then Parker came in, followed by Earl and a couple men that had been in last summer. She poured coffee, served suppers and desserts, and cleared tables. Eventually things slowed down. By the time she could sit down and talk to Parker, he'd gone.

❖ 17 ❖

PARKER LINGERED OVER his beer until everyone had left the saloon, then took one last walk around town. He was tempted to saddle Buckshot and get on with his search, but somehow he had become obliged to the good people of Moose Gulch. He couldn't leave without telling anyone. The worst of it was that the one person he most wanted to talk to would as soon dump his dinner in his lap as set it on the table.

He had overheard talk in the saloon about another robbery and felt he owed it to Kate to tell her about it. It wouldn't change her mind. She hadn't spoken to him in over a week, and he'd decided he should consider himself lucky she hadn't pulled her pistol on him. Right now he wouldn't even mind that, as long as she spoke to him.

Figuring he didn't have anything to lose, he walked to her cabin. The lights were out. It was late. What had he expected? He returned to the hotel, put out the light in the lobby, and went upstairs to his room. He took off his hat, unbuckled his gun belt, and hung it on the headboard, draped the shirt over the back of the chair, and pulled off his boots. It wasn't until he was unbuttoning his pants that he heard the rustle of cloth and realized he wasn't alone. He immediately reacted to the unknown; blood surged through his veins double time as he reached for his pistol.

"It's me, Parker," Kate said, grabbing his arm, her heart pounding in her throat. "You won't need your pistol." He started to pull away, and she tightened her grip. If she hadn't been so unnerved, she would've spoken up earlier, but she hadn't expected him to undress in the dark. "I need to talk to you."

Her voice was deep and soft, and her right hand was holding his arm, so he figured it was safe to assume she didn't have her pistol trained on him. "Mind if I light the lamp?"

She let her hand slip to the bed. "No. I didn't think you'd undress in the dark."

He chuckled, struck a match, and lighted the lamp. The wick was low and cast a soft yellow glow over the bed. Her hair hung down over her shoulder, and she looked sleepy, curled on her side, leaning against the headboard clutching his pillow. She hadn't taken off her coat, a definite reminder, if he needed one, that she wasn't playing games. "Have you been waiting long?"

She shrugged, not sure how long she'd been there. He was a vision standing with such pride. She wanted to run her fingers through the dark curly chair on his bare chest, and she couldn't help wondering how long it would take his pants to slip down over his hips. She quickly sat up and put his pillow back where she'd found it. His shoulders were broad, his chest muscular, and his hips—she swallowed hard and took a deep breath, but the pounding of her heart wouldn't slow. "I've been thinking—"

"About how I take my clothes off?" God, he needed to laugh. It wouldn't hurt her, either, he thought.

She chuckled. "I deserved that." He seemed to loom over her, unsettling her. She scooted over and stared up at him. "If you don't sit down, I'll have to stand up so I don't get a stiff neck."

He obliged, sitting in the spot she had vacated at the head of the bed. "What's so important it couldn't wait till morning?" He didn't care what it was, just that it had brought her there, where he never expected to see her without a dust rag.

Maybe I should've stood up, she thought. The sides of his pants gaped open to below his waist. Her cheeks grew hot, but she refused to be sidetracked. "I've spent a good part of my life avoiding any mention of Hank." Her mouth was as dry as her lips, but she had to finish. "It's time I faced him. It's the only way I can truly get him out of my life." She ran her tongue over her lips. "I'll help you find him—if you agree to let me talk to him before you settle with him." She'd gotten it out: now all she had to fear was his laughter.

Now he knew how it felt to be caught in a trap. The pulse at the base of her neck fluttered like a butterfly's wing. She wasn't as confident as she seemed, but she was completely serious. "You understand, don't you? I *will* draw against him." She didn't flinch. Not too many men were that brave. She was incredible. She was beautiful. And she was the best thing that had ever happened to him.

"I know." She shivered.

"It will be a fair fight. I never intended to gun him down." There was an ironclad determination in her voice that sounded the way he felt.

She nearly smiled. "I didn't think you would. You're an honorable man."

He could have groaned aloud. He wasn't feeling exactly forthright at that moment, not with the thoughts of what he wanted to do with her filling his mind. He put his hand on her shoulder. "Are you certain this is what you want to do?"

"I won't change my mind. If you're worried about that, don't." She smiled. "I'll do everything I can to help you." She was babbling. What she wanted was for him to hold her in his arms. He hadn't been shy the other night. Bolstering her courage, she rolled to one hip and raised her hands to his shoulders, saying, "To seal our agreement," then pressed her mouth to his. When his arms wrapped around her, she deepened the kiss.

Never had he sealed a deal in this fashion. But he'd never known anyone like Kate before, either. She was an exciting blend of innocence and uninhibited passion. She tumbled him back, and he sank his fingers in her loose silky hair. She softly moaned, and his body responded instantly. This was insane, but she felt so damn good. And he needed her, needed to feel her unclothed body beneath his, warm and loving, hear the sound of her voice when he made love to her.

She levered herself up slightly and explored his mouth the way he had hers. He gently rocked from side to side. His hips rubbed against hers, and ripples of desire flowed through her belly and spread lower. She rested her head next to his and savored the aroma of his hair tonic. She tried to snuggle closer, but her coat and jeans were in the way. The room had been cold: now it was almost as warm as the kitchen.

He moved one hand down her back and held her still. "You feel so good, but we'd better stop before you regret coming up here."

Laughing softly, she reached down and lightly ran her fingertips over his ribs. "The first time I saw you, I thought I had you figured out." She kissed his chin. "I was wrong—about a few things."

He grinned. "Such as?"

She brushed his thick, sable hair off his forehead. "You were cocky, scheming—" She kissed the tip of his nose. "And bent on pestering me. You also have a wicked smile."

"You do, too." He rubbed her silky hair on his cheek. "You should wear your hair down more often. Makes you less forbidding." He'd thought talking would ease the tension, but if anything, he wanted her even more.

"*Me?*" She did laugh at that. "At most I put an occasional miner in his place, but rarely you."

"More times than you realized." He fought to keep his need for her under control. This definitely wasn't getting any easier. He rolled to his side, carrying her with him, and ran his hand over the curve of her hip.

Her heart pounded as if she'd been running for miles, but she wasn't tired. She felt a restlessness only he could ease. She pressed kisses to his bare chest and wound one dark curl around her finger. Where she leisurely explored, the muscles beneath flexed, encouraging her search. Her fingers roamed over his flat belly, finding their way down to where the sides of his jeans parted.

She grazed a fiery path he couldn't allow her to complete. He raised her hand to his mouth and kissed each fingertip. "You're playing with fire, Katie." And we're both coming dangerous close to singeing more than our fingers.

"No, I'm not." She wasn't sure what love was anymore, not after learning about her mother's deception, but she knew she wanted him. "And I can't believe you fear me."

"If you were armed, possibly." He took a deep, shuddering breath. "Your effect on me, most definitely."

She grinned. That was the nicest compliment she'd ever received. She unbuttoned the top button on her coat and the next.

He started from the bottom. When their hands met, he pushed the coat off her shoulders and down her arms until her hands were free. He lifted her right arm, loosened the button on her sleeve, and kissed the tender flesh on the underside of her wrist. He did the same to her right hand. She swayed; he steadied her lovely face and traced the line of her lips with his thumb. When she drew his thumb into her mouth, he throbbed with need to bury himself inside of her.

She had never been so aware of her body. With each caress, each kiss, and each brush of his fingertips, she felt a quickening of her pulse. He unfastened the buttons down the front of her shirtwaist, pushed it back, and pulled it off. She loosened the waistband on her skirt, then he kissed her shoulder and her chest above her chemise. Her senses seemed to whirl with the pressure of his lips and the strength in his hands as he removed her chemise. She quickly pulled off her boots. Her skirt and jeans followed.

She nearly forgot to breathe when he kneeled at her side, staring at her. The power of his gaze brushed her from head to toe, and she reached out to him, trembling, wanting to feel his weight on her. He gasped and his chest expanded as he covered her naked body with his. It was the most wondrous feeling in the world. She locked her hands over his smooth back, urging him to join with her, fill her aching need for him.

He moved over her and kissed her hungrily as he entered her. There was a moment's resistance, but she pushed down on him as her legs wrapped around his and moved with him, urging him on. She couldn't imagine feeling any more wonderful and didn't believe she could survive such pleasure. His breathing was as harsh as her own. Her mind spun in dizzying circles, and her heart thundered with deafening force. She cried out and clung to him, trembling uncontrollably, and felt as if she were shattering. He throbbed within her, and she thought she might perish from the beauty of their passion. She had never known such joy, such complete bliss. She pressed her lips to his damp shoulder and sighed.

Her eyes sparkled and her smile sent another tremor coursing through him. Who would have thought he'd find such happiness when he least expected it? He gently kissed her lips. "Oh, Kate . . ." He slid down and laid his head on her breast. "Are you all right? I tried not to—"

"Shh," she said, hoping to waylay his concern. "I feel wonderful."

He kissed her breast and skimmed the back of his hand over her thigh. "I don't know the right words to tell you how very special you are."

"I didn't know it would be like this, so many feelings rushing together all at once." She combed her fingers through his thick hair. She'd come as close to heaven as a body could on earth.

* * *

The next morning Kate stirred to the smell of fresh coffee. It took her longer than usual to come fully awake. She had slid her legs over the side of the bed and sat up before she realized her mother and the dog weren't in bed.

As she watched her daughter, Mary Louise picked up a cup and stepped over to the fireplace. "Good mornin.' Ya were sleepin' so soundly, I decided to let you be."

"Thanks." Kate put on her robe and went over by the fire. She sat in her chair and sipped the coffee. "It's warm in here. You must've gotten up early." And I went to sleep late, very late. She stared at the fire. Parker's face was so clear in her mind's eye, she felt his caress.

"Not really." Mary Louise sat in her chair and petted Shadow. "The sun's been up for a while."

"What time is it?" Kate hurried to the door and yanked it open. "Why didn't you wake me up?" Shadow trotted outside. She closed the door and made a mad dash for her clothes. This was the first time she'd ever missed being at work on time and sent up a prayer that she hadn't put Charlie in a bind.

"Ya were dreamin,' mumblin' an' carryin' on so, I thought you must need the rest."

"Must've been a nightmare," Kate muttered, pulling on her trousers. "If I do it again, wake me." She could only hope she hadn't said Parker's name or anything else embarrassing. After she finished dressing, she ran the brush through her hair, tied it back with a length of red ribbon, and ran to the hotel kitchen.

Charlie set the coffeepot on the stove and grinned at her. "Slow down. I got the fire goin' in the woodstove, and Bishop just sat down," he said, dishing up the breakfast meal.

"Good. I don't know what happened. I slept like the dead." She set the tray out, added the coffee, plate of sliced bread, and the food and hurried into the dining room. Mr. Bishop was reading a newspaper and didn't look upset. "Good morning."

"Hello, Kate. How do you like our mild weather?" Mr.

Bishop moved the paper aside.

"It's nice," she said, serving his food. "For a while, I thought about buying snowshoes."

"Most of us have them." He glanced at her as she set the bread plate on the table. "If it becomes too bad, you can move into the hotel."

"Thank you, we'll be fine in the cabin."

"Don't be too proud to ask for help. You're the first woman who agreed to stay the winter. When we can't find anyone to help, Charlie cooks and serves." He picked up his fork. "Just keep it in mind."

"I will." She started back to the kitchen. She thought he had a peculiar way of running the hotel. He didn't seem concerned about making a profit, but she was grateful for his consideration. She stopped at one table to straighten the tablecloth and glanced out to the lobby hoping to see Parker. Instead, Bert ambled in and waved to her.

"Mornin', gal." He nodded to Mr. Bishop and took his seat by the woodstove.

While Charlie dished up another plate, Kate took coffee in to Bert and set his place at the table. "How's your place? Did the sheriff get those boards fastened for you?"

"Yes, siree. Did a fine job. He sure did." He sipped the coffee. "Heard ja have a dog now."

She grinned. "That we do." She started to turn away, then changed her mind. "He's a big black dog. Friendly. Someone's worked with him. Do you recall seeing a dog like that around here?"

He rubbed his whiskery chin. "Nope. Ain't been a dog 'round here in over a year. Don't ja want him?"

"Yes . . . yes, I do. I just wanted to make sure we hadn't taken in someone else's animal." Each time Shadow returned, she was glad to see him. But one of these days he'll keep going, she thought, and I'll miss him. After Bert and Mr. Bishop left, Charlie insisted she eat.

Parker walked into the kitchen and over to Kate's side. "Good morning. Am I too late to eat?" He smiled at her. She had left her hair down, and she was almost as pretty as she had been the night before.

She was sitting at the kitchen table picking at her food. At the sound of his voice, her pulse fluttered, and she gazed up at him. She hadn't expected the strange sense of excitement that spread through her. ''Hello.''

''That looks goods. I'm starved.''

Charlie grabbed a plate. ''Just in time. I was about to dump everything in the pan for the dog.''

''Thanks.'' Parker gave her shoulder a gentle squeeze. ''I don't usually sleep as sound as I did last night.'' Her cheeks turned the nicest shade of peach. As Charlie turned to him, Parker let go of her and reached for the plate. ''Kate, you want to bring your plate in and keep me company?''

She glanced at Charlie. ''All right.'' She hadn't been too hungry before Parker came. Now she didn't think she could swallow a bite, but she wanted to sit with him. She poured him a cup of coffee, refilled her own, and followed him to his table.

He sat down and eyed her plate. ''Lose your appetite?''

She smiled and shrugged. ''Go ahead and eat.'' She tore off a chunk of bread. There were so many questions she wanted to ask him but didn't dare. Peering at him through her lashes, she couldn't help thinking that she better understood what drove women to make fools of themselves over men. She wouldn't, though. Unlike those women, she knew he wouldn't stick around. However, that didn't mean she couldn't enjoy his company while he was there.

''Last night I overhead talk about another robbery.'' He smiled at her. ''I was going to tell you . . . but I got sidetracked.''

At the mention of last evening, her heart pounded, and she smiled with the memory of their lovemaking. From the glimmer in his eyes, he hadn't forgotten, either. She took a sip of coffee and forced her thoughts back to the robbery. ''Where?''

''Gopher Creek.'' For a minute there, her smile had been wicked. He shifted on the chair and picked up a strip of bacon. "Know where that is?"

"No, but there're creeks all through this area. I'll ask Charlie." She scooped up a bite of pan-fried potatoes. "Did you hear how much was stolen? The miner's name?"

He shook his head, swallowed, and met her gaze. "Are you sure you want to go through with this? You could be returning more gold than was taken."

"I'm not about to weigh it out, unless we know exactly how much was stolen." She waved a piece of bread, saying, "If they get too much, they won't complain. If it isn't enough, some is better than nothing." This was beginning to feel as if they were trying to take apart a beaver's dam more than undo a wrong—several wrongs. She jammed the bread into her mouth. Many wrongs. She washed the dry bread down with coffee. "We have to find Hank and stop him. I refuse to spend the next year trying to return gold he keeps stealing."

He wasn't about to argue. "I agree. If we need to go farther than a couple miles, you'll need a horse. But people might wonder why we only go riding after dark." He grinned, hoping she would, too. He finished eating and sat back. "Why don't we go riding today? If we find any mining camps, you can ask about your long-lost father."

She grimaced. "I'm not very good at playacting."

"Remember why we need to find him and practice." He grinned and added, "You can try your story out on me while we're riding."

"You're right." She saluted him with her coffee. "After dinner?"

"I'll talk to Mac. The horses will be saddled and waiting."

She nodded. "You realize I don't know my way around these mountains any better than you do?"

He chuckled. "If we get lost, we'll let your mount lead us back to the livery." He stood up, finished the coffee, and stepped over to her. "I'll see you later." Bracing her chin with his thumb, he bent down and kissed her lips.

His caress was gentle, teasing, and it didn't last nearly

long enough. As she returned his kiss, he straightened up and walked away. Only then did she think to look around and see if anyone had been watching. I might be searching for shadows in the sunlight, she thought, but it'd only take one person to suspect she and Parker were more than friends to start the gossip. She stacked the dirty dishes on the tray and carried it to the kitchen.

Charlie set a large kettle on top of the stove. "There's more coffee in the pot."

"Thanks, but I've had enough." She rinsed out the big pan, poured in hot water from the stove, added some cold, and scraped the bar of hard soap with the old fork until there were enough pieces to make suds.

"What 'bout the sheriff? He leave a'ready?"

"Mm-hm." She took the long-handled spoon and whipped the water until soapsuds covered the top. She set a pail of clean water to the side for rinsing.

While Charlie peeled potatoes, he kept looking over at Kate. "He's not a bad sort. 'Course, him bein' single an' hardly any unmarried ladies under forty here 'bouts, he won't hang 'round long."

She couldn't believe what she'd heard and glanced over her shoulder. As usual, he seemed to be passing the time, rather than making a point, the sly old fox. "What are you saying?"

"Nothin'." He peered at her. "Not a thing."

She shook her head. "Sounded to me like you think if I were interested in him, he would stay." She laughed and hoped it sounded convincing. "He's not the 'staying kind.' And I don't think he came here looking to keep company with a woman. Not here." She scrubbed the plate she was holding.

"Sometimes ya find what ya ain't lookin' fer." He chopped up the potato and dropped the pieces in the kettle. "That's how I got hitched."

"You?" Well, why not? she thought, looking over her shoulder. "When was that?"

He started peeling another potato. "I was a b'hoy 'n

cuttin' up with my chums one night.'' He shook his head, laughing softly. ''That high-faluntin' gent sure didn't appreciate our mischief.''

She picked up a plate and drying towel. ''Why, Charlie, I never would've taken you for a rapscallion.'' When he looked at her, his eyes were bright with mischief, and she laughed with him.

''Anyways, she stepped out a doorway. I almost mowed her down, but she took my arm and walked me back into the bakery as if we was walkin' out together. That gent's man never did catch me.''

''Clever woman.'' She set the plate down on the work table and reached for another. He had fond memories of his late wife. Kate's hand slowed. She'd also have memories—ones of Parker that would bring a smile to her face and maybe even a sparkle to her eyes.

❖ 18 ❖

AFTER LEAVING HER skirt on the bed, Kate hurried to the livery. Parker was just leading two horses out front. "The chestnut's familiar, the other must be yours." It was light brown with a black mane and tail, a handsome animal, she thought, like his owner.

"This's Buckshot. Mac said this sorrel mare's gentle." Parker handed the mare's reins to her. "Her name's Amber."

Kate took the reins, spoke softly to the horse, and held out her hand. "Be patient with me, Amber."

Parker stepped up behind her and reached under her loose jacket. As he closed his hands on her waist, he noticed the pistol in her trouser pocket. She gasped softly, and he rubbed his thumbs on her back. "Want a leg up?"

She grabbed the saddle horn and grinned. "That's not my leg." She tried to ignore the warmth of his hands, but she couldn't. "I should be able to mount her." She put her foot in the stirrup. As she bent her knee to spring up to the saddle, his long fingers gripped her waist, and he lifted her up. She swung her leg over the horse's rump and landed in the saddle.

He checked and adjusted the stirrups for her before he mounted Buckshot. "Which way? East or west?" Those were the only choices, unless they didn't stay on the road.

For today and until he judged her ability to handle a horse, he'd just as soon stay on a traveled path.

"West." Turning Amber, Kate started up the road. Parker came up beside her, and she smiled. She'd forgotten how much she used to enjoy riding. "There're more camps, cities, and towns east and south of here. Wouldn't he feel safer in a more remote area?"

"Depends on what he's doing." He settled his hat more firmly and glanced at her. "Have you seen any wanted posters on him up here? The last I saw was an old one in Dallas." They rode past the farthest point they had walked.

"No. Not since . . . It's been a long time—" She looked over at him. "Do you think—No. He must still be wanted. Don't you think so?" That hadn't occurred to her before.

"Unless he's imprisoned, I'll settle with him—wanted or not." He glanced at her and realized he probably didn't have to worry about her riding skills. "Are you changing your mind?"

"No!" She brought her horse to a halt, and he did, too. "*We will find him.* The poster only brought us grief." The more she thought about Hank, the angrier she became and the more determined she was to face him. Now that she and Parker had joined forces, she felt even more confident.

He nodded and started up the road again. A half mile ahead, he turned onto a path that wound up and around the hill before it started down. He pulled up at the crest. "Do you know who's down there?"

"No idea. We might as well go see."

"Did you ask Charlie about Gopher Creek?"

"Yes, but he didn't know."

He led the way down to the turn off and followed that trail. "If we find a claim, do you know what you're going to say?"

"The simple truth." She smiled. Not all of it, of course, but hopefully enough. They approached the camp and called out. A man of average height with long dark hair and a beard down to the middle of his narrow chest came to the other side of the fire pit and faced them with a rifle.

It wasn't her father; at least she didn't believe it was him.

"What do you folks want?" The man studied each of them and held the rifle as if ready to use it.

Kate edged her mount forward one pace. "I'm looking for my father." She glanced at her hands and back to the man. "He's been missing for years, but I believe he's got a camp somewhere in these mountains. His name's Hank. Hank Turner—taller than you, brown hair and eyes."

The man shook his head. "Sorry, ma'am. Sounds like half the men in the Territory. Good luck to you," he said, and left.

"Thanks." She guided Amber back up the trail and waited for Parker at the path.

He pulled up beside her and stared down the south side of the mountain. "There must be other camps, but we're losing the light."

She nodded and headed back toward town. When they reached the road, they rode side by side. "What did you think of him?"

"I doubt he was hiding anything." He picked up the pace. The sun seemed to suddenly drop out of sight in the late afternoon.

"He was more pleasant than some of the miners will be."

He grinned at her. "At least he didn't point that old rifle at us."

"I've got my pistol. And I won't hesitate to use it."

"I felt it. I'm armed, too, but this badge should make anyone think twice before firing at us."

"Unless we run into someone who's hiding from the law." Parker slowed Buckshot down, but Amber was heading back to her stall and meant to get back first. Kate shortened the reins and forced the mare to halt. She patted the horse's neck. "Good girl."

Parker caught up with her and gave her an approving nod. She would be fine. "Want to try again tomorrow?"

She gave him a determined look. "As long as the weather holds." They returned to town near sundown.

Mac came out of the livery and took Amber's reins. "You have a nice ride?"

Parker watched Kate dismount and smiled appreciatively. He couldn't remember enjoying another woman's company as much as he did hers.

Kate patted the mare's neck. She hadn't wanted to sell their horse, but the old wagon had barely made the trip, and she didn't have money to waste stabling the horse. "She's a good mount." She wouldn't mind purchasing the mare. But her first concern must be a house. After that, when she had the funds, she would consider a horse. "I'd like to ride her next time, if you don't mind." She idly rubbed her backside, but it was her inner thighs that felt tender. She glanced at Parker and back to Mac.

"Sure thing, Kate. She's a real sweetheart." Mac led the mare into the livery.

Parker grinned at her. "Think you'll work the stiffness out of your legs by tomorrow?"

"Of course." A hot bath sounded wonderful, but there wasn't time now. She'd have to wait until after supper. She looked into the livery, making sure Mac hadn't come back outside. "You didn't tell me what you thought of my story. Did he believe me?"

"He seemed to, but I don't think anyone would argue with you, even if they didn't agree." Parker smiled. "It was simple and true. Don't worry. You were fine." She was a natural, but he didn't think she would appreciate that compliment.

"Thanks." She smiled and stepped back. "I'll see you later. It's time to light the lamps." She walked slowly, deliberately, hoping he wasn't watching her or, more precisely, the way she walked. Lordy, her legs were stiff.

A storm left several inches of snow on the ground during the next twelve days, and Kate went riding with Parker four more times. The results were the same. The men either didn't know Hank or didn't trust her enough to tell her. They rode farther each time, and her patience was about at its limit. They had covered as much territory as possible each afternoon, but they hadn't made any progress. She was beginning to feel like shooting her father on sight—when they found him.

Kate was serving dinner to Mr. Bishop when Mr. Pitt came in and sat at a table near the woodstove. She brought him a fresh cup of coffee. "It's good to see you. How've you been?"

Mr. Pitt shrugged, then shook his head. "Actually, not very well, Miss Miller. I came to speak to the new sheriff and have a good dinner. Since there isn't a sheriff's office, would you be kind enough to point him out for me later?"

"Of course. He should be in soon. His name is Smith. Parker Smith." She'd never seen Mr. Pitt so upset, but she couldn't bring herself to pry into his business. He was so proper, not like the other miners she could tease. "We have venison stew, biscuits, and molasses pie."

He smiled. "That sounds delicious, my dear. I do wish I had Mr. Daw's talent for cooking."

She chuckled. "Wish I did, too. I'll get your dinner." She hurried to the kitchen. "Charlie, Mr. Pitt's here. He seems a bit out of sorts. Why don't you visit with him a while. I can dish out the stew."

"Mebe I will." Charlie dished out a generous portion, set the plate on the worktable, and ladled a smaller one on the next plate.

Kate set the dinners on the tray and added biscuits. "I'll carry it out. Go sit down, give your feet a rest." Since he rarely left town to see any of his friends, she hoped Charlie'd enjoy the visit as much as Mr. Pitt. After she served their food, she kept busy. Mr. Bishop left, and she washed up the dirty dishes. As she was putting them away, she heard Parker in the dining room and took his meal to him.

He smiled at her. Each day it became more difficult to keep a respectable distance from her, when they were with others. The town was so small, it was more like a big family, and he didn't want to cause her any embarrassment. "Thanks for keeping it warm. Why don't you join us? Mr.

Pitt was telling us that he believes he's been robbed."

Oh, no, she thought, not dear sweet Mr. Pitt. "I'll get my coffee."

"Why don'tcha bring the pot with ya?" Charlie called out.

"Sure thing." She returned with the pot and her cup. After she refilled their cups, she sat down by Parker. "When did this happen, Mr. Pitt?"

"I'm not quite certain." Mr. Pitt glanced around the table. "You see, I've been working a ways from my tent. Two days ago I noticed that a few things were out of place." He shook his head. "However, I haven't seen anyone around my claim."

With a quick glance at Kate, Parker asked, "What time of day was this?"

"Late afternoon. Does that make a difference, Sheriff?"

"No. Just wondered." Parker stuck his fork into a chunk of venison. "How much gold was taken?"

Mr. Pitt glanced around, then said quietly, "Three good-sized nuggets," he said, holding up his thumb and indicating the nail. "Enough to see me through the winter."

Parker nodded. "I'll see what I can do, Mr. Pitt. Can't promise anything, but I'll try."

"Thank you, sir. That's all anyone can ask."

Kate waited until Mr. Pitt left and Charlie returned to the kitchen before she spoke to Parker. "Mr. Pitt keeps his camp neat and clean, everything in its place. It won't be easy slipping the nuggets into his tent, where he'll believe he could've misplaced them."

"He's probably a light sleeper, too. We'd better not try sneaking it in at night. We can pay him a call. I'll get him to show me where's he's working the claim and give you the chance to hide it."

"All right. But we'll never find Hank by making these short trips." She gazed at Parker over the rim of her cup. "If I can get away for a few days, would you go with me? I want to get this over with before we're snowed in here."

He stared into her eyes. She wasn't teasing. "Don't you

want to think that idea through, say overnight?''

''I won't change my mind. Don't you see? It's the only way. His camp might be miles from here.'' She held his gaze, willing him to agree.

Traveling alone with her just might be his undoing, he thought. But damn, he wasn't about to turn her down. ''When do you want to leave?'' After years of tracking Turner on his own, he would probably find him in a day or two, now that he'd be traveling with Kate.

''I'll let you know tonight.''

Kate unpacked the dome-top trunk and piled everything on the bed. When she took out the last dress, she found only half the bags that had been there the last time. ''Mamma—'' She glared at her mother's back. ''Where's the rest of the gold?''

Mary Louise kept the rocking chair in motion. ''It's safe, deah. Don't ya worry.'' She beamed at Shadow, as if they shared a secret.

Kate took several deep, calming breaths before she went over and sat across from her mother. ''Where are the bags?''

Mary Louise held up her new dress. ''Don't the buttons look pretty?''

Lovely, Kate thought, wondering how her mother could even think about wearing the dress. ''The gold?''

''It's put away.'' Mary Louise started sewing the last button on the dress. ''In a safe place.''

''Mamma, it isn't ours. It isn't Hank's, either. Think of those poor men he stole it from. It was not only wrong, it was against the law.''

''I told ya, deah. Mr. Turner didn't steal it.'' Mary Louise looked straight at her daughter. ''The first time he tried to give me money, I said, 'I won't take ill-gotten money.' And he vowed he would never give me money he hadn't earned himself.''

Kate buried one hand in the folds of her skirt and made a fist. She'd grown up with her mother's fanciful view of the world, but she had always believed that it was a kind of game. After she confronted Hank, she would have to decide what to do about her mother. "Mamma, I'm going to find Hank. Maybe a marshal or sheriff or a judge will make him return the gold."

Mary Louise stopped rocking. "Ya can't go off on your own. Besides, it'd be like lookin' for a tick in a pack of hounds." She stuck her needle in the pincushion and closed her sewing box.

Kate leaned forward with her hands clasped over her knees. "If you can get a message to him, please help me. He—I need to talk to him."

"I don't know where he's at. How can I get word to him?" Mary Louise shook her head. "If you want to move away from here, we can. And ya can buy a little house and a buggy, too. Wouldn't you like that?" She patted Shadow's head. "Do ya think he'd mind livin' in town?"

Oh, Lord, help her, Kate pleaded, she's deranged. "I'll be leaving with Parker. Hank can't be too far away. We'll find him."

"Katherine Anne Turner! Ya will not take off with him." Mary Louise dabbed her brow with her handkerchief. "A lady simply does not travel alone with a gentleman, even if he is the sheriff."

"You're worried about propriety?" Kate laughed so she wouldn't cry. "You aren't suggesting I marry him so it would look right, are you?" She shivered. Their conversation had gone from bad to ridiculous.

"I most certainly was not. However, since you mentioned it . . ." Mary Louise walked over by the bed and put her sewing box back on the chest of drawers. "He wouldn't be a bad catch. He's quite handsome, and I do b'lieve he's interested in ya."

Kate struggled not to burst out laughing. Oh, he was interested and so was she—but not in the way her mother thought. She went over to the trunk and started setting the canvas bags on the floor. "If you need anything while I'm gone, put it on account at the general store. Mrs. Goody will understand, and I'll settle with her when I get back.''

Mary Louise sat on the edge of the bed, watching her daughter. ''Whatever are ya gonna tell Mr. Daws and Mr. Bishop?''

''The truth.'' Kate reached for a pile of clothes on the bed. Her mother was near tears. As upset as she was with her, she didn't want her crying. ''Don't worry, Mamma, I won't mention the gold. They'll think I'm trying to find my long-lost father. Parker's the sheriff. No one will think twice about it.''

''You're a good girl, Kate.'' Mary Louise handed two blankets to her daughter. ''Please . . . don't do this.''

Kate closed the trunk. ''I have to, Mamma. This is the only way I know to put this behind me. If you can help, I'd appreciate it.'' She set the blankets aside. She'd need to take those.

''He's never told me where he stays.''

Kate believed her. It would've made it so much easier if her mother could've helped, but she hadn't counted on it. She unfolded one blanket, set the canvas bags on it, and rolled it up. Before she left for work, she turned to her mother. ''I'll speak to Charlie about your meals.''

Mary Louise was still sitting on the side of the bed, her brows drawn together. ''Oh . . . thank ya, deah. I'm sure it'll be fine.''

Kate went to the hotel, glad to be out of the cabin for a while but not really looking forward to telling Charlie and Mr. Bishop about her trip. When Parker came into the dining room, she almost hugged him. He really was handsome, and he made her feel softer, more ladylike than she ever had before. Even more important, he understood and shared her need to set things aright. He'd be so easy to love, she thought, too easy. She waited until he was eating dessert to sit down next to him. ''Do you mind if we leave tomorrow?''

He sat back with his hand resting on the back of her chair. ''Can you be ready by then?'' He wouldn't believe she was leaving with him until they rode out of town. His only fear was seeing the pain in her eyes after it was all over.

"Yes, but I need saddlebags, and I have to get a few things at the general store in the morning." He slid his hand to the back of her neck, and her heart beat double time.

"We'll need a packhorse to carry the supplies. It would be foolish to head out this time of year without food and gear." He sipped the last of his coffee. "How about the next day? It'll give us time to pack, and your mother's going to need a supply of firewood."

Once she made up her mind, she usually put her plans into action. But he was right. "Okay."

"Have you told Charlie or Mr. Bishop, yet?" He rubbed his knuckles over the back of her satin soft neck. This trip was going to play havoc with his willpower.

She lowered her head, giving him greater access. "I wanted to know when we'd be leaving. I'd better see if Mr. Bishop's retired for the night." She pressed her hand on his muscled thigh. "Be right back."

He slid his hand down her arm and clasped her hand. "Want me to go with you?"

"Thanks, but I'll be fine." She kissed the back of his hand and went directly to Mr. Bishop's office. She had only knocked twice when he opened the door. "I need to talk with you for a minute."

Mr. Bishop opened the door and stepped over to his desk. "Please, come in."

She stepped inside his cluttered office. "I wouldn't disturb you, but this is important."

"It must be. Won't you sit down?"

She shook her head. "I need to leave for a couple weeks to find my father." She told him the same story she had the miners and hoped he wouldn't ask too many questions. "We're planning to leave day after tomorrow."

"Will your mother be going with you?"

"No. The sheriff said he would help me." He was sympathetic, but there was one thing she hadn't thought about. Would he allow her mother to stay in the cabin? "Would it be easier for you if I quit?'' When she faced Hank, she didn't want her mother there, but she'd take her if that was her only other choice.

''No, certainly not.'' He smiled at her. ''You find your father. Your position will be here for you when you return.''

She didn't realize she'd been holding her breath until she let it out. ''Thank you, Mr. Bishop.'' She smiled and started back to the dining room.

''Kate,'' he said, opening a small metal box. ''You'll need your wages.'' He held out the money.

She'd forgotten all about her wages and felt a twinge of guilt. ''I'll only take half. You keep the rest for rent on the cabin while I'm gone.''

''It's not for rent. I'll hold on to this for you. Good luck with your search.''

She thanked him, tucked the money in her pocket, and went to the dining room. The most difficult hurdle had been crossed. Now for Charlie, she thought. She found him sitting at the table with Parker. She sat down by Parker and looked at Charlie. ''Has he told you?''

Charlie looked at Parker. ''What's goin' on?'' He glanced from him to Kate and back, then began to smile.

Kate gazed at Parker, then spoke up. She didn't want him explaining her problem. ''We're going to find my father. I know my leaving isn't fair to you, but I think he's here in the territory. I have to find him.''

Charlie slumped back in his chair. ''Sure ya do, Kate. When're ya leavin'?''

''Day after next,'' Parker said. ''After we get the gear packed and firewood chopped for Mrs. Miller.'' Somewhere along the way, she seemed to have become the one spearheading this venture and hoped he wouldn't regret it.

''Ya'll have to have breakfast that mornin,' so don't ride out at sunup.'' Charlie grinned. ''Cain't go off on empty bellies.''

19

KATE MADE THE last trip to the cabin. She and Parker had eaten breakfast, and the horses were ready. Her mother was bundled up outside watching Shadow play with a stick. ''We're going now. There should be enough wood to last until I get back. I opened an account with Mrs. Goody for you, and she said you're to have your dinners with Miss Lucy. She's looking forward to your visits.''

''I was plannin' on seein' her later.'' Mary Louise glanced at Kate as she watched the dog. ''Ya know, deah, I think you should take the dog with you. He'd be good protection. No one could sneak up on ya at night.''

Shadow brought the stick to Kate. She smiled. ''That's why I'm glad he'll be here with you. If you should have any trouble, he'll protect you, and he'll raise enough ruckus to bring Charlie.'' She crouched down in the snow, and Shadow pushed the damp stick in her face. ''You be a good boy.'' She gave him a hug and whispered. ''And you better be here when I get back.'' She went over to her mother and put her arms around her. ''Take care, Mamma. I'll be back as soon as I can.'' Unexpected tears sprang to her eyes and coursed down her cheeks. She hadn't cried in years and held on to her mother until she'd wiped off her cheeks.

Mary Louise smiled at her daughter and linked arms with

her. ''This's somethin' ya feel ya must do. I'm glad ya will be seein' him after all these years.'' She started walking down the path and drew Kate along.

''You are?'' Kate couldn't help wondering what her mother was up to now.

''Ye-as, deah.''

Kate narrowed her gaze on her mother. ''You sound sure that we'll find him. What changed your mind?''

Mary Louise shrugged. ''I've thought it over. You're such a willful girl, you'll succeed. Ya always do,'' she said with a touch of sadness in her voice. ''Just keep warm.''

Kate was more than mildly surprised that her mother was seeing her off, showing her approval of the trip. As they came to the road with the dog at her side, she saw almost everyone in town milling around in front of the livery. Of course, by now everyone in town knew they were leaving, but she hadn't imagined they would watch her and Parker leave.

''See, deah? They want to wish ya well, too, and a safe return.'' Mary Louise patted her daughter's arm as they approached Parker. ''It's a fine mornin' for travelin', Mr. Smith.''

Parker smiled at her. ''Yes, ma'am.'' Kate looked a bit overwhelmed by all the fuss. He met her gaze. ''Is Shadow going with us?''

Kate dropped down and hugged the dog. ''Take good care of her,'' she whispered to Shadow. She looked at Parker and stood up. ''He's needed here.''

''Ready, then?''

She nodded and kissed her mother's soft cheek. She suddenly realized she'd been about to abandon her mother and her friends, much the way Hank had them, and she felt she had to reassure her mother. ''I'll be back in two weeks, whether I find him or not.''

Mary Louise shook her head. ''No. Ya do what ya have to, deah. I know ya won't forget me.'' She kissed her and stepped back near Miss Lucy.

Charlie had been watching Kate closely and stepped forward. ''Ya better git b'fore I put ya back to work.''

Parker took Kate's arm. ''Oh, no, you don't.'' He gave her a gentle squeeze, one he hoped was reassuring, and held Amber's bridle, while Kate mounted.

All she wanted to do at that moment was leave. Long good-byes were so difficult. She smiled at Mac and Mrs. Goody, Earl, old Bert, Mr. Ralston, her mother and Miss Lucy, even Mr. Bishop. Parked had mounted and was holding the leading rein for the packhorse. ''Good-bye.'' She turned her horse and waited for him.

Parker tipped his hat. ''Ralston has the key to the only jail cell, so I guess it's up to him to watch over things while I'm gone.''

''Hey, Sheriff,'' Bert called out. ''Yer wearin' yer badge. That mean yer comin' back?''

Parker glanced down at his coat, then at Bert. ''Guess it does. You take care now.'' He pressed his heel to Buckshot's side, and they rode out of town. A half mile down the road, he looked at her. ''Glad we're finally on our way?''

''I thought we'd never leave. Did you know everyone would see us off?'' She was feeling better, now they were alone.

He chuckled. ''Not until they started showing up.''

''What you said to Bert. Did you mean it? You're coming back when we're done?'' She wasn't sure what she wanted to hear. If he did return with her, it wouldn't mean he was interested in her, only his obligation to the town. She simply must keep her mind on what they were about, she told herself.

''Yes. I don't know for how long, but I'll return with you.'' When she smiled, he knew he had to find out if there might be a chance for them after this was over.

She held up her hand and slowed Amber. ''There's the trail to Mr. Pitt's camp.'' She led the way and dismounted at the edge of his camp.

Parker looped the reins around a sturdy branch and stood

at Kate's side. "Anyone could've walked in here and left without being seen."

She called out for Mr. Pitt. When he didn't answer, she motioned to Parker. "Try down near the creek. I'll put the nuggets in his tent." As soon as she heard him calling Mr. Pitt, she peeked in the tent. After glancing over her shoulder, she stepped inside. There wasn't time to be too picky, she decided, and tossed the three nuggets under his cot. She hoped when he found them, he'd think they'd rolled under there. She stepped outside and met Parker coming back from the creek.

He took her arm and smiled. "You all right?"

Her heart was hammering, but she grinned at him. "Now I am. Did you find him?"

"He wasn't too happy to know I'd been calling him and he hadn't heard me." Parker put his arm around her shoulders. "We'd better be going." They walked back to their horses. "Where did you hide the nuggets?"

"Under his cot." She mounted Amber. "He's so neat, he'll find them the next time he cleans. Did you tell him we were together?"

"No. Didn't seem to be any reason."

She grinned. "Good." They went back to the main road and turned west. She hoped dear, sweet Mr. Pitt wouldn't feel he had to tell everyone he'd really misplaced the nuggets. A while later they rode past the turnoff to Thaddeus's cave, and she glanced north. She wished she'd had time to tell him about Parker and finding the gold, but everything had come together at once. When they returned, she wanted Parker to meet him.

"I heard some interesting news last night in the saloon. Pan Handle took me aside and told me his thief was struck with a guilty conscience and returned the gold." He chuckled. "In fact, the guilty fellow returned more gold than he'd stolen."

She laughed, too. "Well, good for Pan Handle. Was he celebrating?"

"Carefully. Said he wasn't looking to be robbed again."

They crossed the western rise and started down into the valley. He glanced at her. "Missoula isn't far. We can ask there about Gopher Creek."

The landscape was white and unsullied as far as she could see. "Since you're a sheriff, think the sheriff there would let you have a look at his wanted posters?" She now followed his lead. With snow covering the ground, she had to trust Parker's ability to stay on the road. She'd heard the weather was unpredictable in the western territory and could only hope it remained clear.

"I don't know why he wouldn't." It was midday when they rode into Missoula. He stopped in front of a wood-framed house with a sign boasting hot meals cheap. "Hungry?"

"Why don't we wait until we're done here? Charlie packed dinner. We can eat by the river." She arched her back. "It'll feel good to walk around. I can go to some of the stores, while you see the sheriff."

He grinned. "Do you always organize everything so easily?"

She glared at him, then shrugged. Wonderful, she thought, I'm ready to snap at him, and we've only been gone a few hours. "Guess I do—out of habit." Grinning, she asked, "Want me to ask for Hank at a few saloons?"

"Your idea was best." They continued on to the center of town. "I'll meet you here. It shouldn't take me more than an hour."

She looked up and down the street before she dismounted. After riding all morning without seeing as much as a hoofprint in the snow, it was comforting to see the many tracks in town. "I'll start at one end and work my way to the other side." She secured the reins to the hitching post. "Good luck."

He tied the reins to the post and put her saddlebags, with the gold stashed in the bottom of each, over his shoulder. "You, too." He headed for the sheriff's office.

She walked into the dry-goods store and went straight to the counter. The middle-aged woman gave her a weary look. She introduced herself and told the woman her story about searching for her father. It was no longer the story it had first been, she realized.

The woman shook her head. ''I'm sorry, but I can't help you. Have you tried the livery or the bank?''

The last idea sent a shiver down Kate's back. ''No, but I will. Thank you.'' She certainly hoped Hank wasn't wanted for another bank robbery. Her backside was sore, her legs stiff, and her temper was rising. She worked her way up the street, stopping in two more stores and a gun shop before she came to the Missoula Bank. It was a small building and inside on one wall were three wanted posters. She read each one and sighed when she didn't find Hank's name or picture. The manager was pleasant, but he didn't know Hank Turner, either.

She caught a glimpse of Parker leaving the sheriff's office and going into a saloon. Feeling as if she couldn't afford to ignore any business, except for the billiard hall and saloons, she spoke to everyone she could. A while later she met Parker at the hitching post. ''I see you did some shopping.''

''Ran into a miner who wanted to sell his tent. It'll come in handy if we get more snow.''

''We won't get anymore. Don't even think about it.''

''If you say so.'' He chuckled. ''Do you want to ride or walk to the river?''

''Walk.'' She grinned. ''We'll probably be riding the rest of the afternoon.''

''Yes, ma'am.'' He tipped his hat to her. ''I'm not surprised you're a bit stiff. You're used to spending the day on your feet, not . . . in a saddle.'' He had the distinct feeling she hadn't really understood how tedious and uncomfortable this journey would be. ''Did anyone know Turner?''

She untied Amber's reins, then Buckshot's. ''If they did, they didn't tell me.''

He tossed her saddlebags over his saddle and secured the tent. ''Lead on.''

"There were wanted posters for bank robbers in the bank, but he wasn't on them." She looked at Parker, really looked at him. She didn't think she'd ever known a man with a better nature. He seemed to handle everything in stride. "What did the sheriff say?"

They stopped near the riverbank and unpacked their dinner. "He was nice enough, he just couldn't help us. He said he'd never seen a poster for Turner." He brushed snow off a log and sat down.

She handed him a sandwich and sat by him. "I wonder how long there's been a sheriff here. We might find his poster in a more established town." She unwrapped the thick meat sandwiches.

"You're probably right." He set it down, filled their cups with cold coffee from the jug Charlie had tucked in with the food, and handed her one. "Too bad there aren't any telegraph lines up here."

"That's another reason why it's a good place for him. If he's smart enough to steal so many miles from where he's hiding, he'll be safe." She ate a bite, mulling over what to do next.

He rested his elbows on his knees and watched her out of the corner of his eye. She was so intent on the search, she was frowning. "LoLo's south of here," he said, hoping to keep her spirits up. "We've only started. I think we should try there next. It's just a couple hours away, and Hamilton's another day's ride. Unfortunately, the rich mines are east of here."

She stared into her cup. "So why isn't he robbing those mines? The men he's robbed don't even have that much gold."

He nodded. "Or we could go north. But it's mostly Indian territory, isn't it?"

"Thaddeus said there're reservations north of here, but I also heard the Flathead Indians lived somewhere around this valley."

He raised one brow. "You don't seem concerned about them."

"They're peaceful, or so they say. But I've never even been to Missoula before." She smiled. They were really going to find Hank. She could feel it. Until then, it had seemed they were on a long afternoon outing. He ran his long fingers through his hair. For one brief moment she imagined him brushing her hair back and trembled as if he had touched her. "You've been tracking Hank for a long time. What parts of the country have you seen?"

"It seems like I've seen a good part of the country west of the Missipp—Kansas—heard about some bank holdups there—Colorado, Wyoming and Utah territories, Nevada, and some of the mines in California." He finished his sandwich and washed it down with coffee.

He'd probably seen as much of the country as any stagecoach driver, she thought. "Didn't you ever get tired of it? Want to settle in one of those towns and forget all about him?" The sunlight cast a golden shimmer in his hair she hadn't noticed before. She sat up and brushed a crumb off her sleeve.

"I worked and stayed in different places for as long as three or four months." He stood up and held out his hand to her. "We'd better start down to LoLo. We'll have to camp a few miles south of there to reach Hamilton by tomorrow evening."

She took his hand and came to her feet, toe-to-toe with him. She felt his hand on her arm, steadying her, and she gazed into his eyes. "Thanks. I should've eaten standing up." She could've spent the afternoon in his arms, if they'd had the time. They didn't, so she stepped back and put the other two sandwiches back in the canvas bag on the packhorse. "Ready?" She moved over to Amber and put her foot in the stirrup.

He came up behind her, circled her waist with his hands, and lifted her up. They couldn't linger there, but they wouldn't be riding all night. Knowing he'd spend the night next to her made it easier for him to let go of her. He mounted and headed for the road leading south within sight of the Bitterroot River.

She still felt the strength of his hands as they rode toward LoLo. He set a pace the animals could keep but made it hard to hold a conversation. The Bitterroot Mountains were across the river in the distance. The valley was immense, and she supposed it would be green and lush come spring. There were few farms, and only one wagon passed them on the road before they reached LoLo. It was smaller than Missoula, but it boasted the Gallatin Valley Female Seminary. They pulled up in front of the general store. She looked at Parker. "This isn't what I expected. Unless he's pretending to be respectable, where would he be hiding out?"

He took off his hat, wiped his sleeve across his forehead, and put his hat back on. "You're probably right, but we're here. You look in the store, and I'll have a beer at the saloon."

As she dismounted, she glared at him. "Beer sounds good," she said, grinning. "Wanna trade?"

"No, ma'am." He dismounted and tied the reins to the post. "I'm incorruptible." He burst out laughing and took her hand. "I'll buy you a beer at Ralston's when we get back if you still want to visit a saloon."

She squeezed his hand. "I won't let you forget." She walked up the steps in front of the store. "I'll be waiting out here for you."

"I'll drink fast."

She grinned, shaking her head, and went inside the store. It was half the size of the Goodys' store and had a stock of farm tools the Goodys' didn't need to carry. The only other person there was the man behind the counter leering at her. She kept her right hand at her side and stepped closer to the counter.

He smirked, spit, and stood up. "How kin I hep you?"

"I'm looking for my father." She repeated the same story even though the man seemed not to be listening.

He shook his head. "Less'n you have a pi'ture, I cain't hep you. I see light-headed men, dark-headed men,'n those betwixt."

She was actually relieved. "Thank you, anyway." As she left, she fought the urge to run. Once she was outside, she went over to Amber and checked the cinch strap, in case the man was watching. Kate looked up and down the road and felt foolish. She couldn't very well sit on the steps now, she thought, and walked down the road to the livery and feed, on the other side of the saloon. A few minutes later she walked back to the saloon and paused in the doorway. The bartender and Parker were the only ones there.

Parker had heard approaching footsteps and glanced at the doorway. She looked ready to enter, and he knew something had upset her. He smiled at her and took another drink of the beer. "Thanks." He walked out the door, offered her his arm, and walked back to their horses. When she clung to him, he hugged her hand to his side. "What happened?"

"Nothing. I just didn't like the man in the general store." She gazed at Parker and sighed. "I'm just a bit tired."

"Too tired to ride for another hour or so?"

She laughed. "No. A ride sounds nice." She didn't want to spend the night there. When he lifted her up to the saddle, she grinned, tempted to ask him if he'd like to ride double. "How far is Hamilton?"

"Day's ride. We can camp by the river tonight." He mounted Buckshot, and they continued south. When it began growing dark, he turned toward the river and stopped in a sheltered area. "What do you think?" She was tired, and he wondered if she would want to keep searching after another day or two of hard riding.

"Perfect. There's forage for the horses, firewood, and fresh water." She helped him set up the tent, got a fire going, and started the coffee, while he cut several low branches from a cottonwood tree to spread under their bedrolls. They didn't talk until it was dark, and they sat by the fire. "I forgot to ask. Did you learn anything from the bartender?" He had to be tired, but he sure didn't look the way she felt.

"He said Turner could've been through there, but he

didn't recognize the name. Seems his saloon is the last one for a while for those traveling to the Idaho Territory by way of the LoLo Pass. It's well traveled, and it's not as mountainous as the northern Coeur d'Alene Trail."

She sipped the cold water in her cup. "I don't think Hank's around here, either, but what's on the other side of the pass?"

"Mines." He finished his sandwich and dug in the canvas bag for the cake Charlie had packed.

"Isn't that too far away?" She yawned and arched her back. "It doesn't make sense that Hank would ride over the Bitterroot to rob a few miners. Maybe he is up north after all."

"This area doesn't feel right." He gave up on the cake and poured another cup of coffee. "Besides, if Turner knows the hills, he might be working both territories." He took a drink of coffee. "Think it over tonight. It might be worth the ride." She weaved slightly with half closed eyes. "Let's turn in for the night. You'll sleep better stretched out."

She smiled at him and nodded. "Sounds wonderful, if I can move." Suddenly he was behind her with his arms around her, and she was lifted to her feet. It didn't feel real. Maybe she was already asleep.

He loosened his grasp on her. She turned in his arms and wrapped hers around him, melting into him. Her breathing was soft. She snuggled on his chest, and her arms slipped to his waist. "Kate—" She had fallen asleep.

"Mm—"

He put his free arm behind her knees and picked her up. She had spread out their bedrolls on the branches, and he laid her down on the one with the little pillow. After he tucked the blanket around her, he bent down and kissed her lips. "Sleep well, my Kate."

Without opening her eyes, she held on to his hand and rubbed it on her cheek. "Aren't you coming to bed?"

He chuckled. "Soon as I check the fire." He pressed a kiss to the back of her hand and stood up. If she were this tired every night, it would be easier for him to keep from making love to her again. He had never used women, and he wouldn't start with her. She meant too much to him.

"Parker, curl up with me. It's cold."

❖ 20 ❖

KATE CAME AWAKE slowly. She was warm and curled around Parker, her arm holding him close. What a wonderful way to wake up. She smiled and snuggled against his back.

He lay there suffering her sweet torment. She had awakened him long before sunup, but it hadn't taken him long to realize she had been asleep. She wasn't now, though. He covered her hand, drew it up to his chest, and rolled onto his back. She looked like an angel with her tousled hair, dreamy gaze that slowly roamed the length of him, and lips parted as if waiting to be kissed. "Morning. I'm glad you're feeling better."

She nuzzled his neck and tipped him onto his back. "Much." She levered her chest over his, her pulse throbbing, and pressed a slow, probing kiss to his mouth. Leaning over him, taking the lead was a heady feeling. She brought her knee up over his thigh, but he pushed it back down with his hand. She knew he wanted her as much as she wanted him. She rolled to her side and ran her thumb over his reddened lips. "Can't we love in the daylight?"

He burst out laughing and felt a bit of relief from the tension racking his body. Her innocence was not only refreshing, it was exciting. "Of course we can, but not now." He pressed her palm to his lips. "We'll need to get going.

We never did talk about which way we were heading.'' He grinned and sat up. ''I don't suppose you've had time to give it any thought.''

''Unh-unh.'' She sat up, too. ''Why would he have gone to Hamilton if there aren't any mines around there?''

''Maybe he passed through?'' He got to his knees and went outside.

Reluctantly she left the warmth of the tent and stepped into the frosty morning air. ''Do you really think Hank may have gone through Hamilton?'' It was a slim chance, but what else did they have? She quickly gathered twigs and got a fire started.

He filled the coffeepot with river water, added coffee, and put it on the fire. ''It's up to you. If we had a sketch of Turner, it would help.''

''I can't draw.'' She held her hands out to the fire. ''We'll try Hamilton.''

''That's what I like,'' he said, pulling her into his embrace, ''a woman of action.'' As his mouth tasted hers, he pressed his wrist on the back of her neck and played with her soft hair. The taste of her sent a surge of desire through him, and he very nearly surrendered.

She groaned and held on to him, as if he might disappear. She knew she shouldn't feel this overpowering need for him, but she did. She molded herself to him, wanting him inside of her. His hand moved down her spine, then both his hands were on her waist holding her apart from him. It took her a moment to understand what he was doing, and she sighed. ''Hank?''

He nodded. ''I have to find him. I've been after him for too many years to pass up any chance of facing him.''

''I understand. I'll start packing.'' When they found Hank, she'd have first crack at him. Right now, she thought, shooting was too good for him.

After a cold breakfast of bread and meat washed down with hot coffee, they mounted up and started south. At midday, they ate by the river and rested the horses. Late that afternoon they rode into Hamilton. She dismounted and looked over the saddle at Parker. "I'll try this general store first." As she tied the reins, she noticed a small sign in the general store window. GUNSMITH. Her heart started pounding. "Why don't you have a beer?"

He smirked with one brow arched. "Do I have to drink all of it?"

She chuckled.

He motioned to a clapboard house across the street. "The sign says 'Hot Meals.' I think we deserve a good warm supper."

"It doesn't say good." She was still grinning. "Okay. I'll meet you here."

"You'd better." He secured the reins, put her saddlebags over his shoulder, and headed for the saloon.

She took a deep breath and walked into the general store. The familiar smells of coffee, kerosene, and wood smoke were strong. As she meandered to the counter, she racked her memory for what Hank had once said about pistols. It was important, if only she could remember. She stopped at the end of the counter, and the tall, rangy man behind it. "Are you the gunsmith?"

"Yes, ma'am. What can I do for you?"

She smiled at him, then looked down at the glass case. She remembered. Hank said he'd never trust any pistol but a Colt '49. "Do you have a Colt '49?"

He shook his head. "I do have a 1873, single-action forty-five. Is it for you?"

She resisted the urge to press her arm against her pocket and her own pistol. "No, but I'm trying to find a man who swears by that pistol. My . . ." Lordy, it was hard to say the word, but she had to to gain his sympathy. "Father. Hank Turner. I was told he'd been through here. I hoped maybe he had needed ammunition or—" She sent him a pleading look. "He got the gold fever. Mamma and I haven't seen him in years."

"Most men don't tell me their names unless they have to leave their guns or pistols for repair." He smiled. "What does he look like? Tall or short, heavy or thin?"

Oh, thank you. "He's taller than I am, brown hair and eyes." She tried not show how very anxious she was to have him confirm he had indeed been in there, but she knew she wasn't succeeding.

"It might've been him. A man came in . . . oh, sometime last summer. I checked the firing pin in his Colt '49, and he was asking about Salmon, in the Idaho Territory." He leveled his gaze on her. "*If* he was your father, it might be worth the trip. Mind you, I can't be sure it was him."

"Oh, thank you. It is definitely worth the ride." Her heart and mind raced. "Where's Salmon? How can I get there?"

"Ma'am, you can't go alone. It's a hard trip down through the pass."

"Down? It's south of here, not north?" That'd put Hank even farther away. Her enthusiasm drained out of her. "I'm not alone. How do I find this pass? And where do I go when I've crossed it?"

"It's pretty much due south. Just follow the road. The Lost Trail Pass'll take you into the Idaho Territory. Salmon's on the river by the same name, a good three, four days from here."

She smiled. "Thank you *very* much." She started for the door and paused. "How's the food across the street?"

"That depends on how hungry you are." He chuckled and added, "But the rooms are clean. Vic don't abide with fleas or ticks."

"Good. Neither do I." She'd brought some money and decided she had better add to their provisions. She left a few minutes later with a smoked ham, a slab of bacon, and a glimmer of hope. She had just packed the food when Parker joined her. "How was the beer?"

He shrugged. "Okay. Let's go eat. I'm starved."

"You'll probably like the food. It's also a boardinghouse. A man named Vic runs it."

"What else did you learn?" He put her hand on his arm and started to cross the road, but an old wagon came barreling toward them. He pulled her back to safety. "That fool's going to kill someone."

Slush and chunks of ice flew out from the wheels, and she glared at the driver. "With any luck, the wagon'll fall apart." They entered the boardinghouse, and she liked the feel of it. The parlor wasn't overly cluttered, it seemed clean, and something smelled delicious. A barrel-chested man greeted them in the front hallway. "Vic?"

"Yes, ma'am. You must o' stopped at the general store."

She nodded.

Parker smiled at her. "Do you have room at your table for two more?"

"Sure do. Rooms, too, if you need 'em."

Without glancing at her, Parker nodded. "We'll take those, too." He was buying himself another night. He wanted her, there wasn't any doubt about that. But when he thought about killing Turner, he knew he couldn't sleep with her before shooting her father.

Once they were seated, she couldn't wait any longer. "Ever heard of Lost Trail Pass?" But the more she thought about it, the more likely it seemed too far away to be where Hank was hiding.

"No one's mentioned it." He studied her a moment, but she seemed lost in thought. "Don't play games, Kate. Tell me."

She was tempted to say, "Later, when we camp for the night," but she didn't really want to wait. She told him what she had learned. "When I saw the gunsmith sign, I remembered Hank's swearing by his old Colt '49. What do you think? Is it worth a two- or three-day ride to check it out?"

"It sure is." He clasped her hand. He felt they were on the right trail.

"We can cover a few more miles before sundown." Watching the gleam in his eyes, she began to think it may not be a waste of time.

"Fort Owen is almost a day behind us, east of where we camped last night. The commanding officer would know if there had been any robberies in the area. He might even know Turner's whereabouts."

She wasn't prepared to face an army officer and admit Hank was a thief. "We'd lose two days. . . . "

"Yes—" He took a closer look at her. She seemed a bit pale, and she definitely didn't sound interested in going back up to the fort. "We don't have to go if you don't want to."

She sighed. "If we don't find him in Salmon, we can come back by the fort." She felt better now. "We can still get a start on the trip after supper."

"We'll travel faster after a couple hot meals and a good night's sleep. I'll stable the horses after supper." He gave her hand a gentle squeeze. "I feel it, Kate. It won't be much longer now."

She nodded. His enthusiasm was catching. "Have you been this close to catching him before?"

"Twice."

Kate mounted Amber early the next morning, and they continued their journey south. Parker seemed to have changed once they decided to go to Salmon. His smile felt as if he didn't quite see her, and his touch was almost careless. She had never seen him so single-minded. As they covered the miles, she had time to think about why she'd come on this long expedition with him—to find Hank.

She had forgotten, for a while, but she must not again, not until it was over. When she glanced at Parker, she saw a hunter on the trail of his prey. She could only hope he wouldn't change his mind about returning to Moose Gulch with her.

Parker set a pace that wouldn't wear out the horses. He had doubted the wisdom of traveling with Kate. However, she was the one who managed to discover a small thread he believed would lead them to Turner. What bothered Parker now was what to do about her when they did meet up with her father. As driven as he was to settle with the man, he did not want to do it in front of her. She certainly wasn't responsible for her father's misdeeds, and she had already paid for his crimes, more than she should have.

Late that afternoon they camped above the tree line by the river. Vic had warned him to store up water for the next day's ride through the pass. They would leave the Bitterroot River and probably not come to the Salmon until the following day. Parker pitched the tent and began unsaddling Buckshot.

Kate started the fire, put on some coffee, and unpacked what they needed. When she went to get their bedrolls, Parker had unsaddled the horses. His coat was over a bush, and he'd rolled up his shirtsleeves. Lordy, he was a fine figure of a man. But he'd been so quiet, she didn't know if she could stand the silence any longer. ''How far do you think we came today?''

He patted the mare's neck. ''Probably twenty-five, maybe thirty miles.'' Her voice was soft, and he didn't have to look at her to know she was watching him. Damn, he'd be glad when this was over, and he felt free to hold her in his arms—if she didn't draw her pistol on him. He went over to Buckshot and raised the near front hoof. ''The next three days won't be any easier than today.''

She untied her bedroll and moved over to his saddle to get his. ''I don't expect it to get any better. I didn't slow you down, did I?''

He smiled and shook his head. ''You haven't complained about anything.'' He lowered the leg and moved to the hind leg to check for stones. ''You can, you know. This isn't a ride in the park.''

His back was still to her, and she smirked. ''No, it's not. I've decided to think of it as an adventure. You've done this before, but I haven't.'' She carried the bedrolls to the tent and started to lay them out but hesitated. Should she place them side by side? This isn't like me, she thought, dropping them on the ground. She marched over to him and planted her hands on her hips. ''I want to know what's wrong. Why you've been so quiet.''

He lowered the horse's leg and faced her. Had he really

thought he could avoid her for the next few days? Her expression made it clear that she wanted answers. "I'd forgotten how direct you can be." No matter how mad she got, he wouldn't let her take off on her own.

"Then tell me why you haven't said anything all day." She narrowed her gaze. "If you're sorry I came along, tell me." One possible answer scared the bejeebers out of her, but she had to know. If he'd changed his mind about her, didn't like her as much as she'd hoped, she would simply have to face that. It was the not knowing that would drive her crazy.

Her pride held her back rigid, but her voice reached out to him, and he couldn't deny her. "It's me." He took her arm and walked her down to the river's edge. "When I face Turner, I can't be distracted by you or my feelings for you. I've waited too long for this."

"What do you think I'll do? Scream and become all hysterical and plead with you not to shoot him?" She made a circle in the dirt with the toe of her boot.

"No. But you can't witness his death. You don't need to carry that memory with you the rest of your life." He hugged her arm to his side.

She gazed at him. "Are you saying you like me, or would even if Hank wasn't my—"

He skimmed his knuckle up her neck and braced her chin with the tip of his first finger. "I can't imagine not knowing you. You're a special lady, and I like you very much." Gazing into her eyes, he brushed his lips across hers. "But you may not care for me after I do what I must." He had come close to admitting he loved her, but that, too, could have become a burden for her.

"I can be as single-minded as you. Believe me, I know what you have to do. I won't hold it against you." She put her arms around his waist and rested her cheek on his chest. "He hasn't been a parent to me since he abandoned us. He's a murderer, robber, and thief. I'm surprised he's escaped the law for this long." She gave him a playful squeeze. "At least I'll have my say first." But Hank wouldn't talk his way out of this, she thought. Not with Parker, and not with her. She wasn't her mother.

He laid his cheek on the top of her head. "You'll have your say." However, he thought it would be impossible for her to care for him after it was over. How could she? And he couldn't blame her.

She tickled his sides and laughed. "So where do I put your bedroll? Can we at least sleep side by side to keep warm?"

He smiled. "That sounds reasonable." And that's all we'll do, he thought, knowing it would severely test his willpower.

Kate followed Parker on the Lost Trail Pass through the Bitterroot mountain range. It wasn't until late afternoon that they finally wound their way down the Idaho Territory side. The day had seemed longer than most, and her backside felt numb. She pulled up beside him and raised the collar on her coat. "Sure is cold here." From the southern to the western horizon, she saw more snow-covered mountains, like ripples in a pond, she thought.

"At least it's dry." He glanced back at the packhorse. "Are you all right? Or do you want to get something from your bag?"

"No. Let's keep going." The snow was deeper on that side of the mountains, and she didn't want to waste any daylight. "Do you still think we're going in the right direction?"

"I do. You getting tired?" He knew he was running on years' worth of pent-up vengeance. She wasn't.

She arched her back, then she noticed the clouds on the western horizon and motion to them. "It may not be dry much longer."

"We can camp in the foothills. Between the trees and the tent, we'll be fine."

She grinned. "I never thought I'd miss that old cabin."

"Are you worried about her?"

"Mamma? No. She's fine. Charlie will check on her, and

she'll have dinner with Miss Lucy every day.'' She laughed. ''She'll be busier with me gone than she usually is.''

He glanced at her. ''Does she know why I'm after Turner?''

''She believes you came along to protect me.'' Kate laughed. ''Mamma knows how well I shoot, but she's old-fashioned and thinks men should defend the women. She doesn't know me very well, does she?''

''I think she knows you better than you realize,'' he said, laughing. Her mother wasn't always too subtle with her hints about the two of them keeping company. But he didn't mind. It had actually worked in his favor more than once.

An hour later the clouds blotted out the sunlight. After they made camp and tended the animals, she fixed supper, and they ate by the light of the fire. ''Think we'll reach Salmon by this time tomorrow?''

''We should. But we'll have to check the area ourselves. If we ask about him, he could easily take off again. I'd rather surprise him.'' He had pictured it so often, he couldn't help wondering if this would be another dead end.

As she chewed the bite of smoked ham, she mulled over what he'd said. ''I could go to the store or the livery, mention my name, and see what happens.''

He shook his head. ''If he doesn't want you to find him, it would only warn him you're looking for him.'' He drank the last of his coffee. ''We can't make any plans until we get to Salmon. Vic said it's a mining town. Gold was discovered there in sixty-six. Let's hope it's larger than Moose Gulch.''

She finished eating and stored their food in the tent. So far they'd been lucky and not had any problems with bears or coyotes. She had heard sounds during the night a couple times, but refused to think about the danger. She shivered. ''It getting awfully cold.''

He grinned. ''That time of year. We've been fortunate. If the weather hadn't held, it would've taken us even longer to get this far.''

He was right, but it was little comfort at the moment.

"I'm turning in. It's too cold to sit out here."

"I'll join you as soon as I shelter the horses." He put out the fire and covered the rest of their firewood with a piece of canvas.

She had just crawled under the blanket on the bedroll near the side of the tent when he came inside. "Your bed-roll is right in front of you."

"Move over. Sleep in the middle. It'll be warmer." His eyes slowly adjusted to the dark tent. He slid in at her side and wrestled with the blankets until he had them tucked around both of them. "Better?"

"Mm-hm." She smiled when he curved his body around hers, and then she snuggled closer. However, when she squirmed her bottom against him, his hand held her still. "I wouldn't mind spending the winter here, like the bears do in caves."

He kissed the back of her neck. "Make me that offer in a couple days." And I won't turn you down, he thought. But he knew she wouldn't, so he treasured the smell of her hair and the feel of her soft, warm body pressing into him. It would be a long night.

❖ 21 ❖

THE NEXT MORNING Kate woke up in about the same position she'd gone to sleep in, and Parker's hand hadn't moved, either. It was still resting on her hip. It was getting light out. She eased onto her back, and when his cheek slipped to her shoulder and his hand moved to her right hip, she had never felt so cherished. He looked sweet and slept so peacefully, she didn't want to wake him. As she watched him, she realized she could see his breath in the air.

She closed her eyes and tried to sleep, but she was wide awake. And she needed to make a trip outside. She shifted her bottom toward their gear, hoping to get up without rousing him, but he pulled her back. She stared at his face and tried again. The same thing happened. Deciding he was teasing her, she covered his hand resting on her hip and moved it lower, and then she moaned. His lip twitched. She pressed his hand between her legs. Liquid heat spread through her belly and her breasts ached to be touched.

He held his hand perfectly still and kissed her jaw. "I like the way you wake up." As he struggled to quiet his need to show his love for her, he eased his hand from her grasp and ran his fingers through her hair. "I think we'd better get up."

"Yes . . ." His deep voice sent another tremor through

her. She pushed the blanket back and sat up. ''It's colder than when we went to sleep.''

After she went outside, he followed. The snow was deeper by a few inches and the sky was still clouded over. ''We'd better hurry. I'd like to get as far as possible before it starts snowing again.''

She fixed coffee, bacon, and heated the last of their biscuits. After they finished eating, they mounted the horses and continued down the mountain. The tree branches were heavy with snow. She might've thought it was pretty if she hadn't been more concerned about looking for mining camps in an unfamiliar area with snow-covered paths.

Midday they came to a creek, rested the horses and had a cold meal, then followed the stream through narrow canyons and gorges. It snowed off and on, but they kept going. As the day wore on, she began to think they could ride forever and never see another person. The rhythmic rolling motion began to feel like a rocking chair, and the mashing noise of the horses' hooves in the snow seemed to be the only sound in the world.

When Parker glanced back and saw Kate weaving on the saddle, he called to her as he came to a halt. ''Come forward and ride by me.'' He had her follow him since he wasn't familiar with the territory, but it was leveling out. ''Keep me company.''

She heard his voice and did as he asked, stopping beside him. She was so tired and the snow was so white. ''Are we there?''

''Kate, you're cold. Rub your hands together.'' He took hold of the mare's halter, walked Buckshot forward until his leg bumped hers. He chafed her leg, arm, and back. ''Look up ahead,'' he said, anxious to give her something to think about. ''See those trees? I think there's a river down there.'' He had been watching, hoping it was the Salmon River, but now, it didn't matter as much as reviving her.

Gracious, he was rough. ''Not so hard.'' He didn't stop and when he held her hands over her face and she felt her warm breath, she finally started to come out of the stupor. She tried to smile. "Was I falling asleep?"

"You sure were." He dismounted and rummaged through her canvas bag until he found a shawl. "Help me unbutton your coat." Once the coat was open, he handed her hat to her, draped the shawl over her hat, down her back and wrapped the ends so the lower part of her face was covered. "Better?" He quickly rebuttoned her coat and pulled the collar up. He didn't want to set up camp out in the open. Trees or brush would give them a little protection.

"Mm—much. Where's the river?" She looked ahead, and then at him. He was more than a little concerned about her, and she felt better by the minute. "Thank you. Mrs. Goody told me what freezing would be like. And I forgot." She rubbed her arms and her legs and the mare's neck. "Let's find that river."

"Yes, ma'am." She moved out ahead of him, and he quickly caught up with her. "That could be a river."

"And that gray point over there could be a town." When she found herself listening to the sound of the horses' hooves crunching on the snow, she forced herself to figure out what kind of trees were ahead. Birches and poplars were bare in the winter, pines weren't, but they were too far away to tell. She had to concentrate, think about the shape of the trees, she told herself.

He scrutinized her carefully. Damn, that had been close. He also knew the signs of freezing, but he hadn't recognized them as soon as he should have. In trying to protect her and himself, he had been careless. "It's getting late. Whether that's a river or not, we can camp there for the night."

"I was teasing before, but doesn't that look like smoke rising from chimneys?"

He stared in that direction and shrugged. "Could be." He thought it was more like wishful thinking, but if it kept her going, he wouldn't argue with her. Or should he? That would keep her alert. "Sit up straight or your back will ache. Don't go to sleep on me!" It wasn't much, but he couldn't think of anything important to debate with her about.

She wondered what difference it made out there in the middle of nowhere. However, she pushed her shoulders back. "I haven't seen wagon marks or horse tracks in the snow for days. Have you?"

"I guess most people have more sense than we do." He kept her talking until they came close to the stand of trees. And within sight of a small town. "You were right about that being a town."

"Can we spend the night in a room with a bed?" She thought a bed and room had never been so appealing. "And the horses can sleep in the livery or a barn." She sniffed. She could smell the wood smoke.

"We'll sleep in a building if I have to buy us space on the floor of the general store." The horses must have sensed it, too. Buckshot wanted to run, but Parker held him back. Soon they were on the outskirts of town. It was no different from the hundreds of other small towns with weathered board storefronts.

She spotted the small boardinghouse sign in the window of a log cabin. It had three chimneys and looked like a palace. "What do you think?" She didn't have many coins left, but she'd spend every last one to sleep beside him in a bed, safe and warm.

"Come inside with me. We're spending the night here." He walked to the door with her and rapped loudly.

The door opened. A tall woman looked them over and stared at Parker's badge. "You lookin' for a room?"

"We sure are." He smiled at Kate. Before he could say more, the woman pulled the door wide open and hauled them inside.

The woman slammed the door shut. "Can't stand here all day with the door open. Got one room left. It has a fireplace. The room's six bits, firewood and meals're two bits each." She looked straight at Parker. "What'll it be?"

He handed her two dollars. "That should keep us in wood and cover two meals."

"This way. Barn's out back."

Kate yawned. She wanted to curl up in bed with Parker with a big fire in the fireplace. A hot meal wouldn't be bad later.

The woman showed them into the room and started the fire in the fireplace. "I'll ring the cowbell when supper's ready. It won't be long."

"Thank you. That'll be fine." He glanced at Kate. "How far are we from Salmon?"

"That's the river," the woman said, pointing at the door, "over there. The town's down the road. On horseback, it'll take you 'bout two, three hours."

He put his arm around Kate's shoulders and gave her a squeeze. "That's good news."

Parker and Kate followed the Salmon River south. If the woman at the boardinghouse was correct, the town lay just ahead, nestled in the snow-covered hills. He smiled at her. "Ready to start following trails?"

"I sure am." With each mile they had put behind them, her anger had grown. She'd remembered every nasty glance, every snicker, every crude remark she'd suffered because of Hank, and every hardship. Yesterday she had nearly given in and let him win. But today she was well rested and more than ready to face him.

Slowing Buckshot to a walk, he searched for signs of a path, but the snow was over a foot deep. The hills were steep with few trees, and he studied the slopes for smokestacks or rising smoke. Finally he saw a wide brush-clear area on the other side of the river that looked as if it could be a path. "We might as well see where this leads."

As she trailed behind him, her heart pounded with excitement. The river narrowed at that point, and they crossed with little trouble. The clearing led up away from the river, then wound back down to it. It had been nothing more than a picturesque ride. They followed the river's course, riding up into the hills and back. Around midafternoon, they came to a definite trail. "This has to lead somewhere."

"We were bound to get lucky." He reflexively felt his pistol and started up into the hills. He figured they had gone about a mile when the path made a loop, and he stopped on a rise. There was a cabin several hundred yards ahead. He motioned to Kate.

She came abreast and stared down the trail. There were pigs in a pen and two horses in a small coral. "Let's go." The clouds were breaking apart, and she took it as a good omen.

He reached out and firmly grasped her arm. "I'm taking the lead. We don't know who's there. Turner's not the only outlaw in the territory."

She nodded and rode next to the packhorse. When he dismounted, she did the same and stayed a few feet behind him. When he raised his hand and rapped on the cabin door, she held her breath. The door opened slowly, and her heart leaped to her throat. She stepped to Parker's side at the same moment a little girl with red curls poked her head outside. The child couldn't have been more than six or seven years old.

"Who're ya lookin' fer?"

Parker smiled and moved his hand away from his holster. "Is your papa here?" A young woman joined the girl. He tipped his hat. "Sorry to bother you, ma'am." This wasn't Turner's place. The child's hair was bright red, the woman's a dirty blond. Turner had brown hair, and the girl didn't look anything like him. Parker quickly improvised a story. "We're looking for Mr. Spivey. Thought this was his place, but he's an old codger."

"My man's Mr. Merckle." The woman pulled her child back and closed the door.

Parker walked back to their horses with Kate. As they mounted up, he noticed the little girl's red hair at the small window. The child's as afraid as the mother, he thought, heading on up the trail. He stopped well beyond the cabin. "This track is too well used not to go somewhere."

She nodded. "That poor woman looked almost as old as Mamma."

"This country'll do that to folks." He pushed on. Years of experience had taught him to heed his instinct, and it told him to keep going.

Kate couldn't shake the image of that woman. If her f— Hank had taken them with him, her mother would've spent her days much like that young woman. Well, she thought, after all these years, I've come up with a good reason for his leaving us. The path wound through the hills. In places the snow was so deep it brushed her mare's belly. Eventually they came to a creek.

He dismounted and walked the horses to the water. "Looks like we'll have to set up camp before long. We'll never make it to town before dark."

She led the mare to the stream. "We still have another hour or more of daylight."

He chuckled. "Aren't you tired? Or hungry? We didn't have dinner." He pulled off his gloves and moved upstream from the horses. After he splashed icy water in his face, he dried it with his handkerchief. He felt as if the burst of energy he'd felt earlier had faded. A person couldn't expect to face trouble around every bend hour after hour without running out of steam. "This's a good campsite. I'll see if I can find some game for supper."

She paced around, working the kinks out of her legs. "Okay. I'll take the packhorse and keep on this trail for a while."

"Kate, slow down. No one knows why we're here." He knocked the snow off his hat and put it back on. "For that matter, there's no guarantee that *he's* around here. It could take us days to search both sides of the river." He walked over to her and held her hands in his. "Don't give up because we didn't find him this afternoon."

She rubbed her cheek over the back of his hands and stared into his beautiful blue eyes. "Just another mile or two. I don't know why, but I can't stop here. It's too early."

"I'll hunt later." He put his arms around her. "I'm not

leaving you.'' She wasn't playing games. That steel edge was back in her voice again. He kissed the tip of her nose and smiled.

''I'll be fine. Honestly. If any man's fool enough to bother me, I'll shoot his toes off.'' She smacked his backside and stepped back. ''Find us a couple jackrabbits, and I'll roast them over the fire.'' The mare came up behind her and nudged her into Parker.

He laughed, wrapping his arm around her shoulders. ''See, she doesn't think I should leave you, either.'' He pressed his lips to her forehead. ''Mount up. We'll keep going until the sun leaves the top of that ridge.''

''Thank you.'' She gave him a quick kiss and walked over to the creek. After she took a drink of cold water, she climbed back on the mare. It had taken them so long to get there, she didn't have time to waste. She'd promised her mother she wouldn't be gone longer than two weeks, and they had already used nearly half that time.

He rode beside her, half surprised she didn't insist on taking the lead. However, when he glanced at her, her expression made him uneasy. ''What are you plotting?''

She shook her head. ''This's taking too long. When we get to Salmon, I'll have to post a letter to my mother. I don't want her thinking I've run off, too.''

''I believe she understands better than you give her credit for. She knows you'll be back.'' He looked up the hill. Seeing a jackrabbit or a deer would have been reassuring, he thought, but they were making too much noise for him to hunt.

''By the way, who's Spivey?''

He laughed. ''I don't know. I must've heard the name somewhere. Couldn't very well use our names, could I?''

''Just curious.'' The road took them higher up the hill. She turned to him, hoping he hadn't noticed the sun had moved. ''The only creatures I've heard during the night are coyotes. Do you think there's anything to hunt?''

''I'd just as soon not try to bring back a moose, but

there's other game.'' He grinned at her. ''I'm not planning on stocking up for winter.''

She laughed. ''Glad to hear it.''

When they came around a bend in the road, he pulled up on the reins and motioned her to do the same. The clearing up ahead resembled a very small valley with the creek running past a fair-sized log cabin with smoke pouring out of the chimney. But the man chopping wood held Parker's interest. The man had opened his coat, but a knit hat covered his head. As he watched the man, he envisioned Turner the last time he had seen him.

It was a perfect setting: a creek, snug log cabin, lights in the windows, fire in the fireplace, everything blanketed with a thick covering of snow, and the man chopping wood completed the picture. Kate glanced at Parker. It had been a long time since she'd seen his cold, deadly stare, and even then it hadn't been so fierce. Did he recognize him? She stared at the man. Could it be Hank? He looked short, or maybe it was the distance.

She urged the mare down the trail and dismounted at the edge of the creek, across from him. With the heavy coat hiding his shape and hat covering his head, she couldn't be sure. But that man was old. . . . Was it him? Or did she just want it to be him? The pounding of her heart seemed to fill her ears and tighten her throat.

Parker pulled up next to her, dismounted, and pushed the right side of his coat back behind his holster. ''Does that look like him?''

''I don't know. It's been eleven years.'' As she stared at the man, she heard Parker step forward.

Parker called out, ''Hank Turner, that you?'' and waited. He had promised she could talk to her father before he drew on the man. He also needed to make certain Turner was armed.

The man lowered the ax and walked closer to the bank of the creek. ''Who's asking?''

There was no doubt in his mind now. ''Parker Smith. You've seen me before.''

"Never saw that badge before." Hank Turner glanced at Kate. "Wondered how long it'd take you to find me this time. What'd'ya bring her along for? Didn't think you rode with anyone."

It was him. Even his voice had changed. It didn't seem possible. His face was weathered, his nose larger than she remembered, and his eyes held no warmth. As Kate stared at Hank, she stepped forward, past Parker. "Is it *really you*?" Her heart was racing so fast she could hardly breath. It didn't seem real, but there she was standing in front of him, with only the creek between them. "You don't even know who I am, do you?"

Hank sighed and nodded. "I've waited all these years for you to change your mind about me. But it doesn't look like you have." He eyed her from head to toe and finally said, "You grew into a fine-looking woman, Katherine Anne."

Her stomach revolted. She was so angry, she feared she might disgrace herself and be ill. She took a deep breath, drew her Colt, and, holding it with both hands, aimed it at his chest. "You shouldn't have taught me how to shoot." She leveled the gun-sight over his shoulder at the very corner edge of the cabin roof and fired one shot.

It had happened so quickly, Parker instinctively reached for her. But she moved quicker than he and dodged him. "Kate, you said you wanted to talk to him. For God's sake, watch what you're doing!" She had caught him off guard, but it had never occurred to him that she might draw on her father.

She grinned. "Oh, I know exactly what I'm doing. This bastard ran out on us, then when he's old and lonely, he sends us gold he stole from miners." She motioned to the mare with her head. "I've brought the gold back to you. *You* can return it to all those men you robbed. I tried but there were too many."

Suddenly the cabin door flew open and a woman ran over to her father. That dress . . . Kate frowned. The fabric was the same as her mother's. Then Shadow ran out of the cabin. No, no, no . . . it couldn't be, that would be too cruel, but it was her. Shadow hesitated at her mother's side, then he dashed across the icy creek and stood up in front of her. Kate's hands began shaking. She set the sight of her pistol to the left of her father and petted the dog. At least he was happy to see her.

"Katie, darlin', what're ya doin'? He's your papa." Mary Louise put her arm through Hank's and pulled her shawl tighter.

Kate didn't dare look away from them. "What—? *How* did you get here? You said you hadn't seen him—didn't know where he was!" Maybe this was a nightmare. It was too bizarre to be real. Shadow sat at her side as if he were guarding her, but she didn't dare pet him. She heard Parker move. "Don't touch me, Parker, or *I'll* shoot him for you."

He stood more than a pace from her, beyond his reach. He had to keep her talking until he could disarm her, for her own sake. "Don't you have a lot of questions you wanted to ask him? Now's the time." What a hell of a fix, he thought. He's the one who'd planned to shoot Turner, dreamed about it, and he ends up playing arbitrator between father and daughter.

Mary Louise shivered. "Katie, can't we go inside like civilized people? It's freezin' out here."

"You're wrong. He's not civilized—no killer and thief is *civilized*. You go on." Kate waited, but her mother didn't move. "There's no reason for you to take sick over the likes of him. He's not worth it. Get inside and take Shadow with you." The dog stood up, tail wagging, and barked at her. She wavered slightly, then said in a gruff voice, "Go on, Shadow, back to the cabin," but he didn't budge.

Parker shook his head. She'd taken over, once again. While she appeared ready to shoot her father, she was worried about her mother's health and the dog to boot. "Turner, tell her why you left them behind all those years ago."

Kate sent Parker a fleeting glare. "What makes you think he won't lie? Just because he looks like any other old man doesn't mean he's honest.'' As she continued staring at her father, part of her pleaded with him to be honest, just once. This would be her last chance to hear the truth, if he even remembered it after all this time.

Hank turned to Mary Louise. ''You'd better wait for us inside. Why don't you put on a large pot of coffee and make sure there's enough supper for them.''

''Mr. Turner, I'll not leave ya out he-ah.'' She glanced at her daughter, wringing her hands. ''When our Katherine Anne's like this, she's so headstrong.'' She lowered her voice and added, ''I fear ya shouldn't've taught her how to use a pistol.''

Hank chuckled and patted her hand. ''She's my daughter, wife. Now, go and let us talk.'' He kissed her cheek and watched until she closed the cabin door, then he faced his daughter. ''What should I have done? Dragged a sick twelve-year-old girl and her mother with me? I was running from the law. Hiding in caves and shacks. Would that have made you happy?''

She shook her head slowly, the pistol still pointed directly at him. ''You didn't even bother saying good-bye. You never wrote and told me why you left us. I had to hear it at school. Do you have any idea how much that hurt?'' She rubbed her lips together and planted her feet to steady her hands, the sting of those insults fresh in her mind.

Parker felt her pain, but there wasn't anything he could do for her until her father finished telling her what had happened. As he watched Hank pace, he moved forward, but again, she anticipated him and stepped out of reach.

''I was shot during that bank robbery, Katherine Anne—''

She interrupted him. ''I'm not that girl anymore.''

''Kate, then. The others took me with them, somewhere in the badlands. It was weeks before I was strong enough to get around on my own. By then, everyone believed I was part of the gang. Once, I went back to Clarksville, tried to explain what'd happened, but I was nearly shot on sight.'' Hank shrugged. ''I thought in time I could clear my name, but it only got worse.'' He stomped his feet and rubbed his arms. ''Are you ready to go in by the fire and finish this talk before we freeze?''

She ignored his question. ''You're lying. You weren't taken for ransom, and bank robbers don't rescue men they've shot during a robbery. Besides, you could've given yourself up anytime, told a sheriff where the outlaws were hiding.''

''When I got shot, they thought I was helping them. That's why they took me along.'' Hank looked from Parker to Kate. ''I must've passed out after they got me on my horse. I woke up miles from town, and I wasn't in any shape to argue. Later, I didn't want to die doing the right thing.''

As she stared down the barrel of the gun at him, tears filled her eyes. ''You didn't give us any thought, did you? We lost the land and the house. *I* worked for room and board.'' She gritted her teeth, ignoring the tears running down her cheeks. ''I suppose you'd call that 'good training.' ''

''I tried, Kath—Kate, but you wouldn't listen to your mother, would you? You didn't have to work so hard. I wrote her and sent both of you every dollar I could through the years so you could grow up like the other girls.''

She shook her head and narrowed her gaze. ''Mamma never got mail. I would've known.''

''Do you think I would've sent cash money or gold by Pony Express?'' He overlapped the sides of his coat across his chest. ''My partner, Davy, he worked out a way of stashing my letters and packages so your mother'd find them.''

Kate hadn't thought her stomach could hurt any worse than it did. She was wrong. Suddenly she remembered the day she found her mother out in the snow snooping around that bush. And there were all those canvas bags in the trunk. It was true. How could she have been so blind? Tears kept rolling down cheeks. Was everything in her life a lie? ''How could you give your wife and daughter stolen cash and gold? Have you no pride? No shame?''

''Good God, girl. Do you really think that of me?'' He stood erect with his arms at his sides. ''I earned every cent of that money and mined every flake of gold myself. But if you don't believe me, shoot.''

As much as Parker would hate to admit it, there was a ring of truth in Hank's words. However, he had skimmed over some of the details of the bank robbery. ''That's some story. You forgot a few things, though. If you weren't with the bank robbers in Clarksville, why did you shoot my father?'' Hank turned pale, then red as a beet, but Parker had been trailing him for too many years not to take great delight in watching him squirm.

''I didn't shoot anyone in that bank!'' Hank shook his fists at Parker. ''You fool. Is that why you've been dogging me all these years?! *I* didn't shoot him. I only got off one shot before I was hit. I was trying to stop the robbery.''

Parker shook his head. ''I saw you. He'd pushed me behind him, but *I saw you* point your pistol at him.'' That day was clear in his mind. He was sixteen, and he had been terrified, then suddenly Hank walked into the bank and stood next to one of the outlaws. He drew his pistol and fired. Parker would never forget that god-awful day. ''He fell back against me and died in my arms.''

''You saw it wrong, son. I walked in on that robbery and drew my gun all right, but I was aiming at that skinny guy filling the bag with cash.'' Hank heaved a deep sigh. ''I'm not about to freeze to death. There's a warm fire in there, and Mrs. Turner fixed supper. I'm going in.'' He turned his back on them and walked to the cabin.

Parker heard the unmistakable click of Kate's pistol being cocked. The moment he lunged for her, the dog sprang up and clamped his teeth onto his arm. As Parker struggled with the animal, he managed to shove her arms up. He commanded the dog to sit, which thankfully he did, then he wrapped his other arm around her waist and spun her away from her father's direction. ''You can't. You're not a back shooter, Kate.'' Her scream resounded through the hollow, and she trembled violently. He held her tight, not knowing if she was angry with him or relieved he had prevented her from shooting out of spite and resentment. He only knew he loved her too much to let her ruin their lives.

22

"THIS'S A MISTAKE. We shouldn't've come in here," Kate said softly. Parker had more or less dragged her into the cabin and insisted she sit on the hearth by him, but she hadn't even felt cold until she'd sat down. She hadn't wanted to see how her father lived. Her first suspicions had been confirmed. He was much better off than she and her mother. His cabin had good plank floors, real windows on each wall with heavy drapes, a bedroom, and an iron cookstove.

Disregarding the Turners, Parker vigorously rubbed Kate's back. "You weren't too steady on your feet. I've searched for years, and we've traveled for days to find him. Did you really want to ride away and hope he'd be here tomorrow when we return?"

She glanced over her shoulder at him. "I should've shot him . . . saved us the trouble." His hands were warm and felt reassuring, but he was sidetracking her thoughts. "How come you didn't draw?" Shadow came over and nudged her hand. He hadn't forgotten her. She rubbed behind his ear and smiled at him.

"I need answers, too," Parker said firmly. "I've never shot an unarmed man. I couldn't tell if he had a pistol." He rested his arm across her shoulders. Right then, he was more concerned about her than revenge. It wasn't over with yet, but he didn't think Turner would run out on his family now.

Mary Louise poured two cups of coffee. She handed one to Parker and held the other out to her daughter. "Are ya feelin' better, deah?"

"Warmer." Kate idly patted the dog. "How did you get here, Mamma?"

Mary Louise smiled at Hank and stepped to his side. "Mr. Ebner, your father's partner, brought me. You were gone, and Mr. Turner had beseeched me for some time to see him. An' Mr. Ebner didn't mind at all." She linked arms with her husband. "I knew ya'd find him, Katie, an' I had to warn him. Ya've been so angry, I wasn't sure what ya'd do."

Kate stared at her mother, completely perplexed. "What if we hadn't found him? Did you at least leave a note in the cabin for me?" She glared at her mother, waving her arms in the air. "Ye gods! What did you tell everyone?!" Shadow barked, and she quieted him.

"Don't ya be blasphemous 'round me, do ya hear?" Mary Louise scowled at her daughter. "I did leave ya a letter and added Mr. Ebner's directions so ya could join us." She glanced at Parker and added, "I told Mrs. Goody and Miss Lucy I was visitin' a friend."

Staring at her mother, seeing her with her father, Kate noticed that Mary Louise looked different, younger, more spirited, not the least bit muddleheaded. Was she drawing strength from Hank? Kate took another sip of coffee and set the cup down beside her.

Hank walked his wife over to a chair and sat in the one next to hers. "Kate, do you remember how sick you were when I took leave from The Rebellion? You were twelve."

"How could I forget? You must've stayed with us for a whole day or two. You told me a story one morning before you left to 'take care of some business.' That was the last time I saw you." She shivered and rested one hand on Parker's knee.

He gave her shoulder a reassuring squeeze. Her color was

back, but she was still shaky. What surprised him most was his reaction. He wasn't yet convinced of Turner's innocence, but he was willing to listen, more than he would've been two hours ago.

Hank held Mary Louise's hand. "Your mamma wrote me how ill you were, and that she didn't have the cash to buy medicine. You were too little to know, but there were no doctors in town. They'd joined the militia. The womenfolk had to make do without them, and medicines were hard to come by." He patted Mary Louise's hand. "When you took sick, she was scared. I got home and learned the bank had also foreclosed on the house and land.

"I went to every bank within twenty miles, but no one would give me a loan—not even money for your medicine. I'd never begged for anything in my life, but I went back over to Clarksville that day ready to beg the banker for a few dollars. I was so caught up in my own problems, I guess I didn't pay much attention to what was going on when I walked into the bank. Before I knew it, I was in the middle of that holdup." He coughed and cleared his throat.

Mary Louise smiled at him. "We made out just fine. When Mrs. Grimley came to stay with her son, she heard how bad off Katherine Anne was. She shared her prized concoction and put Kate on the mend."

Shadow laid down and rested his chin on Kate's boot. She reached for her cup and took a long drink. She had been ill for a while before they'd had to move. "I never—What about the shootings? The other bank robberies? The men you've killed?" Her mind whirled as if it were caught in a sundevil. Nothing made any sense.

Hank jumped to his feet. "*I never killed anyone!* Leastways not till they shot at me."

Kate stood up, glaring at Parker. "Why don't you shoot him?! He killed your father, for God's sake."

He remained seated on the hearth. "I'm not about to draw on him now. Your mother's too close—he's not wearing a pistol." He sent Turner a hard look. "Besides, there's still a thing or two to settle before I do.''

Mary Louise stood up at Hank's side and laid her hand on his arm. ''Give her time, Mr. Turner. She's a stubborn one, like ya used to be, but she's fair. Help me put supper on the table.''

As Hank looked into her eyes, his gaze softened, and he nodded. ''That's a good idea, Mrs. Turner.''

''That's it,'' Kate shouted, ''walk away! Don't tell me why you robbed those banks and held up people at gunpoint!''

''I did what I had to to survive.'' Hank combed his fingers through his hair. ''I'm not proud of what I did, but I've been lawbiding for the last eight years.'' He looked at her. ''Doesn't that count for anything?''

No, she thought, not much.

Parker held on to Kate as she watched her parents. Her tears had dried, but seeing her parents happily reunited was a shock. And so was listening to her father admit stealing from people. ''Let's take a walk outside.'' He was confused himself but experience had taught him to step back when he felt that way, give himself time to think the problem through.

''Yes—'' She grabbed her coat and hat and hurried out the door. It was dark and the lights from the doorway and windows shone like beacons. She was pulling on her gloves when Parker came up beside her carrying a lantern. ''We'd better make camp across the creek and take care of the horses.''

He glanced at her. ''I don't see why we can't stay in the barn.''

''I don't want to spend the night here, in anything he owns.'' She turned to him and put her hands on the front of his coat. But she needed to know her father hadn't hoodwinked him, needed to know they were sticking to their plans. So much had changed, she wanted to hear that Parker hadn't.

He put her arm through his. ''Let's check on the horses.''

They walked around the cabin to the small barn and went inside.

The smells of hay, horses, and leather were strong in the small shed. She straightened her back. She wouldn't beg him. Her life was in shreds, but she had some pride left. "Have you changed your mind about him?"

"If we'd stay in here, the horses'll be more comfortable, and it's warmer than the tent." He set the lantern on an overturned barrel. "I have to see this through, Kate. I've waited too long to walk away now, and I think you have, too." He put a hand on each of her shoulders. "If we leave, he might, too."

She moistened her lips. "He said so much. How can I believe him? I just want to go away and think it over without seeing him—them—across the room."

He wrapped his arms around her, and her hat fell to the ground. "I'm just as confused as you are—that's why we need to stay here." He tipped her chin up and pressed a gentle kiss to her lips. *"I need you with me."*

He couldn't have said anything sweeter than that, she thought. She wanted to cry, but she didn't dare give in to the childish desire—she might not be able to stop. She reached up and rubbed her coat sleeve over his badge, making it shine. "I'll stay."

Mary Louise passed the pan of cornbread to Parker. "Do ya remember the first time ya called at the cabin, Mr. Smith?"

He smiled. "I sure do, ma'am. You made a fine cup of tea." He winked at Kate. "I bet you remember that day, too." She frowned, and he chuckled.

Mary Louise gave Hank a proud-mother kind of look. "He was such a charming gentleman. That was before he was made sheriff."

Parker put two pieces of cornbread on his plate and passed the pan to Kate. "The stew sure smells good."

Hank kept glancing at Kate. But he didn't say a word

when she set the pan of bread in front of him, instead of handing it to him.

"Well, my goodness, ya must be starved." Mary Louise moved the large bowl closer to Parker's plate. "There's more rabbit stew in the pot. This used to be Kate's favorite meal. I want ya to eat your fill." She sent her daughter a haunted glance.

Kate couldn't eat, and the longer she sat at *his* table the worse she felt. She set her plate on the floor for Shadow. Tea sounded good. She left the table, poured herself a cup, and sat down on the hearth. Her mother's voice sounded distant, and Parker's warmed the cold numbness deep inside her. When she idly glanced at her mother, she saw her pass a small crock to Parker and overheard, "Honey." If Kate'd had any doubts before, they vanished. Her mother was finally home. All she wanted was to go to the barn and sort things out with Parker.

Mary Louise watched her daughter. She opened her mouth, as if to speak, then closed it and sank back on the chair.

Hank took a drink of coffee and looked at Parker. "Now that you've found me, are you going to keep that badge?"

"For a while. It has nothing to do with you." Parker eyed him. "Does it bother you?" He was glad Turner didn't press Kate to return to the table. She was exhausted, and if pushed too far, she might pull another pistol on him. Parker didn't want to wrestle with her, again.

"Why should it? I'm not wanted." Hank finished eating and sat back. "Haven't been for a few years now."

Parker broke off a chunk of cornbread. "There's a difference of opinion about that." He wasn't completely convinced.

Kate still felt numb. Parker wasn't quite finished with his meal, but she couldn't stay in the same room with Hank any longer. She walked over to Parker. "I'll see you in the barn."

"No problem. As delicious as this food is, I'm full." He stood up by Kate. "Thank you, Mrs. Turner." He handed

Kate's coat and hat to her and picked up his own.

"Ya can't leave yet. Ya haven't had your raisin custard." Mary Louise wrung her hands, her gaze darting from Kate to Hank and Parker.

Shadow went to the door, and Kate let him out. "Don't forget to let him back inside."

Hank shoved his chair back and came to his feet. "Where're you two going?"

"To the barn." She looked from her mother to Hank. Her mother busied herself collecting the dirty dishes, and he was unquestionably upset. "Never mind. We'll be back tomorrow."

"What's wrong with the cabin? It's warmer than the barn."

She looked straight at Hank. "Parker's welcome to stay if he wants to, but I'm not sleeping in here." She put her hat on and reached for the door latch.

"You're not sleeping with him in my house."

"I'm not. If that includes your barn, I'll leave." She met his glare with an equally furious scowl. "You may not have noticed, but I'm fully grown. A woman. You lost your right to tell me what to do when you walked away from us years ago and didn't have the courage to return." She yanked the door open.

Mary Louise hurried over to her. "Don't do this. There's plenty o' room right in front of the fireplace." She put her hand on Kate's sleeve. "Please, deah, you must stay in here. It isn't proper. Ya know that."

Kate shook her head. "It's too late to worry about convention. And God knows this family's far from proper." She gave Hank a scathing look and walked outside.

Parker grabbed a lantern and followed right behind her. The dog circled them and pushed a stick at his free hand. "You happy to see us?" About the same time he threw the stick, the front door of the cabin slammed shut. Kate flinched, but she didn't break stride. "You can sleep in the loft, and I'll bed down near the stalls, if you'd be more comfortable that way."

She wrapped her arms around herself and shook her head. "It's up to you. I don't feel guilty about sleeping with you." He had an honorable streak that came out at the most inconvenient times, and she wasn't sure what he'd do. She gazed at him and saw the longing in his eyes. It was his decision, but she wasn't ashamed of her feelings for him and prayed he wasn't.

"I don't want to make this any harder for you than it already is." He smiled and closed the barn door, then put the bar in place. "I'd much rather sleep with you in my arms than by a fire." He hung the lantern on a nail. "We could bring the dog in to chaperon us."

"He's good at that." She grinned. "After Mamma and I fell asleep, he'd crawl in between us and take all the blankets."

He loosely encircled her waist with his arms. "If he tries that with us, he'll have a fight on his hands. No one's coming between us." He kissed the end of her nose. "Especially in bed."

"That's good to hear." She slid her hands around his neck and pressed her parted lips to his. When he touched her hair, a delicious ripple rolled down her spine, and she rubbed against him. She needed him with her whole being, naked and caressing the length of her. She needed to feel there was a part of her that hadn't been soiled or taken from her. She wanted his love, if only for a short while.

She had a potent effect on him, and his reaction was powerful and swift. As he tasted and teased, his muscles flexed. He held her close. He wanted to tear off his pants, bury himself in her luscious body, and love her until they were too weak to move. The taste of her created a hunger for more. He drew her lower lip between his and gently sucked. "We'd better go up to the loft while I'm still able to climb the ladder."

"I don't know if I have the strength to move away from you." His gaze sent another tremble of desire through her belly. All of a sudden someone pounded on the barn door, and it was as if ice water had been poured down her back.

"Kate, deah, Mr. Smith—I brought ya more covers. It's awfully cold out here tonight."

Kate quickly tugged at her coat and felt her cheeks. "What does she think we've been using this past week?"

He chuckled and straightened his coat. "She's just checking on her daughter's well being." He combed his fingers through her hair. "How's her daughter doing?"

"Mm, just fine before she disturbed us." Kate took a deep breath and hoped her mother couldn't hear her thundering heart.

"Kate, won't ya let me in?"

Parker walked to the door, slid the bar back, and pulled it open. "Come on in, Mrs. Turner." He looked at the cabin and saw Turner watching from a window. Tomorrow, he thought, closing the door. One way or the other, it will be over with tomorrow.

"I thought y'all'd need these comforters." Mary Louise held out the armful of covers. "There's one for each of ya."

Kate noticed Parker covering his smirk, and she grinned. "That was thoughtful of you, Mamma, but we've managed to keep warm all week." She glanced around, but there was no place to set the covers.

Mary Louise raised her hand. "I don't want'a hear it. Your papa's fit t'be tied."

"Then he should understand how I feel about him." Kate realized her mother hadn't been deliberately cruel to her, just unbelievably loyal to her husband—whether he deserved it or not. "I really am tired, Mamma. I'll see you in the morning."

Mary Louise nodded. "The privy's back by those trees." She motioned toward the corner of the barn.

Kate almost smiled, but she wasn't that ready to forgive her. "We'll find it."

Mary Louise walked slowly to the door. "I can bring ya a pot of coffee and custard. Ya left so—"

"I'm tired. I need sleep more than food. You'd better get back before *he* comes looking for you."

Parker held the door open for Mrs. Turner. "Good night. I'll take that coffee in the morning."

Mary Louise didn't quite meet his gaze. "I'll have a fresh pot ready. Evenin', Sheriff."

When she had walked well into the yard, Parker closed the barn door and set the bar in place. "You all right, Kate?"

She nodded. "Weren't we going up to the loft before she barged in on us?" His slow, enticing smile reminded her exactly what they had been doing.

"Indeed we were."

She handed one of the comforters to him and grinned. "You can carry your own." She partially unfolded hers, put it over her shoulder, and climbed the ladder. Earlier, she'd made up their bed on the straw, but with the extra covers, she wanted one more under them as well and pulled the top blankets off the bed.

He paused at the top of the ladder and hung the lantern on the post. "Change your mind?"

"Of course not. One comforter on the bottom will help keep the straw from poking through." It didn't take her long to remake the bed and pull back the top covers. "Sleepy?"

"No, but I'm ready for bed." As he watched her take off her coat, he shed his, then his boots and put his holster within reach.

She laid her coat nearby and set her Colt under one sleeve. The barn was warmer than the tent and a lot roomier. After she'd pulled her shirt loose, she unbuttoned the top buttons of her pants and stretched out under the covers. She didn't think she could ever tire of watching him, the easy way he moved, and she awaited the feel of his powerful body bearing down on hers.

He crawled into bed, put his arm around her shoulders, and held her close. She fit her curves to his, shifting her weight so she lay half on top of him. He stroked the back of her neck with one hand and traced her thigh with the other. "I thought you were sleepy."

She pushed back the sides of his shirt and pressed kisses over his powerful chest. She flicked her tongue over his nipple, and it grew hard. She moved over him, straddling his leg, trapping it between hers. Rolling her hips, she nibbled her way up to his jaw. "We haven't made love since we left town." She drew his lip between hers with the same deliberate slowness he had taunted her with. "I need you."

They should talk, he thought, but she was bent on seducing him, and he was having trouble putting two ideas together. Pleasure could turn painful, and he was very near that point. He throbbed with his own need to fill her, feel the rush of her hot moist body gripping him tight until she lost control, and he could, also. "What if I sh—"

"Shoot Hank?" she finished for him as she ran her fingers through the dark curls on his chest. "You would've already shot if you didn't have doubts. You won't unless you have no other choice. I want your love, Parker."

"You have it, Kate." He kissed her passionately, giving free rein to his pent-up yearning for her. Then he slipped his fingers under the waistband of her trousers and grazed the length of her with the back of his hands as he took off her pants.

She yanked at his jeans and was none too gentle in removing them. It was her turn to run her hand up his long legs, over his smooth hips, and across his flat belly. Impatient to join their bodies, she lay on top of him and brought him into her.

Dazed by her almost fevered passion, he refused to give in to his release. She claimed and branded him with her tantalizing kisses and her hungry possession of him. He rolled her onto her back and gazed at her. She was so lovely, yet she hid behind her plain clothes and careless appearance. He had discovered a treasure in her, and he wanted to show her how very much he loved her.

She moaned and skimmed her fingertips over his muscled back. The heat of him surrounded her and filled her. He teased her breasts, stroked her belly, and carried her higher and higher. Liquid heat coursed through her, and she tightened around him. Her senses whirled with the scent of laurel and the aroma of their heated bodies. Then the most mind-shattering sensations two people could share carried them to the height of passion.

When his breathing slowed, he kissed her smooth shoulder. He still felt light-headed and aroused, as if he could never have enough of her. She murmured sweetly, and he trailed kisses along her collarbone to the soft hollow at the base of her throat. "I don't think we need the extra comforter."

She wrapped her legs over his and smiled. "You can sleep right where you are."

"I'll feel like a stone wall soon."

"No you won't." She skimmed her palms over his shoulders. "When you move to my side, I feel as if part of me is missing." She still tingled with excitement, but she was too weak to encourage him to do more than rest. She locked her arms around him and drifted off to sleep.

Early the next morning Kate and Parker were startled awake by banging on the barn doors and Hank Turner's raucous shouting. She shook her head. "Maybe he'll bloody his fists."

Parker shoved the covers back. "I'll talk to him."

She grabbed his arm. "Let me." She pulled on her pants, buttoned her shirt, and shoved her pistol in her pocket. By the time she slid the bar back form the door, she'd put her coat on. Before she could open the door, it flew open and Hank was glaring at her. Taking him by surprise, she put her hands flat on his chest and shoved him backward, until he was standing in the middle of the yard. It was barely light. "What do you mean shouting the door down at the crack of dawn?"

"I knew it—your mamma said you'd come back to the cabin, but no, you slept with him!" Hank knocked her hands away. "What turned you into such a brazen bitch?"

She hadn't thought he could do or say anything to hurt her any more than he had, but his words managed to sting her. Sheer determination held her tears back. "*You*," she said bitterly. "I've never been like this before in my life. Of course, I only had one father. Thank God." She paced to the side and back. "I have spent most of my life feeling as if I had to be more honest than most people, better than most—to make up for what you did. By the time I was thirteen *I* was responsible for Mamma. You should've been, but I was."

"That was your choice, but I'll do it now. She'll be staying here with me. Besides, I sure as hell didn't set out to live with a gang of thieves and cutthroats." He raised his hand to her and let it fall to his side. "I sent you money as soon as I could, but your mamma wrote that you'd rather think I was dead. Do you know how much that hurt me, Kate?"

Her throat tightened up as surely as if he'd choked her. Tears spilled on her cheek and ran down to her coat. "I . . . I wanted you . . . to hurt . . . the way I did." She stepped back. "I was a child. What's your excuse?" She kept backing up until she hit the side of the barn and ran inside.

Parker caught her and held her in his arms as she continued to sob. He looked over her shoulder and saw Hank walking back to the cabin. Parker walked her to a bench and sat her down. "You forgot your boots. Your feet must be frozen." He dried her cheeks with his handkerchief and gave her a tender kiss.

She sniffed and rubbed her eyes. "I want to leave today. My mother's happy, and for the first time I don't have to worry about her." She swallowed hard, barely aware he had put one boot on her foot. "I need to get back and help Charlie. I'll pack our things while you have coffee and settle with him."

He got the second boot on and sat beside her. "You're frightened. I am, too, but I want you to go over there with me. Speak with your mother. I'll talk with your father outside."

"He's not my father. He's cold, calculating, selfish—"

She shook her head. "I have no reason to see him again."

He leaned forward with his forearms resting on his knees. "I remembered something last night. Something I may not have understood at the time." He gazed at her. "You might have prevented me from killing an innocent man." He shrugged. "I won't know till I sort it out with him."

"How could that be? You were there." She put her arm through his. "You saw Hank shoot your father. What's changed?"

He rubbed his cheek on the back of her hand. "My memory may be as distorted as yours." She tried to pull her hand away, but he clamped his over hers on his arm and held her gaze.

"Mine was all too clear about the man he's become or always was. How could you be so wrong about him?"

"We lost our fathers in different ways, and we didn't know what our parents did. I was there and all I remembered was seeing your father firing his pistol at mine." He gave her a reassuring smile. "Let's get some coffee. I don't know about you, but I need it." He stood up and held out his hand.

"For you." She held onto his hand until her mother handed her a cup of coffee. She took a sip and walked over to the fireplace. Each time she saw Mary Louise, she looked happier and the way she doted on Hank was positively embarrassing.

"Good mornin', Mr. Smith." Mary Louise handed Parker a steaming cup of coffee. "Looks like it's gonna be a fine day, doesn't it?"

"Yes, ma'am. It could be." He breathed in the steam rising from the cup and looked at Turner. "Let's go outside."

Hank nodded and turned to the door.

Mary Louise caught up with him. "Don't ya be gone too long. Mr. Ebner'll be by to have breakfast with us."

Kate looked at her parents. "Is he the man who's been leaving the bags of gold?"

Hank nodded.

Mary Louise glanced at him. ''I happened to see him quite by accident early one evenin' years ago, but we've hardly spoken all these years.''

Mamma and her little secrets, Kate thought. She hadn't believed her mamma capable of such deception, but she was fast discovering she didn't know her as well as she'd thought.

Hank gave Mary Louise's hand a gentle squeeze. ''Eb won't be by today.'' He went outside and waited for Parker.

Parker carried his cup out and joined him. They fell into step, heading north along the creek. The snow was bright in the early morning light, and the cold air was refreshing. ''You said you were aiming at the skinny guy filling the bag with cash. Right?''

''Yep.'' Hank eyed him. ''What about it? Don't tell me you might change your mind—''

Parker shrugged. ''It wouldn't be the first time.'' The creek bank was frozen and the water ran slow. ''Tell me exactly what you remember, from the time you opened the door to the bank.''

Hank gave a long sigh and recounted everything that he had said before.

Parker took a drink of coffee. ''Tell me about when you drew your pistol, *exactly* what you saw.''

''What're you after? I have a question or two of my own, and I'm tired of saying the same thing over and over.''

''I've remembered something about that day, but it won't mean anything unless you do, too.'' Parker hoped his elusive recollection would clear up his problem. Of course, if he was wrong, it could mean shooting Turner. And he knew if that happened, he would also lose Kate, but that decision could wait a few more minutes.

''I stepped through the doorway and nearly walked into one of the bank robbers, though I didn't know it till I saw the kerchiefs over their faces. I drew my pistol and aimed at the one taking the cash out of the drawer. A woman screamed, I think a couple men backed away.''

Parker could almost hear his heart pounding in his chest.

"The other men behind the counter. Do you remember any of them?"

Hank closed his eyes and rubbed his forehead. "There was a fellow. He must have been behind the post. I didn't see him till I'd fired." He looked at Parker. "Is that what you wanted?"

"There were two others, but, yes," Parker said in a husky voice. "That was my father. He was the bank manager." The long forgotten image became clearer and his words poured out. "He was trying to grab the bag of cash. He must have taken the shot intended for the bank robber." His mother had made him promise not to go after the killers, at least until he finished his education. She died shortly before he graduated, never convincing him to live his life and not try to track down Hank Turner.

"Sorry. I had no idea. The outlaws got off a few shots, and I think another man behind the other end of the counter fired, too." Hank glanced at Parker. "Everything seemed to explode at once."

"He fell back on me, knocking me to the floor." Parker shuddered. He would never forget the weight of his father's lifeless body pinning him down, the terror that had paralyzed him, and the overwhelming frustration of not being able to avenge his father's death. The latter would never happen, he realized.

It was over. Time for him to get on with his life and look to the future.

Kate walked along the creek with Shadow until they came to the bend. He ran into the bushes, and she looked back at Hank's camp. After he and Parker left, she tried talking with her mother. She really did, but her mother seemed to believe all was forgiven—bake a pie or fix a good meal and everything'd be fine. It wasn't that simple for Kate. She was just beginning to understand that letting go of the resentment, something she'd lived with nearly half of her life, would take time.

Hank had given his account of what'd happened and answered their questions, but he expected her to be his obedient little girl—the twelve-year-old girl he remembered. It wasn't possible. She couldn't. He'd have to understand it was too late for that. She'd been an outlaw's daughter too long to change overnight. Shadow ran over to her and pushed a stick at her hand. She dropped down to her knees and hugged him. When she got back, her little cabin was certainly going to feel empty.

She threw the stick up the gully. Shadow caught up with her and followed her into the barn. When she climbed the ladder to the loft, he laid down at the foot of it. She folded the comforters, and she had just rolled their blankets, when Shadow ran to the door and barked once.

Carrying one of the comforters, she went down to see who was there. The fact that his tail was wagging crazily didn't tell her anything. The dog liked everyone. Then she saw Parker. He looked worn out. Her heart leaped to her throat, and she clutched the comforter to her chest. Had he shot Hank? "What happened?"

The blood had drained from her face, and he hurried to her side. "No," he said, understanding her fear. "I didn't." He pulled her into a fierce embrace. "He's with your mother." He kissed her hair. "It's over."

"We can go. Thank God." She buried her face in his coat. She shuddered, and her legs threatened to give out on her. "How? What did he say?"

"When your father came in the bank and surprised the robbers, my father tried to wrestle the bag from the robber emptying the cash drawer." He cradled her head in his hands. "Unfortunately, your father shot at the same man. My father caught the shot meant for the bank robber. It was a tragic accident." He kissed her forehead.

"But you were there. You saw him."

"Mm-hm. But what stuck in my mind when my father fell back into me was seeing your father's face and his pistol."

"Oh, Parker . . ." She dropped the comforter and wrapped her arms around him. "Are you all right?"

"I'm relieved that it's really ended, but it may take me a while to realize it." He held her, enjoying the peaceful moment.

"I'm almost finished packing. We can leave as soon as I take the gold over to the cabin." She stepped out of his embrace and grinned. "Won't take me more than five minutes."

He wanted her to hand the bags back to Turner and make peace with him. "We don't have to go this minute. Don't you want to visit with your mother? You may not see her for a while—unless you decide to remain here." He kissed the top of her head.

"I'm not staying." She rubbed her cheek on his rough coat and drew in a deep breath. "I don't like him and probably never will. And I don't understand what Mamma sees in him." She shrugged. "At least he seems to treat her right."

"They certainly look happy." He ran his fingers through her soft hair. "I could use some hot coffee. How about you?"

She smiled at him. "Sounds good." She picked up her saddlebag. The darn thing weighed a ton, but she managed to get it over her shoulder.

He didn't offer to help her. It was something he knew she had to do. He smiled at the dog. "Come on, boy." He took her arm. "He's going back with us, isn't he?"

She dropped down and petted Shadow. "You want to live with me?" He gave her a wet, slobbery lick over her cheek. She grinned at Parker. "I think that was a yes." She patted his back. "I won't leave you behind this time."

Parker helped her rise with the added weight of the gold, and they walked to the cabin. He glanced at her. Settling down with her would definitely be interesting.

She didn't know what to expect, but when they entered the cabin, her mother smiled. Hank was adding logs to the fire and didn't turn around. She hugged Parker's arm. Shadow came to her side and pushed his head against her hand.

"Gracious, ya two look cold. I've got a fresh pot of coffee right here." Mary Louise set two cups on the table.

When Kate looked back at her mother, she saw tears shimmering in her eyes. Tears sprang to her own eyes, and she knew she couldn't leave her mother like that. She dropped the saddlebags on the floor, went over, and wrapped her arms around her mother. "I'm sorry, Mamma. I didn't want to hurt you. Not really." She sobbed and realized she may as well say it all and put it behind her. "It seemed as if my life was built on lies. No one told me the truth when I needed to hear it."

"Dahlin', ya wouldn't a believed me if I'd told ya what I knew." Mary Louise sniffed. "I tried plenty a times, but ya were so angry and hurt, ya wouldn't listen. Maybe I didn't try hard enough."

Hank wiped his hands on his trousers. "Mrs. Turner, if you two don't stop bawling, their coffee'll be stone cold."

Parked nodded at him. The man wasn't quite as bad as he'd believed all these years, but neither was he a caring father. However, she had replaced him with her friendships with older men, men who treated her better than her own father. "Need some help, Kate?"

She met his warm gaze and barely shook her head. After she dried her eyes, she lugged the saddlebags over to the fireplace. Tossing back the flap, she began setting the canvas bags of gold on the hearth. "This gold is yours. I gave a couple bags to miners I thought you'd robbed. The rest is all here."

Hank waved his hands at the pile. "It's yours. You might as well put that right back in your saddlebags." He stood up at her side. "I've got more than enough to take care of our needs."

She straightened up and stepped back towards Parker. "I don't want it. I've been saving to buy Mamma and me a house—"

"She has one now, Kate. With me." Hank stared at Parker. "Well, Smith, what do you plan to do about my daughter?"

"What?!" She froze in her tracks. "How dare you ask such a thing!" Oh, damn it all, she thought, I should've ridden out of here and left the infernal gold in the barn. "I'm not a horse you can trade off to the highest bidder!"

Hank gave her a stern look. "You *are* my daughter—mouthy, stubborn, and stronger than any woman has a right to be, but I won't stand by and watch you ruin your life." He stared back at Parker. "What've you to say for yourself?"

"Well," Parker drawled, eyeing Kate, "I guess it's as good a time as any." He walked over to her and held her hand in both of his. "We talked about what we would do when this was over. I talked about settling down. I don't know if I want to grow old in Moose Gulch, but I do want to grow old with you." Her eyes were as large as saucers. Could it be that he had actually shocked her? He glanced at her mother. "There's one problem. A man's wife should trust him." He gave her a hint of a smile, just enough to encourage her to take a chance with him.

Her head felt as if it were spinning. "This's insane. He can't force you to do this!"

He shook his head. "That's no answer." The look in her eyes changed faster than a stormy sky. He rubbed her cold hand. "Is it asking that much?"

"Oh, of course not. If I didn't trust you, I wouldn't even be here." She closed her eyes, but when she opened them, everyone was still watching her. "What do you want me to say? I've trusted you with my life . . . and my heart," she whispered. "What more do you want?"

"You, Kate. Just you." He hauled her into a fierce embrace. "You're all I need."

She was so overjoyed, her mind went blank, until she felt Hank slapping Parker's back and congratulating them. She stepped away from him and raised her hand. "Wait a minute. I've got one condition, too."

Grinning, he advanced on her and reclaimed her hand. "Name it." There wasn't anything she could ask he wouldn't grant. He brought her hand up and kissed her knuckles.

"No matter *what* happens, Parker Smith, we'll be together."

Holding her gaze, he said, "Always," knowing he would never make a more heartfelt commitment in his life.

His smile slipped from his handsome face, and her heart thundered. This was too important for her to give up on. He couldn't have any reservations. She looked him square in the eye. "If you ever leave me, I'll hunt you down and shoot you where it counts."

For one split moment she had him worried. Then he smiled. "I know you would." He pressed one chaste kiss to her red lips. "We'll finish this later."

His voice was deep and full of promise. She grinned and wrapped her arms around his waist. "Let's find a cave."

❖ Epilogue ❖

PARKER GENTLY BRUSHED Kate's hands aside and finished buttoning the front of her new dress. After he eased the last button through its hole, he pressed a kiss to her waiting lips. "Mrs. Smith, you're as pretty as a new bride."

"I am. Have you forgotten so soon, Mr. Smith?" She laughed and tickled his sides. "We've only been married—" She peered around his shoulder to the small clock. "Twenty-six hours and thirty-seven minutes, more or less."

He chuckled. "I'll have to think of something to keep your mind off the time." He grinned as he slid his hands down until his palms covered her breasts.

Holding his gaze, she took a deep breath. "You'll have to work harder than that." Then she grinned at him. "But it's a good start."

"Marriage has made you a hard woman."

"I always have been," she said, laughing. "Now let me comb my hair, or we'll be late for our own wedding supper." When she picked up her brush, the light from the kerosene lamp caught on her narrow gold wedding band. She and Parker had stopped at a justice of the peace south of Missoula on their way back to Moose Gulch and were married in a simple ceremony. Neither wanted a fuss made about their marriage, but when she told Charlie, the whole town knew within the hour.

The dog pawed at the door, and Parker let him back inside. Shadow trotted over to the bed, went down on his belly, and pulled his new favorite plaything from under the bed. It was one of Parker's old socks that Kate had knotted in the middle for him. Shadow nosed one end of the sock into his hand. Parker grabbed the end and let him tug on it while he watched Kate brush her hair. "I like that green on you."

"It's dragon green." She set the hairbrush down and straightened the dropped shoulders of her dress. She'd been more than a little surprised when her mother had given it to her. It seemed so long ago when she'd found the cloth in the trunk moments before she'd discovered the bags of gold. "I don't know when Mamma found the time to make it for me." She shook out the full shirt and tugged at the balloon sleeves.

"You'll have to write and tell her about the supper." He yanked on the sock, and Shadow gave a frisky growl. "I'm getting hungry, woman. Aren't you about done fussing?"

She spun around on her heel and raised her skirt, exposing her black stockings. "I'm really dressed up—no trousers."

He leered and winked at her. "Later I'll take a closer look."

She lowered her shirt. "I hope you do."

He let go of the dog's sock and stood up. "Ready?" Her boots didn't do a thing for her best dress. He decided he'd have to see about getting her a pair of slippers. He helped her into her heavy coat and put his own on.

She stepped outside and smiled back at Shadow. "You guard the cabin, and we'll bring you a good supper."

After Parker closed the door, she took his arm. The snow was hip deep and some of the snowdrifts almost came to her shoulders. That morning, he had shoveled a path from the cabin to the hotel kitchen, to the road, and another down to the creek. When he passed the door into the hotel kitchen, she stopped in her tracks. "Where're you going?"

"Around to the front." He gave her arm a gentle tug. "We're the guests of honor."

She fell into step beside him. Snow had piled up on each side of the main road. The barbershop and general store were closed and dark, but shafts of light from the hotel and saloon lighted the boardwalk. They stepped into the hotel lobby and left their coats on a chair by the others. She raised his hand, pressed a kiss to his knuckles, and entered the dining room at his side. A cheer went up. Everyone was there—old Bert, Earl Wilson, Mac and Mrs. Goody, Miss Lucy, Mr. Ralston, Mr. Bishop, and Charlie. Then Kate saw Thaddeus. Her eyes began to fill with tears, and she clung to Parker's arm.

"Good evening," Parker said as they joined the group. "Hope we're not too late for supper."

"Hell, no, Sheriff," Bert called out. "Been waiting fer ya and yer missus. Old Charlie wouldn't even give us a biscuit."

Kate laughed along with everyone else. "I'll see you get supper, Bert." She started to let go of Parker's arm.

He was sure she intended to dash into the kitchen and held on to her. "You're not working tonight."

She glanced around. "I don't see why I can't help out."

Mrs. Goody went over to Kate and hugged her. "I'm so happy for you both. I just wish your mother could be here, too."

"Thank you." Tomorrow, Kate thought, she'd have time to speak with Mrs. Goody and Miss Lucy about Mamma.

Mr. Bishop shook Parker's hand. "Congratulations. I hope this means we still have a sheriff and Kate won't be leaving us, either."

Parker met Kate's gaze, then answered Bishop. "We're not planning on leaving anytime soon."

"And I wouldn't leave Charlie shorthanded," she said smiling at him.

"Good," Charlie said in a harsh voice. "I'd hate to break in a new gal."

Bishop slapped Parker on the back. "Glad to hear you're staying on."

Miss Lucy squeezed Kate's hand. "I'm happy for you, dear. You'll make an honest man of him." Miss Lucy leaned closer. "I told you you'd caught his eye."

Kate grinned and whispered, "You were right about him being a rascally sort, too. Better watch yourself. He hasn't forgotten you."

Miss Lucy giggled and stepped over to Parker. "I hope she led you on a merry chase, Sheriff."

Parker chuckled and kissed Miss Lucy's soft cheek. "She certainly did, but it may not be over for a good many years."

"Just don't take her for granted, and you'll do fine, young man."

"Yes, ma'am." Parker watched Kate make her way over to the only man in the dining room he didn't know, a giant man dressed in buckskins. Then someone grabbed his hand, and he looked back. "Earl. I sure missed your hot baths."

"Glad to hear it. I'm real happy for you and Kate. She's a good woman."

"Thanks, Earl."

Mac Goody worked his way over to Parker. "Good to have you back, Sheriff. After that snowstorm last week, I didn't know if you'd be able to get through."

"It was slow going, Mac. At least we got here before Christmas."

Ralston pressed a cup into Parker's hand. "Thought you could use some libation. Congratulations."

Parker took a drink and grinned. "Thanks. How was your trip?"

"Gets better each time." Ralston winked. "Or maybe

I'm getting older and appreciate her more with each visit.''

Parker chuckled and looked around the room. ''Tullie tending bar?''

Ralston nodded. ''You know he's more comfortable with his banjo than people.''

Kate wrapped her arms around Thaddeus. ''How did you hear about our marriage? Oh, never mind. I'm so glad to see you.''

''Katie—'' He swung her off the floor and spun her around. ''I'm so happy for you.'' He set her down and stared into her eyes. ''Is he good to you?''

She nodded. ''Better than I ever dreamed possible. I've so much to tell you, Thaddeus. Are you staying the night?''

He rested a hand on her shoulder. ''If you'll serve my breakfast.''

''I sure will.'' She linked arms with him. ''I want you to meet my husband.'' The men stepped aside, and she introduced Thaddeus to Parker.

Thaddeus shook hands with him. ''Glad to meet you, Smith. Hear you're the sheriff. Guess you'll be able to keep my girl safe.''

''I'll do my best.'' Parker noticed a gleam in Kate's eyes when she looked up at Thaddeus, and he knew how special this man was to her. ''Glad to meet you, Thaddeus.''

Charlie banged a wooden spoon on the bottom of a kettle until everyone quieted down. ''This food's gettin' cold. So sit yerselves down. Bert 'n' me are hungry.''

''Rightcha're, Charlie,'' Bert called out.

Mac pulled out two chairs in the middle of one side of the long table. ''Sheriff, Kate, you can sit here.''

Parker seated Kate and took the chair on her left and held her hand under the table. ''Supper sure smells good, and poor old Bert's almost drooling.''

''I'll set the biscuits out. It'll only take me a minute.''

He shook his head. ''It won't be long now.''

Everyone sat down at the long table decorated with red,

white, and pink silk roses. Ralston passed out small glasses of wine; Mrs. Goody and Charlie served supper. When he set the plate of roasted chicken, mashed potatoes, and string beans in front of Kate, she looked up at him. "Thank you, Charlie. No bride ever had a nicer wedding supper."

He cleared his throat and gave her a stern look. "If ya don't start eatin', that dog of yors is gonna have a real feast."

When Charlie and Mrs. Goody sat down at the table, Mr. Bishop stood and raised his glass. "Parker and Kate, we wish you a good and long life together."

As everyone raised their glasses, Thaddeus added, "And may your children be healthy."

Tears filled Kate's eyes and blurred her vision. She gripped Parker's hand and glanced at him. She'd never given any thought to having children, and she had the feeling Thaddeus had intentionally planted the idea in her mind. If she'd had any say in the matter, he would've been her father.

After the toast, Parker raised his glass. "To each of you. Kate and I appreciate all you've done for us."

Mac took a drink of his wine and motioned to the far corner table, where Parker usually sat. "Wait till you taste the bride's cake Miss Lucy made for you."

Kate turned to look at the table and saw the cake. Mrs. Goody must have set it out as she served their food, Kate thought. The cake had pale yellow icing decorated with what looked like deep purple huckleberries. "Miss Lucy, that's the prettiest cake I've ever seen. Thank you so much."

"Miz Kate," Bert said, "kin we eat now?"

Laughing, she said, "You sure can, Bert."

Parker leaned over to her side and whispered, "It almost feels as if we never left."

With her hand still in his comforting grip, she turned to face him and brushed her lips over his cheek. They were really home. She stroked his thumb with hers. "I'm glad we did. We needed to complete the journey we started so many years ago and put our past to rest.'' His beautiful blue eyes seemed to bind her in a delicious spell.

''Mrs. Smith, we'll make the years ahead even more interesting.'' He didn't think he would ever completely know her, but it didn't matter. They would create new memories to take the place of the unpleasant ones, and she would never again doubt she was loved.

❖ ❖ ❖

Dear Reader,

I hope you enjoyed *Humble Pie*. Kate and Parker were fun to write about, and Mary Louise was a delight. I'll miss the good people of Moose Gulch. Right now I am completing my next Our Town book in which Emma Townsend considers herself unmarriageable and centers her life around both her store, The Hatbox, which she co-owns with her friend, and the women who drop in to visit. After coming to Emma's rescue aboard the coastal packet that ran aground, Kent Hogarth spends more time than he'd planned in Pelican Cove. Emma inspires thoughts of settling down, something he hadn't planned to do until he was past his prime. Emma and Kent's story will make you laugh, shed a few tears and warm your hearts.

My next Homespun, written as Deborah Wood, will be a 1997 Christmas book. I've been wanting to write a Christmas book, and Caroline and Daniel's Christmas together is wonderful. Caroline Dobbs, a character from *Maggie's Pride* (March '96 Jove Homespun) vows to raise a set of twins, whom she helped birth, as her own. Several townspeople attempt to place the babies in other homes, but she won't give up the children she's always wanted. Daniel Grey, the man she hired to repair her storm-ravaged home, becomes her ally. As he restores her house, Daniel discovers a love that his marriage lacked, and he had dreamed about.

Please watch for my upcoming Our Town, March 1997, and my upcoming Homespun written as Deborah Wood, December 1997.

Best Wishes,

Deborah Lawrence

also writes as Deborah Wood

❖ ❖ ❖

FREE
Romance
(a $4.50 value)
Send in the Coupon Below
To get your FREE historical romance and start saving, fill out the coupon below and mail it today. As soon as we receive it we'll send you your FREE Book along with your first month's selections.